THE CURSED HORDE KING

Cover Art by K.D. Ritchie at Story Wrappers

Editing by Mandi Andrejka at Inky Pen Editorial Services

For more information visit www.ZoeyDraven.com

ALSO BY ZOEY DRAVEN

Warriors of Luxiria
The Alien's Prize
The Alien's Mate
The Alien's Lover
The Alien's Touch
The Alien's Dream
The Alien's Obsession
The Alien's Seduction
The Alien's Claim

Horde Kings of Dakkar
Captive of the Horde King
Claimed by the Horde King
Madness of the Horde King
Broken by the Horde King
Taken by the Horde King
Throne of the Horde King

Warrior of Rozun
Wicked Captor
Wicked Mate

The Krave of Everton
Kraving Khiva
Prince of Firestones
Kraving Dravka
Kraving Tavak

Brides of the Kylorr
Desire in His Blood
Craving in His Blood
Hunger in His Blood

Hordes of the Elthika
The Horde King of Shadow

Standalones
Rescued by the Luxirian
The Midnight Arrow

THE CURSED HORDE KING

USA TODAY BESTSELLING AUTHOR

ZOEY DRAVEN

THE CURSED HORDE KING

A bewitching spy. A ruthless king.
A love that could ignite a war.

Amaia has worked hard to make her family proud. As the star apprentice to the _pyroki_ master in Dothik, she's weeks away from inheriting her mentor's coveted post. But when her desperate brother begs her to take his place in the Heartstone Accords, a diplomatic exchange with their rival nation, she agrees to the unthinkable. Her mission? Cross the sea to Grym, secure work at the dragon hatchery, and _spy_ for the throne.

But Grym is nothing like she imagined—and neither is its formidable king.

Merciless and calculated, Alaryk Arn'dyne is as feared as the ancient dragon he commands. Gifted with powerful heartstone magic that can twist minds, he's impossible to deceive...and a dark temptation Amaia needs to avoid at all costs.

After a deadly curse strikes Alaryk's dragon, Amaia knows she can save him, forcing a reluctant alliance with the very person she's sworn to betray. As their forbidden attraction grows, however, she discovers a male scarred by a painful past, whose wicked needs make her burn.

But when an unexpected crime threatens to ignite a war, Amaia must choose: her home, her heart...or the ruthless king who could destroy both.

CONTENT CONSIDERATIONS

The Cursed Horde King contains some themes and depictions that might be sensitive to certain readers. Please go to my website for a full list of content considerations.

Scan this QR code for easy access:

DAKKARI & KARAG GLOSSARY

Darukkar: Dakkari warrior

Elthika: dragon race; 'death wind' in Karag

Ethrall: death mist

Faryn: stop

Hanniva: please

Illa'rosh: choosing ritual at the Tharken cliffs

Kakkira vor: thank you

Karath: territory leader

Kor anir ji vorak: 'the way of the horde'

Kya'rassa: rider horde

Lomma: mother

Lysi: yes

Mariss: ember

Mrikro: pyroki master

Nik: no

Pattar: father

Pyroki: scaled horse-like creatures on Dakkar

Saruk: outpost

Sen endrassa: thank you *(sen is a respectful term when used to address an Elthika)*

Sorrina: queen

Sy'asha: Elthika song

Syn'ra: pleasure bump

Thryn'ar: flying command

Ty'bara ellrash: stubborn creature

Vorakkar: Dakkari horde king

CHAPTER 1
AMAIA

The heat felt searing along my exposed arm as I grappled for a leg. My seeking fingers found the curve of a tiny claw. A small muzzle next. I reached deeper, and the mother whined, her breathing labored, her scaled flank shimmering in the afternoon sunlight.

Worry knotted in my belly. My head turned a fraction to spy my *mrikro*—the *pyroki* master—watching me keenly from his place along the fence. A crowd was growing, which only added to the pinching anxiousness weaving around my ribs.

Finally, I found the leg. Now to find the other...

"You've really tucked yourself in there, little one," I whispered, feeling a droplet of sweat curve along my brow. I spread my other hand across the mother *pyroki*'s side in a soothing gesture. Witha was her name. She belonged to one of the king's guards, a *darukkar* who'd come to live in Dothik, our capital city, from the wildlands. I'd quite taken to her, though she'd proved to be sassy and belligerent when pregnant. It only added to her charm, in my opinion. But *pyroki* usually birthed in pairs, and she only had the one.

And I didn't want her to lose it.

"You can do this," I said, though it was more to myself than to Witha, who had long taken to exhaustion after laboring for a couple hours in the late morning.

She gave a long, shuddering groan just as I located the second leg, twisted back as I'd thought and jammed up.

I blew out a sharp breath, guiding the leg forward. The first time I'd done this, I'd been scared to hurt the young. But now I pulled hard and sharply, knowing they could withstand it, knowing it would be necessary.

When I finally had both forelimbs in the correct position, I thumped along Witha's belly and she gave a start, beginning to push, the powerful force of which proved more efficient than the strain of my muscles as I pulled. Bracing my shoulder against her backside, my booted feet slipping in the dirt, I thumped again and felt the strain of Witha's muscles.

"Almost there!" I said with gritted teeth, feeling movement.

Then…

Release.

I stumbled back onto my ass as cheers rose through the crowd, the break in the tension pierced through like an arrow. The young *pyroki* slid from Witha, landing in a heap on the ground, sticky and slick with mucus and blood.

For a moment, I grinned, relieved. But the relief was short-lived when I saw the *mrikro* straighten from the fence, beginning to approach with a frown. The *pyroki* wasn't moving as its mother panted from exhaustion.

No, no, no, I thought, scrambling toward the young. I used the edge of my dirtied tunic to wipe the mucus from its passage-ways before thumping my fist just behind its ribs, over the lungs.

Dread rose as I heard the crunch of my *mrikro's* boots.

"Amaia," came my *pyroki* master's steady voice, my name like a gentle warning.

"I have this," I told him without looking up. I knew he trusted me, but I still didn't want to disappoint him. I heard his retreat as he attended to Witha, as murmurings rose through the crowd behind me.

My hand pressed against the young *pyroki*'s still chest.

There's too many people watching, came a warning thought.

I didn't care—I would be quick. But I wouldn't let the *pyroki* die needlessly if it was within my ability to help.

The heartstone magic felt warm and alive inside me, a little ember being stoked to a raging burn. I closed my eyes so no one would see the color of my irises glow as I guided the heat through me, which sprinted through my blood and veins. I channeled it into the *pyroki*, imagining a door as I always did, envisioning crossing over the threshold of it, my body jerking at the impact.

Coldness made me shiver. A coldness like plunging into an icy lake, stealing my breath. But I felt life. All it needed was a little *spark*.

I dragged in a deep breath, all sound and light behind my closed lids and distraction and fear falling away. I heard the throb of my heartbeat, and I sent my magic seeking, like a little warm river, washing through its body.

I heard my heartbeat…

And then I heard the young *pyroki*'s.

Through the quiet, I heard the rasping guttural whine of its first sound, breath gasping, sucking in life, and the way Witha responded, hearing the bleating call of her young.

A wave of dizziness and lethargy sent me sprawling backward, but my shoulders sagged in relief. I fell down onto the earth, letting it support my weight, my eyelids lifting open to peer up at the clear cloudless sky, hearing the cheers and calls from the crowd as they celebrated the new life.

I still felt so cold, my flesh clammy, my passageways narrowed like I was breathing through a pinhole. But I ignored it, knowing it would pass.

Halna crouched over me, his yellow eyes pleased. "Good. Good, Amaia."

I sat up with his help, trying to hide the way I struggled to breathe as I wiped my hands on my already filthy pants.

Halna clapped me on the back firmly but gently. As always, he was a male of very few words and went to attend the mother, who was busy nuzzling her offspring with her sharp snout. It took me a while to catch my breath, and by the time the crowd began to thin out around the *pyroki* enclosure, I felt mostly like myself, though in need of a long—very long—rest.

Just then, I caught the eye of someone in the crowd. Someone achingly familiar as a wide, surprised smile split across my face.

I rushed over as quickly as I could, though it was more like a hobble.

"Don't you dare hug me with all that muck on you," my brother said when I reached the fence line. But he grinned, his gold eyes twinkling in the sunlight. I hadn't seen him in a couple months, but he looked so very official in his armor. "I just had my uniform polished."

One of the *Dothikkar*'s personal guardsmen. Our king. It was one of the most respected positions in Dothik, and my brother had ascended to it. All on his own, through sheer determination and strength and will.

We lived within a few stone throws of one another. And even still, we barely saw him. He lived in the barracks in the palace, was only allowed leave every now and again, and yet our mother always set a place for him at our meals. Just in case.

"I'm coming for supper tonight," Kiron told me. "You can hug me then."

"Am I even allowed to hug you at all?" I teased, gripping the fence with both hands so I didn't fall over. "Or would the *Dothikkar* have me in chains for daring to touch one of his prized guards?"

"I won't tell him if you don't," he said, a quirk of a smile lifting his lips. I laughed, though it sounded more like a wheeze in my state. He nodded behind me. "You did well. Everyone was enthralled."

I was about to run my hand over my forehead but remembered the mess coating it.

"What in Kakkari's name are you doing here, Kiron?" I asked, studying and memorizing every change in my brother. He looked older, lines around his eyes that hadn't been there before. He'd let his brown hair grow. It was braided nearly to the middle of his back, just like a *darukkar's*—a warrior's—might if he lived on the wildlands and belonged to one of the hordes. "We both know you didn't come to see a *pyroki* being born."

Something changed in my brother's eyes at my question. "There's something I'd like to discuss with you. But not here."

I frowned, hearing a strange tone in his voice, one I couldn't place. A bite of alarm went through me. My brother wouldn't have come here if it wasn't serious. "You know I hate that. Just tell me now. What's wrong?"

Kiron glanced around, still hesitating despite most of the crowd having left and no one being within earshot. "I don't think it's the right time. I shouldn't have said any—"

"Kiron. *Tell me.*"

He dragged in a breath. Then leaned closer. "It's about the Karag."

I sucked in a breath, rearing back to meet his eyes. "What? What about them?"

"The accord exchanges are coming up, for a territory named Grym. Your name is among them on the manifest."

I froze, feeling a new wave of dizziness that had nothing to do with my heartstone magic. "What are you talking about? I *never* submitted my name."

"No, you didn't." His lips pressed. "But *I* did."

"You *what?*" I breathed. Shock numbed me. "What possessed you to—"

"Amaia," my *pyroki* master called from behind me. I turned

to regard him in a daze, my heart nearly beating its way out of my chest with the swirl of new knowledge. I waved a distracted hand at him, knowing we had to get Witha and her newborn back to her nest.

I turned back to Kiron, reeling.

"I didn't want to talk here," he reminded me, rubbing the back of his neck. "But I'll explain. It's not mandatory, Amaia. But I have reason for submitting you, and I want you to hear me out before you make a decision."

"Well, the answer is *no*," I told him, already stepping back. "I can tell you that now."

As I turned, a little flint of anger struck inside me. What made my brother think he could do something like that? Without ever *asking* me? We hadn't seen each other in months. And now this?

"Amaia," Kiron called suddenly. I looked back at him. He beckoned me closer, and my nostrils flared as I trudged back over. "You need to be more careful."

His chin jerked over to the young *pyroki*. I swallowed hard, understanding his meaning.

"No one saw," I said, setting my jaw.

Kiron's lips pressed, but he backed away from the fence. "I'll see you tonight."

I watched him go with a frown and a furrowed brow. My pointed ears twitched in worry. Kiron never did anything without reason. I just feared what that reason might be.

The newborn *pyroki*'s bleating cry pierced through my tumultuous thoughts, and I turned. I pushed Kiron from my mind. I had a duty here, one I took seriously, one that would become my future.

Even my brother couldn't sway me from it.

CHAPTER 2
AMAIA

"There had better be *leiso* flour in that sack," my mother grumbled when I stepped through the front door with the remnants of my dirtied clothes in a satchel. I was winded, having climbed up the three sets of stairs to our home, the muscles in my legs threatening to give. Hours later, with the sun slowly melting into the horizon line, I still hadn't recovered.

The older I got, I realized, the more depleting the heartstone magic felt. I didn't want to dwell too much on what that meant, so I pushed it from my mind. Besides, if my mother suspected I had used it again, especially with an audience, she'd have my head.

"Not quite." I beamed, shouldering the crooked door closed before going over to her, stooping to drop a kiss across her cheek. "You'll forgive me though. The young *pyroki* has a line of gold scales and is quite a talker. You'd love him."

"Good omen," said my mother's friend, Avis, who was sitting at the low table, helping to fix a stitch on a leather sleeve. She nodded even as she squinted down at her mending. "Kakkari has blessed the little one. Now you cannot be upset with the washing, Mae."

"*I'll* do the washing tomorrow," I said, falling down onto the floor next to them, my eyes flickering around the cozy space of our little home. The long hours attending to the newborn had softened my ire at Kiron. Besides, he'd said the choice was mine to make, and I'd already informed him what it would be. "Don't worry, *Lomma*." Mother.

"If you wait until the morning, that sack will stink up the entire building," my *lomma* tsked. Despite her scolding tone, there was a light in her eyes. She was in a good mood, happy at the prospect of having dinner with her son. "Did Kiron find you? He said he would look for you."

"*Lysi*, he did," I replied, picking at a stray thread on my clean pants. I always kept a fresh set handy on birthing days. Avis slapped my hand away, and I bit back a smile when she pointed her needle at me in warning.

My mother, Mae, was a well-known seamstress in the Market District, often having a pile of orders dropped at our door most mornings, which I'd have to climb over on my way to the *pyroki* enclosures. Usually Avis, our neighbor—who was truthfully more like a sister to my mother, would be over in the evenings to help her finish the batch in exchange for a meal.

"Good," my mother said, smiling. At fifty, she was beautiful, with smooth, dark skin and bright green eyes. Her silky black-and-silver hair was done up in a neat braid that hung over her shoulder. "He should be here soon. Your father should be cooling down the forges by now. Go wash up and get that sack dumped in some water."

With a barely concealed groan, I climbed to my feet, casting my gaze to the simmering pot in the hearth. "What's for supper? It smells good."

"I'm surprised you can smell anything past that stench," my mother grumbled. Avis cackled and took another sip from her goblet of wine. "*Wrissan* stew."

Kiron's favorite.

These evening sewing sessions were more of a social circle. Sometimes some of my mother's other friends would join them and they'd be up until the quiet hours of morning gabbing and gossiping. I'd fallen asleep to the muffled sounds of laughter and voices more times than I could count. The sounds of people filling a home were always comforting to me, and I'd learned to be a deep sleeper, as had my father, who was the complete opposite of my outgoing and social mother.

It took me longer than usual to get my dirtied clothes soaking and to wash up—especially since I gave my hair an extra good scrubbing. I would sleep well tonight, I thought as I rubbed a clean cloth through my damp hair. I would feel like normal in the morning. Or at least I hoped I would.

When I emerged from the washroom, I saw Kiron had already arrived. Even out of his polished guard uniform, he looked like an older, more severe version of the brother I'd grown up with. He was smiling and chatting with Avis as my mother stirred the stew in the hearth. The table was already set, but my father likely hadn't returned home.

Kiron's eyes connected with mine when I stepped into the family room. Our childhood home was nothing like the *Dothikkar's* palace, the halls of which Kiron now regularly roamed, and I wondered if he found it strange to be back in the cramped space, where we shared so many memories with our family. It had to be jarring for him. As jarring as it was for me to see him here again.

My brother stood from the low table and approached me.

"Now I can claim that hug," he told me, his voice warm. But as his arms enveloped me and I turned my cheek against his chest to rest there, a part of me was wary. "Can we talk before supper?"

The inquiry was quiet, slightly hushed. I felt it rumble against my own chest.

I pulled back to meet his eyes. I cast a glance at our *lomma,* who was still hovering over the pot of stew, neatly shaped *leiso* loaves baking on the hot stone next to it.

I inclined my head, and Kiron announced, "We'll be right back, *Lomma*."

She spun and frowned, hands on her hips. "Where are you going?"

"Just outside for some fresh air. I want to spend time with my sister," Kiron answered, a charming grin spreading across his face, which appeased our mother.

"Don't go far," she said, waving a wooden spoon around. "Your *pattar* will be home soon, and you know how hungry he is after a day in the forge."

"We'll be back quicker than Naruk's horde," Kiron assured her, already shuffling me through the door with a palm on the small of my back, just over the bump of my would-be tail, which had never grown. Too much human ancestry in me, I supposed.

Naruk had been a horde king about fifty years prior. After having been selected to lead a new horde from Dothik to the wildlands of our planet, his horde had caught a disease its first week, which had spread through the members like a fire. They'd had to limp back home to Dothik, and Naruk had never led another horde, a permanent mark of disgrace on his name for eternity, only used in snickering jokes now.

Outside, the night air was warm, residuals of the heat of the day. A slight breeze made me shiver, however, as it wound and curved along the back of my neck, where my hair was still damp from my bath.

We lived on the top floor of a leaning, three-story building. From the balcony of our front porch, we could see Drukkar's Sea, though we were facing the wrong direction to spy the *Dothikkar's* gleaming palace. I liked that better anyway.

Leaning against the banister, listening to Kiron as he firmly tugged the door closed behind us, I waited for him to join me.

"I've missed you, Amaia," he said, sliding into the space

beside me. "I probably should've started with that this afternoon but…made a mess of everything. Like usual."

I felt myself soften. Kiron had often been direct and awkward with his words, something he'd likely had to unlearn working within the palace.

"It's all right," I murmured.

"How are you feeling?" he asked. Those eyes turned on me, scrutinizing me in a way a stranger could not.

"A bit tired. It'll pass."

He sighed, a deep, heavy thing that burst from him.

"Your life is not worth a *pyroki*'s," he told me simply.

I felt a spark burn in my chest, but I held it there. He would never understand. He could never understand the helplessness or the guilt if I *could* do something and chose not to. And why? Because of fear?

"You're meant for much bigger things, sister," Kiron said. And I heard the subtle shift in his tone.

"Just say it," I said, sighing. "Then I can give you my answer. And let's be done with it before *Pattar* returns home. I don't want to ruin supper for *Lomma*'s sake."

"Amaia—"

"I'm serious, Kiron," I said, steeling my voice. Turning to face him, I leaned my hip into the steel banister. I threaded a hand through my damp hair, feeling the wavy, tangled strands catch in my fingers. "I don't know what possessed you to think that I would agree to this and—"

"I need your help."

My words died after the quick, hushed interruption. Dread built in my belly, and I took a fraction of a step closer. "Are you in trouble?"

His nostrils flared, his pupils shifted. "In a way, *lysi*."

"Tell me," I said, inching closer. Down below, a loud group of workers were heading to the nearby tavern for their nightly brews. A bellow of a laugh momentarily cut through the tension between us, and Kiron waited until they'd passed, even though they wouldn't have been able to hear us way up here.

"What do you know of the Heartstone Accords?" Kiron asked.

"What everyone knows, I suppose," I answered. "What they've told us."

Over half a year ago now, the Karag from across the sea had come to Dothik, demanding one of its princesses—Klara of Rath Serok and Rath Drokka. Their shadowed king, who flew on the back of a mighty dragon, had claimed her as his bride, and he'd taken her from the city, to her almost certain death…or so we'd thought.

From that arranged marriage had come love instead, and so the Heartstone Accords had been struck: a tentative and shaky alliance between the Karag and the Dakkari, wherein they would both share the wealth of the heartstones that had been unearthed from below a *thalara* tree on the wildlands. And in exchange, the Karag would teach us, the Dakkari, how to repopulate our heartstones, to grow them for future centuries.

Heartstones were life. Heartstones were power. Heartstones were…magic, infused in the soil that grew our food, sewn like thread into the trees, breathed in from a gentle wind dancing across your cheeks.

The Karag had thought the heartstones alone would be enough to appease the Dakkari.

But the *Dothikkar* and his advisors had demanded one more thing of the Karag, given the immense power imbalance between the two nations. The Karag had a special bond with the Elthika, their dragons, who could breathe out a weapon called *ethrall*. It was a deadly fog that sickened anything it touched…and it would eventually turn lethal, if the Elthika itself didn't snap you in two between its mighty jaws first.

Every half year, a group of Dakkari would be chosen from a highly experienced applicant pool and sent to specific territories within the nation of Karak. To learn from them, to live their way of life, and, for those brave enough, to try their hand at bonding with an Elthika of their own. The riding schools were rigorous, intense, and, at times, fatal. And no allowances or mercies were offered if you were a Dakkari.

But there were other opportunities that weren't rider training. Like working their farmlands or apprenticing under a healer or learning ancient recipes from their seasoned cooks or journeying to their sacred places, infused with heartstone magic, for research.

"The *Dothikkar* and his advisors believe that the Karag are planning an attack soon," Kiron told me in a mere whisper. I sucked in a sharp breath, a spear of fear sliding into my belly.

"What are you saying?" I whispered back, utterly still. "On Dothik?"

"The *Dothikkar* has tasked a select group of his guardsmen," he said with a nod, "with a mission of getting information throughout Karak's territories."

I realized what he was saying. "You mean to *spy*."

He inclined his head. When he said nothing else, I felt an odd prickling sensation across the back of my neck, which trailed down my spine.

"You want…*me* to be a spy for the *Dothikkar*?"

The words left my lips in a tumble that nearly made me laugh.

"*Lysi*," my brother said.

A stuttered breath escaped me. "That's the most ridiculous thing I've ever heard. Are you out of your mind?"

"I wouldn't ask this of you unless I had no other choice."

"Why don't *you* go?" I tossed out, half-panicked when I heard the seriousness in my brother's tone.

When he remained quiet, I felt my panic shift, fear rising for a different reason. "I might have to."

"Not for rider training, surely," I hissed softly, grabbing his arm. "Kiron."

Three Dakkari had already died in the attempt during the last exchanges. No Dakkari had ever succeeded at claiming an Elthika of their own. Well, save for the princess, Klara.

"The territory of Grym has capped the exchange positions to four this season. Two guardsmen are already approved for rider training. Another is the eldest son of a retired guardsman. He'll be there working the land to learn about their food supply, imports, exports. The last position would fall to me. And it would be to fill another slot in the rider training."

"No," I said sharply, my belly dropping. "Kiron, you can't. Surely there's…"

But I trailed off. Knowing that *this* was the other option.

Me.

Something settled inside me. A fresh bloom of fear, but also one of acceptance.

"I'm no fool," Kiron said with a wry smile as he leaned harder against the balcony, looking out over the shimmering of Drukkar's Sea in the distance. The moon reflected off its surface, a faint sliver, like a curved blade, hanging in the night sky. "I have no notable skills other than combat fighting. I learned to be a good guard, to protect, to patrol, to keep the peace. I like to think I'd do well on the back of a dragon…but the truth is that it terrifies me, Amaia."

"You want me to take your place in Grym," I said quietly. "But…if there's a space open in the rider training, then—"

"*Not* as a rider, Amaia," Kiron said firmly, turning to me, catching my shoulder so that I faced him. "I would rather plunge off the back of an Elthika myself than make you take my place there. There is one other position open for the exchanges."

"What is it?"

"A position in the hatchery."

"The hatchery," I whispered, looking at him with an unfocused gaze. "An *Elthikan* hatchery?"

He inclined his head.

I sucked in a sharp breath, my mind hardly able to process it. *A much safer option,* I thought.

"Why can't you take the hatchery position?" I asked.

"I tried already," Kiron said, rubbing the back of his neck. "The Karag have to approve all applicants who volunteer for the exchanges. They give the assignments. I was accepted into the rider training only because of my background as a soldier. But you…"

"They accepted me already? When you submitted my name?" I asked quietly.

"You would be well suited there," Kiron continued quietly. "The star apprentice of the *pyroki* master? No one will think twice about why you're there. You're more than qualified, and the Karag thought so as well. Even my commander thought it would be a good choice, as long as there was someone I trusted on my behalf in Karak. Blood relations only. And it's only for a season. Then you'll be back home."

"Kiron," I said, shaking my head. "I really don't like this. It feels…it feels *wrong*. Me? A spy? What am I even supposed to do? What are we going to tell *Lomma*? And our father? And what am I going to tell my *mrikro*? 'Thank you for training me for all these years as your apprentice, but I'm leaving for Karak at week's end'? The second birthing season is here. I can't leave him right now when—"

"Amaia," Kiron interrupted.

And with just my name, he struck me silent.

I realized that I was being selfish because the choices were clear: let Kiron risk his life every single day trying to claim a dragon, or go in his place to work, safely, in a hatchery.

To be a spy for my homeland.

I glanced back at the closed door of the home we'd grown up in. I thought of my mother and had the vivid image of her grief if we learned of Kiron's failure in Karak. I thought of my own grief, knowing I could have done something and had chosen to turn my back on my only brother when he'd needed me.

Just like the heartstone magic, there was no choice. Only the illusion of one.

I heard heavy footsteps making their way up the wooden stairs. I would recognize the slow and steady thumps anywhere, and when my father finally appeared on the porch landing, seeming surprised to see us there, Kiron went to him.

"Son," our father said, brow furrowing. He hadn't known Kiron would be here tonight, evidenced by their tight embrace. My throat burned when I spied my father's eyelids squeeze tightly together, a male who rarely showed emotion save for his quiet contentment.

"I'm staying for supper tonight," Kiron told him, pulling back and cutting me a look. "We're just catching up."

Our father didn't say much, merely bobbed his head in a nod. "I'd better go wash up, then. You know how your mother gets," he said before disappearing through the front door.

The warm, spiced smell of *wrissan* stew floated out to us, followed by our mother's quick exclaim of "*There* you are! I was beginning to worry. Did you see—"

The door closed, and it was just me and my brother once again.

"You have a choice in this, Amaia. I know I ask too much of you, but—"

"There is no choice," I said, cutting him off. "I'll go."

Silence spread between us. It seemed as though Kiron was holding his breath. "You will?"

"*Lysi,*" I said, feeling that answer settle in my bones. It didn't feel real. But I had a feeling reality would catch up with me in the morning. I would enjoy tonight, I decided. With my family. "And like you said, it's only for the season. My *mrikro* will under-stand. I'll figure out something to tell him. But *Lomma*...and *Pattar*..."

"Leave them to me," Kiron said. "I'll explain. I can have a missive signed from the *Dothikkar* for your *mrikro* so that he knows you're going in duty to Dakkar."

"It's settled, then," I said quietly, gazing out over Drukkar's Sea and Bekkar's Shield, the mountain range just before it.

"Amaia," Kiron said, catching my hand when I turned toward the front door. "*Kakkira vor.* Thank you."

I pressed my forehead to his when he embraced me. "I missed you too."

He released me, and I could see a large weight had been lifted off him. I wondered how long he and his group of guardsmen had been discussing me as a potential alternative.

A pressing question rose. "When do I leave?"

"In three days," Kiron replied.

I swallowed. Hard.

So soon. So much to do before then.

But Kiron was wrong. I wasn't doing this for Dakkar. Or the king. I was doing this for my brother only. And that was all that mattered.

"Let's go inside and eat," I said, a little numb, turning to the door. "They're waiting."

CHAPTER 3
AMAIA

The pounding thud of my heart was all I could hear as I stood outside the gates of Dothik.

It was early enough that the sun hadn't yet crested over Bekkar's Shield. Though the air was crisp, sounds felt muffled, breaths held from the hundreds that had gathered, all anticipating the dark shadows that would appear in the lightening pink sky.

Waiting on the compact earth beside me were the other travelers. Currently only two places accepted Dakkari for the exchanges: a territory in the south called Sarroth and a territory in the east called Grym—which apparently bordered an enemy nation, as my mother had hysterically pointed out to my brother when he'd broken the news to them over supper a few nights ago.

The supper hadn't ended well. Kiron had left in frustration, and as I'd lain in bed that night, I'd listened to my mother cry, my father and Avis trying to console her, hushed through my bedroom door.

Kiron hadn't told them about the "spy" part, curiously, which might have soothed our parents' ire. If they understood I had no choice. But I'd been forced to tell them that it was a direct order from the *Dothikkar*, a high honor considering my position at the *pyroki* enclosure.

And it's only for a season, I reminded myself now, dragging in a deep, slow breath, pushing back my shoulders, brushing my arm against the Dakkari male standing next to me.

It was as quiet as a gravesite. Behind me, the families of the travelers made a crooked line in front of the two towering steel doors of the East Gate of Dothik. A neater line of guardsmen were off to one side. And peering through the East Gate, I saw a massive crowd had gathered, all angling for the best view of the impending visitors and their mighty dragons through the steel columns.

My *mrikro* hadn't come. Halna hadn't said much when I'd given him the missive from the *Dothikkar*. He'd read it over with an expressionless face, and then he'd scanned my face afterward.

"Learn from them," Halna had eventually murmured before continuing to shovel out one of the enclosures for another nest build. "They have much to teach us about these creatures."

"They don't have *pyroki*," I'd reminded him. "As far as I know."

He'd leveled me a stare, a slight quirk of his lips. "All creatures are made from the bones of Kakkari. Elthika too."

Still, I wished Halna had come, but I knew that it was another birthing day, that he was preparing with his other apprentices. I wondered if a new apprentice would take my place before I could return. If anyone would, it would be Myre. He had been waiting for a chance to pounce at my position, and I'd successfully fended him off for years. My leaving probably delighted him.

Halna was retiring his position soon. He'd hinted that it would be mine to take over. Now? I wasn't so sure.

But Kiron's life was more important than any position on all of Dakkar. I would shovel *pyroki* shit for the rest of my life under Myre's smirk if it meant my brother was safe. At least I would still get to work with the creatures I cared for so dearly. Not everyone could boast that.

Suddenly a rippled murmur went through the gathered crowd, and I caught a flinch from a young Dakkari male next to me. My gaze darted over Bekkar's Shield, and there I saw them. At first they appeared like large *thissie* birds, silhouetted black against the sky.

But as my heartbeat built to a crescendo, they grew much, much larger than mere *thissie* and their wings became monstrous things. I could hear the beat of them, like drums, as they worked against the air. I could hear the crackle of joints, the whisper of their scales, the heaved breath from throats that I knew could unleash *ethrall*, a powerful deadly fog.

I'd been frightened stepping out onto this plain. Building up a monster in my mind, for I had only caught a mere glimpse of a dragon, once before, when it'd flown over Dothik. A flash of an image.

But now…

I counted a total of ten Elthika. When they reached us, half landed, while the other unit broke out to fly over the city. Patrolling, I figured, to make certain there was no threat against them.

I'd never thought of myself as a coward. So I was glad that it wasn't only *fear* that rose inside me like a crawling, strong vine, gripping onto my lungs and twining around the cage of my ribs. Instead, it was *awe*—and I felt it spark inside me until it seared.

The fear was there too. How could it not be when faced with the mightiness of not one but five Elthika, stomping the earth as they landed, sending shock waves out from their weight that made my bones quake in my flesh?

But mostly it was awe, and I was glad for it.

To touch one…to feel them with my heartstone magic…to feel the essence of their souls…

A shuddered breath escaped me, and for the first time, I couldn't wait to cross an ocean I'd only ever seen the shores of.

The group of Elthika held back. Three Elthika, I noticed, had different saddles strapped around their backs. Ones with strong leathered sides, built up to form half walls, like a sturdy basket. Instead of one rider, they would carry five or six, easily.

Behind me, I turned to look at my parents. My mother's face was pale, my father's arm wrapped in support around her hip. My heart squeezed, wishing I could tell them I would be okay. I settled on a smile, hoping it wasn't like a grimace. I wished I could open my soul to her, so she would know that I was not afraid, that this *excited* me.

My gaze cut to the line of guardsmen. Kiron was looking directly ahead, hand on the hilt of his sword, his expression impassive, cold. A replicant of all the others. I wished he could look at me.

My belly swooped low when a large shadow cut across us, blotting out the rising sun. When I looked up, I caught a flash of red. Human-blood red, like mine.

The Elthika landed in front of all the rest. And suddenly I *did* feel a sharp, momentary bite of pure terror. My hand flew up to my pendant, a nervous habit, as if I could pour my fear into the gem enveloped in the metal.

This Elthika was the largest I'd ever seen, with maroon scales like dried blood. The flare of its wings alone could decimate my entire block. I even doubted it could land comfortably within the large paddock of the *pyroki* enclosure.

When it lowered its head, I saw that the eyes were a blazing red—a striking color matching its scales. Given the Elthika's size, I couldn't make out the rider on its back, if there was one. It studied each and every one of us, slow like an inquisitive serpent might.

Next to me, the Dakkari male's tail twitched uncontrollably, batting at the back of my calves repeatedly. He made a sound when the Elthika's eyes cut to him, a cross between a choke and a gasp.

Dropping my pendant, I snatched up his hand, giving it a squeeze. Though we didn't even know one another's names, he gripped it for dear life.

There were four of us going to Grym, and we were separated from those going to Sarroth. They were a group of eleven, a stark difference. I wondered how many of them were spies for the *Dothikkar*.

The guardsmen—who would go into rider training at Grym—looked like all the rest I'd ever seen patrolling the city. Standing tall, chins held high, eyes narrowed, as if anticipating the worst. One of them was a handsome male with black hair and hooded red eyes. He sported the look of someone afraid who could not show it…and so he overcompensated with a look of indifference, though I could see the way his lips were pulled tight around the corners. The other was unassuming, a male with brown hair that shone russet in the sunlight, slightly leaner and taller than the first.

The male whose hand I held…I assumed he was the one who'd be working the croplands, to gain intel of the Karag's food supply for the capital. He was no trained solider. He looked to be around my age and he was strong. I felt the callouses on his palms from farm work to prove his reason for being here.

He was a farmer. And I had only ever worked with *pyroki*. We were the outliers here, the weak links in the armor the *Dothikkar* had patched together for this ridiculous mission.

The thud of someone landing on hard earth made my pointed ears twitch. The red Elthika's wing raised…

And there was its rider.

Vorakkar.

That was my first thought, which whispered through my mind like a certain thing.

A horde king, like one of the ancient kings who'd roamed our wildlands, a fearsome leader, a merciless warrior.

Though he was no horde king. How could he be?

He was a Karag, who rode on the back of a terrifying Elthika, who had come from across the sea. And I wondered who was insane enough to try to claim an Elthika such as *this* one.

Its rider stepped forward, his wide palm pressed against the scales of his dragon. I wondered if they felt like *pyroki* scales, like unyielding metal.

The hush that drenched the crowd was almost too intense. The silence was only broken up by the thud of wings of the patrolling Elthika still flying overhead…and by the booted footsteps of the rider as he approached.

His hair was silver, though his age seemed at odds with the color. The top half of the silky strands was pulled back from his angular face, and the rest fell past his wide shoulders. His jaw was a hardened line, cut so sharply as though with a whistling sweep of a sword, and a long scar ran down his face, curving to his neck.

The scar, however, did nothing to diminish his otherworldly beauty. It only made him more menacing, and I had to fight the urge to flinch when I saw his gaze sweep over us all.

It was disrespectful to look a horde king in the eye unless you were a friend, a blood member of his family, or a mate. And so, briefly, I lowered it on impulse. I'd never met a horde king in my life, had only ever lived in Dothik, but the stories had been imprinted on me from birth.

When I remembered that this was no horde king but a Karag rider, I lifted my chin and looked up. His gaze had moved on, but I saw they were a bright blue…crystalline and icy.

The rider went to the line of travelers going to Sarroth first. He was at least a head taller than all of them, I noticed. I'd thought, foolishly, that riders might have a more sinewy bulk, might be smaller in size. Only to realize I'd been very, very wrong.

He inspected the travelers, walking in a slow line, meeting each and every eye he came across. Remaining utterly silent. And I thought one or two of the Dakkari might wet themselves where they stood, the way they trembled under his inspection.

I didn't know what he was looking for…but then he gestured back at one of his riders, who came forward and ushered the Sarrothian group toward two of the Elthika with the larger transport saddles on their backs. I didn't watch them climb up the mighty wings, each unsure of how to ascend, because then he came to us.

The four of us, held apart, going to Grym.

I was at the very end of the line, and he did the same thing as he did to the Sarroth travelers. He inspected the two guardsmen first, his face impassive.

Then he came to the farmer, whose tail flicked again, striking my legs, whose sweaty palm I could feel quake in my nearly numb grip.

Then I heard the soft thud of his boots come closer, crunching earth and gravel, though my eyes were still trained on his Elthika.

When his shadow fell over me, I remembered he was not a horde king…and so I lifted my eyes to his.

Up close, his eyes were even more piercing, even more haunting than I could have imagined. Craning my head back, I held them steadily, determined to show no fear. If he was trying to intimidate us, or to size us up, I wanted to give him no reason to find me lacking.

Something strange happened.

Our gazes held for impossibly long, time slowing. The rider frowned, a subtle and slight downturn of his full lips, as he peered at me more closely, his observation sharpening.

Then in a desperate panic, my heart lurched. I felt the pull of my heartstone magic wiggling in my chest, as if summoned by an unseen force. I nearly gasped as shock withered my veins.

Not here, not here, I thought.

Then where? a mocking voice replied. Not mine. A male's voice.

His?

Impossible.

Don't tell me what's possible, little Dakkari, he replied, his voice a seductive whisper, threading through my mind and body like we were one. *Shall I turn your mind inside out and see all your secrets spill?*

I felt a surge of magic inside me—my own—and I envisioned a blade.

The connection broke, and I felt it like a cord pulled tight, severed. Relief came.

Suddenly I could breathe again. I bundled my magic up tight, shoving it back, locking it away as I struggled to calm my racing heart. Praying that no one had seen, hoping my eyes hadn't been glowing.

The rider stared down at me, though I couldn't read his expression. Behind him, his Elthika's gaze sharpened on me.

Finally, the rider stepped back, and I almost went limp, as though I was a puppet controlled with strings. My hard swallow felt loud. I realized the farmer boy was trying to shake off my hand because I was holding him too tight, and I let go, feeling cool air rush against my sweating palm.

He was inside my mind, I thought in disbelief.

"I am Alaryk Arn'dyne," the rider said. His voice sounded as it had in my mind. A rough velvet that made goose bumps spread over my arms. Calm yet cutting. "Rider of Samryn."

He gestured back to his Elthika, who stomped its legs at the sound of its title, making the earth boom and my bones rattle.

Alaryk Arn'dyne's gaze cut back to me when he said, "I am the *Karath* of Grym."

Shock made me freeze.

Karath.

So this was the king of Grym…

I hadn't expected him to make the journey personally.

My jaw was clenched so tightly I thought my teeth might pulverize. Maybe there was a reason you never met the gaze of a horde king. Maybe *Karaths* were the same. Maybe they could steal one's soul. Maybe it was a warning.

"We will be seeing a lot of one another…though I doubt you'll last the season," Alaryk continued. His head inclined toward the remaining Elthika with a transport saddle. "There's your way to Grym. Ascend. Or it's your last chance to stay in your homeland."

I cut a glance over my shoulder when the two guardsmen stepped toward the Elthika without hesitation. I looked at my mother and father. The tears streaking my *lomma*'s face shimmered in the rising sun. I offered a smile, one I didn't feel.

It'll be okay, I wanted to tell her. My father's face was solemn at her side, though he offered me a small smile back, a slight nod. The steady pillar, always.

Then I looked at Kiron. He *was* looking at me now. He inclined his head, subtly, before straightening. They were the only representatives from the *Dothikkar*'s palace. Not even the king had come.

Crouching, I snagged my single satchel off the ground, everything I'd be living off of for the next season, before looping it around my shoulders. Then my feet carried me to the dragon, noticing that the *Karath* of Grym had gone to one of his other riders, was speaking with him in low tones, the words of which I couldn't make out.

The wing of the Elthika was stretched out toward the earth, the guardsmen having already ascended up it, taking a prime place next to the Grym rider sitting at the helm. The farmer was halfway up, his strides well balanced and surprisingly agile. I reached my hand out to touch the Elthika's wing—though my prior awe was now shrouded in worry. The wing membrane felt like layers and layers of thick, hardened leather.

I climbed up after the farmer, navigating the thick bones of the wing, the climb getting steeper and steeper the higher I went. Finally, I fell down into the saddle, taking my place beside the farmer, in the second row behind the guardsmen.

I looked over Dothik on the back of an Elthika, at the crowd that had gathered. At the towering building of my home in the Market District and then down at my family.

Samryn, the *Karath's* Elthika, flapped its wings. I noticed the other Elthika had given it a wide berth, clustered together away from the red dragon. Alaryk had already returned to his place on Samryn's back, and he was looking at *me*.

I remembered the whisper of his voice in my mind and forced my gaze away, just in case he could wiggle his way inside through the brief connection.

He had heartstone magic—that much was clear. But I had bigger issues now. Because if he could let himself into the door of my mind, this had just made the mission all the more dangerous. I'd never given thought to what would happen to us if we were *caught* spying for the *Dothikkar*.

Now I worried it would mean a certain death. For *all* of us.

"*Thryn'ar*," came Alaryk's call, the word short and commanding. An order.

The Elthika below us vibrated with energy, like it was pulling it from the ground around it. I heard the farmer cry out beside me, huddling deeper into the side of the saddle, hands scrambling for purchase on anything as we catapulted into the air on dragonback.

The shimmering scales of the Elthika caught sunlight. I pressed my fingertips over the half wall of the saddle, to touch the plating of its side. Just like *pyroki* scales—hard like metal, but flexible and shifting with its movements.

Familiar.

Halna was right. There was much to learn. Maybe we weren't so different from one another. Our beasts certainly weren't.

Behind me, I saw the stretch of Dothik, the tiny dots of people below, of everyone I'd ever loved made small and unrecognizable. The city sparkled, smoke rose from turrets, people milled in the markets.

Overhead, I heard a mighty roar. Samryn, bloodred, flew above us, taking the very tip of a flying formation.

Before us stretched the glimmer of Drukkar's Sea.

And beyond that?

Karak.

CHAPTER 4
ALARYK

Samryn's amusement strummed through the bond as he watched a Dakkari stumble down the wings of the Elthika.

"Amusement" with a heaping dose of derision. Samryn was a Vyrin, after all. An ancient. He could be impatient and temperamental because he'd lived long enough to run through his supply of patient understanding.

It was my duty to keep him tethered, and so I pressed my hand to the side of his wide jaw, a heaping huff falling from him, blowing back my hair. I sent a rebuke of my own, funneling it down the thread of my own magic.

"Because of the Dakkari, we have heartstones once more," I reminded Samryn. His red gaze flicked to me. There was a strain there. Something he'd been trying to shield from me. I could feel it grow in conjunction with my own worry. *Not again.* "We should show…gratitude."

Elthika could not understand our language. They had one all their own, which the Karag could not replicate. But Samryn and I were bonded beyond imagine…and so we communicated with shared emotion.

He shook off my rebuke, raising his head so my palm fell

away, and made a chortled growl when a young Dakkari male took a topple to the ground.

"You're impossible," I murmured, trying to hide the way my own lips twitched. A feeling within me bloomed, one of annoyance, but it was my Elthika's. "Very well. Sit here and enjoy the spectacle."

Samryn's smug satisfaction had me shaking my head as I walked away. The ground quaked behind me when he curled himself down onto the earth. I tried to shake the feeling of unease. I feared the sickness was returning. Samryn's breathing had been labored during flight, but every time I'd tried to squeeze beyond the gap of our natural bond, he'd shut me out, an edged warning following the simmering rejection.

Though we were bonded and had been for years, Samryn was still an Elthika. I could not break his trust, and he deserved his privacy and my respect. Even if I was only trying to help the stubborn ancient.

Myzalla was instructing my *kya'rassa*—my rider horde—to be ready within the next hour for the final leg of the journey. There was a group of trusted riders from Sarroth—Sarkin's territory— that would lead their Dakkari to its borders. This was our resting place, and then both groups would break away to their final destinations.

"Anything you want to add, *Karath*?" Myzalla asked me when she saw my approach. She was my second-in-command, my wing commander. A damn good rider, a longtime friend, and she kept a tight leash on the *kya'rassa* for me...if I was otherwise distracted.

I looked around the small circle. A rider horde I had handpicked for this brief journey, many of whom I still made uneasy.

"Nothing at all," I replied. "We'll leave as soon as the Dakkari have rested. Take advantage of the break."

I dismissed the group, catching sight of the Dakkari female over Myzalla's shoulder. She'd helped up the Dakkari male who'd fallen on his descent, the one who'd be helping to work the crop-land. Brune was his name.

But my eyes were drawn to the female in particular. I recalled her name on the list from the *Dothikkar*'s own advisors.

Amaia of Rath Savenal. The *pyroki* master's apprentice in Dothik, who was said to be particularly gifted with the beasts.

"See something you like?" Myzalla's voice cut through my observation.

"I see something I don't trust," I told her, keeping my voice low so I wouldn't be overheard. Her teasing smile faded, and she darted a look over her shoulder. "That's even worse."

"The girl?" Myzalla asked quietly. "She's so young."

"Irrelevant," I said, thinking that she could only be a handful of years younger than Myzalla.

"What did you feel?" my wing commander asked.

"Wildness. Untamed magic. She's powerful," I said softly and without thinking. I met Myzalla's golden eyes as she digested the words. "But what she can do remains to be seen. Heartstone magic isn't a crime against her. But she was able to break my tether easily. That's what worries me."

"The Dakkari didn't mention that—"

"The Dakkari are afraid. Likely, so is she," I said. "I'd bet the *Dothikkar*'s advisors don't even know what they sent to me."

A gift. Or…trouble.

"I'll keep careful watch of her," Myzalla promised me quietly, "when we reach the Arsadia."

I inclined my head. "She's assigned to the hatchery, correct?"

"Yes," she replied. "Do you think we should split them up? Keep the Dakkari rider acolytes in the Arsadia and her and the other boy in Grym?"

"No," I decided. "They all go to the Arsadia."

"Do you want me to alert Tarkosh about her, at least?"

"Not yet," I replied. "I'll dig into her more before I decide.

But I'll make that decision when I join you in the Arsadia. Keep them out of trouble for the week."

Myzalla threw me a dry look. "Running off to Grym and leaving me saddled with a bunch of Dakkari? When you chose me as your wing commander, this wasn't exactly what I had in mind."

I grinned, warm and hopefully charming, because I knew she was only teasing. "You were my *only* choice. Never forget that."

Her expression softened. "I know, Alaryk."

I inclined my head at her, one of my oldest friends. She'd known me ever since I was a Hartan boy, with strange hair and even stranger eyes, dropped into the unforgiving place of Grym as a hybrid child. We'd grown up in the same village. And, well, children could be mean, I knew. But I'd shown I could be meaner, and she'd never been frightened of that. She'd *understood*.

I looked to the sky, seeing the sunlight waning. "I'll leave now. If anything changes, send a missive to the citadel. I'll finish up there as soon as I can and be in the Arsadia before the moon wanes."

"Fly beneath Muron's wings, my friend," she murmured, something she always said. A superstition she clung to, just as she always kissed the pendant her husband had gifted her before she got onto the back of her Elthika.

"You as well," I replied, knowing it would bring her comfort.

The Dakkari were huddled together, sitting on logs of the forest clearing we'd landed in. They were tearing into the bread they'd been given and drinking from water skins. I felt a strand of pity wind through me. They weren't used to being on Elthika-back, but they would learn. Especially the ones who wished to be acolytes.

My gaze landed on the girl. As if sensing my gaze, hers rose to meet it. She straightened in mild alarm to find my sudden obser-vation, the lump of bread that had been afforded to her resting in her palm, forgotten.

Her black waves were windswept, making a wild but beautiful mess around her head. Her skin, a light tawny brown, looked irritated from the violence of the flight. The whites of her eyes were bloodshot, red veins branching towards the luminous green of her irises. *Fascinating,* I thought.

She was tall for a female, I'd noticed. Her build athletic, strong. No doubt from handling *pyrokis* for years. While *pyrokis* were no Elthika, I'd observed the wild beasts during my time in Dakkar and knew they possessed a strong will coupled with their sheer power. It couldn't have been easy.

Puzzlement filled me. She'd broken my tether so easily on the wildlands, and yet I'd sensed no steady, certain root within her magic. It was likely she didn't know how to wield it properly… and *that* was a dangerous thing. Unrooted heartstone magic was unpredictable. I would know that better than anyone.

Amaia of Rath Savenal broke my gaze first, darting it back down to the lump of bread in her hand, as if surprised to see it there.

She was a problem I'd deal with in the Arsadia, I decided.

But for now, I had one too many of those in Grym. And so I turned back to Samryn for the next leg of my journey home.

CHAPTER 5
AMAIA

"Amaia," came the voice, followed by a jostling of my shoulder. I gasped, shaken awake, though it was a mystery how I'd fallen asleep to begin with.

Brune's hooded eyes were peering off to the left of me, into the yawning darkness of night.

"Look."

After nearly three constant days on Elthika-back, with very little sleep or privacy, all I wanted was to plant my feet on the ground and never leave it again.

My back hurt something fierce, an unpleasant crick in my neck from being hunched down in an awkward position while sleeping in the saddle. The constant rhythm of the Elthika's flight made the hard leather of the seat press into places I would definitely feel in the coming weeks—places I could already feel ache. I was bruised, I knew. Just like I'd been when I'd first started riding on the backs of *pyrokis*, only I had a feeling this would be worse.

We were still flying, into the dead of night. While the moon was nearing full brightness, there was a heavy cloud cover tonight that obstructed nearly all of its light. Before I'd fallen asleep, I could make out the tops of trees and the dull shimmer of lakes as we flew over them.

But when I turned my gaze to follow Brune's, I pressed forward, against the steel of the rail that kept us safely enclosed on the seat.

Just when I thought it might never end, I saw lights below.

A village? I wondered, my lips parting in hopeful, excited awe.

In the distance I saw towering, darkened mountains, their tips and cliffs clean and sharp like blades. Below were forests, thick and seemingly impenetrable. When a misty cloud passed by the moon, I saw the light reflect off what I thought was a tumbling waterfall, so massive that I swore I could feel the spray thousands of feet off the ground.

And nestled into a flat valley on the edge of a forest, bracketed by mountains, was a village, not unlike a *saruk* in Dakkar. An outpost. I could make out the shadowed dwellings and larger structures illuminated by soft golden light.

When I felt the Elthika tilt, swinging in a sharp left to circle back around, I felt my heart leap in relief. Maybe tonight I would be able to sleep on the earth. And I never wanted to leave it again. I wanted to press my cheek into the hardened ground, and I would be thankful for the stillness, the calm.

Next to me, Brune groaned, "Thank Kakkari."

In the front row of the cramped seat saddle, I eyed the backs of the two *darukkars'* heads. They'd said not a word to either of us, had barely even spoken to one another. Now that we were descending to the village, I realized I had no inkling of an idea of what I was supposed to *do* once I got there. But at the moment, I didn't care. All I wanted was to get off this dragon's back.

Tomorrow I would worry about the blue-eyed *Karath*, whose smoky voice had whispered through my mind like a touch. Tomorrow I would worry what that would *mean* for us, for our mission.

Tonight, however? Food and sleep.

When the Elthika landed with a hard thump onto the earth —in a large clearing a few stone throws around from a perimeter fence, I saw—I nearly sobbed with giddiness. Brune nearly tumbled again as he clamored down the dragon's outstretched wing. At the bottom, he did trip and fall, but he seemed relieved, lying on the ground for a moment, even though the *darukkars* merely stepped over him.

I was the last to descend, brushing my hand against the Elthika's scales, thinking that I was grateful it had worked so hard to get us to this place. Its breathing was labored, as if the long journey had been strenuous on it too.

"Please tell me we're staying put now," I heard Brune say in a tired voice to the Karag who'd been at the helm of our Elthika. "Please tell me this is Grym."

"This is not Grym," the Karag grunted back. "But we are staying."

Not Grym? I wondered, frowning, my legs shaking as I navigated the large wing of the Elthika. When my feet hit the ground, I could swear my whole body vibrated in pleasure, even as I crouched down beside Brune.

"You all right?" I asked, placing my hand on his back.

I felt his sigh vibrate his entire body, running up my arm.

"*Lysi,*" he replied. *Yes.*

He pushed himself up from the ground, and I helped him stand until he found stability in his trembling legs again.

Brune looked around, peering at the perimeter fence and the plethora of Elthika that had landed with their riders nearby. "If we're not in Grym, then where are we?" he wondered.

"No idea," I breathed out, wiggling my toes in my boots, needle pricks zinging down my legs from the cramped riding seat.

"This is their outpost for the rider season," came one of the *darukkar's* voices.

I turned to look at him. He was handsome—a full-blooded

Dakkari male, from the looks of him…and from the sweeping tail that brushed the ground. One of the *Dothikkar's* loyal guards.

"We haven't gotten a moment alone, so let's take advantage," came the other guard's softened voice. His reddish-brown hair was curled around his tipped ears, his golden eyes flashing in the moonlight.

"I'm Ryak," the first guardsman said. He had hooded eyes, the color red. His black hair hung to his shoulders, half of it pulled back from his face, secured in a bone clip. I thought it impressive it hadn't fallen out for the duration of the flight. "This is Nevin."

"Brune," the farmer's son chimed in, placing a hand over his chest.

"And you're Amaia," Ryak said, turning his gaze on me before cutting it back to Brune, baring his teeth in a half smile. "We know."

I heard Brune's hard swallow, felt the slap of his tail against my leg again.

I hugged my arms around my waist. It was cooler here than in Dothik this time of year, and all I had were the clothes stuffed in my travel pack.

"What are we meant to do, exactly?" I asked Ryak quietly. Because I had a feeling he was the one in charge, not Nevin. If I hadn't come, it would've been my brother at Ryak's side.

"Whatever we tell you to do," Ryak answered simply.

I frowned, my shoulders tightening at the cold arrogance in his voice. The way he'd said it set my teeth on edge. And whether it was my exhaustion or frustration from being here in the first place, I didn't know. Even I knew to hold my tongue, but I simply didn't care in that moment.

"I came here as a favor to my brother," I said with gritted teeth. "I did not agree to take orders from one of the *Dothikkar's* pets. If you don't have a plan you can give us, then what in Kakkari's name are we doing here?"

"Watch yourself," Ryak murmured, observing me with narrowed eyes. "In Dothik, I could cut out your tongue for speaking to me that way."

And it was on the tip of my tongue to tell him to try it, but I took in a deep breath, especially when I felt Brune's tail swat at me, this time seemingly intentionally.

"My apologies," I said woodenly. I added, "*Darukkar.*"

Ryak let out a sharp breath through his nostrils as he regarded me, tipping his chin back. We would not get along. I could already tell that outright.

"Just relax," Ryak told me. Told us both. "Get an understanding of your assigned positions. Then we'll talk."

They aren't telling us something, I thought. But it didn't make sense because I knew my brother wouldn't have deceived me about coming here. He wouldn't have lied to me about my purpose here.

So why did I have a bad feeling in the pit of my stomach, especially when I saw Nevin exchange a look with Ryak as they turned from us both?

Brune met my eyes. He shook his head, looking at me beseechingly, as if asking if I was nuts to speak to a guardsman that way.

"Dakkari!" came the voice. A female rider, one I'd seen speaking with the *Karath* a couple days prior before he'd taken off on his Elthika. I hadn't seen any sign of him since, which was relieving. Maybe he wouldn't even be here. Wherever here was. Maybe he was back in Grym, where he belonged.

The rider was beckoning us over, near the fence perimeter of the village. A crowd had started to gather, people inspecting us and murmuring to themselves, despite the late hour.

It was difficult to wrap my head around the fact that I wasn't in Dakkar anymore. I was in a place where very few of my people had ever stepped foot.

There was excitement at the prospect, especially in regard to working in an Elthikan hatchery. But there was also fear. And now an even deeper sense of paranoia if we were caught doing… whatever the hell we were meant to do.

Only a season, I reminded myself. *Take advantage. Then you can go home. Back to your family, back to your* pyroki. *Back to your life.*

And Kiron would be safe.

I felt better knowing that. And so I followed behind Brune when he started to approach the perimeter fence.

The rider waited until all four of us where there. She peered at the group that had gathered. Karag looked no different than we did, especially in Dothik where bloodlines mingled. Some had darker skin, some lighter. Some had tails, some did not. The coloring of their eyes were all different shades, catching in the moonlight—some blue, some yellow, some red, some brown.

There were both young and old. Children hiding behind their parents' legs to peer up at us with wide eyes. I smiled down at a boy who couldn't have been more than five years, and he turned his face to bury it into his mother's hip, shy.

I thought of my own mother, hoping she wasn't too worried about me.

My heart was beating quickly, uncomfortable with so many eyes on us after the long flight we'd had.

"These are the exchanges from Dakkar," the rider announced to the crowd. "And since I know you lot love the gossip, let me assuage some of your curiosity." She pointed to the guardsmen. "Ryak and Nevin. They'll be trying their hand at rider training this season."

I heard snickers and murmurs rise up from the crowd, and I nearly arched in satisfaction at what a blow to Ryak's ego that would be.

"Better head back to Dothik now, boys," came a roughened voice. "Wouldn't want you to hurt yourselves."

Laughs erupted, and the female rider bit out a sharp, weary sigh.

Ryak spoke, his arms crossed, voice firm: "I'm claiming an Elthika, or they'll send my lifeless body back home. There are no other options."

"That's if there's a body to find," came another voice. "A death fall at Tharken? You'll be splattered into pieces."

I nearly shuddered, thinking of Kiron.

"Enough," the female rider said. She gestured over to me. "This is Amaia. She'll be training at the hatchery."

Dozens and dozens of eyes turned to me, momentarily freezing me in place when I was still imagining the horrific vision of my brother falling off the back of an Elthika, his mouth in an open scream.

I inclined my head, dropping my gaze. Luckily no one had anything to say. No baby dragon maulings of their handlers in the hatchery, apparently.

"And this is Brune. He'll be working the outer croplands for the season."

Brune's tail was flicking in apparent nerves, braced for barbed words. His shoulders relaxed when he received none.

"Right." The female rider sighed. "Rider acolytes"—she gestured to Ryak and Nevin—"you'll stay in the bunks for now. Erm, Syris? Where is she?"

"Here, Myzalla," came a soft, husky voice. A female stepped forward as the crowd parted, dressed in a thick brown dress that brushed the tops of her booted feet. She had long indigo-colored hair, as dark as the night sky, braided in a neat plait. Her eyes were yellow, and there was a deep scar running vertically through the outer left of her lips, leaving a gash like a thick seam.

"Ahh," the female rider murmured. Myzalla, I would endeavor to remember. "You have room in the hatchery, yes?"

"Yes, Beyla stayed in Grym for the season."

"Good. Take Amaia and get her settled there. Bring her to Tarkosh in the morning."

My gaze connected with Syris, and she gave me a hesitant smile, one I returned.

"And Brune…Nysa and his son have agreed to let you stay with them for the season. You'll be working with them closely."

An older Karag male stepped forward, his silver hair tied at the nape of his neck. There was a streak of mud on his black trousers.

"Well, what are you waiting for? I'll be sleeping for two days, so no one bother me," Myzalla barked. Laughs rose from the crowd. I knew the dozens of Karag who were in attendance couldn't possibly be all of the village we'd seen from above…but it was late.

"Good luck," I said to Brune when he turned to me.

"See you around?" he asked.

"Of course."

Then with a deep inhale, though eager for a bed and a meal, I approached Syris, who stood waiting on the outskirts of the crowd.

"You must be tired," she said when I reached her. She was shy, a little uncertain of her words, which were spoken as if they were a question.

"I am," I said.

"Follow me, then," she said after studying me, her eyes flickering across my face. "I'll show you to your new home."

CHAPTER 6
AMAIA

The entrance of the hatchery was protected by a fenced-in stone courtyard and illuminated with glowing orbs that sat atop alabaster pedestals. The orbs shone a warm amber, casting deep shadows across the double doors, set into the wide archway.

I couldn't make out the sheer scale and size of the building but truthfully was too tired to care much about it at the present moment. Beyond the entrance, there was a small empty chamber, and Syris led me through another doorway directly forward.

There was a hushed quiet that seeped into these stone walls, the kind of quiet that made me hold my breath as I followed after Syris.

"This is where we usually keep the hatchling pens," she announced, her quiet voice incredibly loud in the echoing chamber. I nearly jumped, a sharp exhale escaping me. "But it's not mating season yet. The only eggs we have are rescues and a few late-nesting broods from some of our Elthika. Rythbacks, specifically. But their kind are more prone to late nestings anyway."

My mind reeled with the stream of information. "It's not mating season?" I asked, my voice bouncing through the empty chamber, as if to amplify my unspoken question.

If there were no Elthika eggs, then why open the position for the exchange?

"Oh, no," Syris replied. "Riding season is here. After the *illa'rosh*, the Elthika will begin to nest."

The *illa'rosh*? It was apparent I had much to learn.

"Right," I said softly, as if I had any idea what she was talking about. "So what am I meant to do here?"

"Don't misunderstand," Syris said, casting me a glance, biting the unscarred section of her mouth with worry. "There is still plenty to do with the eggs we have. Rythbacks are always more... needful than others. But you'll learn."

I gave her a small, tired smile. "I'll take your word for it."

We entered another chamber after Syris slid open the bolted latch on the door. When we stepped through, I felt the heat hit me like a wall, a strange earthy smell that reminded me of *pyrokis*, making me suck in a sharp breath. Suddenly, longing for home cut through me. The memory of the *pyroki* pens in the early mornings as I made my rounds gave me—

There they were.

Elthika eggs.

Each nestled into little alcoves along the stone walls. The alcoves themselves were oval in shape, similar in curvature to an individual egg, with a flat base. My heart picked up in excitement, my exhaustion and sore legs momentarily banished as I approached one.

The alcove base was flat because each egg was nestled into a bed of what looked like glowing embers. I could feel the heat radiate from them, but it didn't look like fire. There were no flames, I noticed, perplexed.

"Starstone," Syris explained, joining me. "Clusters of them fall in the Arsadia during winter. We break them up because they're a constant heat source for incubation."

"The Arsadia?" I asked, my eyes pinned to the stones. They looked like rubies, like fire gems, glistening in the darkness like each trapped a pool of lava. Like the gem around my own neck.

And the egg itself…it was larger than I expected. The size of a large water jug with overlapping scales that resembled a *pyroki*'s.

"This is the Arsadia," Syris explained. "This land. Elthikan territory."

My expression must have been one of frustrated puzzlement because Syris gave me a smile filled with amused sympathy.

"I'm certain it will get easier with time. Especially after a good night's rest. Whenever I have to travel to Grym, I just want to sleep for days on end."

Before I could ask any more questions, she ushered me through the chamber of eggs. I counted a dozen or so. Most of them were similar in color—a pale beige with tones of copper— but a few I spied tucked into their separate alcoves were vastly different shades. One a deep bloodred, the color of the *Karath*'s dragon, Samryn. Another was black with shimmering scales tipped in silver. Another was a beautiful shade of light blue, almost iridescent like *thissie* feathers from home.

Wonderment filled me, and while I was loath to leave the chamber, I realized that I would be patient. I would learn every-thing. Not for the *Dothikkar*, but because I wanted to. Because I thought I might love these creatures as much as I did *pyrokis*.

Syris latched the chamber door behind us, going through another hallway that cut through the building. I saw door after door, some open, some closed.

She went to an open one and gestured inside. "Your cham-bers," she explained.

I stepped inside, seeing the candle sconces already lit on the wall, their wax dripping, one making a little puddle on the stone floor, which was partially covered in a thin rug to keep the chill away.

There were two small beds on either side of the room, a large window along the wall between them, moonlight streaming through it. A table sat next to the door, and I saw a tray there, with a carafe of water and dried meats, nuts with wrinkled flesh, and a thick crust of bread.

"I prepared the room," Syris said, her cheeks pinkening a bit. "I hope you'll be comfortable."

"You're too kind," I told her softly.

"It's all yours," she explained, casting her eyes to the empty, unmade bed. "It's offseason, so there are only a few of us working in the hatchery right now. I'm right next door if you need anything. Oh, and you'll find the washroom at the very end of the hallway. We all share it."

I nodded my head.

"Get some rest," she told me as I set down my travel sack against the table leg. "I'll come get you in the morning so you can meet Tarkosh."

"Tarkosh?"

"She oversees the hatchery," Syris explained. "We all apprentice beneath her."

Just like home, then, I thought, thinking of my own *mrikro*.

"*Kakkira vor*, Syris," I said. When her brow furrowed, I amended sheepishly, "Thank you."

"Oh," she said, looking flustered. "That's what Dakkari sounds like. I've always wondered."

My half-hearted chuckle echoed as she gave me another smile and bid me good night, taking her leave. She closed the door behind her, leaving me on my own.

Finally, I thought, eyeing the bed. Though it was raised from the earth, on wooden legs, I wouldn't question it. In fact, I thought of nothing else—not the food, not changing out of my dirtied clothes—as I headed straight for it.

I might've already been asleep by the time my body met the thin mattress.

"She can be…harsh at times," Syris told me as she led me through the hatchery hallway, streams of sunlight pouring in from the windows. "But you will find no one with more knowledge of Elthikan hatchlings in all of Karak."

She said that last bit proudly, though her voice was nearly a whisper, as if she was worried Tarkosh would overhear.

"I'm glad," I said truthfully, squaring my shoulders. "I want to learn from the best. That's why I'm here."

A small lie, perhaps, but also a partial truth. Why wouldn't I take advantage of being here? Last night had sparked determination and wonderment in me, which had only amplified after a good night's sleep.

"I trust you slept well?" Syris asked me. "Were you comfortable? I know it can get cold in the rooms at night—"

"It was perfect," I told her in assurance. "I don't think I moved once. And that washing tub this morning was probably the best thing I'd ever experienced after flying for who knows how long."

Her slight giggle was cut short when someone pulled open a door to our right suddenly. Another bedroom, I saw. A male stepped through, bleary-eyed, swiftly tying the laces of his trousers. Behind him, I caught a flash of naked legs, still in bed.

He looked surprised to see us standing there. He only glanced at me momentarily, his eyes narrowing before they cut to Syris. "Is Tarkosh up?"

"For hours," she replied, her tone a little stiff. "You know the rules. No outside visitors when we have eggs in the—"

He tugged the door firmly closed behind himself and snorted. "Like anyone follows those rules."

"You're the only one who breaks them," Syris sniffed.

"Then who's *this*?" he growled, jerking his head at me.

He was a handsome male, I noticed, with dark skin that made his green irises appear darker, and a commanding presence.

"This is Amaia," Syris answered, her tone defensive, almost snappish. I held back a smile. "Our new apprentice. From Dakkar."

"Pleased to meet you," I said.

His gaze was assessing. Mistrustful. "A true Dakkari," he murmured. "Huh. I'm disappointed."

My brows rose. I nearly laughed. Not in offense. In incredulousness. I also knew what he was doing. Sizing me up. Testing me. I'd dealt with it for years with Myre, since we were both after the same position.

"Maybe you can write to the *Dothikkar* about your displeasure," I suggested, lifting a shoulder in a shrug. "I hear he loves to take complaints from the Karag."

He tilted his head at me. Then he snorted again, shaking his head. "Washroom free?"

"Yes," Syris replied, her gaze going to the closed door behind him meaningfully. For someone seemingly afraid of her own shadow, she wasn't backing down. "Please show your guest out before Tarkosh finds out."

His heavy sigh followed him down the hallway. I could feel Syris stiffen with annoyance, and then she scoffed a little under her breath before resuming our path down the hallway. We went past the incubation room from last night, though I could feel the heat seep from it like flesh.

"Former lover?" I asked softly.

Her face flooded red. "Me and Moak? On Muron, no."

I suppressed a smile, nodding. Interesting.

Syris cleared her throat. "He just thinks he's above the rules. He forgets they're there for a reason."

She guided us through a heavy wood door, and I heard a strange animal sound. The door led out to a fenced-in courtyard, decorative tree plants along the perimeter for privacy. Beyond the courtyard, around trunks and boughs of the gnarled trees, I saw stone houses, smoke rising from chimneys, all shadowed in the morning light from the mountain behind them. I swore I saw the dark flash of an Elthika disappear into the side of the jagged rockface.

The sound I'd heard came again. A rumbling growl coupled with a low chirping that reminded me of a young *pyroki*.

I saw wings first. Small wings, the membranes so thin that they were nearly translucent. His scales were a sleek gray threaded with black strands and he had two small horns protruding from his thick skull.

"Is that…?"

"Yes," Syris answered me.

A baby dragon. Or whatever the term was that the Karag used.

"A hatchling," Syris told me, as if reading my mind. Which, for a moment, I'd worried she might've.

You're being silly, I thought, shaking off the worry as I watched the hatchling dart around the courtyard on strong limbs. It was no bigger than a newborn *pyroki*. Small enough that I might be able to cradle it in my arms.

"Hatched only three days ago," came a voice.

There was a Karag female, seated on a bench in the shadow of a tree to our right. She had a small silver cup in her hand, and she took a sip from it as she regarded me carefully over the rim. She had golden eyes and dark gray hair. And when she stood from her place, I saw she was taller than even me, dressed in black fitted trousers and a silvery blue long-sleeved tunic.

There were wrinkles around the corners of her eyes and mouth, which made her look like she was perpetually frowning.

"You must be Amaia," she murmured, setting her cup down on the small metal table next to her. The hatchling dragon scampered past my leg, like it had energy to burn. "Amaia of Rath Savenal."

I blinked, not having heard my bloodline's name addressed by a Karag before.

"Yes, that's right," I said, inclining my head at her in respect.

"What exactly do you wish to discover here?" she asked quietly.

My brow furrowed, and I glanced up at her, meeting her golden eyes. "I want to learn."

"What?"

"*Everything,*" I said, waving my hand to gesture at the hatchling, to the hatchery behind me.

"A tall ask for a single season," she replied. I assumed this was Tarkosh, the master of the hatchery.

"I know," I said. "But my *mrikro* told me that our creatures might not be so different from one another, that they were all given life by Kakkari. I've worked with *pyrokis* nearly my entire life. I hope to apply some of that experience here. It's why I'm here."

Tarkosh assessed me, her eyes narrowed. Then she smiled. I relaxed, but only briefly, because she then said, "And yet we are very different. We don't believe in your Kakkari. We believe in our Elthika. And if you think that your little earthen beasts are anything like them, then you have much to learn."

My smile died slowly. "What shall I call you?" I asked, not one to be defeated by words.

"By my name. What else?"

"In Dakkar, we address the masters with a title of respect, befitting their knowledge and experience."

Tarkosh said, "But we aren't in Dakkar, Amaia. Call me Tarkosh and nothing else."

I swallowed, then forced a smile. "Tarkosh."

"This is a Rythback," she told me, changing the subject entirely, since our first meeting wasn't going as smoothly as I'd hoped. "A species of Elthika that dominate the northwest of our homeland. His egg was found rejected by the mother. While you're here, you'll likely be primarily handling Rythbacks. We have another ten in incubation currently."

"Yes," I said, glancing at Syris, who was standing back. "Syris explained that they tend to nest late?"

Tarkosh nodded, her lips pinching. "We expect another to hatch in the coming days. So be careful what you wish for. Rythbacks are menaces at this age. Today you can acquaint yourself with this one. Enjoy the reprieve while you can."

With that, she walked past me.

"And where is Moak?" she asked Syris. "Ulin needs help with the nests."

Syris's voice squeaked as she said, "He's in the washroom… he'll be out shortly."

I noticed she didn't snitch on his guest, but I turned my attention to the hatchling that was scurrying around the courtyard. Not even my less than wonderful meeting with Tarkosh would deter my awed smile as I crouched down.

"Hello, little one," I greeted when the hatchling approached me with wariness. Tarkosh had referred to it as a "he." I wanted to know how to discern that for myself. A *pyroki's* sex, to an untrained eye, was difficult to determine, but I could tell almost immediately at birth. The slant of a jaw, the width and breadth of the ribs, the angle of a limb as it tapered down into their claws, the distance between their tall ears and horns.

The hatchling snapped at my hand, and I bit back a smile, in case he thought I was baring my teeth like a predator. He grunted, a constant huffing sound, before he snapped again. I felt his teeth that time, dull and nearly painless.

I could feel Tarkosh watching me and figured this was a test. I couldn't afford for her to write me off as a silly Dakkari fool.

I built up a little thimble of my heartstone magic, closing my eyes briefly as I imagined it shooting out of my fingertips, like warm currents of energy that would seep into the Elthika.

I could feel the hatchling's curious wariness, the thunderous beat of his heart against his ribs. I nearly gasped at the raw magic I felt flowing within the Elthika, so potent and surprising that it nearly brought tears pricking my eyes.

Awe channeled through me. I reached forward and felt the Elthika's snout sniff at my hand.

The moment I felt him arch into my palm, I cut off the current, sealing it back inside me. I couldn't afford to be exhausted by it, but I'd never connected with an Elthika before. Only *pyrokis*. Only my family.

"We'll be good friends," I murmured, my eyelids lifting to watch the Rythback male nuzzle into my hand, as if seeking more of the warmth of my heartstone magic. "Won't we?"

Footsteps approached behind me. Tarkosh peered down at me, her eyes flickering to the Elthika. Her gaze was assessing, puzzled. Maybe I could still make a good impression after all.

"It seems you aren't afraid," she said. "Good."

I felt a little pleasure bloom inside me.

"But we'll see if you last the day," she finished.

Clearly I had my work cut out for me.

CHAPTER 7
ALARYK

Grymia lay nestled at the base of the Rykish, a mountain range that stretched southwest all the way to the Tharken cliffs. In the lowering afternoon sun, glass gleamed in house windows and the circular skylight of the hatchery glowed like a beacon home.

Only the Arsadia had never felt like home to me.

Grym did…perhaps because it lay so close to the Hartan border. To the wide, rushing river that acted as a natural perimeter. Our land and their land.

The Arsadia was one of the most beautiful landscapes I'd ever set my gaze upon. Yet I'd take the blustery East Lands, the gray days, and the sheer rawness of my own territory at any moment's notice. Being in the Arsadia was a *Karath*'s duty during the rider season, though I was more lax with my time spent here than others might've been.

Especially now. Especially since I'd felt the familiar curse rising within Samryn these last months. I worried that even my own heartstone magic wouldn't be able to banish it this time. My magic had been a bandage on a forever-seeping wound, keeping it clean but never healing it.

The curse had been courtesy of a Hartan witch—or, rather, a

group of them—placed upon Samryn but with the intent to hurt *me*. And now I could feel its winding, nauseating tug, like creeping vines along a forest floor, sucking the life from the earth.

Samryn would feel it all the worse.

I could feel him, annoyed at the direction of my emotions. It wounded his pride when I thought him ill, the hard-skulled Elthika he was. Not only an Elthika, but a Vyrin. One of the ancients, from an even older bloodline. They deserved reverence, respect, and yet Samryn was brooding, his temper prickly with my worry.

He let out a low, huffing groan as if in answer.

I tethered my fear for him tight, not letting it escape its imprisonment because I knew what he would do in retaliation.

When he landed at the outpost field, I saw that Myzalla was already waiting for me. As I jumped off Samryn's back, he wouldn't quite meet my eyes.

"*Sen endrassa*," I murmured to him. My thanks, my respect. It was on the tip of my tongue to ask him to stay, for me to get Tarkosh, to see if she could do anything for him.

I could feel the wane of his strength, the budding rot building inside him. My hand shook as I placed it upon his jaw. But when he felt my heartstone magic, warm and pressing, he shook me off, the earth vibrating with his intake of energy before he leaped into the sky.

"Fuck," I ground out lowly. My chest ached. The sickness was spreading fast. It only seemed to get worse every single day. "Stubborn creature."

"Welcome home, *Karath*," came Myzalla's voice, the crunch of her footsteps behind me making me turn.

I hid the lines of my worry. I was only *Karath* because Samryn had chosen me.

I wondered the unthinkable: What would happen when death finally took him away?

I'd always been too afraid to even give weight to the thought.

Samryn was my bonded Elthika. And our bond stretched beyond others, deeper into the realm of heartstone magic. The loss of Samryn would be like the loss of half my own heart. A half-life. I would lose not only my Elthika, my friend, but would I lose Grym as well?

"You were meant to be here two days ago," Myzalla said with pursed lips.

"I got held up," I told her. "I'm here now, aren't I?"

She sighed. "You crossed the border again, didn't you?"

"The Hartans want to renegotiate the terms of their surrender."

"Did you tell them that's not how it works?" Myzalla grumbled. "Especially since it was nearly a decade ago?"

"The discovery of the heartstones in Dakkar changed their minds," I said, though I didn't have to. Myzalla knew something was bothering me. She'd asked me directly a few times, but I'd always used the rumblings in Harta as an excuse.

In reality, the life of my Elthika was coming to an end, and I…was lost. For the first time since I'd been a boy—before anger and bloodied determination and sheer spite had given me purpose.

I was in uncharted territory and struggling to come to terms with the inevitable. But all I could do was try to ensure Grym's safety, to keep the Hartans accountable, to remind them of what happened when they crossed the Karag.

"I'm not worried about it," I told Myzalla. "I just want them to feel my presence. To remember. I've upped flyover patrols in my absence. I have a meeting with their council at the end of the riding season."

"Does Elysom know?" Myzalla asked quietly. Elysom was *our* governing council. They lived apart from Karak, on a vast island west of the Arsadia. Their city was a jewel of our nation—a glittering, obscenely wealthy jewel that sucked the marrow from the outer territories' resources.

"About the meeting? Not yet."

"Alaryk," she chided softly, meeting my eyes, worrying her bottom lip. "You know they can—"

"I deal with the Hartans," I told her. "That was my deal with Elysom when I took over Grym. They already proved themselves incompetent in that matter."

Myzalla grabbed my arm when I turned away, and I swung my gaze back to one of my oldest friends.

"I just worry that Elysom will use any excuse to cut you out, Alaryk," she said quietly. I huffed out a breath. "They thought you were a spy, on Muron's blood! There's no telling what they'll do if another Hartan war comes."

"And it doesn't matter that I ended the last one?" I asked her. But we both heard the sarcasm in my tone.

"*Especially* because of how you ended the last one," Myzalla hissed.

Elysom might get their wish sooner then they think, came the dark thought.

"They'll only ever see me as a Hartan," I told Myzalla. I'd come to terms with that a long time ago, as she well knew. "But they can't take Grym away from me." I grinned. "And I will enjoy how much that cuts them for as long as I retain my position as *Karath.*"

Myzalla sighed.

"Probably even until I'm dead," I added. We resumed walking toward the perimeter of Grymia, a stone road that wound and slashed its way throughout the outpost, leading to every door, every building. "Otherwise everything's in order?"

"Yes."

"The riders?"

"Training well."

"Even the Dakkari?"

She made a face. I knew how she felt about Dakkari being inserted into training. She thought it a joke, a farce. "Passable."

"And the other two?"

"They're both settling in well," Myzalla told me. I could hear the surprise in her tone. "Brune is much-needed strength for the old farmer, and he knows a lot about soil nutrients."

"And the girl?" I asked.

Myzalla cast me a knowing look. "Amaia is…exceptional with her assigned hatchling."

I threw a look of disbelief over my shoulder. "Tarkosh actually said that?"

"I heard it directly from her myself," Myzalla said with a small tug on her lips. She shrugged. "A Rythback hatchling, apparently."

The girl was another problem I'd deal with in due time…but it pleased me to know she wasn't incompetent. Or that the Dakkari hadn't lied about her qualifications.

"Feast tonight," Myzalla called after me. "Don't forget."

As if I could.

CHAPTER 8
AMAIA

"On Muron, I love feast nights," Ethrisha cried out, creating a rumble of laughs around her as people cheered in agreement.

Syris crossed her arms, throwing a look over to Moak across the numerous couples dancing to the beat of the drums, accompanied by a stringed instrument that sounded like wailing to me. Combined, they created a strange but intoxicating music, one that made me sway, my arms lifting over my head as my hips rocked.

Ethrisha was a delightful new friend, a childhood friend of Syris…though the two females couldn't be more different. Ethrisha worked as a craftswoman, her specialty in jewelry, using precious gems she mined herself from the Arsadian mountains. She was occasionally gone from the outpost—which I'd discovered was called Grymia—for a week or two at a time, on the hunt for more materials.

Her prices were high, but I'd discovered that blood borns—those from bloodlines that were mostly made up of riders—believed that certain gemstones attracted Elthika and brought them good fortune during the rider season. And those blood borns paid a hefty price for a pendant or a sturdy cuff imbedded with such gems.

Ethrisha herself was chiming and glittering as she danced. The bracelets made a long trail up her forearm, making music all their own, as gems shimmered from piercings along her pointed ears, which I'd never seen before.

Syris looked uncomfortable as her friend's dancing grew more and more frenzied, as more wine flowed and the music pounded louder, vibrating the very earth.

Brune watched Ethrisha over the rim of his own goblet, his swallow heavy, his cheeks flushed from the heat of the bodies…or perhaps from the way Ethrisha moved.

"Come dance with me, Dakkari," she teased, crooking her finger at him. As if pulled by a string, Brune stumbled forward once he rose from his seat. His big body was awkward, but Ethrisha grinned up at him and taught him steps he couldn't have possibly known.

I laughed, slumping back down into the seat Brune had just vacated next to Syris, who sat stiffly, sipping on her own goblet. Not of wine but of unfermented juice.

"Are you having fun?" I asked her, shouting over the music and the laughter and the voices.

I was used to large gatherings like this. My mother knew half of our district, and every moon, the streets of Dothik were filled with food and dancing just like tonight. *This* felt like home…and instead of making me sad, it helped the ache. Or maybe that was the wine.

And Karag wine, I'd discovered, was a bit stronger than Dakkari brew.

"I hate when people ask me that," Syris shot back. "Of course I'm having fun."

I hid my smile at her frown, especially when that frown turned into an even deeper scowl when she caught sight of Moak flirting and kissing yet another girl who wasn't her. As well as the girl he'd brought back to the hatchery my first morning there.

Syris harrumphed, tossing back her dark indigo hair.

"Wine?" I asked, offering my goblet to her.

She seemed to debate for a moment before accepting it from my hands and taking a steady chug.

"Easy," I laughed, snatching it back. "We might have a new hatchling tomorrow."

The egg was on the verge of hatching, or so Tarkosh believed. I couldn't wait to witness it, had even been hesitant to come tonight, almost volunteering to stay behind at the hatchery. But Tarkosh had waved us off. We'd been cleaning out nests all morning, continuing their prep, as the Rythback hatchling, who'd been named Kyr, had raced around us, creating havoc. She thought we deserved the break.

Now that I was here, I was glad I came. Nearly all of Grymia was in attendance, spread out on the landing field, which was the only large enough open space to accommodate everyone. The loom of the forest directly around us made the gathering seem more intimate, torchlight and glowing orbs casting the party in shimmering gold. The wine flowing over my tongue made everything seem softened around the edges. I was having fun with these Karag, and even Ethrisha had commented how at ease I seemed with such a large group of strangers.

But I was used to people around all the time. Being alone was what scared me. That was when I was out of my element, when I felt the most vulnerable.

And maybe that was why I'd felt so betrayed by Kiron leaving us. I knew it was necessary, but there was still a part of me that mourned his absence when he had always been part of us. Like a limb he'd willingly severed.

But tonight I was far from alone, and I was enjoying the feast with my new friends. I laughed as Ethrisha teased Brune, dancing around him in a circle while his eyes traced her. I observed the

Karag all around me, old and young, coming together. And while I saw certain looks cast my way, I liked to imagine that they were only in curiosity, not distrust or malice. It was only natural, I knew, so I didn't let it worry me.

The feast, it seemed, was in celebration of the *Karath* of Grym, finally returned to the Arsadia, where he would apparently stay until the end of the rider season.

My gaze was unwillingly pulled to his form, sitting at a table with a group of his chosen riders, Myzalla near him with her husband. They were speaking while Alaryk looked at ease and relaxed in his chair, which he made look more like a throne. There was a laziness to his surveillance of the gathering. I'd caught the prickle of his gaze on me once or twice, but I had refused to assuage my curiosity, only sneaking peeks at him when I thought it was safe.

Only this time, when I looked at him, his gaze snapped to mine, like he'd been waiting for it. I was so startled that I found my eyes trapped, unwilling to leave his, trying to figure out what he wanted, what he would do.

The blue of his eyes seemed to shimmer across the field. He still spoke with Myzalla, but his attention was on me. I felt my heartbeat begin to thunder. My blood rushed in my veins, but whether it was from the music and the wine or the *Karath's* pretty, dangerous eyes, I couldn't be certain.

When I felt the prodding of his heartstone magic, seeking like tendrils, I nearly gasped, conjuring something like a shield in my mind and tearing myself away before he could get inside.

The moment made the wine in my belly turn sour. I needed to remember myself and the danger I could be in. The guardsmen hadn't approached Brune and me in the last week of our being here. I could almost believe that we were just here to experience the life of the Karag. Desperately, I hoped that was all it would ever be.

"Are you all right?" Syris asked, looking at me with a frown. "You've gone a little pale."

"Too much wine, I think," I lied, thrusting my goblet back into her hand. "You finish mine."

She nodded. When I chanced another look back over to the *Karath* a long time later, I found that his attention had been pulled by a female who had perched herself on the edge of his chair, leaning down to speak into his ear.

Fascinated, I watched.

"Who's that?" I asked Syris. "Speaking with the *Karath*?"

"Rivenna," she answered. "She works in the smithery."

I cast a look over at her, my brow raised.

"Yes, if that's what you're asking," Syris told me, a little smirk perched on her lips, the wine already relaxing her. "They've been…involved."

"Interesting," I murmured.

"She's one of the only ones who dares," she added, sparking my interest.

"What do you mean?"

Syris pressed her lips together, her cheeks going a little pink. "I shouldn't have said that. This is why I don't drink wine. It turns me into nothing more than a gossip."

"And don't we love to see it," Ethrisha exclaimed, throwing herself down into the seat across the table from us, Brune taking a place next to her. "What are we gossiping about?"

They were both breathing hard, and Brune was smiling.

"The *Karath*," I supplied when Syris wouldn't. "And his lover."

"Which one?"

I laughed.

Ethrisha looked over her shoulder. "Ah. That one."

"How many does he have?" I asked.

"Enough for an unclaimed *Karath*, I suppose," Ethrisha said.

Then she grinned, wicked, her eyes twinkling. "And not nearly enough for someone so beautiful."

Brune coughed into his fist.

"Have you ever…?" I asked, fighting a smile.

"Me?" Ethrisha asked, eyes widening comically. "On Muron, no. I wouldn't know what to do with a *Karath*. Especially Alaryk." She leaned across the table, and I leaned over to meet her, like she would tell me a secret I desperately wanted to know.

"Tell me," I mock-whispered.

"His father was Hartan, you know. His mother was Karag."

"I don't understand," I said. I'd gathered that the Hartans were a neighboring people in the east, on the borders of Grym. So, naturally, it would make sense that bloodlines would mix, wouldn't it? Just like humans and Dakkari. It was inevitable.

"Hartan males pierce themselves," she told me with a smirk. My gaze flashed to her ears. She touched one. "Like these. But…" She looked over at Brune, placing her fingers on his chest, trailing them down until his face grew hotter and hotter. "Down…here."

Just before Ethrisha's touch landed on his pelvic bone, she snatched her hand back, laughing. Poor Brune looked like he was torn between throwing her over his shoulder or expiring on the spot.

But her meaning wasn't lost on me. "They pierce their…"

She nodded, the jewels in her ears flashing in the light, twinkling almost as brightly as her mirth-filled eyes.

Brune's wince was loud as my jaw hung. "With gems?" I gasped out.

Ethrisha, and even Syris, giggled. "No! With metal."

Brune groaned.

"But *why*?" I asked, unable to keep my gaze from drifting back to Alaryk. Rivenna was nearly in his lap, his hand spanning across her hip lazily.

It might've been the wine, but I was…intrigued.

"Warrior sons of Harta get them when they come of age,"

Syris said, her voice positively prim, like we weren't talking about the *Karath*'s cock piercing. "It's custom."

"Surely he had a choice if his mother was Karag," Brune chimed in.

"Oh, he did," Ethrisha said, laughing. "And he chose the piercing. I respect it."

I laughed in disbelief. "How can you even be sure?"

"Because when a *Karath* beds a female, they all like to brag about it. You hear the same story so many times, it becomes a well-known fact," Ethrisha informed me, taking a long sip of her brew. I saw her hand move beneath the table, going to Brune's thigh. He shifted in his seat, while the temptress herself suppressed a smile. "And who doesn't love to gossip about an unclaimed *Karath*?"

When I looked back to the head table, I saw that Alaryk and Rivenna were gone. I gazed around, searching for a silver-haired male, but found none.

Ethrisha leaned into Brune. "Let's go."

Some things, I realized, as I watched a red-faced Brune and a grinning Ethrisha rise from the table and disappear beyond the landing field, were the exact same among the Dakkari and Karag. After all, I'd lost my virginity at a gathering much like this one, with a Dakkari boy who'd worked at the docks. Years ago, he'd whisked me away from the party after a night of brew and dancing. And to this day, the scent of the briny sea reminded me of that clumsy night.

Syris sighed. Her eyes flicked back over to Moak, saw him kissing a pretty Karag girl. She looked down at her lap. "I'm going back—I'm tired."

"I'll stay a little while," I told her, not ready to return to my quiet room quite yet. "I'll see you in the morning."

She nodded. And left. And even though I was surrounded by dozens and dozens of people, I found I *was* quite alone after all.

I was humming to myself, an old tune my mother would sing late into the night as she finished up her sewing. I would hear it on occasion, seeping into the walls of my bedroom, a muffled song that helped lull me to sleep.

I'd been in Grymia for nearly a week, and I was sleeping horribly. At first I'd thought it was because the bed was too high, so I'd dragged the mattress to the stone floor. But I still tossed and turned.

I realized, belatedly, that it was the quiet more than anything else. The hatchery sounded like a tomb. Empty and echoing. Even Kyr slept soundly in the nesting area and only roused when dawn light broke.

Syris had told me that once more hatchlings were born, I might not be able to sleep at all for all the noise. And truthfully, I welcomed it. I could feel the silence crawl over me at night like a nightmarish creature. And in those early-morning hours when I couldn't sleep, I roamed the grounds of Grymia, walking by torchlight, encountering not a single soul. But the looming darkness of the forest or the jagged peaks of the mountain ranges scared me less than my sleeping quarters.

And so, long after the feast had ended and the landing field had gone quiet, the embers of the bonfires glowing as they slowly died, I walked. My cheeks felt flushed and warm from the wine, my legs a little heavy. I'd thought maybe it would help me sleep, and so I hadn't protested whenever my goblet had been filled up…and I'd drunk every last drop.

The outpost was quiet, but the cool wind across my flesh helped distract me. As I passed stone houses along the road, some were dark, but in others I could still make out muffled laughter and the weaving of two or three or four voices, which made longing fill my breast until it was hard to breathe.

Overhead, I heard the unmistakable sound of Elthika wings slicing through air. I looked up sharply, thinking it odd a dragon would be out this time of night when they were usually tucked away in the mountain.

In the darkness, I saw the mightiness of a fully grown Elthika, shooting off the mountain cliff, circling over Grymia. It was too dark to make out its color, but something in the way it took flight made me still on the path, cocking my head as I studied it.

Its movements were sluggish but jerky. It began to veer left, toward the line of the thick forest before it righted itself sharply. It circled again but then seemed to…fall.

I gasped, then frowned, the haziness of the wine dissipating. The Elthika resumed flight, but only for a moment. It let out a call, low and rumbling, a mournful thing that tugged at my rib cage like a metal thread imbedded into the bones.

Then it *was* falling, and I was running.

CHAPTER 9
AMAIA

Deep in the forest, I finally found the Elthika. I heard it before I saw it, over the pounding of my heartbeat from my near sprint over fallen tree trunks and thick, spiky brambles.

The labored breathing sounded like the rush of a waterfall, the hum in the air seeming to vibrate the very ground I stood on. I pushed into the clearing without thinking about the consequences of encountering a fully grown Elthika.

And I got the shock of my life when I recognized it.

Samryn.

The *Karath*'s own bonded Elthika.

His bloodred scales appeared dulled in the darkness, but I would recognize the glow of his eyes anywhere.

"It's all right," I found myself whispering, as if he could understand the universal tongue. "I won't hurt you."

I remembered a conversation I'd had with Tarkosh a few days prior. All Elthika could be testy with strangers, especially if they were bonded already.

Especially if they were Vyrins—Elthika from ancient bloodlines.

Just like Samryn. Only Samryn was apparently the worst of

them all…of all the bonded of Grym. *No one* dared to approach him, with the exception of Alaryk Arn'dyne.

Not even Myzalla, from what Tarkosh had told me.

"It's important for the Elthika to feel respected," she'd said. "And each one has different boundaries on what they will and will not accept."

Just like *pyroki*, I'd thought at the time.

Only now, facing Samryn, whose head was larger than my entire body and whose jaws could tear me apart in a moment…I realized how wrong I'd been.

A low rumble shook the ground. A growl. Of warning? Or of pain?

A twig snapped up my foot when I stepped further into the clearing, holding my arms away from my body and keeping my movements slow. I didn't know what to do, but I felt my heart-stone magic gathering, warming my entire body, a default I fell back on when I was uncertain with a creature.

"Are you injured?" I asked, envisioning my magic like a spool of thread, slowly beginning to unravel, its string stretching across the clearing to make contact with Samryn.

Blue light reflected on his scales, so I knew my eyes were beginning to glow.

His growling lessened, his head raising to regard me, as if he could feel the magic. I'd heard stories that Elthika were sensitive to the heartstones, that they needed their energy to survive.

Could I help him? Just like I had countless *pyroki*? Just like I had my father when he'd been ill? Or my brother when infection had taken root?

"I won't hurt you," I breathed again, my magic gathering. I reached out a hand. Samryn was so big that he'd toppled a few trees when he'd fallen, their ancient trunks uprooted, and I thought I could scent the metallic tinge of blood in the air. Had he injured himself in the fall? "I want to help you."

My hand was so close to the heat of his scales that I could feel it seep into me, warming the flesh. My touch hovered over his jaw, recognizing that he could snap his fangs at me and I'd lose my entire arm.

I pressed my magic forward, crossing over a threshold, and I saw the blue glow of it in my mind's eye, tracing Samryn's scales, highlighting them, running like a current beneath them as it looked for a way *in*.

A groan from the poor creature. I pressed my hand to his jaw with the last of my courage and felt the bond of my magic latch tight.

I gasped, a flooding of heartstone magic being reciprocated back at me like a funnel. Tears nearly blinded me. Everyone had been right—Elthika were so deeply intertwined with the heartstones that it felt like a deep pool of pure magic. It felt like I was sinking into it, getting swallowed up, while *wanting* to.

I wanted to delve deeper. I'd never felt anything like it before —this raw, wonderful bliss of what I'd always felt inside me.

But the longer I twined my magic with Samryn, the more it began to hurt.

I knew something was wrong when I felt something thick and cloying, sickeningly sweet mixed in with the magic. Like muck in a clear river that threatened to clog it up like a dam.

My brow furrowed. That was when the pain started. And I nearly cried out when I felt that deep, deep pain. Because I realized it was what Samryn was feeling. He was funneling it into me, trying to find relief, the poor beast. Seeking any way out he could.

"I can help you," I gritted out, "but I need time. Stop giving me—"

I was wrenched away, a heavy, tight grip on my arm that sent me sprawling back. When the connection was ripped away, I nearly screamed, going dizzy from it.

When I gained my footing, I looked up.

Blue eyes clashed with mine.

Alaryk.

And he looked pissed, fury seething from him. Heartstone magic *flooded* from him, crawling up my flesh like ropes that wanted to strangle me. Like it wanted to consume me.

I nearly choked on it.

Such power, I thought as harsh panic began to chase away the remnants of Samryn's suffering. *He'll kill me with it.*

In a deadly calm voice, Alaryk asked, "What did you do to my Elthika?"

CHAPTER 10
ALARYK

The intoxicating problem with rage was that sometimes I could sink into it so deep and never want to surface. For me, rage was like pain. And pain centered me. It gave me something to focus on when I felt like I was out of control of a circumstance.

Pain was my oldest and most reliable companion. And rage fed it.

So, while I felt the fury whipping through me, manifesting my magic quickly, I also felt in control. A calm in the maelstrom of my anger. I wasn't like others. I didn't yell or grow violent when I was angered.

I punished quietly, feeling a swell of malicious pleasure in its wake.

"What did you do?" I asked again, my voice low. I felt a touch in the back of my mind. Samryn. Trying to break my attention…but once I latched onto something, it was difficult to let go, and so I ignored him, shutting off the bond with a firm rejection.

"N-Nothing," the Dakkari girl gasped out, struggling in the grip of my own magic, while her own eyes glowed with the remnants of hers. "He…he fell. I saw him. I—"

She gasped when I delved deeper. Thoughts were not always clear. They were more like impressions, like footsteps in the earth after it rained, but I'd learned to read them. To fill in the gaps, to bend the mind to my own will. Sometimes I took it upon myself to fill in those empty places with my own wants and desires. Like filling a mold.

And I did it right then, urging the truth to fall from her lips.

"He fell," she whispered again, staring up at me with pretty, glassy eyes that reflected a withering moon behind the clouds. "He's hurt. I can feel it. Like rot."

My stomach clenched. She was telling the truth.

I released her from my power, wrenching it away, and she fell to the earth, struggling to breathe.

I whipped around to look at Samryn. I could still feel the touch of her magic along his jaw, the crawling warmth of it. He'd *allowed* her to touch him?

Opening the connection, I felt how weak he was. I felt the surge of my own guilt mingle with it. He'd hid this from me until he couldn't any longer?

I'd pushed him too hard, I knew. We'd been on patrol for days in Harta, and then we'd come to the Arsadia. He'd done so willingly. He'd never given me any indication of his growing weakness.

And yet...I should have known better. I knew from last time how quickly the curse spread once it gathered its strength. Exponentially. Just this morning, we'd flown over the Arsadia.

And by nightfall, Samryn could hardly raise his head from the earth.

I'd been roused from a restless sleep, fueled partially by my lust but mostly by my dissatisfaction from my encounter with Rivenna. I took her as my lover in Grymia because she shared certain proclivities when it came to sex. But even still, I was growing more and more restless, the anger coming quick and hard and merciless. And when I spent it inside her body, I didn't feel the relief I usually did.

I'd stumbled from Rivenna's home, leaving her sprawled on her bed where I hadn't meant to fall asleep, lacing up my trews as I'd sprinted toward Samryn's call. I'd left my tunic behind in my haste.

Rot, the Dakkari girl had said. A peculiar word that had me rounding back on her, stalking to where she was sprawled.

"What did you feel?" I asked, crouching down to meet her eyes, only feeling marginally guilty for unleashing the full force of my magic on her. It must have been…shocking.

"Don't," she whispered, having the audacity to glare up at me, her finger pointing in accusation, even though it trembled. "Don't do that again."

"I will do whatever I please," I hissed softly, "if I think my Elthika is being threatened."

I thought my eyes might've flickered with heartstone energy because hers went wide. "I'm telling you the truth. I would never hurt him! I was trying to help him, you bastard."

My nostrils flared.

"What did you *feel?*" I growled, repeating the question, feeling my frustration finally snap. A rare moment of lost patience.

"Rot," she growled right back, making me still. "Sickness. Disease. Pain and waste. He's *dying.*"

The forest floor met my backside when I fell, untrusting of my own legs to keep me steady. The words weren't anything I didn't already know.

But…hearing them spoken from another's lips…it felt final. It felt certain.

And I felt the *grief.* Riding me hard, sitting on my chest until I felt like my lungs had collapsed and I couldn't find the air.

"But I can help him," came her voice.

My head snapped up as I trained my gaze on her.

"I can try," she amended, raising her chin. She didn't want to meet my eyes, I could discern that clearly. But she did, bravely, though it was tinged with her righteous anger.

"How?" I rasped, grasping onto a small, slippery thread of hope I didn't dare feel.

"He's in a lot of pain," she told me. It felt like a blade to my own chest. "I tried to root out what's causing him so much of it, but he's fighting me, using me to help find relief. It feels like a dam of a river. And now that I've unblocked some of it, he's desperate to find a pathway out."

What she described…how could I have been so blind to it?

Because the proud creature wouldn't have let you see it, I knew. For him to get to this state, to finally expose his pain…he couldn't bear it anymore. Perhaps it had been exacerbated by how hard I'd been pushing him, with very little rest.

"What do you want?" I asked.

"I want to help him," she said, rising to her feet. Her eyes were still a little glassy, perhaps from the wine I'd seen her drink at the feast. I remembered her wide smile as she'd danced, remembered thinking that she had a special talent for making strangers like her. She'd had no problem fitting in at a feast full of them. And I had envied her for that gift as I'd watched her dance and sway in the crowd. I'd been…*enthralled*, though I'd never admit it.

"What do you want really?" I asked her, standing to meet her, to gaze down into those eyes so she wouldn't misunderstand my meaning. "Because nothing is freely given."

"Your Elthika is suffering, and you want to talk about payment?" She glared, her eyes like ice. "Get out of my way."

I was too surprised to respond as she pushed past me. I felt the shocking heat of her shoulder against the bare skin of my chest as she nudged me back, perhaps purposefully and with intended force.

I trapped any hope I felt in a fist as I watched her approach

Samryn. I could feel the magic radiate off her like a hum. The energy made my flesh prickle uncomfortably, my own power beating at my bones to be let out…but I didn't want to dare risk her helping my Elthika.

Blue light glowed off Samryn's scales. The hair on the back of my neck rose. Where Rivenna had bitten me, on my shoulder, hard enough to draw blood, ached as my heart pounded. The base of my spine, where my tail had once been, tingled, making my flesh itch.

The forest grew quiet. Still. Like the life had been sucked out of it.

I heard the exhale of my own breath, loud. I didn't have to open up my own magic to know Amaia's was a powerful thing. I hadn't felt power like hers in a long, long time.

Samryn made the first sound, a loud cry I'd never heard before, aching and raw, just as her back bowed. An unseen wind rose in the clearing, whipping her hair around her face, but when I strode toward her side, I knew her eyes were unseeing.

"So much," she whispered, tears beginning to drip from her eyes, tracking down her cheeks in little rivers. "I can take it. Give some to me. Let me help you."

A guttural sound left my throat as I rounded to Samryn, looking into his eyes even as his head thrashed. His pupils were blown wide, reflecting the glow of her own magic.

I couldn't help it. I unspooled my power. If I could take some of the pain for the both of them, maybe it would help her.

I opened the flood of my magic.

I heard her scream. I felt the flood of aching muck infuse itself into my own veins. And I felt *her*, a pure river of heartstone energy sweeping through.

It was building. Building. The pain came. Searing. Like it was slowly eating my body from the inside out. I wanted to bellow with the suffering that Samryn was experiencing. I wanted to marvel at the pain that Amaia was taking on for him.

It seized up every part of my body, making my jaw grit tight. I couldn't help him. But maybe I could help *her*.

If only a little.

Her magic might've been pure, but it was also a wild thing. Untamed. Untrained. I felt it begin to falter against the mightiness of this…almost certain death.

All the while, Samryn's groans began to quiet. I felt a strange sense of relief, felt the rise and fall of his breath in my own chest.

Amaia's tears turned to blood.

And when I saw her sway, I broke the connection to catch her. She fell limp in my arms, her eyes closed, cheeks stained in red.

Samryn collapsed too, his mighty body rumbling the earth.

Only when I saw both their chests rise and fall could I breathe again too.

CHAPTER 11
AMAIA

When I woke, it was to dim golden lighting and the scent of light, earthy smoke. My vision was blurry when I peered around the unfamiliar room.

No—a home.

The bed I was lying on was in one corner of a much larger room. A simple kitchen—a warm stone hearth and a small table —was on the opposite wall. The floor was peppered with a plethora of soft multicolored rugs of different patterns and types of threads, to soften against the stone.

I saw a door, a small window beside it, which showed a starry night, clear and bright. Next to the door was a riding tether, a sheathed sword, a pair of thick, muddy boots.

My body ached fiercely. It felt like I'd been pulled apart, my muscles and tendons and bones stretched to the extreme, only now I was shrinking back into myself.

I remembered Samryn falling, a clear vision in my mind's eye, and the racing panic as I'd sprinted toward him in the dark woods. I remembered the pain—the *rot*—and then I remembered…*Alaryk*.

Struggling to sit up in the comfortable bed, I saw that a thick quilt had been laid over me, the material soft as silk, keeping the chill away. I thought at first there might've been a fire going in the hearth I'd spied beside the kitchen, in the middle of a lounging area, but no. The smokiness I smelled was coming from a little glass pot on a round wooden table with spindled legs beside the bed. It looked like a pot of blue ash on first inspection, but in the middle there was a tiny ember that was smoking, a wisp of smoke rising into the air.

My head was pounding as I pushed my body up, but even that winded me. I'd woken up in this state only a few times in my life, but I recognized the lingerings of my heartstone magic. A gift and a curse, perhaps.

For a moment, I thought I might be alone in this strange dwelling. But then I froze when I heard the telltale splash of water, coming from a room off the lounging area, which I couldn't see.

A skipped heartbeat later, a thin, gossamer curtain was spread and I saw Alaryk stepping through it.

Naked.

Well, nearly. He had a drying cloth wrapped around his hips, tied in a neat knot like a sarong, as water droplets from what I assumed was his bath rolled down his bare chest.

My swallow was loud. The ends of his long silver-white hair were damp, turning nearly translucent. His blue eyes, gleaming in the low light, tracked to me as my own dipped down the surprisingly stunning line of his body in disbelief. The scar trailing over his jaw shone silver in the light.

A warrior's body, I couldn't help but recognize. Only Alaryk was much larger. Rippling muscle led to a tightly packed abdomen. His shoulders were impossibly wide—if anything, his riding clothes made him look smaller than he truly was.

And he was halfway across the room.

When he walked toward the table in the small kitchen, I saw a carafe of what might've been water or wine. He poured it into a goblet—wine—and took a sip as he regarded me over the rim. My tongue was still stuck to the roof of my mouth, tracking him like I would a dangerous, wild *pyroki* I was trying to tame.

When he drained the contents of the goblet, his hair fell back from his chest, and I saw a flash of metal. His dark nipples were pierced through. Suddenly my face flamed, remembering the conversation I'd had at the feast last night.

Had that been last night? How long had I been recovering?

Another clink came. He filled another goblet from a metal spigot in the wall, the hinge squeaking when he turned it off. Then he finally approached me, and I straightened in the bed.

I was still wearing the dress I'd worn to the feast. One of my only dresses I'd stuffed into my travel pack when I'd left home. The hem was covered in mud and forest grime, stained, but thankfully not *off.*

I thought of what Ethrisha had told me with twinkling eyes during the night of the feast. That Alaryk had many lovers…and here I was in his bed, even though I knew nothing had happened.

But it still begged the question…

"Why am I here?" I asked when my tongue finally unstuck itself from the roof of my mouth.

Alaryk peered down at me, close enough that I could feel the heat of his naked body, radiating off him like a crackling fire. His gaze tracked to the little pot of blue ash, as if ensuring it was still lit. The blue nearly matched his eyes.

"You've been sleeping for two days," he informed me.

My belly twinged in alarm. Had I missed the hatching?

"That didn't answer my question."

I saw his shoulders rise with his deep breath, the metal through his nipples flashing with the movement. I forced myself not to look at the small, distracting, intriguing things.

I rose from the bed, feeling that my being in it was too strange, too intimate. But my legs were wobbly when I stood, and Alaryk caught me against him when I stumbled, water sloshing over the goblet.

"I'm fine," I said, pushing him away, trying to forget the shocking heat of his skin. "Just…just tell me why I'm here. What happened?"

"At least sit down," he said, nodding his chin toward the lounge. Deep cushions were sprawled across the floor. It reminded me of illustrations I'd once seen of *voliki* layouts in the old hordes. Sitting close to the earth, to feel more of a rooted connection with Kakkari, our goddess.

Dakkari kept our beds on the floor. Our tables were low to the ground so we could sit while eating. The only thing high in Dothik, for my family, had been our home. We lived on the top floor, only reachable by a winding staircase, and that was because we'd been too poor to afford a lower unit.

But from my week in Grymia, I'd discovered that the Karag didn't sit on the earth as the Dakkari did. They had tall chairs, tall beds, high tables. Even their stone homes were raised from the earth on a stone foundation, a small set of stairs leading up to the front doors. As if they wanted to be closer to the sky, closer to their Elthika.

It might've been more comfortable, but it was certainly less… grounding. Stabilizing.

So I stumbled over to the lounge area in something like relief. And when I sank down onto the floor, I nearly sighed in contentment, my free hand spreading across the soft rug beneath me, pressing my palm into it wide. A cushion was at my back, and I finally took a sip of the cool water from the goblet, letting it quench my dry throat. I drained the contents in three swift chugs.

If I'd been asleep for two days, I certainly felt like it. Dehydrated, hungry, and dazed.

Alaryk refilled my goblet without a word, taking me by surprise. Only after my third did I shake my head, and he finally dropped down across from me, the long cloth around his hips lifting dangerously high. As he settled back into the cushions, he looked perfectly at ease. Like a hedonistic god of pleasure and flesh. Arrogant and patient, because he knew he would eventually get exactly what he wanted.

"You're here because I don't trust anyone but myself," he said quietly.

I frowned, licking my lips. "I don't understand."

"If you can do what you claim," he said, "then you just became very important to me, Amaia of Rath Savenal."

My shoulders hitched up at the sound of my name falling from his lips, like a mere caressing whisper but edged like a blade.

"You mean Samryn," I clarified.

"You were right," he told me. "He is dying. But you claim you can heal him. Perhaps I'm desperate enough to hope you might."

My brow furrowed. I remembered whatever was plaguing the poor creature. Heavy and poisonous. I'd never felt anything like it before. The deeper I'd tried to root out the seed of it, the more intense the pain had become. I thought I might have siphoned some of it away, giving some relief to the Elthika…at cost to myself. But there was always a price to pay.

"I said I could *try*, not that I could," I told him. Perhaps I was afraid at what I'd felt within him. But I couldn't stand that he suffered when I could help him.

"Tell me what your ability is exactly," he ordered.

My spine stiffened. "So you can use it, you mean."

He didn't even flinch. "You would be rewarded. Whatever you desire."

I glared, though it made my head throb even harder. "A simple thank-you would be nice."

Alaryk scoffed, a dry humorous sound. His arms spread over the backs of the cushions beside him. "*Endrassa,*" came the velvety purr of a Karag word I didn't understand. "Thank you."

But his voice was dripping in what I thought was sarcasm.

"I don't need this," I said, beginning to rise to my feet.

But Alaryk moved like a serpent, so quick he was like a blur. I felt the warm strength of his hand on my throat, making me gasp and still. He was on his knees before me as I stood over him… but there was no mistaking who held the power.

His thumb smoothed down the side of my neck. Back and forth. I was certain he could feel the wild thumping of my pulse. His grip wasn't hard, but it was firm, meant to catch my attention. We regarded one another with mistrust, bordering on glares. When I moved to jerk my neck from his grip, he tugged me down so I stumbled to the cushions.

"Why, you *bastard*—"

"If Samryn dies, my soul dies with him," came his gentle hiss, hovering over me.

The words made me freeze. He was close, pressing me back into the cushions, his long forearm pressed between my breasts, his hand still on my neck, though it was to keep me still more than anything. He was heavy. Hot. Water from his bath dripped against my dress. His thigh was pressed between mine, keeping me still.

"We are bonded. Deeper than any bond a *Karath* has with his Elthika. My magic has been intertwined with his for years. And…" He blew out a rough breath but met my eyes with an intense ferocity that would keep me pinned in place, even if he released me. "I'm scared for him."

There was a startling vulnerability to the words, one that made my glare soften. I heard the strain, the worry, the fear in the timbre of his soft voice.

Maybe I was just easy to manipulate…but I believed him. And it made me want to help him, help Samryn, even if he was an arrogant bastard.

But if *Karaths* were anything like *Vorakkar*, horde kings, was I really surprised?

"Tell me you'll stay and speak with me. And then I'll release you," he said, his thumb still moving against my flesh, his eyes bright as they seared me.

"I'll stay," I said. "But if you do that again, I'll leave."

A sound chuffed from his throat, and he inclined his head. "Agreed."

He maneuvered off me, releasing my neck from his grip and leaning back into the cushions, though he was closer to me than he'd been before, the side of his thigh nearly touching mine. I shifted farther away.

"You cannot escape your blood," he told me, "and sometimes the Hartan in me comes out. Forgive me."

I swallowed, touching the lingering heat of his hand. "Everything you say sounds like an order," I informed him.

The edge of his lip curled. "I wasn't always so high-handed. In fact, once I rarely spoke at all."

"I'll take your word for it," I said, eyeing him carefully. After the tussle, the slitted end of the drying cloth revealed even more of him. I saw the softened edge of his cock, a glint of metal before I sucked in a sharp breath, my gaze darting to the wispy white smoke from the blue ash across the room.

My heart was beating, my face felt hot.

"I heal," I said finally. "That's what Kakkari gifted me with."

"How?" he asked, leaning forward, his eyes pinned on me, seeking answers he was, apparently, desperate for.

"What do you mean, 'how'?" I asked, a humorless smile passing over my features as my stomach rumbled. I ignored it. "The same way you use yours, I imagine."

His chin tilted back. "And your gift works on creatures and beings alike?"

"Yes," I said. "Though I've really only used it on my own family and *pyroki*."

"Has it ever failed?" he wanted to know.

"Only…" I hesitated, a memory of a *pyroki* I'd tried to save, only to feel her soul already gone. Until all I could feel had been an iciness so bitter that it had hurt. "Only if they're already gone."

Though, on rare occasions, I had managed to claw a *pyroki's* soul back to life. But that was only if their heart had stopped beating while my magic was already threaded through them. I kept that to myself.

Because regardless, those *pyroki* hadn't lived very long lives after that. They'd been sick, a sickness I hadn't been able to cure.

Sometimes, I thought, it was better to let nature take its course. It was Kakkari's will, after all, for her creatures to be returned to her in the earth.

"Tell me what happened with Samryn," he said quietly. "During the night of the feast."

I blinked, but my memory was in pieces. It took me a moment to find them, to stitch back together what happened that night.

"I saw him fall into the forest, and I went after him, thinking he was injured and needed help," I said. "I didn't know it was Samryn at the time. But I came upon him, and he let me touch him. And what I felt…"

"Tell me," Alaryk said. An order but also a plea.

"I've never felt anything like it," I said, worrying my lip as I bit it. "It's some kind of disease, eating him from within. The pain was…unimaginable."

I was growing nauseous just thinking of it.

"How is he?" I asked.

"Resting," Alaryk told me. "In his mountain hold. Whatever you did, it *did* help him. He was out today, patrolling the territory."

A small sense of relief at least. "Good. I'm glad. But…"

"He's not healed," he finished for me. Once again my stomach rumbled in hunger, and once again I ignored it.

"Do you know what's wrong with him?" I asked, thinking

that if I knew the root of the disease, it might make it easier to help him.

Alaryk regarded me. Then he stood, snagging my water goblet to refill it. He pulled a wooden tray from a cabinet. From another, he gathered a plethora of cured meats, fruit, and a small loaf of dense brown seeded bread. He brought it all over to me. And if I was surprised that I'd be served a meal by a *Karath*, I tried not to show it.

"It was a curse," he finally told me, settling back into his seat, though farther from me to make room for the tray of food between us. I didn't touch it, however, listening, rapt. "By a Hartan witch."

My belly sank, churning. "A witch? Like a…*sorceress?*"

He inclined his head.

A sorceress was a powerful thing. And a Hartan, no less? I knew they were an enemy nation to the Karag, though there was an uneasy peace for now. How much malice and hatred had been imbedded into a curse like that?

"Why?" I asked.

"The *why* doesn't matter," he told me firmly. "Only the *what*. She placed it upon Samryn nearly a decade ago. It was meant to be a slow death. She said it would 'rot his heart,' like mine had been."

He let out a humorless dark scoff.

"A decade," I said softly. "So it's taken root. And for a long time."

"I've used my own magic over the years to help slow it," he admitted. "But even my own power has proven to not be enough. I don't have the ability to heal. Only to…change. And twist."

I didn't know what he meant by that, but I wouldn't ask right now.

"But you took his pain for him. I tried to take some too," he continued. "That night. Yet it hurt you."

I swallowed. The pain had become so much that it had eventually turned me numb, until I couldn't feel my limbs or feel the cool wind against my cheek. It was like I'd been suspended in it.

I nearly shuddered, remembering it. "Yes," I replied. "That's always been the nature of it. I can heal, but it requires me to siphon away the sickness and pain. It takes a toll. It doesn't usually knock me out for a couple days though."

"What do you want?" he asked, face suddenly serious. "What do you want for trying to heal him?"

The nausea was rising, but I took a hasty sip of water. The cowardly part wanted me to lie, to tell him that I didn't think I could help Samryn, if only to spare myself the suffering.

"Can I think about it?" I asked instead. There was a flash of wildness on Alaryk's face, one I didn't want to try to decipher, but it had me adding, "Not about helping Samryn. About what I want for it."

There was a hesitant relief in his gaze. "Very well."

"It might take a lot of time," I warned. "And I'm not certain I can save him at all."

Alaryk wiped a large palm over his face. "We aren't in the position to turn away a thread of hope."

He meant Samryn and himself, I knew.

He stood swiftly, rising silently, towering over me in the small lounge space. "I know it's unwise to show you all my fears. It gives you power. But truthfully, I don't care what it takes, what you want. I would give anything. And you should know that... because I felt an inkling of what you would take for him. I would be forever in your debt merely because you *tried*."

My lips parted in shock, hearing a gruff vulnerability in his voice I hadn't expected. He loved Samryn. Deeply. Even I could sense that plainly. And it made me soften toward this arrogant, high-handed male.

"Think about your price," he continued, "once you've recovered fully."

He walked from the lounge area, going to a built-in wall of

drawers near the bed. Steel, polished drawers came out smoothly from the wall. I watched as he unknotted the drying cloth, let it fall to the floor.

My breath hitched, spying the firm, rounded, strong backside and the telltale scar just below his spine where his tail had once been. I'd heard that the Karag riders cut them off after they completed their training, a final commitment.

I looked away swiftly, reaching forward to take a chunk of cured meat from the tray, popping it into my mouth as I tore into the bread. When I chanced another glance up at him, he was lacing up his dark trews before pulling on a riding vest, one made of scales.

"I'm going to check on Samryn," he informed me. "Eat. Rest. We'll discuss this more in the morning."

Before I could say anything else, he was gone.

CHAPTER 12
AMAIA

"There's been some gossiping about you," Syris informed me in a hushed tone as we wound our way through the village.

I frowned, casting a quick look over at her though I felt a dip in my belly, thinking I might know what it was. Still, I played dumb. "What about?"

We were on our way to get feed from the outer fields for Kyr. Another hatchling was expected to come this afternoon, and I was eager to get back so I could witness it. Hatchlings, I'd learned, ate a specific type of grain, soaked in animal fat and blood. It sounded disgusting, but Tarkosh assured me it was the only thing hatchlings ate without fuss. It was soft enough for digestion and high in nutrients, supporting their accelerating growth.

The outer boundaries of Grymia were apparently rich in cropland and grazing livestock, which were sometimes used for Elthika consumption. But Syris had told me that most Elthika liked the hunt and while they were large beasts, they didn't need to consume food as often as one might think, replenishing much of their energy on heartstone magic, which the land was still seeped in.

And now that new *thalara* trees, which grew heartstones, were being replanted throughout Karak *and* Dakkar, they would need the livestock even less. There had apparently been worry over the growing demand, sometimes entire fields of them wiped out by a passing wild Elthika pack.

It was a long walk to the outer fields, and Syris was apparently waiting for some semblance of privacy away from Tarkosh to lay the news on me.

"You were seen leaving the *Karath*'s dwelling," she told me. "Last night. When no one had seen you since the night of the feast. You're lucky Tarkosh didn't have your head. Kyr was unmanageable that day."

I sighed. "I told Tarkosh the truth. I had been unwell. She said she'd verify it with the *Karath*, and she told me this morning that she had."

"I'm just trying to look out for you. Grymia is small—people know everyone's business here. It's not like Grym, which is so vast you can at least walk down one of the roads and not know everyone's name. And believe me, you don't want to catch the attention of the gossips."

"It's not what it looked like," I assured her.

"Then what happened? Because it *looked* salacious. They said you were still wearing your dress from the feast night."

I let out a small groan. I thought I had been careful when I'd crept from Alaryk's home that night. It had been late enough that I hadn't seen anyone around, and I'd scurried back to the hatchery, already wondering how I would explain my absence to Syris and Tarkosh.

But someone had seen. And they'd drawn their own conclusions.

In my mind's eye, I remembered a flash of Alaryk's bared backside and the glint of metal piercings—

I coughed, my cheeks heating, which didn't make me look

any more innocent. The only thing that could prove it was the truth. Or perhaps a half-truth.

"I collapsed in the forest after the feast night," I told her.

She gasped, stopping on the path. "Are you okay? I told you not to drink so much wine—"

"It wasn't that," I said, trying and failing to meet her eyes. We'd just started to descend down a dirt path that hugged the line of the forest. We were already past the landing field, and at the base of the path, I could spy fields of tall grain. "I get these… episodes. Where I get sick. I don't remember much. But he brought me back to his dwelling, and I woke up two days later."

The story felt flimsy even to my own ears. "Why wouldn't he just bring you back to the hatchery?"

"I don't know," I grumbled, a little frustrated that I'd done nothing wrong and yet I was getting all of the suspicion. "Maybe I'll ask him that the next time I see him. But I swear…nothing happened."

Syris inclined her head, and we resumed walking. "And these…episodes. How long have you had them?"

"All my life," I said.

"Have you seen a healer?"

I almost scoffed out a laugh. If I'd gone to a healer for my heartstone magic back in Dothik, that would've been a sure ticket straight to the *orala sa'kilan*, the priestesses' stronghold in the North Lands.

"Many," I said, my only willful lie. "It's always the same thing from them."

"Maybe a Karag healer," she suggested. "Our healer here in Grymia, Raran…she's quite knowledgeable about all kinds of ailments, both heartstone-induced and mortal. Perhaps you can consult with her."

I smiled because I knew Syris was only trying to help. "I think that's a good idea. While I'm here, of course. It couldn't hurt."

She beamed. But then her smile slowly died. "Just be careful. With Alaryk. Did you know that Elysom thinks he's a spy for the Hartans?"

"Surely, you're kidding," I said, frowning. "How long has he been a *Karath*?"

"Oh, over a decade now," Syris said, her tone breezy. "But you never know. People talk."

"Well, maybe that's the issue," I said. "People seem to talk too much here."

To our right, just past the landing field and on a steep incline, I spied rider training. A large group of acolytes, being barked orders from an older female, Myzalla close by.

The riders had a rucksack filled with stones strapped to their backs as they tried to sprint up the incline. I nearly winced in sympathy, imagining how much their lungs and legs must've burned. But then I spied Ryak, nearly doubled over. I imagined Kiron in his place and looked away.

"He's handsome," Syris said quietly as we walked past. Ryak had turned his head to regard us, glaring. "What's his name again?"

"Ryak," I told her. "But I wouldn't go near him."

"Why not?" she asked, though I knew she was probably too shy to ever approach on her own.

"Just a gut feeling. I don't really know him. But, well, back in Dothik, all the females know to stay away from a guardsman."

"Like a rider, perhaps," Syris said. "All they want is to be on dragonback. My father was one."

"Oh?"

"And he left long ago," she said pointedly.

"Oh," I said quietly. "I'm sorry."

"Don't be. My mother and I aren't."

"Does she live here?" I asked as we were nearing the grain field. There was a path that cut to the right, curving around the fields, and in the distance there were a few stone buildings where we could see people milling around.

"No, she has a shop back in Grym. She can't leave it for the season unless she hires on help. I used to help her run it…but she always knew I wanted to work with the Elthika. And there's nowhere better to do it than here."

I took her hand, giving it a squeeze. "Well, I'm glad you're here," I told her.

She gave me a smile, her scar pulling at her mouth.

"Now, let's go get these awful oats."

After we left the farmstead, our baskets overfilled with satchels of the heavy, stinking grain, we both struggled up the incline back to the village.

"On Muron's blood, I know why those farmers are so fit," Syris grumbled through her heaving breaths. "Usually Moak does this, but of course he's nowhere to be found today of all days."

"We should've asked Brune," I said. While I was feeling much better today than last night, I still had a prickling headache and felt like I needed a solid day of sleep. But I hadn't wanted to give Tarkosh another reason to mistrust me if I lay in bed all day.

"Yeah, we should've. He'd been quite eager for the chance, actually," Syris said.

"He probably just wanted to go into the village for a chance at spotting Ethrisha," I panted through gritted teeth.

Syris's exhausted giggle drowned out my heaving breath. Momentarily, we paused for a break close to where the riders were in training, though they were all sprawled out on the ground, listening to their instructor. The instructor clapped, and they all pushed themselves to their feet, beginning to disperse with weary shoulders and slow limbs. Perhaps it was their midday break.

"Think he'll carry these for us?" Syris asked, hands on her hips, as she spotted Ryak, who'd caught a glimpse of us.

"Maybe if they were filled with gold and he got to keep it," I said, watching as he approached, my eyes narrowing on him. We'd been here for a little over a week already, and we hadn't spoken with the exception of that first day upon arriving.

"You have a moment, *pyroki* girl?" he asked when he drew close. For Syris's sake, he flashed a charming smile when he looked over at her. "You don't mind, do you? In fact, I'll have my friend help you back to the village with that. Nevin!"

The second guardsman came walking gingerly over.

"Help her back to the village with that basket, would you?" he told Nevin.

Nevin hid the flash of frustration on his face valiantly. "Sure."

Syris looked back at me. "What about you?"

"I'll be okay," I told her. "I'll see you back at the hatchery."

"Don't be too late," she warned. After a brief nod, I watched her and Nevin begin walking up the slope, growing more and more distant.

Ryak crossed his arms over his chest, nudging the basket at my feet with the tip of his muddy boot. "What in Kakkari's name is that awful smell?"

I wiped my arm over my forehead. "Feed. Soaked in blood and fat."

Ryak scoffed. I didn't know why his derision annoyed me, but I bit my tongue.

"Did you want something?" I asked pointedly.

His eyes regarded me as I watched a drop of sweat run down his tanned temple.

"Heard something interesting this morning," he said. "About you and their *Karath*."

Unbelievable.

"I would think idle gossip beneath you, *Darukkar*," I said, raising my brow. "And regardless, it's not true."

"I don't need to remind you what we're doing here," he told me.

"Actually, you do," I said, my palms upturning in frustration. "Because I actually have no idea what we're doing here. Beyond what my brother initially told me, that is. And you haven't exactly been *illuminating* either."

He stepped closer. "If you want to fuck the local villagers to fit in, fine. I'd even applaud your dedication. But do not fuck their damn *Karath*. Are you out of your mind?"

"*I. Didn't,*" I bit out, glaring up at him.

He blew out a sharp breath of disbelief, his gaze cold. I imagined that he was the son of a wealthy noble. He'd probably lived in Dothik all his life—in the upper districts, of course. He'd probably passed warrior training easily, a paved little path laid before him, whereas people like my brother had limped home bloody and bruised just for a chance at hearing their name called for assignment.

He had that air about him. As if he couldn't imagine someone doing something he didn't want.

Gleefully, I remembered him hunched over with a rucksack full of stones. I only wished I had time to witness every session of rider training. His name, or who his family was, didn't mean anything here.

"How's the hatchery?" he asked.

I blinked, thrown by the question. "Why?"

"I don't need a reason to ask. You answer to me, remember?" he informed me.

"It's fine," I told him, trying to unclench my jaw when I spoke.

"I heard they have some eggs this season."

My eyes narrowed. "Yes."

"How many?"

I frowned, suspicion pricking the back of my mind.

"Why do you want to know?" I asked, my eyes darting back and forth between his.

"We're acquiring information about *every* aspect of their lives, which is reported back to the *Dothikkar* himself. Elthika eggs being high on that list because it gives us an idea of how many are born each season, how many they expect to add to their armies each year," he said, glaring cooly. "Or do you have a problem with that? Can you suddenly not count?"

This condescending bastard, I thought, my hackles rising, imagining wiping that smirk off his face.

"So, I'll ask you again. How many eggs are in the hatchery?" he asked slowly, but his tone was clipped.

I focused on breathing in and out, slow and controlled.

"A dozen or so," I finally answered.

"Or so," he repeated. Then he growled, "*How many?*"

My nostrils flared, and I hated that I nearly jumped in surprise. "Thirteen."

His expression smoothed. "Was that so hard?"

I wouldn't last a season without punching this smug bastard right in the jaw, I knew.

"About to be twelve, so I need to get back. Or will you take issue with that too? Doing my assigned duties?" I asked, reaching down for my basket. "In addition to fucking *Karaths*?"

The look he gave me could've shriveled a lesser person, but I didn't give a shit.

His hand reached out to grip my arm. Hard. Hard enough to make me cry out, the basket toppling from my grip, nearly spilling its content.

"Let go of me," I hissed, glaring up at him.

"Your brother made a grave error in judgment in sending you here," Ryak finally told me, his voice low. "You're not right for this. And if you fuck up, it'll be on him."

My body went cold. "What are you talking about?"

"The *Dothikkar* doesn't take kindly to people who are liars. Kiron vouched for you. He told the *Dothikkar* himself that you would do whatever it took to help Dothik, to help *him*." He released me, tutting with his tongue. "But that's clearly not the case. So when I send my weekly missive back to Dothik and I tell the *Dothikkar* that your brother lied, what do you think they'll do to him? To your family?"

Alarm bells were going off in my head. A weekly missive? How was he sending reports back home? Across the sea? Not only that...I was rooted in place, hearing what went unspoken as icy fear began to prickle across my flesh.

"My family has nothing to do with this," I said quietly.

"You know what I think?" Ryak asked, shrugging his shoulders, which I wished ached something fierce. "I think your brother was scared to come here. Always a weak link, that one, but desperate to prove himself. Whatever it took. And so he threw you into his place because he knew you wouldn't deny him."

"You don't know what you're talking about," I hissed softly, never breaking his stare, though he was obviously trying to intimidate me. "And my brother isn't *weak*."

He grinned. "You don't know him like I do. He doesn't have guts. But me? I'm not afraid to get my hands dirty in service to my king." He toed the basket again, righting it with the edge of his boot. "So what did we learn from this *illuminating* conversation, *pyroki* girl?"

My heart was beating fast, frozen in place.

"Shall I recap?" he asked, tilting his head at me. He jabbed a finger at me. "You do whatever I say. You answer whatever questions I have. And if you don't...?" He waited for my answer expectantly.

"*Enough*. I understand—"

"Then your brother might find himself thrown into the *Dothikkar's* dungeons for...treason? Does that sound like a good enough offense? Or should we go with malicious conspiracy so that he can be tried and executed?"

"Enough," I whispered, my body numb. "I understand perfectly."

He leaned down until he was eye level with me. "Good. I'm glad we're in agreement."

He stepped back, already heading back up in the incline. And I felt like I could breathe again, if only barely.

The reality of what was going on, of what was at stake, was finally tumbling down onto my shoulders.

Kiron, what have you gotten me into? I wondered.

"I'll see you around," Ryak told me with a smirk. "*Pyroki* girl."

CHAPTER 13
AMAIA

When the thick shell cracked and split, my gaze felt hollow on it. Syris nudged me, and when I looked over at her, she gave me a hesitant smile. She'd known how excited I was to witness the birth of an Elthika.

But now?

All I could hear was Ryak's threat in my mind.

I conjured a small smile just for her, so she wouldn't think anything was amiss. But I thought she'd noticed my quiet once I returned to the hatchery, lugging the basket of oats, my arms trembling. My hands too, but that had had nothing to do with the weight and strain of the walk back.

Tarkosh was standing at the edge of the small, raised pen. It had low sides enclosing the squared space—apparently because sometimes Elthika were *jittery* at birth. Syris told me one Elthika a couple years prior had emerged from his egg in the middle of the night and taken a topple off his nesting place. They'd found him limping the next morning. And while he'd eventually healed, Tarkosh preferred the added assurances to keep the newborns safe.

One thing I'd learned in my week at the hatchery—and in

Grymia, truthfully: Beyond all else, the Karag revered the Elthika. Especially *their* Elthika, the bonded of Grym…and their hatchlings. Tarkosh, I'd learned, was one of the most respected residents in the Arsadia because of her talent and expertise working in the hatchery.

I admired that. It reminded me of how the *pyrokis* had once been treated, centuries before, when the ancient hordes had known that their sacred and special way of life wouldn't be possible without their revered creature companions.

Now?

At least in Dothik, *pyroki* were seen as a status symbol, if one could afford to purchase and keep one. But many owned creatures had still been relegated to our care. And it saddened me to know that the respect they deserved was long past, deadened with time.

I saw the edge of a long snout, pointed rather than rounded, poke from the egg. And for a brief moment, I felt awe. For a brief moment, I felt reprieve from the fear that Ryak had installed within me and I could marvel at this wonderful little miracle, which was only possible in Karak. I felt blessed by Kakkari that I was *here*.

Because in that moment, as I watched a hatchling—another Rythback—break through the egg with all the might and strength of a creature three times its size, I found that…

I was exactly where I was meant to be.

The feeling, the realization was startling. It stole my breath for a moment. The only thing that could distract me from looking away as the hatchling emerged in a tumble, a thin mucus covering its body, as it let out a rasping squawk, was the smile on Tarkosh's face.

I figured she'd witnessed a hatchling birth more than a hundred, perhaps a thousand, times by now.

But that smile struck me. Because it was like she was seeing it for the first time. That same sense of awe lining her features, when I'd never seen an expression that wasn't drawn and stoic on her face before.

A lump lodged in my throat.

Would I have to betray these people?

Tarkosh approached the small pen. "Never wipe away this lining, Amaia," she told me, gesturing to the glistening mucus coating the hatchling. "Always let it dry naturally. We don't handle the hatchlings until that happens. Unless they are born injured."

"The lining gets reabsorbed into their scales," Syris informed me. "Makes them stronger, until they have their first shed. It's what makes hatchling scales so important. It's used in clothing, armor. Nearly impenetrable. Everything that makes us strong… it's because of them."

Fascinating, I thought, watching the hatchling stretch its wings. Off balance and clumsy. I couldn't help but grin.

"Kyr, get down," Tarkosh ordered. "*Faryn.*"

I knew that word meant *stop*, and I watched the hatchling I was meant to monitor clinging to the stone walls of the incubation room, halfway up.

"Sorry," I apologized, racing over to him. I plucked him off the wall, his sharp talons scratching against the stone as he tried to resist my pull. "*Kyr.*"

At my firm word, he nearly went limp. I almost laughed because it felt like he was pouting. Elthika, like newborn *pyroki*, had little personalities that usually involved seeking trouble.

I held him up, but my arms shook. He weighed as much as a small boulder, solid and thick. Even in the last week, he'd grown. I'd watched him devour the oat mixture, which Tarkosh merely called their "feed," just moments before Syris had pulled me away for the birth.

"You little troublemaker," I scolded softly, looking into his bright gold eyes, feeling a swell of affection, which I tried to tamp down.

"He'll be ready to start flying soon," Tarkosh told me when I returned to the ground, Kyr firmly tucked into my side. "All the hatchlings only stay here for a short time."

"What happens then?" I asked, knowing she probably meant that as a warning for me. I didn't want to get attached to the hatchling. Because I knew, like some *pyroki*, they wouldn't stay in my care.

"If they have a known lineage, we present them to the mother or father," Tarkosh told me, taking hold of Kyr's snout and giving it a small little wiggle, which he huffed at. Her lips quirked. "If not, like Kyr here, then we present them all the same. Another Elthika will usually step in and take them under their care and guidance. They are very protective over young, even if they're not their own. They have a higher consciousness in that regard, even more than we do."

I nodded, relieved.

"But don't feel too sad," Syris said. "Letting go of a hatchling is a happy thing. And you'll always see them around the territory. Besides, we'll have our hands full soon. You might even be relieved once they're ready to fly."

My eyes tracked around the incubation room. It was warm in here, a constant heat that made a trickle of sweat run down the back of my neck. Twelve more hatchlings to come. It was only the beginning.

"I think you might be right," I said.

As if Kyr understood me, he gave a growl of displeasure.

Later that night, I was tucked into my room, sitting by the window, which looked out to the courtyard and the mountain behind the hatchery. I'd been watching the Elthika come and go.

There must've been a cave entrance where they nested on the western face.

I'd put Kyr back into the nesting room for the night, where he could climb the walls to his heart's content. Had the evening meal in the kitchens with Syris, Moak making a brief appearance, which had only made my friend blush. And then I'd locked myself in my room for the night.

In my palm, I held a gift my father had given me. A beautiful piece of metalwork, smooth around the edges, with a gleaming red jewel imbedded in the face. The symbol of our family line—Rath Savenal, which had once been the horde of my grandparents—was etched above it, a looping line that resembled an ocean wave.

The dips and edges had developed a patina over time from my touch. It was one of the only things, besides clothing, that I'd stuffed into my travel sack when I'd left home.

My father had spent a lot of time making it. A gift on the eve of my coming of age. And I knew that my parents had saved and scrounged for the gold needed to buy the jewel—a fire gem.

I rubbed my thumb over it. Like it had a light within, it glowed from my touch before fading, responding to heat.

It was one of my most cherished possession…and I felt a desperate ache for home. To walk into the home I'd grown up in, on the top floor that had a beautiful view of Bekkar's Shield, to smell a stew cooking in the hearth and my mother's laughter as she hosted whatever friend that night. To hear the sound of my father's heavy footsteps ascending the rickety staircase after a day in the forges, and to see my mother's warm gaze land on the door, just as it opened to reveal him. She'd always chide him for being late—though he never was—an old joke between them that Kiron and I had never quite understood, but I always watched the way they looked at each other.

I'd always hoped to find a love like theirs. Warm. Familiar. Rooted.

I wiped away the stray tear that fell down my cheek, the silence of the hatchery filling my room.

Just then, my door opened, and I gasped, turning in the stone window seat with a quickened heartbeat.

And when I saw who filled the doorway, it did nothing to calm my racing heart.

"What are you doing here? Gods, did someone see you come in here?" I asked, rising from my seat with parted lips, already fearing the gossip that would get fed back to Ryak.

"Embarrassed to have a *Karath* enter your dwelling late at night?" Alaryk asked, raising his brow, his voice nothing more than an annoyed grumble.

"Shut the door," I hissed, wiping at my cheeks again, just in case there was evidence I'd been crying. My thumb was moving over the fire gem nervously, and I only felt a small relief when the door finally shut.

Alaryk's booted feet treaded heavy on the stone, making a crisp sound, before it was dulled by the rug. He looked around the small room, his eyes hovering over the empty bed on the other side of the wall, not that there was much to see.

"Do I really need to clarify why I'm here?" he asked, his voice low. "When I left that night, I had meant for you to stay in my dwelling. Not sneak back to the hatchery before I could return."

My brow furrowed.

"I wasn't going to stay there," I said.

"I want you close and safe, where I can—"

I cut him off, which made his jaw tighten. "Where's the danger within the borders of your own village, *Karath*? Am I in danger of a vicious attack from the seamstress? Or maybe one of the acolytes might bludgeon and rob me blind as they're limping home from training? Is that what you're afraid of?"

"I'm afraid you might change your mind," he growled, his blue eyes glowing in the dark, even brighter than my fire gem ever could. "So yes, I'd like to keep you close."

A thread of realization shot through me. "So you can…*twist* if necessary."

That was one of the words he'd used when he'd mentioned his own heartstone magic. That he could "change"…and "twist."

I remembered our first meeting. The slither of his magic within me, getting into my head. His voice, deep and velvety smooth, almost like he'd enjoyed making me fear him.

Shall I turn your mind inside out and see all your secrets spill?

I thought of Samryn. The deep aching pain. I thought of the hatchling just born. I thought of Ryak, my new fear that there was much more going on here than Kiron had led me to believe.

Secrets. I had a lot of them these days. And if Alaryk uncovered them…

Even still, I wouldn't turn my back on Samryn, on a creature that I thought was within my power to help and heal.

"I know what I want from you," I told him quickly. "I know what my price is."

"I'm listening," he said quietly, stepping forward.

"I want you to promise to never use your heartstone magic on me. *Ever* again."

His expression was watchful, carefully cataloging my reply in his mind, as if he was already looking for loopholes.

My eyes narrowed into a glare. "I mean it," I bit out. "If you use it on me, if I feel it even once…I'm done. And Samryn will battle his curse alone."

Now his expression looked thunderous. Perhaps my words had been a touch too rough…but after my encounter with Ryak, I *was* shaken. And until I knew exactly my purpose here, I couldn't let Alaryk get inside my head again.

"I agree to your single term," he finally said. "An easy enough thing."

I almost snorted. I knew it was a lie.

"For a moment, I thought you might ask for riches. For jewels. Perhaps even to become my wife."

I jerked. Shock spun in my veins. Now *my* expression was thunderous. "How could you think that?"

He said nothing at first. Finally, he said, "A relief that you ask for so little. Because I would've done any and all of that."

I swallowed hard. "You're out of your mind if you thought I'd want that."

His sardonic brow raise told me he noticed the way my cheeks were flushed. He ignored the slightly barbed words. "Have you recovered?"

"Yes," I sniffed.

"Good," he bit out. "Let's go."

CHAPTER 14
ALARYK

"You'll need to learn how to better control your ability," I told her as we made our way to the landing field. "I can help you with that."

"Who knew a *Karath* could be so generous?" Amaia muttered back. I barely suppressed an amused smirk. She was a cantankerous little Dakkari. Then, after a long moment of quiet, the only sound the crunch of our boots as we walked the gravel pathway, she asked, "How would you help me if you've promised not to use your magic?"

"I promised not to use it on *you*, not that I wouldn't use it at all. There's a difference between using it and bonding it," I informed her. "I used it that night. To take some of the pain from you and Samryn."

She absorbed the words. Grymia had been quiet, most people asleep at this hour, except for the night watch, who were posted at the towers. Once the Karag and their bonded Elthika could travel and live in the Arsadia safely. But over the last few decades, with the heartstone magic depleting from the land, the wild Elthika had grown more…restless.

Villages had been attacked, livestock slaughtered. It was rare, but it still happened. And so every night, the watch continued. A necessary precaution.

"I remember," Amaia said. "I think I do, at least. I remember the pain lessening. I felt like I could breathe again."

Samryn was waiting on the landing field, having felt my tug on our bond.

My Elthika regarded Amaia with slitted eyes as she approached.

"Good evening, friend," she said quietly. "How are you?"

As if he understood, he let out a huff of derision at the question. He jerked his head away when the Dakkari tried to press her fingers into his jaw. To Amaia's credit, her lips only twisted in wry amusement, not offense.

"He dislikes everyone," I informed her. "Don't take it personally."

"Then however did *you* claim him?"

I ignored the subtle dig. "With my charm, I suppose." I grinned, but it felt more like a baring of my teeth. "And because I wasn't leaving the *illa'rosh* without him."

Amaia swallowed. I swore I caught an edge of a smile. Then she looked back at Samryn, her expression going quizzical. "You want to do this here?" she asked. "But what if someone sees?"

I reached out my hand to press against Samryn's side, and he lowered his wing, the membrane stretched over bone making a creaking sound as it shifted.

"Heartstone magic isn't persecuted here, Amaia." Though I thought it might still be wise to stay hidden. "We'll go into the forest. We won't be disturbed there."

She nodded. Whatever fears she had about using her own ability would need to be quelled—and soon. It was horrendous what the Dakkari had done to their own people in search of power. But the Karag were not the same. Or even the Hartans, for that matter.

Amaia ascended up Samryn's wing, though the Elthika let out a low growl when she did, as if he couldn't help himself.

"Enough," I murmured quietly to Samryn, chastising him through the bond. He responded with an ice-cold flood of annoyance, but the growling ceased. I followed after Amaia, who sat uncertain in the riding seat.

"Like this?" she asked, peering up at me. For a moment, I had a strange feeling as I looked down at her, where I was still standing at the joint of Samryn's wing.

The moonlight reflected in her eyes, which flickered back and forth between my own. Her wavy hair was pulled back into a messy plait, though tendrils had escaped. Her lips were pursed, resembling a small pout, as she peered up at me, awaiting my instruction.

I swallowed, huffing out a rough breath.

Not her, I decided firmly. Even if she was beautiful.

"Lean forward," I ordered. "Yes, like that."

I swung over, tucking into place behind her, with her seated between my thighs. I had no use for tethers when it came to my Elthika—with our bond they were unnecessary, so I only bracketed my arms around Amaia, gripping onto the handle at the front of the mount, pressing low over her back.

"Hang on," I murmured, her heat seeping through my clothing as I sent the command through the bond. She smelled good, like spiced soap.

The energy rippled through Samryn's body, and then he was launching into the air, the mighty gust of his wings drowning out Amaia's gasps. The ascent was rougher than it needed to be, and I gritted my teeth, knowing he'd done it on purpose.

When he leveled out, Amaia was trembling.

"Riding with a Vyrin," I told her, "is much different than the transport you took here, yes?"

"Y-Yes," came her breathless reply.

My lips curled as I looked out over the Arsadia. Bright stars peppering a cloudless sky, illuminating towering mountains, which billowed out to deep valleys and lakes in the lower region, closest to the coast.

In the far distance, I spied a formation of wild Elthika, making their way north.

"It's *beautiful*," Amaia said when she'd finally caught her breath and dared to chance a peek up.

"How does it compare to your Dakkar?" I asked curiously, wondering what she might say. I'd flown over her land. I hadn't been impressed, though it had reminded me of Harta, in its own way.

"I…I don't know," she replied. She looked over her shoulder to look at me. Her cheeks were flushed, her eyes wild in worry but also in excitement. She liked this. "I've never stepped foot outside of Dothik."

"What on Muron's blood possessed you to come here, then?" I asked, frowning.

"*This,*" she replied, as if it were obvious. But she didn't gesture to the magnificence of the Arsadia. Instead she risked releasing her grip on the side of the mount to pat Samryn's side. "*Them.*"

I thought I understood, but it still surprised me to know she'd stayed in one place her whole life. Even when I'd been a boy in Harta, we'd moved around a lot. It had taught me how to adapt. I'd assumed that Amaia had had a similar experience, considering how easily she'd assimilated into the Grymia horde.

Samryn dipped suddenly, descending fast, making Amaia's breath catch in a silent scream. He was heading for a lake, not in the forest surrounding our territory but a stone's throw outside of its boundaries.

He landed roughly, nearly knocking the breath out of my own lungs and sending a sharp reverberation up my spine and through the backs of my legs. I let a growl of my own out, one of displeasure.

"*Ty'bara ellrash,*" I muttered. Hartan for *stubborn creature.*

Amaia was breathing hard, trying to suck in air.

"All right?" I asked Amaia, lifting off of her.

"Yes, I think so," she wheezed out. I helped her stand, and Samryn had the good sense to lower his wing without hesitation so she could descend, likely due to the flood of biting annoyance I sent rippling through the bond. He knew he was riding the edge of my patience.

When I followed after her, I went to him. "Do that again, and she might not help you. She might not help us," I warned quietly. A hot stream of breath escaped his nostrils.

Amaia was staring at the shimmering lake, one that stretched so wide it looked like an ocean. But I could just make out the tree line on the opposite shore, dark, tall shadows against the night sky.

When I approached her, impatient to begin, she glanced over at me before gesturing to the lake. "Have you ever seen something so beautiful that it just doesn't seem real?"

I peered at the lake, then flicked my gaze back to hers.

"No," I said, answering her question. "A lake impresses you more than the view of the Arsadia?"

"I've seen mountains before. I've never seen a lake. Only the edge of Drukkar's Sea. But I've never even stood upon its shore." She met my eyes. "Are you so used to being surrounded by beautiful things that you don't notice them anymore?"

Her question surprised me. It made me still, made a strange snap of irritation whip down my spine. Once I had been surrounded by muck and squalor, my mother so poor that we'd lived inside a hollowed-out tree on the edge of a Hartan village.

A half-blood, desolate Hartan boy like me? He would've never *dreamed* of being a *Karath* who had claimed a Vyrin.

You don't know anything about me, I wanted to say. Only it sounded like a petulant child's words, even to my own ears.

"Are you ready?" I asked instead, deciding it wiser to ignore the question.

She gave the lake one last lingering look as I studied her with a furrowed brow. The urge to use my magic on her, to sink it into her and uncover what she was truly thinking, surprised me. I'd only ever used my ability for a specific purpose. To protect, which sometimes meant edging toward the borders of my own morality.

Now that I wasn't allowed to use it on her, the urge to do so grew ever stronger. A temptation I could no longer satisfy, which made me hunger for it all the more.

I was always a greedy bastard.

"How would you like to do this?" she asked, but I couldn't tell if she was speaking to me or Samryn. She approached my Elthika, stilling in front of his wide jaws, which could snap her cleanly in two. The slit of his pupils narrowed on her.

Following, I said, "Just like last time. I'll use my magic to bond to yours, to give you time. I don't know how yours works, but I might have a better understanding if we take it slowly."

"I don't know how it works either," she admitted. "It's just a connection. It comes naturally. I always imagine it's like an entrance into something. I might not know what I'll find, but I'm still willing to cross the threshold."

"Then when you feel my interference," I told her, "think of my power like a pillar. Something to ground you, something to rest upon if you need the reprieve."

She darted a quick look over at me, surprise evident in her expression.

"You understand?" I asked.

"Yes," she said quietly, swallowing hard. I realized she was nervous. Her face had gone a little ashen, her throat bobbing.

I didn't know why that bothered me so much, but I was too selfish to give her an out. This was about Samryn. I would never turn away an opportunity to help him, no matter what. Even if the obvious fear in this Dakkari girl made my stomach turn.

I also couldn't understand why she was doing this. No one was this altruistic, were they? Or was I so jaded that I couldn't see why someone would resign themselves to suffering in return for nothing?

Though I had my suspicions, I still intended to use her, as much as she'd willingly let me. And then…if there came a point of her refusal, what would I do?

If there was a chance to save Samryn…I didn't think there were any lengths I wouldn't go to, even to corrupt my own morals. My own promises.

I could *make* her do it. That was the ugly truth.

"Let's begin," I said, my voice gruff from my thoughts. "Ready?"

She nodded with hesitation. "As I'll ever be."

CHAPTER 15
AMAIA

The curse—whatever wretched curse this was—felt like a tangle of disease. Like a decaying forest, vines hanging, grasping for any form of life to consume. I felt like I was walking through it, and yet every step was like treading through thick sludge. The vines got tangled in my hair, one wrapping around my limbs and then my throat, until it was difficult to breathe.

But just as panic set in, I felt a surge from Alaryk's magic, as if he could feel when I needed him most.

I gasped.

His magic felt like a warm current in a nearly frozen river, giving me some semblance of life as I felt the threads of it inter-twine with my own. I imagined it splitting the darkness of the forest, a glowing river winding through, and I raced toward it.

I sank into it, desperate.

It was a lifeline he was throwing to me, pulling me through the muck until I could feel blood rush to my limbs again. From a river to a rope…I tied his magic to me so I could let it guide me home. He took the pain, so much of it that I could actually try to make sense of what was hurting Samryn.

I could see it all. An intricate woven mess…and I just had to untangle it. And quickly. It was a vast undertaking. And the more time I wasted, the more the curse would bind, weaving itself through Samryn's veins and sinew. Even now, I could feel it moving. Crawling like a worm through him. And to reach its center, I had to heal everything that shrouded it from my view.

I didn't know how long I lasted this time. It felt like I'd been lost in that dark place for weeks, counting each moment by my labored breath, wishing it could be over and fearing the possibility that it could be endless. I'd never felt a curse before. But for the first time, I wondered if it could ensnare me too. If I meddled and poked too much.

"Let me in, Amaia," I heard Alaryk's gritted command. "You're resisting."

Fear and panic swelled. He sounded so far away, and I felt his magic going slippery. The tighter I tried to hold on to it, the more it evaporated in my grasp like a mist.

"I...*can't*," I breathed. The mutated forest in my imaginings seemed to amplify in its power, looming over me until it was just a black wall of endless decay. *Growing. Growing.*

It would crush me. It would swallow me whole—

I was ripped from the curse, and it felt like a tearing of my very soul. And then I remembered nothing at all.

When I woke, I was flying. The wind was whipping my hair, but I pressed my cheek into the heat at my front.

A hand was supporting my back. I was cradled in Alaryk's arms, on the back of Samryn. My eyelids felt so heavy, my body numb. I could taste the acrid bitterness of the curse on my tongue. It was inside me. But I could heal myself. I had to trust that.

My tongue felt heavy when I said, "The hatchery."

Alaryk's hand tightened on my back.

"I felt you," I whispered. "I felt you there. Thank you. *Kakkira vor.*"

"Rest, Amaia," he commanded, his voice gentle. If I didn't know any better, I'd say he sounded worried.

"*Kakkira vor.*"

I succumbed to the relief of sleep again.

For a moment, I didn't know where I was. For a moment, I thought maybe I was home. I had been dreaming of my family, I thought, could very nearly smell my mother's *wrissan* stew bubbling in the hearth.

For a moment, I was *relieved*, all my worries gone. Ryak, my brother, Samryn's curse, the pain…Alaryk.

But it was only my dream crossing into reality for a brief second. I blinked my blurry gaze, salted tears having crusted around the corners of my eyes, and I knew I was in my room at the hatchery.

At first I thought it was dawn, pink light from the sun stretching against the room. But then I realized it was sunset, given the orientation. I hoped I'd only slept the day and not two. My body wasn't as stiff as it'd been when I'd woken in Alaryk's bed.

But my belly rumbled in hunger.

I sat up with a wince and a groan, my head pounding as the room spun. There was a bitterness on my tongue as I swung my legs gingerly over my bed. Someone had placed my mattress back up on the frame.

The cool stone beneath my bare feet felt nice. I let it center me before I rose, my legs a little shaky but growing stronger with every step.

The smell was coming from the kitchens, and I heard the rattle of dishware and the low murmuring of voices when I crept out into the deserted hallway.

Moak, Ulin, Syris, Tarkosh, and I were the only ones who lived in the hatchery—at least during this offseason. Syris told me during the hatching season, the rooms were usually filled, more apprentices having traveled from Grym. Ulin was someone I rarely saw, a quiet male who lived two doors down from me and often had the nests cleaned out before I even woke.

They were all in the kitchen when I leaned against the frame of the entrance. Tarkosh saw me first, her expression one of careful observation.

"There you are," she said, which made the others look at her in confusion before they followed her gaze to me. "You must be hungry."

"Amaia," Syris said, jumping up from her seat. "On Muron's blood, I've been worried sick."

"I'm all right," I assured her, but I gladly took her arm as she guided me to the long table where the rest of them were sitting.

"Up for some stew? The farmer sent over a fine cut of meat," Syris said. "I made it myself. I think it turned out well."

"It did," Moak chimed in. "Very well."

He flashed a charming grin at my friend, who flushed but was already scurrying over to the pot.

"What's been up with you?" Moak asked pointedly, pinning those eyes on me. "You look horrible." His nostrils flared. "And smell horrible."

"Thanks, Moak," I murmured. I slid my gaze over to Tarkosh. "How long have I been sleeping?"

"Two days," she murmured. "We have another hatchling."

A stab of regret and frustration went through me. Two days. Lost again. Tarkosh must've thought I was a flake. I'd wanted to prove that I *should* be here. Instead I'd barely been showing my face this last week.

It looked bad.

"A Rythback?" I asked.

She inclined her head just as Syris slid a heaping bowl of stew in front of me, steam rising from the top. I was hungry, but I also felt vaguely nauseous.

"Go slowly," Tarkosh murmured. "Moak, Ulin, out with you since you're done. Leave her in peace. Moak, you don't smell so great yourself. Go bathe while the washroom is free."

Syris sat across from me, taking Moak's place after he got up with a grumble. They left the kitchen, but Tarkosh lingered.

"I feel…I feel like I should explain," I murmured, even though my throat was clogging up with fear. It was so imprinted on me that heartstone magic was something to be hidden. My mother had worried so much when I'd been growing up. She'd thought I'd let it slip accidentally and I'd be taken. I remembered her fearful whispers with my father late into the night, the timbre of his voice reverberating through my bedroom door in assurance.

Alaryk had told me that heartstone magic wasn't persecuted here. I knew that. Logically, it didn't make sense for me to be so concerned with shielding it.

Then again…there were Dakkari here. Dakkari with connections to the throne. And while the priestesses' power had been snipped when the Heartstone Accords had been made last year, those with magic were still wary to show themselves.

"The *Karath* brought you here in the middle of the night," Syris told me, her voice edged in hesitation. "When I saw you, I thought you were…*dead*."

"Eat a bite first," Tarkosh ordered me quietly. "I spoke with Alaryk. But I would like to hear whatever you wish to tell me. Syris…perhaps you should—"

"She can stay," I said quietly as I picked up my spoon and dipped it into the stew. It tasted like ash on my tongue, combining with the lingering bitterness. But at least it was hot. I felt it warm my frozen bones. And my second and third bites were much better, the flavor smoky. "It's good, Syris. Thank you."

She nibbled on her lip.

I sighed, replacing my spoon in the bowl and looking at both of them sitting across from me.

"What did Alaryk say?" I wondered.

I wanted to know exactly what he had revealed about Samryn, about what I was doing.

Tarkosh's gaze darted to Syris, but she was too busy peering at me in worry to notice.

"That there is a Grymian Elthika who's been sick. And that you are helping to heal him," Tarkosh finished. I had a feeling she knew which Elthika it was, which would explain Alaryk's presence in all of this. But she likely didn't want to betray her *Karath's* trust.

"That's right," I said quietly. I looked over at Syris. "I...I possess heartstone magic." My friend blinked, straightening in surprise. "I can help to heal creatures. I can draw out sickness and pain, so they can recover."

A flash of surprise crossed Tarkosh's face, and I realized that Alaryk hadn't told her everything. I didn't know why that comforted me. Because...perhaps he had been respecting my privacy to keep my trust?

"You can?" Syris breathed. "But that's wonderful!"

I didn't tell them that it worked on people too. I preferred to downplay the extent of my ability. There was a reason I had used it in secret, mostly on *pyrokis*. My *mrikro*—the *pyroki* master I'd apprenticed under—had had his own suspicions, I knew. But he'd never said a word, and I knew he never would.

But I'd apprenticed under Halna for nearly a decade. I'd known Tarkosh and Syris for not even two weeks. And while I knew no one here in the Arsadia would capture me in the middle of the night to ship me off to the priestesses for *experiments*... there was still a good reason for me to worry with Ryak and

Nevin roaming around, who both had close ties with the *Dothikkar.*

"That's an amazing thing during hatchling season," Syris breathed. "Or *any* season. On Muron's blood, Amaia, do you realize how rare, how powerful an ability like that is?"

"I don't know," I admitted quietly, sitting unmoving in my place across from them, my eyes darting back and forth between them. "I don't know at all. Because in Dakkar, heartstone magic is never spoken of. It's a dangerous thing to have. I've kept it a secret all my life."

Syris blinked, her brow furrowing. Sobering. Tarkosh understood it a little better, I thought, because she inclined her head. Listening to me speak, saying little.

"So…*lysi*…I saw an Elthika fall into the forest the night of the feast. I tried to help it. But what's ailing it is *powerful.* Alaryk found me. I'm determined to help the Elthika, but it'll take time to heal. And it takes a lot of my own energy, which is why…"

I gestured to the state of me with a half smile. A nervous one.

"I'm sorry I haven't been in the hatchery. Watching Kyr, helping with the nests—"

"Don't worry about that," Tarkosh said, interrupting me. "Do what you have to do for the Elthika. But watch over yourself, Amaia. You were in a terrible state when Alaryk brought you here. I don't want to see you like that again."

I swallowed, struck by the soft honesty in her voice. "I can't promise that," I said quietly. "But I'll rest more between our sessions. It looks worse than it is. It really only hurts me in the moment."

"Does it?" Tarkosh asked, her question pointed.

Then she surprised me most of all by reaching across the table to take my hand.

My lips parted.

"You're wise to keep knowledge of your ability quiet," she said. "I wouldn't tell anyone here."

My brow furrowed. "I thought…"

"You're right in believing that Karag are more accepting of heartstone magic. But we also value *strength*. And if you knew how to protect yourself—like our *Karath*, for example—or if others feared you enough to never try to *use* you…you would be safe."

Syris sucked in a deep breath.

"But you, Amaia…" she continued quietly, her voice making me lean forward. "Your ability is highly valuable. To anyone, but especially to a Karag with a bonded Elthika. I would like to say that any of the territories would respect that you are protected under Grym…but I've lived long enough to know that greed makes people dangerous."

"You…you think I would be in danger here?" I asked softly.

I thought back to Alaryk's annoyance that I'd left his dwelling. I'd teased him that he thought I'd be in any danger in the Arsadia—other than perhaps from a passing wild Elthika, which I thought I could handle regardless—but now I wondered if there had been more behind his insistence at keeping me safe.

"If word got out about your ability," Tarkosh said, glancing at the open door, "then yes."

Syris sat, nibbling on her lip again. "Surely you don't think another territory would try to steal her away. She's still a Dakkari."

"I have no doubt," Tarkosh said, her words final. "The *Karath* is right to be worried."

I wondered what he'd confided in her when I'd been passed out.

"I don't mean to frighten you, Amaia," she said. "But you're right to be cautious, even here." Tarkosh rose from the table. "And don't misunderstand me—I find it exceedingly fortunate to have an apprentice in Grymia with an ability such as yours, considering we lose a few hatchlings every year to sickness. Fair warning, I will likely do everything in my power to convince you to stay beyond the exchange agreements."

Surprise fluttered through me. But as flattering as it was, I couldn't imagine leaving my family. Still, I understood what she was saying about the hatchlings. "I will help them, if I can," I assured her. I added, "While I'm here."

She nodded. Her gaze flicked to Syris when she said, "This doesn't leave this table. Not even to Moak."

"Of course, Tarkosh," Syris whispered, as if aghast it needed to be said.

"Get some rest," she told us both, walking toward the door. "We expect another hatching sometime in the night. I'll wake you both when it begins."

When she left, a heavy silence fell between me and Syris.

Then she said, "Eat some more. You need your strength."

I captured her hand when she pushed the bowl closer. "You've been a good friend to me here, Syris," I told her. "I just wanted you to know that. I didn't mean to keep the truth from you. But I'm always so afraid of it."

Understanding crossed her expression, compassion knitting her brows together. "Maybe you should consider what Tarkosh said. I would be so very happy if you decided to stay. Not just because of..." She glanced at the door, dropping her voice in an almost comical way. "What I know now. But because you really belong here. And I would miss you terribly."

I smiled widely, even though it felt like my face would crack with it. My skin felt tight. "I would miss you too."

But I can't stay, I wanted to add. I decided to keep that to myself for now, even as an anxious dread settled into my belly. My sole purpose in being here was to observe...to spy. On people who were becoming dear friends.

It made my flesh feel like crawling. But with Ryak's threat in my mind, I knew that I would always choose my family, if push came to shove. All Kiron had ever wanted was to be a guardsman.

All his life, he'd watched them patrol Dothik in their uniforms and watched them train through the fences with wide eyes. He'd spent years in training, had worked for it through his blood and sweat and broken bones.

I wouldn't be the reason he lost what he loved. It would break him.

And we were all still a little broken from when he'd left.

"I'd never seen the *Karath* like this," Syris whispered. I darted a look up at her from my stew, my spoon poised in midair. "When he brought you here a couple nights ago."

"What was he like?" I asked, infinitely curious.

"*Worried,*" she said, finally settling on that word. "He's… I don't know what other *Karaths* are like. But they've always felt so untouchable, almost godlike, to me. Like a beautiful statue you're never allowed to go near. Alaryk feels that way, only more so because…well, there's his ancestry. We always learned to fear the Hartans. And maybe that's wrong for me to think, to fear him like we were trained to. But it's always there."

She sighed, giving me a half smile.

"But that night, he looked…like anyone could touch him. He was worried for you, Amaia. I was in your room, washing away the blood that was pouring from your nose, but I heard him speaking with Tarkosh in the hall. I couldn't really make out what they were saying, but I did hear him tell Tarkosh to make sure you're protected. Or else he would take you from here to do it himself."

I swallowed. "He did?"

I remembered the heat of his hand on my back. The warmth of his magic. I thought back to that dark forest and wanted to shudder as nausea rose.

There was a strange intimacy in the bond of heartstone magic. I hadn't realized it until Alaryk had showed it to me. I'd never experienced it before. But I *had* felt him. And he *had* been like a pillar to me, just as he told me he'd be. Someone to run to.

"Anyone could've touched him that night," Syris finished softly. She peered at me. "But I think it was you who had touched him most of all." She made a face. "That sounds silly. But I don't know how else to explain it. What happened between you two?"

It's complicated, I wanted to tell her. But I didn't want to reveal the bargain I'd made with Alaryk, because it would only lead to more questions.

"He wasn't himself that night," I informed her. Then added, "I mean, I don't know him well enough to say that, but…he helped guide my ability with his own. I'm sure it took a toll on him too."

Understanding went through Syris. But then she looked worried. "You bonded your magic?"

"Yes."

"Just be careful," she told me. "Bonds are strange things. Scholars in Elysom dedicate theirs lives trying to understand them and have failed. Sometimes they can latch and hold, even if it's unintentional."

"What?" I whispered, frowning. "What does that mean?"

"Just that bonds can be hard to break without consequence," she said. She rubbed her arms. "But ask Alaryk. I'm sure he'd know more than I do."

CHAPTER 16
ALARYK

The sharp rap of knuckles on the door sounded just as I was pulling on my boots. I heard a quick retreat of steps down the stairs to my dwelling, and my lips twitched in knowing.

When I pulled open the door and stepped down to meet Amaia, my brow was raised.

Her temper was spiked. That much was easy enough to discern from a mere glance.

"What have I done now, *mariss*?" I asked. *Mariss* meant *ember* in the Hartan language. In Karag, *ember* was *marisha*, reminding me that once, our people had been one.

She frowned at the word, and I wondered for a brief moment if she thought I'd forgotten her name. I didn't correct her assumption, watching with slight amusement as her shoulders tightened even more.

Amaia glanced around the quiet village. Even though the moon had long risen and there wasn't a soul in sight, she was nervous people might see her, standing at my dwelling, alone with me, in the dead of night.

I wondered if I should be offended or not. But I ended up settling on intrigued.

"You sent someone to come retrieve me at the hatchery," she whispered. "To come to your *home*. I don't want more rumors circulating."

I descended the final step, my boots thumping against the stone road. "And what rumors are these, I wonder?"

I knew. But I wanted to see what she would say.

Her cheeks darkened. Even still, she gave me a tiny glare that made interest burn in my belly. She was even more beautiful when she was angry...and truthfully, I was more relieved to see that she'd regained her strength enough to exhibit her temper.

Amaia said, "You know exactly what I'm speaking of. I will *not* be made into some Dakkari concubine with the only desire to join...your...your...your harem!"

"My...harem," I repeated slowly. Why did I get such a strange thrill watching her bristle? "A shame. I've always loved variety."

The words nearly made her eyes bug out of her head. I chided myself, however. It wouldn't benefit either of us if she decided she disliked me. While it was entertaining to push and prod and tease, it was a passing amusement when there was something much bigger at stake.

Samryn had had more energy these last two days than I'd seen in months. And it only made me realize how much pain he'd been shielding from me. I didn't dare *hope*. Not yet.

But Amaia was a blessing to both of us. I needed to remember that so I didn't fuck it up with my glib tongue.

"For the record, I don't have a harem," I murmured, stepping closer.

"That's not what I've heard," she grumbled under her breath.

I ignored that. "Come with me."

Her brows lowered slightly, and for a brief moment, her expression turned stricken, her face losing a bit of its color. Sudden enough to make me still.

"So soon?" she asked. "I just woke this afternoon."

Even the realization of what she feared didn't make me feel any better. I knew how much I asked of her. And for a price so little that it was laughable.

"I know," I said. I'd had Tarkosh sending me missives. I knew she'd woken today. But when I'd visited her last night in her sleeping quarters, she'd still been…dead to the world. I didn't know how long I'd stayed at her bedside, watching the rise and fall of her breath. But it had been the only thing to keep me grounded. "Not tonight. When you are ready."

The bright relief in her eyes made discontent roil in my chest.

"I wanted to try something tonight," I informed her. "But I'm not sure if you'll like it. Or if you'll think that it's breaking our agreement."

Her expression turned suspicious. She was silent for a long moment before she surprised me by simply saying, "Lead the way, *Karath*."

I made a sound in the back of my throat but turned toward Ny'am Mountain, situated toward the back of Grymia's village. My own dwelling was nearer to it than the hatchery.

An Elthika—one I couldn't make out, though I knew it wasn't Samryn—flew overhead, crashing into the mountain side, taloned claws latching onto the stone. High above, it disappeared into one of the inlets, rubbed smooth and wide by centuries of consistent Elthikan scales.

"It's hard to imagine the mountain can hold them all in," came Amaia's soft comment, eyeing the same thing, "now that I've seen them up close."

"Ny'am is vast," I told her as she fell into step beside me. "The mountain extends for miles eastward. This is just the western face. The Elthika have their own tunnels inside. Bonded pairings have their own nests. You'd be surprised by what the mountains can hold."

She went quiet, even reaching out to touch the rocky face as we neared. I led her along the face of the mountain, walking for long moments in quiet as the moon drifted over the sky. Finally I saw the entrance I sought, hidden by overgrowth of the forest that directly abutted it, making borders around Grymia.

Her expression was trepidatious when she saw the opening, but she said nothing.

The entrance was littered with rotting leaves and dead vines. A striped rodent scurried out with a squeak when we stepped inside the mouth.

I led her down a long tunnel, but halfway, I heard her say, "Alaryk, I can't see anything."

Were Dakkari senses so dulled she couldn't see in the dark? I wondered, frowning. But then I remembered—she had human blood. Human senses, I'd heard, were noticeably…disadvantaged.

"Wait," she said.

Then a glow of red light filled the tunnel. Dull but enough that she blinked up at me, like she was seeing me for the first time. She smiled. The light was coming from a pendant around her neck, and I watched as she rubbed the gem there with her thumb.

Even still, it wasn't enough light to illuminate more than a couple feet in front of her, so I took her hand in my own and guided her through the maze of darkness looming before us.

Her hand was soft in my own. Small, but she gripped mine tight. When we reached the worn stone stairs, descending even further, that was when her hand spasmed in my own.

Looking over my shoulder, I asked, "Frightened?"

My voice seemed to echo against the walls of the tunnels. Her chin lifted. "*Nik.*"

My lips twitched. *No* in Dakkari. She might deny it, but I saw her hesitation.

"Afraid of the darkness?" I asked as we started to descend.

"Afraid of…being enclosed. Caged in with nowhere to go," she answered quietly.

"It's only a little while more. You'll see," I told her, hoping the words brought her comfort. "You won't feel caged down there—I promise you."

Her small hand tightened in my own, and I made quick work of the stairs. Amaia tripped on one of the last steps, the edge more worn and slippery than the others, and she crashed into my back. I wedged myself against the wall, catching her before she could stumble again.

"I'm sorry," she whispered, giving me an uncertain, shaken smile.

I nodded, righting her, my hand lingering on her waist to make sure she was steady. The curve of her hip was generous and soft. She was so close, I could smell her warmth. My hand curled into her flesh before I remembered myself and released her.

When we reached the bottom of the steps, there was a curved archway before us. Beyond that…moonlight.

Amaia dropped the gem pressed between her fingertips, the red glow fading in the presence of the silver light. I let her surpass me as she went to peer into the cavern.

"What…" she breathed before turning to me with wide eyes. "What is this place?"

I looked beyond her, stepping out onto the half-sunken ledge of stone at the entrance of the room. A whisper of a touch glanced across my skin, and my neck prickled, feeling a sense of icy stillness here. It was why I'd brought her *here* specifically.

"The Arsadia used to be inhabited by an ancient people. One who lived in peace with the Elthika…until they didn't. Until war drove them from the land, across the sea, to Karak."

"I thought *this* was Karak," she said softly.

"This is the Arsadia," I corrected. "It's an island, albeit vast. It's Elthikan domain. Karak is cleaved into two by the sea. The Arsadia is in the middle of it all. It's said to be where Mokag, the first Elthika, once lived. Here, where he first cried and each tear that landed on the earth grew a *thalara* tree, laden with heartstones."

Her eyes roved around the cavernous room. Water was trickling down from a small waterfall at the north end, filling the bottom at a constant rate, though there was an outlet along the east wall, which I knew was the source of a wide stream that cut through the forest outside.

Overhead, there was an opening in the side of the mountain, despite how deep we were, showing bright stars and a large moon. On this side, it was shallower than the western side, no upper caverns overhead. What this place had been used for, I wasn't certain. But I thought it'd been chosen because of how it opened to the sky. Perhaps, once, it had even been used as an Elthika's nest.

Stone walkways and bridges had been constructed over the lake that flooded the bottom of the room. Amaia stepped from the ledge onto one of the walkways, which wrapped all the way to the center before shooting off to various points of the room. To different tunnels, different staircases, all of which I'd already explored. Most had been caved in.

She crouched to look down into the water. It wasn't a steep drop. If she waded in, it would likely only come up to her waist. The moonlight reflected off the surface, and I peered down as she inspected her face in the water.

"It feels…" She trailed off, but the frown on her expression was puzzled. She stood.

"What *do* you feel?" I asked, curious.

"It feels strange here," she decided on, looking around. "Like…something is waiting. But it's not threatening. It feels… *good*. Welcoming."

I inclined my head, drawing her away from the crumbling edge of the stone walkway.

"Some believe that the early Hartans used to live in these mountains," I told her. "That they built cities inside them. Hartans are a mountain people, even today. So when they were banished from the Arsadia by the Elthika, many scholars in

Elysom think they made their home northeast of Karak, where Harta lies."

She peered up at me, her green eyes darting back and forth between my own. "What do you think?" she asked.

"I think it's a valid theory," I told her. "Hartans are drawn to mountains. Like Elthika to heartstones. Whereas to the Karag… this place would feel like a tomb."

"What is it that *you* prefer?" she questioned curiously.

I bared my teeth in a smile but didn't answer. Which might have disappointed her, but I changed the subject back to common ground.

"There is at least one heartstone in this mountain," I informed her. "Likely here. In this very room. Because it's where the energy is most concentrated. That's what you feel. Have you ever been near a heartstone?"

She shook her head. "No. There's one in Dothik, but it's deep within the *Dothikkar's* palace, below ground. The nearest I've been was with my face pressed to the gilded gates."

I thought it a shame that the Dakkari were so stripped of their nourishment. Heartstone magic had seeped into Dakkar, evidenced by the *thalara* trees, the trees which grew heartstones at the tips of their very roots. The magic had imbedded itself into the earth, the wind, the creatures, the people.

But like the Elthika, if one had heartstone magic, one would forever feel deprived of it if the heartstones all died out. Like a missing limb.

"If you know one is here," she continued, "why not find it and take it?"

"The Elthika need it more than we do," I told her. "The mountain too, for that matter. It benefits no one to go looking for it, though many have tried. Tonight it will benefit us."

"I'm not understanding."

"When we were both joined with Samryn a couple nights

ago," I said, "you were fighting me. Trying to shake me off like a net you'd gotten tangled in."

"I…I didn't mean to," she confessed. "It was all so overwhelming. It's new."

"It would be beneficial if you could get used to my magic. To my touch. So you can recognize it. So you can let me in when I'm trying to help."

She sucked in a sharp breath. "That reminds me…"

There was something in her tone that had me crossing my arms over my chest. "Of what?"

"Syris told me something interesting today," she started. "That bonds can be created if you join your magic with another's. Bonds that can be hard to break. When were you going to tell me that?"

My lips pressed, my tight jaw ticking. "It's an improbable risk," I told her.

"But a risk nonetheless," she countered. "One I didn't know."

I would give her that.

"Bonds can be broken," I assured her.

"I don't even know what that *means*, Alaryk," she said, bristling, throwing her hands wide. "I feel like I'm navigating this with half-truths. In darkness. Blind. I'm trusting you to tell me the truth. But how can I trust that you'll keep me safe when all you care about is your Elthika?"

"It doesn't benefit me to bond with you, Amaia," I growled. "I already *feel* too much. I don't need someone else under my skin! Believe me, I can control how deep we get before there's *ever* a risk of a bond."

I dragged in a deep breath, taking a step closer to her. When she turned her face away, a scoff on her lips, I cradled her cheeks in my palms, surprising her. I forced her to look at me, keeping my gaze locked with hers, my thumb rubbing against her skin.

"Heartstone magic is unpredictable. You know that. It's drawn to certain threads of magic, and if it latches, then it will catch. But I think our abilities are so different from one another's that there's little risk of it."

"What does it mean if it *does* happen, though?" she asked. "That you'll be inside my head all the time? Like you were?"

Like what I'd promised her I wouldn't do was what went unspoken.

"Not like that," I told her, shaking my head. "I'm bonded to Samryn. Our magic caught and held at the Tharken cliffs during my *illa'rosh*. The choosing. It means I can feel him…always. A constant touch in my mind, until the day either of us dies." Her lips parted. "I can feel his emotions. I can give him direction when we fly. I know when he's in distress, when he calls for me. The same for him. Right now, I know he's resting in this very mountain. He's at peace.

"But there is still agency and decision in what we share across the bond. He hid the depth of his own pain from me. I didn't realize how much until I was able to feel it through *you*, Amaia."

I finally released her, but I didn't step away.

She swallowed hard, licking her lips, then asked, "And if you are bonded…what happens if…if…"

"If he dies?" I asked, lips twisting. "Part of me dies with him. There will always be an emptiness where the bond once was. I will forever feel it. But it goes for Samryn as well. Only it will be worse. Because he was bonded once before too."

"He was?" she whispered, compassion lining her face.

"To a rider, two centuries ago. But we are all mortal creatures. The Elthika just live much longer than we do, and so they are cursed with bonds. It's rare that it happens. But…I think he knows that if I die before him, it will mean his death too. Because he might not withstand it again. He still mourns his last rider. I feel it."

Part of me thought he might even view this curse as a mercy. One that took his life before mine had the time to end.

I cleared the tightness in my throat. "So believe me, little *mariss*—the last thing I want is another bonded."

"Then why even risk it?" she breathed.

Then realization shrouded her expression, answering her own question. Because of Samryn. She was finally understanding. I was fucked either way.

"Then don't help me," she insisted. "Don't use your magic if there's a risk of a bond!"

I shook my head. "The curse is too strong for you alone. Especially without direction. Your magic is pure. It's rare. But you also don't know how to wield it."

Her spine stiffened. "I've been doing just fine on my own."

"I don't doubt that," I said carefully. *Proud little thing,* I thought, trying to hide the way my lips quirked. "But can we agree that this curse is much more powerful than anything you've encountered before?"

After a long moment, she finally inclined her head. "I've never even felt a curse before," she admitted softly.

"Then let me help you," I said. "Let me *teach* you." When she still hesitated, I continued with, "You know how many recorded bonds have happened in the last two decades? Of all the riders? Of all the wielders of heartstone magic in Karak?"

She waited.

"Three. I'm included in that number," I said. "Out of *thousands*. And like I said, bonds can be broken."

Most, I amended silently. *And not without consequence.*

"Fine," she said. But her giving in didn't fill me with relief. "What do you want me to do?"

"Open up to me," I told her simply.

"A tall ask," she breathed, staring up at me with luminous eyes. I remembered her standing on the plains of Dakkar, outside her city gates, when I'd first come to her. I remembered thinking she was wild. A puzzle. Something to be untangled, especially since she'd been able to cut off my magic within her so easily.

"But necessary," I told her softly.

CHAPTER 17
AMAIA

My heart was beating like a drum, so hard that I thought Alaryk might be able to feel it throb into his own skin.

"You won't be inside my mind, will you?" I whispered.

"Something you don't want me to uncover?" he asked.

I tried to keep my expression impassive, hoping he didn't see how much alarm saturated my eyes. He would be able to tell. It seemed he saw everything. "I don't like the feeling of it," I said quickly. "It feels…violating. Like I'm not my own."

"Yes, it does," he agreed, surprising me. He rubbed a hand down his jaw. "No, I won't be able to dig around in your mind, Amaia, if that's what worries you."

"And I should simply believe you? Because you've been so forthcoming about everything else?"

His gaze snapped to me. I thought I might've offended him with my comment. "Do you have a choice?"

"I do, actually," I said, feeling my spine straighten at the words. "Because I could walk away right now. From *all* of this. At no cost to me."

He sobered. "Yes, you could. But I don't think you will."

I couldn't even bring myself to deny those words. Maybe that made me a fool. But I realized that in helping Samryn, I would help save *two* beings. Even if the other unexpected one was infuriatingly smug and irritating.

"I was told you were worried about me," I found myself shooting back. "When you brought me back to the hatchery a couple nights ago."

"Does that fill you with satisfaction?" he wanted to know, cocking his head to peer down at me, eyes narrowed in shrewd observation. He was closer than I'd originally realized. But now I could see the strands of silver in his stunningly blue eyes, mesmerizing. His lips were full, surprisingly soft-looking for such a severe face.

No matter what I replied with, I realized he would have the upper hand, and so I bit my tongue. He smirked, and I stepped back. But I forgot the edge of the walkway was right there.

Alaryk's hand flashed out, quicker than I could gasp when I felt my foot slip, and he tugged me forward. A blur of reflexes that made me realize just how powerful he was.

"Be careful," he warned, releasing me, stepping back himself. He ran a hand through his silver hair. I didn't know if I just imagined it, but I thought it might have been shaking. "Are you ready to begin?"

"Will it hurt?" I asked, ignoring my near fall.

"No," he said. "Just the opposite, in fact."

What did that mean?

But I realized I would find out.

"Close your eyes," he murmured. "And quiet your mind. You'll feel the heartstone. When you do, latch onto it. Let it lead you. I'll be there, waiting."

His voice was quietly fading away as I did what he told me. Closing my eyes in that strange place, I'd never felt more vulnerable, except perhaps on the back of an Elthika. I focused on my breath. I'd never called my heartstone magic to me unless there was a *purpose* for it, unless it was needed to calm a *pyroki* or to heal a loved one. There was no urgency here, no heart-pounding danger or desire for it.

And the more I searched for it, the more it eluded me. I felt a breeze against my arms, but I knew there was no wind here in this crumbling, ancient, desolate cavern. It tingled against my skin, sinking into me like a silken oil. I felt my magic wiggle, like it was summoned. But the more I tried to grip it, the more it slipped away.

My eyes opened. Alaryk was watching me, his handsome face drawn in observation across from me.

"Resisting again?" he asked.

"I can feel it," I said, frustrated, "but it's not coming forth. I…I've never had to use it unless I needed to."

"*I* can call it forth," he reminded me. "But you need to learn to do it yourself."

Easier said than done because it had always felt effortless. I'd never had to *think* about it.

I closed my eyes, trying again.

"You're *too* focused," he declared a moment later when I could feel my frustration rise even more. "It should feel like breathing. We'll need to coax it from you until it becomes familiar."

"And how do you want to do that, exactly?" I asked, my eyes popping open, propping my hands on my hips.

"I was taught with pain," he told me, making me freeze. "But that's because I responded to it most. That won't apply to you. But maybe another's…"

Crouching, he unsheathed a dagger that I realized he had strapped to the side of his calf. When I realized what he would do, I gasped. "Don't!"

The tip of the blade was poised over his hand.

Even still, I felt my magic rise, and I gripped onto it with desperation. "Don't do that because it'll drain me to heal you."

"Then don't heal me," Alaryk growled. "Can you feel it?"

"Yes…but it's slipping. Because I'm annoyed with you," I snapped.

The wrong thing to say because he brought the blade swiftly across the palm of his hand.

I gasped, dismayed, as black blood bloomed. "You're insane!" came my shrill cry. "Why would you do that?"

The magic rose, beating against my chest. But no, I wouldn't reward this. I didn't like this. And so I snuffed out whatever tendrils I felt winding their way around me, like little ribbons encasing me.

"I'm not doing this," I said, beginning to turn on my heel, feeling suddenly cold. "I don't care if *you* used pain to help train yourself. But I won't participate in this. It's twisted and—"

His uninjured hand gripped my arm and turned me back toward him. He'd moved so fast, one moment crouched, the next looming over me.

"I think you're afraid," he murmured, his voice silken, like hot blood wasn't dripping from his palm, tinging the air with a metallic scent. "You're afraid to embrace it because you've had to keep it secret your entire life. Because you thought it was your own curse, one that could get you and your family punished. And so you've shoved it down so deep it won't respond unless threatened."

"What are you doing?" I asked, struggling against him.

"*Threatening you*," he growled.

I looked up at him in surprise. This close, I realized how much larger he was. How much stronger. All of these things I'd known, of course. But knowing and being fully pressed against that realization were two *very* different things.

"You won't hurt me," I murmured, keeping his eyes as his heat sank through my clothing, until I could feel it warm my skin. "I know you won't."

"No, but I'll hurt myself to get you to respond," he told me. His vision went cloudy. "Maybe a part of me will even like it."

Shock funneled through me. At the rumble of a confession in his voice, like it was one I hadn't been meant to hear.

"I don't want that," I said, my words brittle. "I don't want you hurt."

There was a wildness in his gaze that hadn't been there before. Had it been brought on by the pain? Something sharp but something unpredictable…it was tangible. There was a buzzing energy rising between us. I realized I didn't know him at all. Especially as a *Karath*, I thought that he might toe the edges of boundaries more than most. Because he needed to.

"There are those who would take advantage of you, Amaia," he rasped. "There are those who would hurt you for what you possess. And throughout history, pain has been more enticing and more easily controlled than anything else. Love. Kindness. *Lust*. It would serve you to identify what you need to control your own magic…before someone else does."

What Tarkosh had said had been right, hadn't it? Was I in danger in Karak?

I could see the pain in his eyes. Perhaps it was foolish of me, but it made me soften. If only slightly. I reached down to brush my fingertips across the back of his sliced palm, feeling my magic bloom. Not hurried or rushed though. *Steady*.

"Don't do this again," I whispered, feeling my magic ball up inside me like yarn waiting to unravel. "I use my magic when it's needed because I *don't* want pain when I can give relief instead."

Something flickered in his eyes.

"Ah, I see," he whispered. He tilted his head down. "No pain for you, *mariss*. You only need softness. Pleasure. How opposite we are."

The cavern seemed to sway when he reached up to trace my face with his fingertips. Confusion swam in me as I stared at him in surprise. At the warm glide of his touch and the way it made a shiver race down my spine.

"Let me teach you this, then," he murmured. "Seduction has

its own place within magic. But seduction is just another method of control. It's more pleasant than pain, perhaps, but also more cutting when wielded recklessly."

I blinked, my thoughts thick and syrupy. "I...I don't understand."

"Using one's magic is like seducing a lover," he told me, making me suck in a low breath, my heart beating in my throat. "There is a push and a pull. There is power in holding it back and knowing when to release it."

"And that's all well and good *if* I could summon it," I answered, once my thoughts had quickened. My cheeks felt hot, but I narrowed my eyes on him nevertheless.

His hand moved, drifting to my shoulder. Something strange happened. I felt the rasping touch of heartstone magic, but it was like I was wrapped in it. I heard the distant murmurings of whispers, but it wasn't alarming. It felt like a comfort as I stared up at Alaryk.

"I...I can hear something," I told him quietly, my eyes widening. His hand moved over me, skimming down my arms. I realized it was *him*. He was calling the heartstone energy toward us, like a magnet. Funneling it straight to me, to make it easier for me to grasp.

"Follow," he whispered, leaning down to murmur the word into my ear. His lips brushed the pointed tip of my ear, making my toes curl in their boots. "Follow where I guide you. Or push me away, Amaia."

My eyes drifted shut as my hands found his wrists. So thick and wide, my fingers didn't meet on the other side. I could feel the pulse of his heartbeat, strong and steady. I shivered, feeling my magic grow warm and languid. Like metal in a forge, malleable and molten. It rose. Tangible. My breaths went heavy with it.

This was what I wanted to learn.

"Show me," I said, determined. I didn't care if my voice

sounded like a plea. *This* was power. Alaryk had wielded his with mastery for much longer than I had. And I wanted to know how. Maybe then I wouldn't be so frightened of it. Maybe then I wouldn't feel like I was risking my own life every time I had to call it to me. "*Hanniva.*"

Please.

He made a gruff sound in the back of his throat.

Then his hand rose. It dove into my hair, and I felt him tangle it into the strands, pulling back my head so he could peer down into my gaze.

"Know this was not meant to happen like this," he told me. His expression looked wildly furious, though still simmering in his own control. For a reckless moment, I wanted to see that control snap. Even I knew I shouldn't want that.

The magic rising made a droplet of sweat roll down the back of my neck. Why was it so *hot*? A strange desire pricked my body, swirling in my lower belly. Perhaps magic and seduction were intertwined, just as he'd said. But it embarrassed me to feel it.

"Nothing has happened," I breathed. "Maybe nothing has to."

His scowl lightened. "You feel it?"

"*Lysi.*"

"Practice keeping it there," he told me, his tone hushed. "I'll show you."

I felt it then. The familiar touch of his magic. Only it felt different. Before I had likened it to a warm current in an icy river.

Now it felt like the drag of his calloused fingers against my bare flesh, making me arch. A moan fell from me, but I couldn't even be embarrassed by it. Had he done that on purpose? *Could* he have even done that? It felt *good*. Sinfully good.

My lips parted as I stared up at him. His eyes began to glow a bright blue. Heartstone blue.

I could only describe it as threads intertwining when his

magic met my own. I felt the *color* of it, and it felt like a burst of gold within me. Beautiful and pure.

Only then I panicked. Because it felt like he could just claw his way up my throat and he'd be inside my mind with no resistance. I would give him *anything* like this. Every secret spilled for him, just as he'd wanted that first day I'd met him.

It was vulnerable and shocking.

"You're fighting me again," came his voice, sounding far away, just as it had in the forest. "Hold on to it. Let me guide you. *Trust me*, Amaia."

Could I?

I didn't know.

"You'll come to know my magic with the familiarity of my touch," came his smoky voice. "That is when you'll stop fighting. When you know I won't hurt you. Or break my promise to you."

This felt more intimate than I ever thought possible. His wrists were firmly in my grasp. I could push him away at any time. There was a laughable comfort in that.

But he *was* joined with me. More than anyone had ever been before. Even sex had never felt this intimate.

It felt raw. It felt aching. I wanted more, and I wanted it to stop. I was both breathlessly greedy and breathlessly frightened.

"Just for a moment," he murmured, his lips brushing my ear. "Let me show you what's possible, *mariss*."

I closed my eyes. With my heart beating its way into my throat, I pushed into him, just as I did when I used my ability to heal. I heard him hiss out a low breath as I surrendered willingly.

Giving in, I leaned forward, pressing my forehead to his chest, running my hands up from his wrist to skim along his arms. I rubbed my lips against the rough material of his shirt, feeling his heartbeat throb against them.

"That's it," I heard him say above me, his deep voice sending a flood of warmth rushing through my limbs. He groaned, clutching me to him, like he was afraid I'd pull away. "You feel so good, *mariss*."

It felt like I was floating. On an endless sea, water rushing in my ears, drowning everything out. But Alaryk was there, holding me up. There was no pain, though the threads of his magic felt sharper. The edge of it skimmed across my skin like a dulled blade. The threat of danger was present, but there was a part of me that recognized it like…his scent. Unchangeable. That was just how his magic felt, perhaps honed and sharpened through pain and experience, as he'd admitted. It didn't mean he would wield it against me.

But where he was sharp, I was soft, encasing his magic until he was forced to sink into me. To give in.

I felt him stiffen.

He'd called this seduction. A push and a pull. And so I dragged him deeper, envisioning pulling him down beneath the water. I could feel his heart thundering against my lips. I heard a breath in his throat catch. It sent my own pulse soaring.

He was right. There was no pain. Only pleasure. Sublime pleasure. It was alarming how good it felt.

But where there was a push, there should be a pull.

And so, when I felt myself getting too wrapped in him, when I began to feel his magic press harder into my own, I surfaced, imagining a blade cutting the threads of our magic.

"*Fuck,*" came his anguished groan as I stumbled back. Only this time, my foot went flying over the edge of the stone walkway. I still felt wrapped up in our connection, confused about what was real and what wasn't. When I felt the water rush over my head, I felt…calm. Tranquil, even. The water was deeper than I expected. It was icy cold, too, shocking me back to reality. The reminder I desperately needed.

When I surfaced, I looked up at the stone walkway, only a few feet above my head. Alaryk was sprawled on the ground, as if the broken connection had taken him by surprise. He stared down at me, breathing hard, expression unreadable though the intensity in his gaze made my nipples pebble tight beneath my thin tunic, the reverberations of heat still weaving between my thighs. His cock was hard, eye-catching and distracting, pressed against the laces of his trews, straining them so tight that I thought they might break. My hand curled beneath the water in *want*.

That had been…entirely unexpected.

As we regarded one another, neither moving, I thought that might've been the case for *both* of us.

And the way he was looking at me?

He was looking at me like he'd never seen me before.

My tongue felt glued to the roof of my mouth as I stood in the water. The surface came up to my shoulders, and I waded closer to the walkway. By then, Alaryk had regained some of his control, crouching at the edge, reaching a hand down toward me.

That was when I realized…the cut on his hand had healed. Unblemished skin met my gaze. I felt more energized than I had in years. I flicked a curious, puzzled glance up at him before taking it, and he effortlessly pulled me up.

I stood, dripping wet, before him. His hand came to my hip, his thumb nestled against the bone there. His jaw tightened. His lips opened, like he was about to speak, before he stopped himself. And I didn't know why that brought awareness crawling over my skin.

"Let's head back so you can get warm," he finally said, his voice guttural, like he hadn't spoken in days.

All I could do was nod as he moved to the hidden stairwell through the archway.

I was flushed, aroused, reeling as I followed.

The most alarming thing, however, was that I wanted to feel him—his body, his magic, his touch—again. I thought that if I wasn't careful, I could come to crave it.

CHAPTER 18
ALARYK

As the desire curled tighter and tighter around me, I lashed out at the sand-filled sack harder and harder. Which only made the former all the worse.

It was before dawn. I'd lain in bed, sleep only coming to me in fragments, teasing me with moments of relief before my mind had pulled me into reality. So I'd stalked to the training grounds near the landing field, the desolate little building that only a few ever used. Dusty and forgotten, but I preferred it that way.

The punching bag never toppled. The leather was worn, but the inside was lined with hatchling scales. Even if the leather failed, the scales never would against my fists.

The pain felt centering. I felt relief the longer I worked on the upright bag, until my knuckles were bleeding, my bones aching, the skin feeling raw and stretched too tight.

I didn't stop until after the first rays of morning sun peeked through the glass window near the door, gleaming off dusty practice blades and bows, hung haphazardly on hooks along the far wall. I didn't stop until my hair was damp from sweat, until every flex of my hand felt like a searing burn.

Only then did I feel like I was back inside my own flesh.

But the desire wouldn't leave. For a brief moment, as I stalked back to my dwelling at the top of Grymia before the village woke, I thought of veering east toward Rivenna's dwelling. She wouldn't deny me. I could shake off the memory of lust for Amaia onto her willing tongue. And wouldn't it feel wonderful, to feel her teeth graze against metal and *tug? Hard?* Just the way I liked it?

But when I imagined the scene, all I could conjure was Amaia's face peering up at me, the sensation of her soft, untouchable magic all around me like a shroud I wanted to stay buried in.

I recalled the punishing tease of her magic. I'd never felt anything like it before. I almost worried that she could do more than heal. I worried she could *ensnare.* Because I hadn't been able to think of anything else since we'd left the cavern in Ny'am. Only her. Desperate and aching to feel her again.

"Fuck," I hissed under my breath, veering toward my dwelling, the stone road familiar. The moment I entered my humble home, I bolted the door and stripped where I stood.

I sighed in relief, feeling cool air over heated skin as I maneuvered to the washroom, drawing open the thin, gossamer curtains to reveal the sunken stone bath.

As I waited for it to fill with steaming water from Ny'am Mountain behind us, I ran the backs of my raw knuckles down the metal piercings of my erect cock, breathing deep and slow. The metal felt cold against the heat of the injuries. I could feel the piercings pull and shift beneath my flesh, sparking pleasure, which coiled in my heavy sac.

Pre-come pushed from the tip, dripping over the head. I spread it with my thumb before stepping into the bath, the water so hot that it burned. Steam rose as I sat on the small ledge beneath the water and leaned back. The heat made me hiss, especially when the water met my sore knuckles, but it only made me grip my cock harder.

I was too far gone to draw this out. I'd been hard for hours, punishing lust fogging my mind ever since I'd been down in the cavern with Amaia. Ever since she'd opened up her magic to me. Ever since she'd emerged from the water like a tantalizing siren hellbent on stealing my soul, her clothes clinging to her lush body, her eyes burning like the namesake I'd given her, like embers.

A desperate sound clawed its way up my throat as I stroked down my thick cock, squeezing hard at the base before running my palm back up. My fingers dragged along the piercings lining the underside of my shaft, each click and subtle pull making my abdomen tighten.

I breathed out, my hips beginning to rock and thrust. I leaned my head back along the edge of the sunken bath, the hard stone supporting my neck as I closed my eyes. Imagining her. Those wide eyes. The curl of her full lips. I imagined the sounds she'd make if I fucked her like this, how good she'd feel around me. She'd demand her pleasure. She'd demand *softness*. Gentleness. She wasn't at all right for me…but on Muron, I wanted her. I wanted to be soft for her, so she could use me up.

The drag of my hand grew rougher, tightening along the piercings. The water's surface went choppy, little waves from my rapid thrusts. The tantalizing mixture of pleasure and pain brought me right to the edge.

And when that pleasure seared me, my vision went white with it, and it felt like a delicious brand on my skin, sizzling until I bellowed with it.

In the aftermath, I recovered, my chest heaving.

I didn't know why she came to mind right then, but I remembered the Hartan witch. The first one that my mother consulted. The prophecy…that I would cut out the heart of my first love before I offered her mine in return. That I would be a king forever torn between three worlds.

I scoffed. My mother and her witches and her prophecies. She'd go from seer to seer when we'd lived in Harta because you could find them at nearly every mountain or village entrance. Whereas in Karak, you'd never encounter a single one.

I understood now why she'd done it. She'd been lost. Looking for someone to give her an answer—or hope, perhaps—that she could cleave to. But none of them had ever offered her any peace. Except that last one, who'd told her that she'd never find what she was looking for in all of Harta, after she'd whispered into my mother's ear about me.

That was why we'd left.

My mother saw riches if I was meant to be a king. A comfortable life. Everything she could ever want and more. It didn't matter that we had nothing except the clothes on our backs and a bundle of dried meats for the journey to Karak. It didn't matter that I'd been a young boy, that the journey had been dangerous, navigating steep mountains and blustering valleys and frigid nights.

Regardless, my mother hadn't lived long enough to see me become a *Karath*.

As for the other prophecies that witch had whispered into my mother's ear…well, I didn't know what love was. I preferred it that way. And so I didn't need to fear it.

And if I was to be torn between three worlds, then let it be Harta, Karak, and the next world in death.

CHAPTER 19
AMAIA

"He's gone?" I asked, frowning. "Where?"

I hadn't seen Alaryk for three days, ever since that night in the mountain. Nor had I seen him around the village, though I would be embarrassed to admit that I'd been searching for him, taking longer walks during meal times and breaks.

"Summoned to Elysom, apparently," Ethrisha told us all, plucking a small fruit from the bowl she'd brought to our picnic lunch. It was a rich purple in color, so dark it appeared black, but the flesh inside was pink. Tart but sweet.

I watched as she bit into it before leaning back against Brune, whose arms came around her. Ever since the night of the feast, the pair had been inseparable. She held another fruit up to his lips and giggled when he splattered juice with his sharp bite.

"But why?" I asked Ethrisha, because she seemed to know everything about everyone. Even me apparently.

"Sad you don't get any more late-night rendezvous with the *Karath*?" she teased, waggling her brows, a smirk on her fruit-stained lips, which I was certain Brune would kiss away later.

Next to me on the spread blanket, Syris shot me an unreadable look. Only she and Tarkosh knew what Alaryk and I were really doing. Though I'd told her *nothing* of the night in Ny'am. Just thinking about it made me shiver and blush.

"You don't know what you're talking about," Syris sniffed, "and you should be shutting down those gossips if you ever hear them."

I took a bite of my bread, stifling a smile. It was a lovely day, and Tarkosh had given us the afternoon off to enjoy the weather. No more hatchlings were expected for another couple days, and Kyr was currently resting in his nest, along with the other four newborns.

"I can't do that," Ethrisha argued. "How will I know what people are really saying about her if they think they can't trust me?"

"You'd make an excellent spy, *kalles*," Brune murmured. My gaze flicked up at him. He seemed to realize what he'd said because his smile faltered, his eyes darting to me.

I'd never told him what Ryak had threatened me with. But now I wondered if Ryak had made similar threats to him.

"*Kalles*," Ethrisha said dreamily. "I just love that word. Say it again."

"*Kalles*," Brune rumbled into her ear, nipping at the lobe.

Syris gave me a look that nearly had me snorting. She was long over the affectionate couple. "What does that even mean?"

"It means *female* in Dakkari," I told her. "But...it's a soft name. One of our ancient horde kings would call his *Morakkari*, his queen, that name. It's sweet. It stuck for centuries."

"How romantic." Ethrisha sighed.

"I wouldn't want anyone going around calling me *female*," Syris sniffed.

"You're just jealous," Ethrisha singsonged, no true malice in her tone as she leaned her head back against Brune's chest.

We were sitting under the shade of a tree along the forest's edge, with a great view of the village below and all of the comings and goings. The sharp slant of the gray roofs, the riders training in the field—mounting practice, from the looks of it—and Elthika flying overhead on occasion. It was peaceful here, I realized.

And every day I settled deeper and deeper into place, my dread and nerves only multiplied.

"When do you think he'll return?" I asked.

Ethrisha peered over at me. "Careful, Amaia. Villagers will *really* think you're warming his bed if you go around pining for him."

"I'm *not* pining," I said.

My friend took pity on me. "Hard to say. It depends why Elysom requested his presence…but I imagine it's about the Hartans. Yesterday I overheard Myzalla saying a formation of wild Elthika got close to the border. Maybe something's drawing them there."

"Does he still have family in Harta?" I questioned.

"Not sure," Ethrisha said, her lips pursuing like she was trying to remember something. "I think it was only him and his mother who fled across the border when he was just a boy. His father was Hartan."

Syris chimed in, "But I heard he never knew him."

Ethrisha's eyes twinkled at Syris actually participating in the gossip. "Well remembered."

"And…the Karag don't take issue with the fact that he's from their enemy's territory?" Brune asked.

"Our territory of Grym is different than the rest of Karak," Ethrisha told us. "There was a time when Hartans and Karag crossed the borders freely because of the short distance. It's only been in the last century when peace has been fractured. It was a lot worse before Alaryk claimed Samryn, before he became the *Karath*. We were actually at war during that time. And Alaryk ended it swiftly."

I frowned. "How?"

"All political, I'm sure," she said, waving her hand. "Elysom was heavily involved during those days too, from what my mother told me. But regardless, very few Grymians actually care that Alaryk was raised in Harta. There's a vocal few, yes, but…he claimed a Vyrin. And not just any Vyrin. *Samryn.* Hard to fight against that. Now, if it were anywhere else and he was their *Karath*…"

"Like in Sarroth," Syris snicked, with an eye roll.

"Yes, now, Sarrothians *hate* outsiders," Ethrisha said with a laugh. "I visited my mother's sister there once. On Muron's blood, the amount of looks I got…I just thought they'd never seen anyone as pretty as me. I jingled as I walked down the streets in my jewelry, and you would've thought I'd spat at their feet. It's so…militant there. I thought *I'd* end up in rider training before I could leave."

Just as our laughs peeled out, as we all tried to imagine Ethrisha in rider training of all things, there were raised, frantic shouts in the distance that quieted us all. Brune stood, squinting into the sunlight as we all tried to figure out what was happening.

That was when I saw it. A fight in the field, where the acolyte riders were. And even from this distance, I could see the familiar form of Ryak, all broad brawn like a true *Dothikkar's* guardsman, struggling with someone in the dirt. He got the upper hand as a gasp sounded from Ethrisha, straddling whoever it was and pummeling them. Over and over as the riding instructor and a few of the other acolytes tried to pull them away.

Even from a distance, the sound seemed to funnel straight toward us, and we could see the ferocity of the fight. The sickening sound of Ryak's fist meeting flesh, the gurgle of blood, and desperate grunts.

It was brutal. And horrifying. And it made my gut churn with nausea to see what Ryak was capable of.

It took three riders—*and* Nevin, I saw—to pull Ryak off his fellow acolyte, who lay limp and unmoving on the ground.

Later that night, I was pacing the hatchery, unable to sleep. I wound down the hallway outside the sleeping quarters, drifted into the kitchen, picking at little bits of bread in the basket, checked in on Kyr—sleeping in the nest, along with the other hatchlings—and then observed the remaining eggs in the incubation room before the heat grew too uncomfortable.

Outside the night air felt blissfully cool against my heated flesh. I sat down on the stone bench, closing my eyes. But all I saw was Ryak being dragged away, his expression thunderous but almost…gloating. They'd locked him away in an empty dwelling, apparently, with guards posted outside the door and windows.

I couldn't ignore the long looks that had been cast my way in the evening as I returned to the hatchery. The whispers and abrupt conversations that ended when I drew near. I knew what they were saying, but the only thing I *could* do was ignore it.

Before Syris had gone to bed, she'd told me that Alaryk had just returned to Grymia at the urging of Myzalla. Maybe that was why I couldn't sleep. Well, one of many factors.

The acolyte still hadn't woken up, apparently. And I'd begged Tarkosh to let me go to him, but she'd looked torn. She'd told me to wait for Alaryk's decision, the worry of exposing my magic at the forefront of her mind.

So I was waiting. But as the moon rose and the hour grew later and later, I knew sleep would elude me if I didn't do something about it.

I didn't go back to my quarters. Instead I jumped over the half wall of the courtyard, my feet landing on the stone road that wound all throughout Grymia, and I went searching myself.

I didn't know *why* I felt guilty. I wasn't responsible for Ryak's brutal actions. I'd learned that he and the acolyte had been at each other's throats for days, barbed comments and prickly smirks being exchanged, before it had apparently erupted this afternoon. I wasn't responsible for Ryak, no…but I felt guilty that I could've helped the acolyte on the field earlier.

I'd been *frozen*, my mind reeling with consequence and fear, an old habit.

And so I'd done nothing.

But that night, I scoured the village. I avoided the dwelling that I knew Ryak was being held in, knowing I wouldn't get any help from the guards—most of them trained Grymian riders, apparently. But most of the village was quiet. As was Alaryk's dwelling, to the point that I wondered if Syris had heard wrongly that he'd returned.

At the base of the village, however, where the road looped around the landing field and cut through the land that led to the farms below, I saw a glow of torchlight and the familiar silken sheen of Alaryk's silver hair as he spoke with a guard standing outside a small stone dwelling. I recognized Myzalla and a handful of riders who had been present when we'd been transported from Dothik.

When he heard the crunch of my boots and one of the guard's eyes flicked to me, Alaryk turned, his expression unreadable as his blue eyes met mine. I hadn't seen him since that night in the mountain, since that strange, electric energy had been shared between us, sweet and aching on my tongue.

He turned back to the guard, said something I couldn't hear, and then approached.

"Is he in there?" I asked, nodding my chin at the dwelling that looked like any other.

"Yes," Alaryk told me.

I moved to step past him, but he snagged my wrist.

"Don't."

I heard something in his voice that made me still. I frowned. "I want to help him, Alaryk. I've waited long enough. I don't care if anyone finds out anymore."

And I hoped he heard the seriousness in my tone because I wouldn't be sent away. I'd waited for his decision, but I didn't want to wait anymore.

Alaryk's soft curse met my ears, and he took my wrist in his grasp, pulling me away.

"What are you doing?" I asked, struggling against him. "I *can* help him."

"No, you can't, *mariss*," he told me, bringing me to a stop a short distance away from the dwelling. He took my face in his palms so that I met his eyes steadily. His voice was almost gentle when he told me, "He's dead."

Everything went still. Even the wind.

At first I thought I hadn't heard him correctly.

"What are you…" I trailed off. Frozen in place as I looked up at him with wide eyes. "What are you saying?"

Alaryk's expression softened marginally. His thumb stroked over my cheeks, like he knew I'd pull away.

"He's dead, Amaia," he told me, keeping my eyes. "Where he's gone, you can't help him."

"No," I said. I didn't even know the acolyte's name, but I still felt a spiral of heartbreak. My own. A splintering in my chest. "No, you're lying."

I wrenched myself from his grip, the sharpened edge of one of his nails catching below my jaw, a sting taking its place.

"Amaia," he warned.

But I was already running to the dwelling, a lone little light on inside. My heartstone magic was gathering wildly in my chest, spurred on by panic and desperation as I sprinted.

Myzalla saw me first, and she tried to hold me back, the guards coming closer in a formation around me as I tried to get through them.

"I can help, I can help—let me through," I heard myself say, my voice watery and brittle, gasps escaping me. I saw blue light reflect off Myzalla's face, making her frown. My eyes.

"Let her through," came Alaryk's roughened order. "Let her see."

Myzalla backed away immediately, as did the guards, and I barreled through the door, only to be greeted by the sight of an older Karag woman, one I recognized, who worked on the farm with Brune. She wasn't crying, but there was a cold grief drenching her expression as she sat at the bedside of who I now realized was her son.

The acolyte's face was an unrecognizable mess, bruised and swollen, though a lot of the dark blood had been washed away.

I spread out the tendrils of my magic, seeking, pressing, hoping.

"What are you doing to him?" came his mother's alarmed bellow. "Get away!"

I felt the iciness wash over me. Familiar. So cold that it nearly stole the breath straight from my lungs, and I wrenched my magic away before it could be withered.

Dead.

Gone.

Lost.

There was nothing I could do. Not anymore.

I met the pained eyes of his mother, angry unushered tears in her vision.

"I'm sorry" was all I could breathe. "I'm so sorry."

"You should never have come here. Any of you. Now my son is dead! Because of *you*. All of you!"

She pushed at my shoulders, shoving me back.

"Saran, that's enough," came Alaryk's firm voice. He stepped into the dwelling, taking my wrist, and pulled me back. "The person who killed your son will pay the price. I promise you that."

"And where were *you*?" Saran asked, turning on Alaryk. "*Gone*. You never should've allowed them to step foot here. This is sacred land. They only poison it."

"Come," Alaryk told me softly. I realized he'd tried to spare me this…but what did it matter?

The only person allowed to hurt here was his mother. The one left behind.

I glanced at the acolyte's lifeless body on the bed one last time as Alaryk guided me from the dwelling, as I heard his mother break down in wrenching sobs that felt like blades across my skin.

I'd never known his name, but I would carry this moment with me for the rest of my life. A curse of my own. Until the day I died.

That would be my own punishment.

CHAPTER 20
ALARYK

"Is she all right?" Myzalla asked me quietly, her gaze flickering to Amaia, who stood on the edge of the road, her unseeing eyes pinned on the shadowy boundary of the forest beyond.

"She's in shock," I told her.

"Her eyes…" Myzalla said, trailing off. She frowned before peering up at me. "What exactly can she do, Alaryk?"

"We'll talk later. But not now. Not here," I told her, rubbing the back of my sore neck. Samryn had pushed himself hard to reach Grymia quickly, soaring over the sea that kept Elysom and the Arsadia separated. It wasn't a long journey, but we'd encountered a storm system off the coast of Elysom. It hadn't been pleasant.

But what I'd encountered in Grymia?

Even less so.

"Want me to escort her back to the hatchery?" Myzalla asked.

I shook my head. "I'll take her."

My wing commander blew out a sharp sigh, her eyes troubled as they swept the quiet village. "What are we going to do, Alaryk? He's Dakkari. There was nothing in the exchange accords about this. How to handle it."

"The crime was committed in Grymia," I told her sternly. "He will be punished according to our laws."

A punishment befitting the crime.

So, it would mean Ryak's death.

"We can't just sentence a Dakkari to execution. You know it's more complicated than that," Myzalla said, keeping her voice low.

"Doesn't have to be," I told her. "I'll notify Elysom soon. And I'll send a missive to Sarkin. Perhaps one of his riders will deliver my message to the *Dothikkar* himself."

Myzalla looked troubled.

"For now, keep him closely watched. No one goes in without my approval," I said.

"And what of Nevin?" she asked. "His friend? What of *them*?"

She gestured to Amaia.

"I'll have an answer for you in the morning," I told her.

"They can't stay here," Myzalla told me. "Not after this. It's safer for them if they leave. And soon."

"*She* stays," I told her firmly. "And if anyone has anything to say about that, they will answer to me."

"Don't tell me you have feelings for the girl," she hissed. "No lover is worth an uprising, *Karath*. I don't have to tell you that."

"She's more valuable than you realize," I growled, narrowing my eyes on her. "You know me better than that."

Myzalla sucked in a long breath, centering herself. "Gethrin was a promising acolyte. He'll be missed. A tragic waste. I hope she's worth it."

A flash of Saran's anger, her palpable, stabbing grief, made me turn away. So Myzalla wouldn't see the way my expression drew up.

"I'll address the village in the morning about what's happened. Will you stay with Saran tonight?"

"I'll try," Myzalla told me. "Though she might not want the company."

I left my wing commander with the others, making my way toward Amaia, who had her arms wrapped around her body.

She stiffened when I came up next to her, but when she saw it was me, she turned forward again, peering into the trees.

"Are you all right?" I asked, turning her until she faced me, so I could study her fully.

She laughed, the sound disbelieving though there was no true bite to it. "You should be asking his mother that. Certainly not me."

"It's late," I told her quietly. "Let me take you back to the hatchery."

"No," she said immediately, shaking her head. "I don't want to go back there. Not right now."

If she wouldn't go back to the hatchery, then I would take her to my dwelling. But it would do us no good to be standing outside for the rest of the night. I pressed my hand to the small of her back. She felt cold, so different than how brightly she'd burned in the mountain.

"Come," I told her softly.

"Not the hatchery," she pleaded, looking up at me with panic I didn't understand. "Please."

"I heard you," I assured her and then ushered her forward. She fell into step beside me as I wound us around the village, which was thankfully empty this far back, away from where most were gathered at the base.

We said nothing along the way, not even when she saw my dwelling come into view, its darkened windows and smokeless chimney looking uninviting. She didn't say a word. Only climbed the short set of stairs as I shouldered open the front door.

Once we were both inside and I had the door bolted, she lingered inside the entryway, her head down, as I went to light the hearth and a few tapered wax candles for light.

"Why didn't you want to go back to the hatchery?" I found

myself asking once a soft bloom of golden light had chased away the colder shadows in the main room.

I gestured to the lounge area, which was much the same as since she'd been there before, and after she toed off her boots gingerly, she shuffled forward. She nestled herself down into the pillows, sitting on the ground, curling her legs beneath her.

"It's too quiet at night," she told me, her eyes pinned on an old snag in the rug. "I can't stand it. Because it reminds me that I'm not home."

I felt a sizzle of worry dart through my belly. Because if I had any say in the matter, she might never go home again.

But that was a dangerous thought. I shook off my protective riding vest, made of hatchling scales, hanging it up by the door. Then I went to join her. Though I desperately wanted sleep, I knew it wouldn't come. Not after tonight. Not with what I knew loomed at dawn.

"I've been around people my entire life. My family, our friends. I've hardly been alone. And so, when I feel like this, it becomes more difficult to face that I *am* alone here. Very alone," she admitted, picking at a stray thread in the pillow. I listened to her speak, wondering what growing up in a family unit like that would be like. My own upbringing couldn't have been more opposite.

Then she took in a steady breath and met my eyes head-on. "I know I didn't kill him, Alaryk. But I'm the reason he's not alive. I don't know how to come to terms with that."

"Amaia," I said, my tone edging on warning. "You know this is *not* your fault."

"When I have the ability to heal and I choose not to…then that certainly feels like my fault."

"You're not a *god*, Amaia," I growled, catching and holding her eyes so she would understand. "You don't get to choose who lives and who dies."

Her lips parted, her eyes widening. "I didn't say that. Only that there *had* been a choice and I'd chosen to do nothing."

"People die every day," I said simply, knowing the words might sound callous and cold, given the circumstances. "In Karak, in Harta, in Dakkar. Are you responsible for their deaths too?"

"Of course not," she said. "But he was *right there*. For how long did he suffer? While I *waited*?" she spat, self-loathing evident in her tone.

"Do you want me to tell you that you're a terrible person?" I asked, eyes narrowing on her. "That this is all your fault? So you can feel worse about a situation that was not your doing?"

"Of course not," she whispered, eyes pained.

"*Enough*, then," I said. "I don't have patience for victimhood."

She looked stricken by the words, staring at me wordlessly across the cushions. If I had to be cruel to make her see reason, then I would be. "I'm not...I'm not..."

"Don't make his death about you," I told her simply. "It's not about you. Do you understand? You *could've* helped him. Just like I *could've* been here. Myzalla *could've* stopped the assault earlier. But she let them fight, thinking it would get their pent-up aggression out. But ultimately...*Ryak*, and Ryak alone, could've stopped. And he didn't. He's a trained guardsman. A trained soldier, a warrior. You think he doesn't know his own strength? He intended to harm, to kill...and he did. It's as simple as that. The only question is *why*."

Amaia flinched, but I thought that maybe the raw honesty of the words would prick her, make her see reason.

"Do you think I feel guilty?" I asked her.

"I...I have no idea what you feel," she answered.

"I do," I answered her, and she looked surprised by the soft confession. "I'll remember Saran's face and words tonight forever."

Her lips parted, and it was a sentiment I knew she shared.

"There is more than enough guilt to go around. And you know what I've realized when I have more than a lifetime of it? It accomplishes nothing," I continued. "Because in the morning, Grymia will want the truth. Grymia will want justice. And the guilt *I* feel serves neither."

Amaia was quiet for a long time as the light of candle flames flickered across the walls. We were both lost in our own thoughts, and I debated what would come next, especially when it pertained to the female across from me.

"What will happen to Ryak?" came her soft question.

I regarded her closely. "If we were in Dakkar, what would happen to him?"

She scoffed, shaking her head. "He's a *darukkar*. A guardsman. A high-ranking one, from my understanding. The same laws don't apply to him. Everyone knows that."

"If he weren't a guardsman?" I prodded, curious.

"*Kor anir ji vorak*," she said quietly, the Dakkari words flowing like wine from her lips. I straightened when she flicked her gaze to me. "It means *the way of the horde*. In Dakkari hordes, if one murders, then they pay in their blood. All of it. He would be executed by a *Vorakkar*, a horde king. In front of the family whose son or daughter or husband or wife he took. But in Dothik…he would be sent to the dungeons, perhaps. It depends whose life he took, I suppose."

"I prefer the way of your hordes," I told her. "A life for a life."

"What would they do in Harta?" came her hesitant question.

My gaze snapped to hers. I tilted my head back. "The Hartans value strength. The murderer would be cast into the wilderness. Anyone who wished revenge or justice could do whatever they wished to him if they hunted him down. But if he survived them all, then he would live and could return home."

Her brows furrowed down into a troubled expression.

"If I have my way, Ryak will be executed," I said simply.

She gasped, her head snapping up.

"We aren't in Dothik. He is no *darukkar*, no guardsman, here. He is an acolyte in training. And he is not above our laws," I said.

"And if that threatens the Heartstone Accords?" she asked. "The *Dothikkar* won't take kindly to it. He'll twist the truth. He already…"

"He already what?" I prompted, gaze pinned on her.

She took in a small breath. "He already looks for cracks. He thinks the Karag are too powerful with your Elthika. You know this. It's no secret."

My lips pressed. "If Elysom intervenes, then I will take their concerns into consideration. But they know it is ultimately my decision. Not much will sway me from it. I have my people to answer to. It is them I listen to, them I serve. No one else."

"Then I don't envy you," she said quietly.

Very few would, I thought.

But this was the life that I'd chosen. The life that had chosen me, the moment my magic had bonded with Samryn's during the *illa'rosh*.

I wasn't one to believe in fate. But circumstance had forged me into what I was now.

"What will happen to *us*?" she asked next, after another long silence. "For me? For Brune? For…Nevin?"

That was a more difficult decision to make.

"It changes nothing for you," I finally replied. "For your place here."

We both knew I was lying, however. I would likely *have* to reveal the extent of her ability—when I had wanted to keep it secret—for Grymia to accept her. But I'd have to do it in a particular way.

"And Brune?" she asked.

I knew she was close friends with the farmhand.

"He would want to stay," she insisted when I said nothing in reply.

"I haven't made a decision yet," I informed her, my tone hardening, shooting a pointed look.

"How would it look if you played favorites with the Dakkari?" she asked, frowning. "They already think…"

"Already think what?" I asked sharply. I let out a small laugh. "That you're warming my bed?" Her cheeks heated. "Well, you have once before already, and you will be tonight. So what? What they think doesn't matter. There's more at stake."

"You're right—it doesn't matter," she whispered, shaking her head. She pressed her palms to her face, rubbing against her eyes. "What am I even saying? I care about my reputation here when someone is dead? I didn't even know his name."

"Gethrin Osa," I told her. "That was his name."

She peeked at me from behind her hands, understanding going through her eyes. She nodded solemnly. "*Kakkira vor.*"

Thank you, I knew it meant in her language.

"Amaia," I said, regaining her complete attention. "I already told you…I'm a selfish bastard." My expression was stern, I knew. "I don't care how it looks if I keep you here and send the others away. *You're* more valuable to me than anyone else here right now. I won't deny that. And I will do whatever it takes to keep you here. I'm warning you now."

Her expression settled into one of knowing and wariness. "You have me until the end of the exchange. One season. Nothing more. And even then, this might change things. If the *Dothikkar* calls us home, I will go. If I think I'm not safe here, I will leave."

"Decisions can change."

Especially if I set my mind to it.

"I'm serious, Alaryk," she said, tone hardening. "I have a life back in Dothik. A family I miss. A future I've worked hard for. I won't give that up so that I can be *used*."

"We'll see about that," I said coolly.

CHAPTER 21
AMAIA

"What happened?" Syris asked in a whisper. "What did he say?"

I sighed, watching Kyr leap from the tree he'd been climbing up, his wings flaring wide. I couldn't pick him up anymore—he was too heavy, and rapidly growing at a rate that I'd never seen in a *pyroki*. Any morning now, I expected Tarkosh to declare that today was the day we'd present him to the Grymian Elthika, to see if one would take Kyr under his or her wing as he came of age.

One thing was becoming very clear. He couldn't stay here much longer. We had four more hatchlings already, two of which were tumbling with each other in the courtyard.

"Nothing happened," I said, scrubbing a hand down my face and over my tired, stinging eyes. "I fell asleep in the lounge, and when I woke before dawn, he was gone."

"But what about you?" Syris demanded. "What did he say?"

"I don't want to talk about it," I said quietly. "Please."

She went silent, in the process of scooping out the feed from the tight container we kept it sealed in. There were little troughs in the courtyard and in the nesting room, and I watched as Syris plopped ladlefuls of the stinky feed, the hatchlings coming racing.

"It's not your fault, Amaia," she finally said after a long silence had stretched between us. "You know that, right?"

Tarkosh appeared at the courtyard entrance, saving me from having to answer, from having to lie. "We're being called to gather at the landing field."

Alaryk's address, I thought, wondering what he would possibly say.

When Syris and I both stood, Tarkosh stepped forward. "Amaia, his orders are that you stay here. Syris and I will go. We'll tell you what happens."

I frowned. "Alaryk told you that?"

She inclined her head. "Stay with the hatchlings. We won't be long."

Before I could protest, both of them retreated, Syris throwing me a concerned look over her shoulder. I gave her a half smile, crouching down to stroke one of the hatchlings' scales, which were already beginning to molt.

It only took me a few moments alone, however, to realize that I'd feel like a coward hiding at the hatchery. I didn't care what Alaryk wanted. I needed to hear whatever he said for myself.

Luckily the hatchlings were quick eaters, having gobbled up their first of many meals of the day in a flash, and I corralled them back through the small door at the end of the courtyard, which led directly into their nesting room. Kyr was the last to obey, but I pressed my hand underneath his jaw, giving him a gentle scratch.

"I'll be right back," I whispered, like he could understand me.

Once I was certain the doors were secure, I didn't bother heading through the hatchery to reach the front entrance, merely climbed up the stone half wall of the courtyard, dropping down on the other side. The road that met the soles of my boots would take me all the way to the landing field.

I didn't see a single person as I wound down through Grymia. Only when I was beginning to descend the hill that led to the field did I see the large crowd, like every Karag was in attendance, having left their duties and posts for the morning.

And even from a distance, I could see Alaryk, standing before a line of his chosen riders, and Myzalla, his wing commander.

He was already speaking by the time I arrived, with my heart lodged in my throat. Immediately, even across the crowd, I felt his gaze find me, his eyes narrowing, but his words never faltered.

"Ryak is being held and watched by chosen guards, and I will decide on his sentencing after I consult with Elysom's council and the other *Karaths*," he was saying. It sparked a ripple of protest from the crowd, which Alaryk quickly silenced. "When I'm done speaking, I'll open this forum up to comments, but until then, I don't want to hear *anyone*. Understood?"

I saw the familiar figures of Tarkosh and Syris, Moak and Ulin close by, their arms crossed over their broad chests. Syris's eyes widened when she saw me, and Tarkosh shook her head when I silently slipped beside them.

"You shouldn't be here," Tarkosh hissed.

"Nevin is," I said, my eyes finding him with the rest of the acolytes, though I could see the tension lining his shoulders, his expression cold and impassive. But I didn't see Brune.

Tarkosh's nostrils flared, but she didn't see the point in sending me away *now*.

"This is a delicate matter," Alaryk continued, his voice carrying, strong and unwavering. "The Heartstone Accords that our nation made with the Dakkari were set in place to encourage peaceful and *mutually* beneficial relations with each other."

I heard the scoffs, the shared expressions, the shaking of heads throughout the crowd. I only felt the pit in my belly grow, the dread tripling. I could feel Syris glance over at me, but I kept my gaze pinned on Alaryk.

"It's no secret that the Dakkari possess a fully mature *thalara* tree. And that it will take years for new trees to grow from the seeds we planted here in the Arsadia only *because* of the Accords. But they will grow nonetheless," Alaryk said. "We are honor-bound to see the Accords through, though we will consult with Elysom, the different territories, *and* Dakkar on the appropriate sentencing for Ryak."

My brow furrowed. So different than what he'd told me last night.

"Are you asking me to forgive my son's murderer for…*politics?*" came a familiar voice. Saran stepped forward, her voice nothing more than a spat. A rumbling went through the crowd.

Alaryk's jaw clenched as he regarded her. "Not forgive, no. That is your choice. I am asking for time, Saran. This is an unprecedented situation. I will not act rashly, despite what I personally believe should happen."

"You promised me justice last night," came her hiss. "So give it to me, *Karath*. Blood for blood—that is the way. The only way. I want him *dead*. Just like my son is."

Movement in the sky made the crowd raise their heads. A dark shadow momentarily blotted out the sun, wings flared wide. A flash of red scales. *Samryn*.

Had he felt Alaryk's call through their bond?

Alaryk said, "I can't give you that right now. For reasons I just explained, Saran."

"You would rather bow to Elysom, to *Sarroth*, than to your own people," Saran spat. "Oh, but of course, it's because you're a Hartan. A serpent who slithered out of the mountains, who promises one thing and does another."

I wasn't the only one who gasped. The earth trembled when Samryn landed on the field behind Alaryk, his riders slowly backing away, and I was awestruck and terrified by the image they both made. One of Samryn looming behind his chosen rider, red eyes glowing. His movements were jerky and quick as he prowled closer to the crowd, belying his own anger, but Alaryk never flinched from Saran's words.

"You're grieving," Alaryk said, "and so *I* will forgive that intended insult because you are not of your right mind. But remember, Saran, any insult directed at me is an insult felt by my bonded Elthika. And he will be much less forgiving if it happens again."

As if to drive home the point made by his rider, I watched Samryn's jaw widen, and a mighty roar, ear-splitting, shook the earth, making Saran stumble backward with a cry of alarm. The entire crowd backstepped, some falling over one another. Even though we were in the rear of the crowd, we still had to stumble away as the wave of people rippled.

In the aftermath, it was so quiet that I could hear the way Samryn's talons latched into the earth. I watched as Alaryk stepped forward, reaching down to help Saran to her feet. I saw her step back, her head bowed, her face paler than it had been before. She was shaking.

My mouth was bone dry as I looked from Samryn to Alaryk. As if Samryn had decided his horde needed to be *reminded* of who Alaryk was…he'd showed them all.

"Now…would anyone like to speak to give their opinion on the matter?" Alaryk asked, raising his voice so that it rippled through the shocked crowd.

A brave soul called out, "What…what of the others? The other Dakkari?"

Syris squeezed my hand. Across the way, I saw that Nevin was as still as a statue. But the moment the Karag ended her question, his gaze cut straight to me.

Alaryk said, "They will remain and see out the terms of the Accords."

More hushed protests rose up.

"And what if they snap like Ryak did?" came another voice. Whoever spoke stepped forward. A male that I recognized worked in the forges, making plating for the Elthika. "They cannot be trusted. I, for one, want them gone."

A chorus of tentative agreement floated up from the crowd with his words, even in the presence of Samryn.

"That one there was a friend of his," the male continued, gesturing over to Nevin. "What's to say he won't do the same?"

Nevin's jaw tightened as he fastened his eyes on the male. "Because I am Dakkari, I am now a killer?" he asked.

"Your friend was. We all know you are *both* trained soldiers," someone else argued. "I can't believe Elysom would approve of warriors for the exchanges, especially to come here to the Arsadia of all places. This is sacred land. Ryak's act defiled it, spilling Karag blood here."

"I think they should be sent back to Dakkar," came another voice.

Voices rose, all of which were in agreement, as my heart thudded harder and harder in my chest.

"They will not be sent away," came Alaryk's words, final and quiet, but they carried across the entire crowd, drawing scoffs and protests. And I knew that what he meant was that *I* wouldn't be sent away.

You're *more valuable to me than anyone else here right now. I won't deny that. And I will do whatever it takes to keep you here* was what he'd told me last night.

"We don't need them. There's no reason for them to stay!" came a rebuttal.

Alaryk fastened his gaze on me. He could only protect my secret for so long, couldn't he? But the crowd was becoming louder and louder, even in the presence of Samryn, all spurred on by each other.

"Can I speak?"

Only belatedly, I realized it was *my* voice that billowed out across the crowd. Heads turned.

Syris hissed, "What are you doing?"

My heart was in my throat, but all I could feel was Alaryk's eyes. His arms crossed over his chest, regarding me over the crowd. He shook his head subtly, warning edged in his gaze.

I took in a deep breath, frozen in place when I saw that most had turned to regard me, whispers weaving through the hundreds of people in attendance on the landing field. All of Grymia… looking directly at me. I was on the incline of the hill, so everyone could see me clearly.

What in Kakkari's name possessed me to speak? I thought, dazed.

"I…I'm sorry about Gethrin's death," I found myself saying, my voice rising. "We all came here to Grymia together, to…to learn from you and to exchange any knowledge we ourselves have. That was always our intention and purpose here. What Ryak did…it's inexcusable. I have no idea why he did what he did. I don't know him well enough to be a judge of his character, but I do know that…" My eyes flicked to Nevin, whose jaw was clenched, his eyes narrowed in a similar expression to Alaryk's. One tinged in *warning.*

I swallowed, hard, closing my eyes for a brief moment to center my thoughts. "I do know that I feel equally responsible for Gethrin's death."

Confused murmurs erupted.

"Amaia," came Tarkosh's quiet voice. "Be careful."

I opened my eyes. Maybe it was the guilt I'd felt lingering from the night before, or maybe it was being confronted with all of Grymia, with everything I feared. Alaryk couldn't keep my secret much longer, but I realized *I* didn't want to be afraid anymore. I'd lived my entire life in fear of others knowing the truth. I'd tamped down my magic so deep because of it.

And maybe if I hadn't been so afraid…Gethrin would still be alive.

And so it felt like my own punishment—while also being in control of my own freedom—when I said, "I possess heartstone magic. I have the ability to heal. I could've saved Gethrin's life. But I was too afraid to do it."

Gasps and a cacophony of voices erupted through the crowd at my declaration.

I heard Tarkosh's deep sigh.

When I met Alaryk's gaze, it was assessing. His lips pressed, and even from this distance, I could see his jaw ticking from how it was clenched. Myzalla moved to his side and was speaking to him, her brows drawn. When I looked to Nevin, I saw that he, too, looked thunderous.

Tarkosh put her hand on my shoulder. I realized I was trembling.

"What do you mean you could've saved his *life*?" came a voice near me. Moak. His expression was confused, troubled, even.

"I—I could have healed him," I confessed, "when he was still alive."

The crowd was surging forward, but then the earth rumbled again, Samryn stomping his limbs to try to bring order. When I peered over at the Elthika, I felt a tinge of fear when I saw red smoke billowing from his jaws. *Ethrall,* I knew the Karag called it. Poisonous fog that could kill with long exposure. Once Dakkar had seen its likeness, and it'd killed an entire race called the Ghertun in the Dead Mountain.

Only some of the Vyrin possessed such a lethal ability, which was why they were so revered. And feared.

The mere sight of the *ethrall* quieted the crowd.

"Enough," Alaryk said, but the word was directed at Samryn. "*Faryn.*"

The command seemed to be enough, and Samryn banished the *ethrall,* the red curls disappearing instantly.

"What does she speak of?" came Saran's voice when no one else spoke in the wake of Samryn's interference. "She could've saved my son?"

The question was directed at Alaryk and Alaryk alone.

He said something to Myzalla, and she inclined her head, beginning to cut through the crowd. Toward me.

"It's true," Alaryk announced. "Amaia of Rath Savenal possesses a rare heartstone magic. A powerful one, which will not only help our people but our Elthika too."

"And yet my son is dead," came Saran's wooden tone. And it cut me deeply. I heard the depth of her grief in the brittleness of her voice.

"If you want someone to blame," Alaryk told her, "then blame me. I told her not to use her power here, in fear that it would put her in danger. She was waiting for *my* order to act, and as you know, I was not here to give it."

"She's your *weapon, Karath*. And you wanted to keep it a secret instead of saving one of our own. My son."

"Make no mistake, Saran," came a rider's voice, "one person and one person alone killed Gethrin, and he will get what's coming to him. But pushing blame onto *anyone* else, including your own *Karath*, gets us nowhere. We all respected Gethrin. We all feel his loss. But you're making it worse."

"How dare you," Saran snapped.

Arguments broke out at the front of the crowd, voices rising.

Myzalla was still pushing through the crowd, coming up the slight incline where we were standing. She looked blurry, only for me to realize it was because tears had pushed into my eyes.

"He wants you away from the crowd, Amaia," she said quietly. "Let's go." Her hand took my wrist.

My eyes met Alaryk's as Myzalla pulled me away. I thought that my admission might make things better, like I'd feel absolved if I confessed my own guilt, if I came clean about what I could do…about what I *could've done*.

But it had only made things worse.

For Alaryk…and for me.

CHAPTER 22
AMAIA

I wondered if this was how Ryak felt, pacing the dwelling he was being kept in. For *hours*, I stayed in Alaryk's home—the door, I saw, guarded by Myzalla at first before another rider came to be her relief, likely called away to help clean up the mess I'd caused. The other rider didn't let me leave either, had actually forced me back into Alaryk's dwelling when I'd felt my patience finally snap.

From guilt, from worry, from sadness… I'd felt each emotion chip away as the hours passed, morphing into something else entirely.

When I finally saw Alaryk, the sun had already set. Long enough for the heat of my temper to simmer toward a roiling boil.

Though two meals had been sent throughout the day while I'd waited, I was still furious that I'd been kept caged. My skin was practically crawling with it. It was the one thing I couldn't stand—and he knew that.

The moment he stepped through the door of his dwelling, his electric-blue eyes found mine from across the room, where I was seated in the lounge. My fingers were twisting against the frayed edge of the rug. The tension was palpable, zapping electricity over my skin, especially when he never took his eyes off me.

We hadn't been alone since the night in Ny'am. Seeing him again was jarring, especially when I remembered the way our magic had intertwined. How it had *bloomed.*

My nostrils flared, met by his cool glare. The iciness on his expression should've been a warning. But I still opened my mouth and asked, "Am I your prisoner now too? You can keep me locked away like Ryak? Like your own personal Dakkari pet?"

The silence was so thick and heavy in the aftermath of the question.

"Be careful, *mariss*," came his voice, oddly soft. But no less terrifying, coupled with his piercing glare. "Do not push me right now. You won't like how it ends."

Dismissive. The words only stoked my ire.

I stood, drawing myself up to my full height before I started to stalk toward the door. I was over this. I felt trapped. This entire exchange, me coming to the Arsadia at all, had been a disaster.

"If it ends with me leaving this place, then I'll take my chances," I couldn't help but snip. "I shouldn't even be here. It was all a mistake."

Alaryk's hand flashed out to grip my arm before I could move past. "You don't get to decide that," he hissed, pressing my back against the front door he'd just come in from. "You think it's a mistake? You couldn't be more wrong."

My temper burned. If it wasn't so overwhelming, I might've given a second thought to the consequences of inciting a *Karath's* wrath.

"I'm done, Alaryk. *Done*," I said, struggling against his grip, but he kept me in place with the whole front of his body, pressing me back until I couldn't move. My emotions were a frayed, frazzled mess. A combination of anger, punishing irritation, loneliness, guilt, *embarrassment.* "I want to go home."

"Oh, you're like a petulant child," Alaryk bit out, those blue eyes sparking dangerously. I stiffened, my defensiveness rising. "Selfish, you know that? I just spent the entire day negotiating to keep you here after what you announced today, in front of everyone. If my horde had any say, you'd be on an Elthika heading back to Dakkar as we speak."

"Good," I hissed, struggling against him, tears beginning to push into my eyes, burning and hot. "Let me go, then. I don't want to be here anymore."

Deep down, I knew I didn't mean it. I didn't truly want to leave the hatchery, all the hatchlings, Syris, Tarkosh, Samryn… Alaryk. But I was at that point where I didn't care. Where the burn of his own responding anger might even feel good. I wanted the fight. I wanted his ire. Because it was what I deserved. At least I thought so.

"*Let me go!*" I cried out, tears dripping down my cheeks even though I was glaring at him. "What was it all for anyway? I fucked everything up! Someone is *dead*, and I made it even worse. You should want me gone."

In front of all of Grymia, I'd finally revealed the truth, one I'd kept locked away for so long, been taught to fear. I'd finally stopped being afraid, for a mere moment, thinking it would bring me some relief from the guilt. But in the end, the truth had made me all the more fearful. It had made everything worse. Just as I'd known it might.

"Amaia," came Alaryk's growl. His big hands were gripping just below my shoulders, his thigh pressed between my own to keep me in place. "You're not going anywhere."

"You *don't* get to decide that," I disagreed.

He leveled me a look, part arrogance, part rage. His hand tipped my chin up, his thumb firm just below my jaw.

"Watch what I'll do to keep you here," he purred, but it was tinged in warning.

A threat.

The spark of my own fury surprised me. I felt a surge of my

heartstone magic, because I felt trapped, because I felt hopeless, and it was the only thing I could think to do to react.

If I surprised Alaryk, if he sensed the tendril of magic weaving across his skin, it was only momentary.

"You have no idea what you're doing," he growled, his eyes flashing blue. "*Enough*—before I make you regret it."

My magic wasn't a weapon. Not like his. He knew it. I knew it. But in Ny'am, I *had* gotten control of him, hadn't I? He'd been *wanting*. I'd felt him. And when I'd cut the tendrils, he'd felt it, aching and deep. He'd underestimated me. If that was the only way I could control him, could get the upper hand, if only for mere moments to prove a point, I'd do it.

Especially now. With tears pushing into my eyes, as frustration and hot anger and an aching, bone-deep sadness coursed through me...what did I have to lose?

My magic grew, uncontrollable, fed by the wild tangle of my emotions. They were beginning to scare me. Everything I'd held bottled up—the disappointed feeling of betrayal by my brother, the fear I'd had ever since Ryak's threats, the worry that I'd be in danger if my secrets ever surfaced, my inability to be alone—came bubbling to the surface.

"Amaia," Alaryk growled, his eyes flickering. In concern? Could he feel it? "Stop."

But it was like a boulder rolling down a steep hill. I didn't know if I could stop it. The heartstone magic was too strong inside me, it felt like it was flooding and seeping into every part of me, beating at my very bones, trying to break free, trying to escape. But I couldn't let it loose. It was trapped and growing. Growing so fast—*too* fast.

"Alaryk," I choked out.

I felt his magic rise in response, flicking over my skin. I wouldn't be able to control it. I'd never experienced this before in my life. I didn't know—

Alaryk's lips pressed hard and firm into my own. Shock raced down my spine. I felt his hand drift from beneath my jaw to my waist, the other cupping the back of my head to keep me in place.

"Give it to me," he breathed against my lips, his voice gentle and soft. Like a lover's. "I'll take it all for you, *mariss*."

Just like in Ny'am, I felt the press of his magic. It wasn't an intrusion, however, not like it'd been on the Dead Lands outside the gates of Dothik. This felt like a seeking question, a skimming touch across my skin.

And momentarily, blissfully, it gave me relief.

The panic ebbed. I was still crying, could taste my salty tears on his lips, but I latched desperately onto his magic like it was a lifeline he'd thrown to me.

I kissed him back in complete surrender. Like if I stopped, I might drown. I poured everything into that kiss.

His fingers dug into one of my hips. I heard the reverberating growl in his throat when he felt me submit to him, but I couldn't tell if it was in relief or pleasure. And when his magic intertwined with my own, as it had in Ny'am, it felt like a golden bloom of warmth slowly seeping through my chest, chasing away the cold, icy panic and raw, desperate emotions that had built and built within me.

I knew what he was doing.

He'd discovered that I responded to pleasure. To softness. Not pain, like him.

He was distracting me. Giving me what I needed to shock my mind into regaining control before it was too late. The emotions were dulled but still present, but I poured everything into him selfishly. My hands came up to grip the front of his sturdy vest, the silver catches scratching against my forearms. I was afraid he'd pull away. That he'd leave me to navigate this alone.

I was still furious with him. For keeping me locked away when I'd told him that one of my fears was to be trapped, for having the biting arrogance to think he could control me, like what I wanted—and needed—didn't matter.

I didn't have to like him. I certainly didn't trust him.

Instead I wanted to use him…just like he was using me. I wanted to feel the wash and strength of his power, I wanted him to teach me how to control it, I wanted to feel that tantalizing and addicting desire deep in my belly.

And if I was being honest with myself, it had been much too long since I'd felt another's touch. I felt *starved* for it.

The low rumble in his chest made my fingers curl. The way our magic was connected…it made me feel like I was floating, all while being pinned against the door by Alaryk's strong thigh wedged between my legs, pressing into my core.

He pressed harder, stooping down to angle our mouths against one another better, like he wanted *more*.

I knew Alaryk had a string of lovers. There were probably a million reasons why this was a terrible idea. I didn't care. I wanted to *feel* something other than guilt and anger. Alaryk was offering me a reprieve. Consequences be damned.

I bit his lower lip, keeping it between my teeth, and felt the hot rush of his sharp exhale. I felt his body shake, felt what I could only describe as electricity through our joined magic, zipping down my spine. He pressed his hips into me more firmly, and I felt the shocking hardness of his cock.

I didn't know who stepped over the invisible line we were both about to cross first.

Maybe it was the way I'd dragged my hands down the firm, solid wall of his chest, the edge of my little finger skimming over his cock, making him hiss.

Or maybe it was him, devouring my lips in a deeper kiss, his tongue sweeping against mine, a tantalizing tease that only made me mew in frustration in the back of my throat. His knee pressed to the throbbing place between my thighs harder, the movement making a spark of pleasure rise.

Being connected to his magic, however, only added to the sensation. I could feel it caressing my sensitive skin, skimming across my taut nipples, weaving its way up the column of my throat, making my pulse jump.

My clothes began to feel too scratchy, too *much*.

"Get them off," I gasped before I dragged his mouth back toward me. He tasted divine. He smelled like the blue smoke that had risen from the little tray on his bedside table, earthy and addictive.

And if he stopped touching me, kissing me, I thought I might wither away, consumed by the uncontrollable pressure of my own heartstone magic. Killed by the very thing I'd been taught to fear.

He growled, the only warning I got, low and rumbling in the back of his throat, before I was up in his arms.

The table was closer than the bed. And that was where I found myself being placed. I arched up when he left me, and I wanted to scream at the flood of sensation that rose. He'd been keeping my magic at bay. Without him, it felt like I was being torn apart.

Alaryk looked feral, a darkness gleaming in his crystalline-blue eyes, like he wanted to hunt for his meal before he savored it.

"Does it ache?" came his voice, smoky and husky. "Do you need me to ease it, *mariss*?"

I didn't have shame. Not when I felt like this.

"Yes," I hissed, arching my back, thrusting my nipples up toward him. My hands flew to my tunic, the material too scratchy against my skin. I tore it off, dropping it down onto the floor as his eyes flashed, narrowing in on my breasts. "Come here."

I was pulsing between my thighs. Wet and aching. Needing *something*.

"Touch me," I pleaded. "Gods, Alaryk, please!"

His hands were rough when they tugged at the laces of my trews, the only sound in the dwelling my rapid breaths and the strong thud of my heartbeat. With one firm yank, Alaryk had me naked, spread out on his own personal dining table, like a willing feast.

I didn't even have the good sense to be embarrassed. How easily I'd folded. How desperately I would beg.

I'd done this to prove that he *didn't* control me. That I could still have power over him. The flicker of that realization made me reach up and grab the back of his neck. I pulled him down until his head was at my breast.

The only thing that brought me some semblance of comfort in the tumultuous maelstrom was that Alaryk was panting hard, that his cock was so thick and pulsing that the laces of his pants had begun to come undone of their own accord. I thought he might split the leather.

When his mouth latched onto my breast, I cried out, stars exploding behind my closed lids. My nipples had always been sensitive, and the heat and silky rasp of his tongue made me tremble.

"*Fuck*, I feel you," he breathed against the taut bud, pressing a little kiss to it. "I feel how much you like this."

My brows furrowed.

A stray, fearful thought filtered into my mind, even as I arched into his mouth. Had he done this to me? Had he used his power on me, when it had been all I'd asked him not to do? Had he…*twisted* me into this? This ball of need and pleasure and flesh, where nothing else mattered but relief?

"What did you do to me?" I asked, feeling the spark of my anger intertwine with the heat. "Did you do this?"

A scoff of disbelief whispered over my breast. The bright blue of his eyes met mine, the glare hot. His hand skimmed to my other nipple, his gaze never leaving mine as he gently plucked it, making me stifle a moan.

"You think I'm a liar? That I would break my promise to you?" he asked, his tone like a purr, but I heard the cutting barb to the words.

His head dipped, but his eyes awaited my answer as the flash of his teeth gently teased my nipple. Back and forth. Back and forth, making my gut tighten more and more, a flood of wetness bathing my thighs.

I was too far gone. I didn't even think it mattered. If he admitted to me right then that he *had*, would I have the strength to stop this? Or was I too frightened of what would greet me if he left me to the hunger of my own magic?

I thought he saw the flash of surrender in my eyes because he chuckled, low and taunting, making me grit my teeth.

"*You* did this, Amaia," he accused. "You spun us both up so tight, we can't escape it now."

His words made a shiver race down my spine.

His mouth returned, clamping down over my breast, sucking *hard* like he was ravenous for me, making me cry out. The scratch of his vest, the silver catches lining the front, abraded my soft belly, likely leaving marks in their wake. And even still, my hands dove into his thick, silver hair, holding him there.

The heat of his tongue dragged through the valley of my breasts as Alaryk slowly rose. He licked up my collarbones, up my throat. There wasn't much space between us, but I felt the urgent pulse throbbing through my veins, likely shared between us. He tugged roughly at the laces of his pants, shoving them down, and bodily dragged my hips to the end of the table.

When my gaze dropped to his cock, my lips parted.

The rumors are true, came the delirious thought.

Silver metal piercings were lining the bottom of his cock. I thought I counted eight…nine? I couldn't be certain. Like a ladder, the piercings were straight metal, capped with a small metal ball at each end.

It wasn't only the piercings that gave me pause. He was

massive. Much, much larger than my previous two lovers. Precome was dripping from the slit, a silver sheen to it, making the swollen head slick and glistening. His *dakke,* the protruding, pleasurable bump at the base of his shaft was firm and perfectly positioned to hit my clit when he was deep inside.

My core clenched in shocking *want.* A flood of wetness dripped from my pussy, pooling down onto the table underneath me. Alaryk's nostrils flared when he saw it, running a hand down his mouth and jaw, his teeth seemingly clenched.

Briefly, he stooped, as if unable to resist. Between my legs, I watched with parted lips as he licked up the wetness, tasting me, his hot tongue flattening and running up my pussy slowly as I held my breath. The drag of it made me buck, made me see stars as pleasure coiled tighter. Once more, he licked me slowly, and my thighs shook around his face.

He murmured something, perhaps in Hartan, under his breath before that gaze flashed up to mine. I nearly gasped at the intensity there. So visible I almost mistook it for anger. But it was desire. And then he was shooting up, leaving me shaking.

I gasped when he laid his heavy, hot cock against my pussy. My eyes widened when I registered the cold gleam of the piercings against my delicate flesh. And when he gave a few small, teasing thrusts of his hips, letting the metal glide over my clit?

I nearly came outside of my skin, pleasure racing through my veins, tightening in my core.

Alaryk laughed. He had the audacity to *fucking* laugh, like it amused him how much control he had over me. When I looked into his eyes, I was assuaged when I saw his own burning need.

"If I pushed you away right now, what would you do?" I couldn't help but ask, narrowing my eyes on his even as I took his hands in my mine, bringing them to my breasts.

He cracked his neck as he tugged and teased my nipples, rolling them between those calloused, rough fingertips, as he continued to give short little thrusts of his hips, making me see stars.

Then, all at once, he pulled away. His hands left me, his cock too, and I felt the flood of my desperate magic swarm. "No!" I cried out in protest.

"You are spoiled," he declared with a maddening smirk. "Maybe I should leave you like this. To teach you—"

I reared up and grabbed his cock, making a harsh groan release from his throat.

"Like you could," I hissed. Loudly, he groaned as I ran my hand down his shaft. It felt so foreign, so strange with the metal, but I was emboldened when I heard his ragged inhale and saw a fresh flood of pre-come at his tip. The piercings pulled when I ran my fingers over them. I pinched one of the metal balls, tugging, and he growled low.

I pulled him closer by his cock and used the tip of his slick head to tease against my clit. He let out a rough exhale when he looked between us, at his pre-come dripping against my sex.

"You're so fucking needy," he rasped.

"And you want me so much, you can't help yourself," I shot back. "Look at how much you're dripping."

I heard his hard swallow, unable to deny the words. He kissed me again, the kiss rough, meant as a punishment for my mouth.

"I thought about how much I don't like you all day," I found myself whispering against him, even as I gripped his vest with my free hand.

"No one said you had to like me to want this," he growled, pushing me away. He pressed me back onto the table. "Enough. I need to be inside you. I feel how much you need it, but what you don't feel is how much *I* need it too."

Was his magic his own curse? I wondered.

His hand joined mine on his cock, and he circled the head at the entrance of my pussy.

"Sink down onto it," he ordered, his hands coming to my

hips, gripping them tight, positioning me so my ass was nearly off the table, my legs splayed wide. "Let me feel how greedy this little pussy is for me."

The naughty words made heat spread, low in my belly. I hated how *hungry* I was for him. I hated that he knew that.

"Fuck," he hissed when I wiggled down onto the tip of his cock. "You're tight, *mariss*. And so *fucking* hot."

With that, he thrust into me slowly, making my teeth clatter together, a pleasured groan reverberating around the room. My own? I couldn't be certain.

"Look at me," came his order. My eyes had fallen closed, but at his command, I obeyed. The bloom of our shared magic felt like a second touch against me, though I was certain he felt it too. There was an expression of disbelief on his face, as if he'd never felt it before. Had his lovers never shared in his magic before? Was it only me?

My gaze dropped between my legs. My lips parted, feeling as each piercing disappeared inside me. Four, five, six, seven…eight.

I registered the heat and firmness of his *dakke*, nudging perfectly against my clit, when he had nowhere else to go. He groaned and I felt it vibrate with the sound, making me gasp. The sensation of fullness—too much fullness—came, even though I could feel the maddening glide of cool, hard metal against my sensitive walls.

I felt too much with him. It was always *too* much, like he was deconstructing me, to build me anew. In Ny'am, that was exactly what it'd felt like. Only, what he uncovered surprised even him.

Thinking about that, as he began to fuck—really fuck, with teeth-rattling thrusts and a controlled, pounding rhythm— between my thighs, I envisioned crossing over the threshold of my magic, as I did whenever I used it, only I pulled him through with me. His body was bathed in blue light. Were my eyes glowing again?

His body jerked, as though he could physically feel the sensation.

"Gods, Amaia," he breathed in disbelief.

I cried out, feeling his pleasure connect with my own. I could feel the heady, sizzling sensation of need, the throb of his heart joining my own, the slide of me around him, while also feeling the overwhelming thickness stretching inside me.

"*No,*" he bit out, a flash of what I thought might be panic stretching across his expression before he pulled out of me.

Frustration ate at me, a growl of my own on my lips. Alaryk flipped me, quicker than I could blink, until I was pressed face down into the wooden table. He kicked my legs open.

"Don't do that, Amaia," he warned, his voice so deep and thick, it sounded like a stranger's.

A sharp crack came, his palm striking my ass, hard, the pain harsh enough to jolt me, the magic fading…*loosening.* Draining. That was the only way I could describe it. He nudged my legs apart more forcefully, his hands coming to the flesh of my ass, gripping it.

I didn't have to wait long to feel the familiar stretch and burn and pleasure as his cock sank into me. The metal rubbed me perfectly, differently in this position, and I moaned, my nails curling into the surface of the table in need.

"Don't bond your magic to mine right now—it's dangerous," came his sharp command. "If you do, I'll pull away. Do you understand me?"

The sound that left my throat was a cross between a whine and a moan.

Another slap on my ass came, making me rock forward, the edge of the table pressing into my clit, making my back arch. His hand came around my throat, a steady pressure, as he growled into my ear, the words clipped, "Do you understand me?"

Right then, I would've agreed to anything. His cock was fully seated inside me, and I tried to wiggle so he would *move*, dammit.

"Yes!" I cried out.

"Good," he murmured, pressing a soft kiss that belied his gruff tone to my temple. His hand never left my throat, and he pulled me until my back was arched, my ass up, the rounded flesh of which was tingling from his palm. I hated that this turned me on so much, as if Alaryk knew every string to strum when it came to me.

Because he'd been connected to me…in a way no one had before?

"Perfect," he breathed.

There was a part of me that wanted to see him, that wanted to look into his eyes as he used his body like a weapon against my own. But this position also felt more fitting. This was a need, a relief to an ache—nothing more. His magic was beginning to feel more and more familiar to me, which was only an added bonus, considering we were reluctant allies now. He was trying to teach me how to control mine, how to wield it more efficiently, while I helped Samryn.

We didn't even have to be friends, truthfully. It didn't matter that he was so handsome that it made me weak. It didn't matter that he could be a smug, condescending bastard or that he always tried to get his way. Because I knew that I could still meet him head-on if I needed to.

"Yes," I breathed, my lips parted, a steady pant falling from my lips, the curl of pleasure unfurling inside me. "More!"

The rough reverberation of a groan met my ears. His hand spasmed at my throat as his thrusts became more and more demanding. The stretch and slide of him, the shocking pop and drag of his piercings, the shameless sounds of our bodies meeting, the slap and primal ferocity.

One of his fingers pressed to my lips, and when he shoved it inside, I sucked on the digit, hearing the sharp intake of his breath.

"Bite," he growled. And so I did, my teeth digging in. He fucked me harder, the heat between my legs growing hotter and hotter. I was getting close. With the table's edge a constant stimulation against my clit, with Alaryk relentless at my back, pressing me into the wooden surface, surrounding me, filling me up until all I could do was surrender to him.

I bit harder, one of my hands coming up to his forearm, my nails curling against his skin with the pleasure.

"*Feels so fucking good,*" he rasped, his hips punctuating each and every word. I could feel each piece of metal slide against my entrance—an erotic, strange, addicting sensation.

On his last thrust, I felt the world tilt. His *dakke* was *there*. Ecstasy. The orgasm that came felt like it was ripping me apart, tearing me into little pieces until I didn't know what was left of me. Little tattered remnants that only became whole again when I sucked in a deep lungful of air like I'd been drowning.

The almost violent pulses in my core made me see stars as my teeth dug around Alaryk's finger, hearing his responding groan. He continued to fuck me through my orgasm, never letting up, never letting me breathe. I went dizzy with it, couldn't catch my breath as the pleasure continued to climb and climb. Belatedly, I realized it was his own. His magic was still roving inside me, prowling like a beast, demanding its due.

When I felt it peak, he flipped me around, quicker than I could blink, until I was staring up at him. His eyes were so dark they were nearly black, and he pulled his cock out of me, bellowing his own pleasure as he thrust into his palm between my thighs.

Dazed, I watched as silver come lashed against my sensitive sex, spilling across my slick, pink flesh and the bud of my clit. It glistened in the low light.

Our breaths and the pounding of my heart were the only things I heard.

And when I met Alaryk's eyes, I couldn't tell if what we'd just done had been a mistake…or inevitable.

CHAPTER 23
ALARYK

Staring down at the mess I'd made between Amaia's thighs, I didn't bother to lace up my trews.

My cock was still pulsing with the aftershocks of my orgasm, the pleasure of which was so intense it had nearly bordered on pain.

I could feel her eyes on me. Had I expected her to shy away? No, I didn't think so. But the steadiness of her gaze surprised me.

Her taste was still on my tongue, my mouth watering for more as the remnants of our magic drifted in the air between us like a thick fog, heady and dizzying.

She'd nearly bonded our magic.

I'd felt her…sinking into me.

For a moment, I'd been tempted. It had felt too good. The reckless part of me wanted to see what would become of a bond like that. The selfish part of me knew that if I allowed it, she'd never go back to Dakkar again.

I wouldn't allow it. Some semblance of reason had cut through the cloying haze of lust and power. But now…I knew what could be. And I craved it.

"It wasn't meant to happen like this," I found myself saying.

My voice was thick, husky from my groans, from the soul-wrenching bellow I'd unleashed when I'd spent myself between her thighs.

"But you believed it would happen?" Amaia's voice was husky too. Soft. Though, fortunately, not laced in the desperate anger I'd meant to guide her away from.

I ran a hand down my jawline. I had been exhausted before I'd stepped foot in my dwelling. A representative from Elysom—Gevanth—had flown through the night, had landed in Grymia shortly after the gathering had finally dispersed. The arguments with Gevanth and my own riding council had been…extensive.

"After Ny'am…" I said, "I thought it likely."

I'd wanted her then. Fiercely. And I knew myself well enough to know that when I coveted something, I usually did everything in my power to get it.

That ambition served me well as a *Karath*. In other ways…it made me high-handed and arrogant.

She was still naked, sprawled out on the table, but she'd come up onto her elbows, her lush breasts tipped up toward me. My cock stirred, her eyes flickering down to it.

"We should clean up," I said, tipping my chin toward the washroom at the back of the dwelling, hidden from view by the curtain. "And we need to talk."

Perhaps my intent of fucking the anger out of her had worked because she wordlessly rose from the table, her legs a little shaky. I steadied her, my palm grazing her hip, and led her to the washroom.

The tension was palpable as I filled the sunken bathing tub, larger than my bed, with a set of stairs leading down into it. Amaia watched the water rise wordlessly, the steam beginning to brush against her flesh, as I—finally—undressed.

I couldn't help but notice that my come was dripping down the inside of her thigh. How much restraint it had taken not to spend my seed deep inside her…

"Ignore it," I commanded when Amaia's gaze cut to my hardening cock.

"That would be hard to do," came her flippant reply with a raised brow.

I huffed out a sharp breath. "Get in—the water's high enough."

"Can you speak without it sounding like an order?" she shot back, but unlike earlier, there was no bite in her tone.

Fair enough. I unclenched my jaw. "Will you please get in the water? It's high enough."

Amaia shook her head, but when she stepped down into the bath, I watched her breasts bounce, making me blow out a sharp breath. I wanted her again. But this time, I wanted to take my time. I wanted to *savor.* I wanted to torment her a little more, to see what fire I could unleash.

The small pendant that hung around her neck gleamed as she settled down onto the ledge opposite where I stood. She looked up at me. Her hair was a wild tangle, her lips red from my punishing kiss, her nipples puckered from my sucking.

I was fully hard again, the need I thought might've been satisfied roaring back in merciless force.

"You desire me," she said softly, her eyes rapt on my cock.

I cut her a withering look as I followed after her. "What was your first clue?"

I surprised her by coming close, by pressing her back into the edge of the pool, standing between her thighs where she sat on the sunken ledge. My arms caged her in, one hand landing on the stone behind her and the other drifting beneath the water.

She went a little breathless when she asked, "Is it me or my magic you desire?"

My fingers grazed over her pelvis, sinking down, making her breath hitch when I caressed her sensitive flesh.

"I can't exactly fuck your magic, now can I?" I rasped. "But I might do a lot of uncharacteristic things for another taste of this…"

Her hand gripped my wrist when my fingers parted her folds, when I teased the small bud of her clit. Her cheeks were flushed, and in her eyes, I saw…curiosity. Mingled with wariness.

I drew my hand away but stayed where I was. Her eyes dragged down my chest—to the piercings through my nipples, to my tensed abdomen, to my cock head bobbing at the surface of the rising water.

When her eyes returned to mine, that curiosity had only grown.

"I suppose you do like variety," she murmured.

For a moment, I had no idea what she was talking about. Then I remembered. Her odd comment about my "harem" in Grymia and my responding flippant words.

"For the last damn time," I murmured, my tone slightly exasperated, "I don't have a harem of lovers just waiting at my beck and call."

Amaia lifted a shoulder, as if the words didn't have any effect on her. But I saw right through it. "If you say so."

My gaze dipped to her lips, full enough that they looked perpetually in a pout.

"Now that we're both calmer," I started, guiding the conversation away from any mentions of *lovers*, "we can talk."

Her expression sobered, and she pressed a hand to my chest, right in the center between my pectorals. I thought it was because she was about to push me away, but then her expression flickered and she kept it there, feeling my heat radiate into her palm. The steadiness of my heartbeat.

"It's still…agitated," she finally said, settling on that word. "I…I'm sorry about earlier. My emotions felt so heightened, so volatile. It feels like it's feeding on them and it's hungry. What if it never stops?"

I cupped her face, rubbing my thumb along the top of her

cheekbone, and her breath hitched. Her eyelids fluttered closed, a shuddered sigh falling from her lips as she gave in, accepting the warmth of my touch, my only intent to bring her a sense of comfort. I could feel her magic still sparking, little zaps across my flesh, and I sent a small river of my own to help soothe it.

"Better?" I asked.

"Yes," she murmured, her shoulders sagging. When her eyes opened, her pupils were dilated. "Thank you."

"It's not uncommon, what you felt," I told her. "Karag who exhibit heartstone magic are placed with tutors from a young age, regardless of class or status in the territories. To help control it. I'm honestly shocked you haven't felt it uncontrolled before now. Which means you do have some restraint over it."

She absorbed my words like she was a sponge. "You speak about it like it's a separate entity. Like it's different from me."

"In many ways, it is. Depends on the individual, I suppose," I replied. "And each individual learns to control their magic in different ways, using different methods. You said you envision a doorway, that you imagine walking through it or crossing some invisible threshold. That's a technique some tutors utilize, or so I've heard. Like manifestation. You learned to do it yourself, which is impressive."

"You had a tutor to help you?" she asked.

My lips lifted in a wry smile. "Not quite."

But I didn't offer up anything else, not wanting to delve into my history with Kamora right then. I'd learned much from her... but at what cost?

"My instruction was...different, as yours will likely be with me," I finished.

Sex would complicate matters, as it always did. But I didn't think I had the strength and discipline to stay away now that I'd been offered a taste.

There was the danger of a bond, to add to that. Amaia hadn't known what she'd been doing, had only done what had probably felt good at the time. But even I had recognized how perilously close we'd come to bonding our magic.

Kamora was the only other female with heartstone magic I'd had sex with…but she'd used hers as a weapon against me during it. Amaia had used it like an embrace, one I wanted to sink into and never leave. That was even more dangerous, in my opinion. There had never been a bonding risk with Kamora.

"Still, I'm not surprised if there are unfortunate flare-ups of your magic, especially given the events of late," I finished, steering back to a more unpleasant conversation. "You were angry with me. I was angry with you. Let's start there."

Her jaw tightened, but she took a steadying breath as she shifted on the stone ledge.

"Can I have some soap, please?" she asked pointedly, making my lips quirk.

"Certainly," I said, releasing her cheek, sensing her small flinch when I had to retreat before wading to the opposite end of the bathing pool, where I kept a small jar of lathering granules. I poured some out into her palm when I returned, taking a seat on the ledge when she stood.

Crossing my arms over my chest, I watched as she scrubbed herself clean, erasing all evidence that I'd left on her skin…or between her legs. The heat of the water started to loosen my muscles and I felt more relaxed than I had all week.

"Don't lock me away again," she finally said, the words calm and even, so unlike the spitting fury I'd spied in her eyes when her temper had been bright and hot. "If you need me to stay out of sight, fine. But keeping me confined…I won't allow it again."

"I wanted you safe," I replied. "I didn't think I'd be gone as long as I was. But someone from Elysom arrived today, and we've been in talks ever since."

"Then tell me that," she replied, her eyes flashing. "I could've been in the hatchery, where no one is allowed to go anyway. I would've been safe there. And useful. Instead of wasting every minute stuck in my own head here."

This went beyond keeping her locked away, I realized belatedly. This was about her having to face the rawness of her own emotions, with no distractions…and she resented me for it.

"Very well," I murmured, my stubbornness softening. "I'm sorry."

Amaia blinked, her hands pausing in her washing. "It's…all right."

She bit her lip, looking a little embarrassed now.

"I didn't really mean what I said earlier," she said quietly. "About me…about me wanting to leave. About not liking you."

That was what she was worried about?

"I know," I said simply. "You have a temper. I don't know why that surprised me."

"Not usually," she said, "but when I get worked up…I really get worked up. It just takes a lot to get to that point."

"And I pushed you over that edge."

"Not just you," she replied. "Obviously. I…I did make a mess of things today. I didn't mean to. I thought that maybe it would help. Though I don't know if it was selfish, me trying to absolve the guilt I feel with truth. But what's done is done. I know that."

"Your admission was ill-timed," I finally said. "But it can't be helped now. Grymia would've found out eventually, I'm certain. But now we have bigger problems."

"And those are?" she asked, stopping in her washing to gaze at me firmly.

I slung my arms back onto the edge of the tub, leaning back. "Elysom's council wants Ryak executed."

Her eyes went wide. "What? They actually agreed?"

It was political posturing…and nothing more. I didn't want a part in sending a message to the *Dothikkar*. I only wanted justice for a murder that had happened in my own territory, justice I'd promised to a grieving mother.

But Elysom…

They had spies placed in Dothik, of course. Spies that had been there far longer than the Dakkari even realized. Far longer than when Sarkin Dirak'zar had been tasked with making contact with the Dakkari last year.

And those spies had heard the rumblings in the *Dothikkar*'s own palace. That he was paranoid that the Karag would strike Dothik first, that it was our ultimate mission to gain control of the Dakkari capital city and slowly dismantle the nation from within until we took it for our own.

His argument was that we had Elthikan power.

He wasn't wrong. Elthika were the most powerful weapon in existence, even over heartstone magic. To know that your reluctant ally possessed that kind of might and power…it would make anyone fearful if you were so lacking in strength.

Elysom's council thought it was an opportune moment to remind the *Dothikkar* of that very thing he feared. To force him to reveal what Elysom already knew: that he didn't trust the Karag in the slightest and would take the first opportunity to weaken us.

The Heartstone Accords were a formality and nothing more. They were the illusion of peace between our two nations, but when it really came down to it, the only thing that was important was control over the heartstones.

Ryak's execution would be less about justice for the life he cut short, the life he stole, the son he took.

Instead it would be a political message. It put a sour taste in my mouth.

And that wasn't all.

"Elysom also wants all the Dakkari sent back to Dothik. From here and from Sarroth."

Amaia's shoulders moved with her heavy inhale. "When?"

"I won't allow it," I told her, the water trickling when I

moved slightly. "Elysom can only make requests, not demands, of a *Karath*."

She blew out a breath. "What about Brune and Nevin?"

"Do you want them to stay?" I asked, cocking my head to the side, eyes narrowed on her.

"Brune," she said, looking down at the water.

"Not Nevin?"

"I—I don't know him well enough," she replied truthfully. "But it's up to Brune to decide. Maybe this has changed things for him. Maybe he wants to return home."

"And what about you?" I asked, curiously. "What do you want?"

Her gaze connected with mine, steady. There was something in her expression I couldn't read, something that made my brow furrow in confusion.

Finally, she said, "I want to see all the hatchlings born. I want to see Kyr fly for the first time. I want to see Samryn healed."

A gruff sound fell from my throat.

"If I left before then," she said, "it would feel unfinished…for a long time. Maybe even forever. I don't want that. But…it's become *more* than I thought it would. With you."

"Because of your heartstone magic," I guessed. When her face flushed, I asked, "Or something else?"

"There's a lot here for me, Alaryk. That's what I'm trying to say. You're included in that."

I inclined my head, a swell of something I didn't want to give a name to rising in my chest.

"I know I said something different earlier," she added. She sank down into the bath, the surface of the water lapping at her lips. Amaia looked like she had in Ny'am, when she'd fallen into the water at the base of the stone walkways—like a goddess as she'd emerged, her magic prickling over my skin, electrifying the air as desire had pumped hotly through me. "But I wanted you to know how I really feel."

Was it a little fucked that I'd *liked* her temper? That I'd liked that she'd submitted to me, trusting me, at the very least, to give her some relief? That she'd been passionate? That she'd been unafraid of stoking my own temper?

Amaia of Rath Savenal had surprised me at almost every turn.

"Why are you looking at me like that?" came her soft question, which floated across the arm's distance we were apart.

"Like what?" I asked, a challenge.

She shook her head, not giving a voice to what she was thinking. Shy now? Maddening female.

"What does this mean for us?" she asked after a brief lapse of silence.

"Sex, you mean?" I asked to clarify.

She nodded.

I wasn't going to stop—that was all I knew.

"It doesn't have to change anything," I answered. "Besides your living arrangements."

She frowned.

"I already told you before—I don't trust anyone to keep you safe," I said. "You'll live here with me. You can go about your duties at the hatchery during the day, but I'll have a guard assigned to you throughout the village. One of my own riders."

Her lips parted, an indignant flash crossing her features.

"After today's meeting," I added, "it's best that you have a guard with you anyway. Not just because of us." I gestured between our naked bodies. "I expect you won't like this arrangement, but I think it's necessary. Elysom knows about you now, about your ability."

"Someone told this councilmember?" she asked, frowning.

"Gevanth." I inclined my head. "It was what I didn't want to happen, but now that it has, we'll deal with it. That means I want you near. I'm committing myself to the Arsadia through the rest of the riding season. And if you decide to stay beyond the exchange agreements, you'll return to Grym with me after the choosing."

"I won't," she replied. "Change my mind, I mean."

I let it slide, but she didn't know how wrong she was.

"Are we in agreement?"

"And what do I get if I agree?" she asked, raising her brow. She rubbed the gem of her pendant, casting the bath water in momentary red light before she let it drop. "To stay here with you?"

"What do you want?" I asked softly, curious what she would say. Another deal between us, another barter.

She nibbled on her lip. I saw when the answer came to her, but oddly, she didn't voice it right away. Like she was weighing the consequences if she said it.

"Tell me."

"I…I don't want to fall asleep alone if I stay here," she finally said.

The words surprised me. The quiet stretched in the bath as she shifted, waiting for my reply.

Because she didn't want to be alone, I knew. She'd said something similar to me down in Ny'am.

"All right," I said, making her gaze snap up toward me. "Then you won't be."

Easy enough.

She sniffed, as if she hadn't just asked me to lie beside her each and every night she was here. "So we are in agreement? Again?" she added.

"It seems we are."

That was easier than I'd thought it'd be.

"What…what are you going to do about Ryak?" came her hesitant question.

I looked down at the rippling of the water.

I didn't want to be a tool for Elysom, used to relay a strong but clear threat to a distant king.

Then again, I risked the backlash and uprising of Grymia's citizens, who knew the precedence for a murder. If I let this one slide, what would become of the order and law that we were all bound to?

If one murdered, their life was forfeit.

If one stole an Elthika egg or hatchling, their life was forfeit.

If one harmed an Elthika maliciously without provocation, their life was forfeit.

Three simple laws that led to the highest form of punishment.

I knew what needed to be done. What always should've been done. The knowledge settled deep into my bones, the answer clear.

I met her eyes.

Then I said simply, "Ryak will be executed."

There was no other choice.

CHAPTER 24
AMAIA

Walking to the hatchery the next morning, I could practically *hear* the stares. So loud that I felt my throat slowly tightening with every step.

Myzalla was behind me, marching me the—thankfully—short distance between Alaryk's dwelling and the hatchery. She seemed perturbed that she'd been assigned as my guard for this morning, but I knew it was because Alaryk likely didn't trust many. Myzalla was the exception.

"I can walk from here," I informed her, turning to look at her over my shoulder when the circular dome of the hatchery building came into view.

"Not a chance" was her reply.

I sighed. "I didn't ask for this," I informed her, grumbling it under my breath.

"That makes two of us," she replied, "but I understand his caution. So let's just pretend that I haven't been assigned to be your nursemaid for this morning and say nothing more about it."

I wisely kept my lips pressed together, trudging down the road, trying to ignore the Karag who physically stopped in their morning routines to stare at me passing. Some gazes held wariness. Others, shrewd curiosity. And then there were the ones with blatant mistrust, shaded glares.

My feet picked up pace, though the resulting twinge between my thighs was a constant reminder, adding to my growing list of impulsive and reckless things I'd done yesterday.

But I'd slept—irritatingly—well. I'd woken in the middle of the night once, to find Alaryk sleeping beside me, his warm thigh crooked and pressed against my leg, his hand resting on the soft part of my belly. The closeness, the strange newfound intimacy had made my chest flutter, but in my sleepiness, I hadn't questioned it. His warm, solid presence beside me in bed had helped me drift back to sleep. The steadiness of his breath and the heat of his hand were the last things I remembered until dawn light had filtered across the bed.

And Alaryk had been gone. I'd wandered outside to find Myzalla already waiting for me, telling me that Alaryk was meeting with Gevanth, the representative from Elysom.

I pushed the memory of his bed from my mind. I pushed the memory of me spread out on his table from my mind…and the way his fingers had brushed over my clit in his bathing pool. I *certainly* didn't need to remember that.

When I stepped foot in the hatchery, I blew out a shaky breath of relief. Myzalla stayed outside, telling me not to leave the building unless a guard was present with me. Only after I agreed did she let me out of her sight.

"There you are," Syris breathed, looking a bit frazzled, when I found her in the courtyard. She was alone, trying to corral four hatchlings, Kyr included, into their nesting room. My friend looked me over, long and assessing. Then, to my surprise, she said, "Tarkosh is prepping another hatchling. Help me get them inside, because she wants us in incubation."

We would talk later, I knew. But maybe Syris sensed that I needed a state of normalcy right now. Something distracting, something that would give me purpose so I didn't sink into my own emotions and regret.

"On it," I said, already setting my sights on Kyr.

It was nearing evening when I was finally able to catch my breath, stepping outside into the courtyard. Pink dusk light was filtering through the heavy cloud cover overhead. A cool breeze swept through my hair as I chugged a goblet of water. Hatchery work was less messy than working with *pyrokis*. I wasn't covered in birthing aftermath and blood at the very least. But it was no less strenuous. Hatchlings were mischievous and much more intelligent than *pyrokis*. Outsmarting them was tiring, and keeping them occupied was a job in itself. I didn't know how Tarkosh and Syris handled it year round, especially since this was supposedly the quiet season, right before the storm of hatchlings would come.

A tapping sound made me snap my head up, frowning as I peered around the empty space. Syris and Tarkosh were in the kitchens. Ulin was in the washroom, Moak was down in the main village. I'd come out for fresh air before we all ate.

At the end of the courtyard, I saw a familiar face watching me from over the half wall that lined the perimeter.

I jolted, my heart speeding in trepidation.

Quickly approaching, I kept my voice hushed when I asked, "What are you doing here? How did you get past Myzalla?"

Nevin leveled me a look, as if my question was insulting. "We don't have a lot of time. The guards are on rotation," he said. "What are they saying about Ryak?"

I swallowed hard. "I don't know—"

"Cut the shit, Amaia," came Nevin's words. His tone was even, bordering on cold. Stern. "I know what Ryak threatened you with. Just because he's gotten himself locked away doesn't mean you're in the clear. And now I know something about you that Ryak doesn't."

My heartstone magic.

I realized that he was dangerous in a way that Ryak hadn't been. Nevin was measured. Calculated.

"I'll ask again. What are they saying about Ryak?"

His golden eyes were like mirrors. They made a shudder work down my spine, and I had to look away.

His arms flashed over the half wall, digging his grip into my forearm. His thumb pushed into a tender muscle, making me bite my tongue to keep from crying out. "Tell me."

I glared, trying to pull away. "Ryak is the one who fucked up, Nevin," I hissed. "Not me."

"I won't ask again," came his soft words. And those soft words terrified me more than Ryak's threats ever had.

"Let me go, and I'll tell you."

He released me, but not after squeezing harder. I stumbled a step away when I finally had my arm back, the goblet still in my hand, though the water had sloshed over it when I'd tried to get away.

My heartbeat was in my throat.

"They're going to execute him," I found myself saying through a clenched jaw.

There was no expression on Nevin's face at my pronounce-ment. A wiggle of guilt and shame moved in my chest. Why did I feel like I was betraying Alaryk's confidence?

Because you are, I thought.

"How you'd find out?" he asked.

"From Alaryk," I said with gritted teeth. "Last night."

Nevin huffed out a sharp breath. "Who knew we only needed a whore to get the *Karath*'s secrets?"

I hid my flinch.

"Maybe you're smarter than I thought you were," he told me.

I couldn't even deny his words. Was that what I'd become now? A whore for secrets? Alaryk had been between my thighs last night. I'd used him, just as he'd used me.

"Ryak didn't want you getting close to him because he thought you couldn't be trusted," Nevin admitted to me. "But I disagree. I think you've positioned yourself perfectly."

"I didn't plan this," I grated.

"But you'll take advantage," Nevin ended, his eyes cutting to me. "When are they planning to execute him?"

"I—I don't know," I confessed.

"Then find out," he ordered, his eyes like flint.

"What are you planning?" I asked, frowning. "Surely you're not thinking—"

"Amaia," came Syris's voice. "We're ready to eat."

I whirled, just in time to see Syris come into view. She frowned when she saw me.

"What are you doing over there?"

"I…" I turned back to find Nevin had disappeared, likely ducked down beneath the wall. "I thought I saw an Elthika going into the mountain. I was trying to get a better look."

"Well, come on," Syris urged, jerking her head toward the hatchery. "Everything's hot, and Ulin is starving."

With one last glance at where Nevin had just been, I turned. The only evidence he'd been there at all was the throbbing along my arm where he'd grabbed me and the tightness in my throat.

I might've been worried about the wrong guardsman, I thought.

CHAPTER 25
AMAIA

If Syris or Tarkosh noticed my quiet mood at dinner, neither commented on it. In fact, the entire meal was slightly awkward and stilted, given Ulin and Moak's presence, neither of whom knowing what to say after yesterday's events. Any questioning by Moak, Tarkosh had cut off, eventually sending him away from the table when she'd had enough of his prying.

I didn't want to talk about it. The hustle of the day had been a bandage, covering up a wound so I didn't have to look at it directly. But as the quiet stretched at dinner, I knew that the wound had begun to seep.

I was relieved when Myzalla showed up, rapping her knuckles against the kitchen door, alerting us to her presence.

"Ready?" she asked. "I can't stand out there all night."

"Thanks for the meal," I told Syris, who only inclined her head, a worried expression on her face. "I'll see you in the morning."

"Good night, Amaia," Tarkosh said.

I passed by my quarters, heading inside to grab my travel sack —everything I'd brought with me to Karak, stuffed into a small bag. After I collected the items, I gave a quick look around my temporary room, but I was, truthfully, happy to leave it. I wouldn't miss the solitude.

I followed Myzalla back to Alaryk's dwelling. Before I went inside, she told me, "Another guard will be assigned to you tomorrow. I have to make preparations to travel to Elysom."

I frowned. "Is Alaryk going?"

"No, I'm going in his place," she said.

Because of the deal we made? I wondered.

"I, for one, wanted you gone, Amaia," she told me. "I thought it would be safer. I think we should've sent you all back, Ryak included, and washed our hands of it."

I frowned.

"But he wanted you here," Myzalla said, her voice low, her eyes narrowed. "And he's willing to risk everything just to keep you here. I hope you're worth it."

I couldn't stop my flinch then. I hoped my guilt didn't show on my face because my gut was swimming with it.

I didn't reply. Instead, I watched her walk away, and then I turned up the steps to Alaryk's dwelling, feeling those perilous emotions begin to press against the cage of my breast.

For a moment, I almost knocked on the door, but then I remembered…this was where I lived now. There was no need to knock.

When I opened the door, I found Alaryk sitting at the table, a spread of parchment scattered around the very place where I'd been face down, this time last night.

I tried to keep my neck from getting too hot, shutting the door behind me.

Alaryk had been eating as he worked. On what, though, I couldn't be certain. It looked like typography maps.

"Is that Karak?" I asked, nodding to the rolls of parchment.

"It is," he replied. "Would you like to see?"

I would. Dakkar had no idea the expanse of the Karag's country. I was curious, and when I stepped up behind Alaryk, I looked over one of the parchments, seeing two different land masses, separated by two smaller islands, one of which I knew was the Arsadia. The other must've been Elysom. And on the maps of the land, I saw mountain ranges depicted, lakes, valleys, rugged coastline, vast forests.

"Where is Grym?" I asked, leaning down for a better look.

"Here," he said, running the edge of his thumb, which had strummed between my legs last night, to the northeast. A nearly vertical line had been drawn on the map, following a mountain range and what I thought was a river.

"And is that Harta?" I asked, running my hand over the line.

"Yes," he replied. "Are you going to report this back to your *Dothikkar?*"

I stiffened. I shot him a sharp look, realizing that our faces were closer than I'd thought. His tone was serious, making me wonder if he somehow knew about my conversation with Nevin today...

But I didn't think that was possible. We'd been alone, at the back of the hatchery, our voices low.

"Of course not," I replied, trying to hide the stab of shame I felt. Because truthfully, when it came to protecting my family, I didn't know what I would and would not reveal. I thought I might do anything if it meant that my parents and my brother were safe.

Alaryk rolled up the maps, wrapping a leather cord around them and stacking them on the table. There was a nearly empty tray of food, a sliver of blue fruit with fat black edible seeds remaining, which he popped into his mouth. He stood, and I backed up a few steps, feeling out of place and thrown off balance, wondering if he did somehow know I'd been sent here to deceive him.

When the silence stretched too long, I said, "I'm feeling well tonight."

He regarded me with a long look. "Oh?"

"I think we should take advantage and go to Samryn."

"I think maybe you don't want to face what happened," came Alaryk's words. His fingers came beneath my chin, lifting my face up so I was forced to meet his eyes. "Afraid of what might happen tonight?"

A flash in my mind—Alaryk's silver hair dipping, a warm tongue, seeking and soft, on my clit.

I sucked in a breath. "I'm recovered. So let's go."

Alaryk said nothing, only regarded me carefully.

When the silence stretched and he didn't make to move, I narrowed my eyes. "This is what you want, isn't it? This is what I'm here for. I'm offering to work with Samryn tonight. I'm giving you what you want. So why are you hesitating?"

Whatever was going on behind those eyes, I couldn't be certain. But I had a feeling that Alaryk knew *exactly* what I was doing. Masking. Again. Bandaging something so tight, hoping I wouldn't bleed out.

Hiding.

"Very well," he said, eyes sharp. "I'll summon Samryn."

Out on the landing field, it was so dark and quiet, the slivering moon barely enough light to navigate the stone road weaving through the village. But Samryn was waiting for us, and for once, he didn't huff at the mere sight of me.

"We can do it here," I told Alaryk quietly. "There's no reason to hide it anymore."

"Amaia," he said, grabbing my arm when I stepped past him, right over where Nevin had. I couldn't hide my surprised wince, and he looked down, confused at first. At least until he spied the bruise, then his expression went eerily cold. "What happened? Did someone do this to you?"

His voice had taken on a quiet tone, and I looked at him in surprise. He was…furious? At the mere thought that someone might've harmed me?

"No, it happened at the hatchery," I quickly said, tugging my arm back, placing my hand over the budding bruise. "Kyr is getting bigger. It's harder to keep him contained."

How easily the lie fell from my lips shamed me. But what else could I do? What else could I say?

Alaryk's jaw was clenched, making his scar flash, and he was glaring at me. But I didn't know if it was actually directed at me or not.

"You're a terrible liar, Amaia," he murmured. "And if there is someone who's threatening you, who's hurting you because of what happened…I'll find them. They'll answer to me for it. That's why I have a guard with you. So something like this—"

"I told you—it was Kyr," I repeated. "How would anything else have happened? Myzalla was out front of the hatchery all day."

"Moak?" Alaryk rasped. "Ulin?"

"Please," I scoffed. And at least that was convincing. "You think Tarkosh wouldn't have sniffed them out if one of them had done this?"

His lips pressed. I turned my attention back to Samryn, stepping up to the bloodred Elthika. I reached out a hand to touch him, my fingertips meeting the cool resistance of his hardened scales, smooth like glass but unyielding like Dakkari steel.

"Are you ready?" I asked, wanting to end this conversation, wanting the distraction of Samryn's curse. The *punishment* of it.

"So eager for pain," Alaryk rasped knowingly, still pissed… because he knew I was lying? "Fine, *mariss*. But if you think I'll let this go, you'll find out how wrong you are soon enough."

Then he surprised me. He stepped up to me, dragging me toward him.

When his lips met mine, I gasped into his kiss. He took

advantage, sweeping into my mouth with his tongue, a tangle of dominance and heat between us...before he won the battle. Before I was forced to melt into him, momentarily forgetting everything but his kiss, a brief reprieve. I closed my eyes, simply letting go.

I wanted it to last forever. To prolong the inevitable.

Alaryk cursed softly—a Hartan one, I was certain—before he pulled away, though he kept his palm firmly around the back of my neck, where it had drifted during our kiss.

"Why'd you do that?" I breathed, my gaze unfocused, staring up at his lips. "Because you were angry?"

He glared. "Because I wanted to."

"Oh," I murmured, uncertain how to reply to that. All I knew was that I liked it. I tilted my head up, meeting his eyes, asking for something unspoken.

His lips met mine again. Softer this time. Deeper. The back of my throat tingled with its sweetness.

A sharp exhale drifted from his lips when we finally pulled away. If I didn't know any better, I'd say he looked...lost. Like he didn't know what to do with me. I probably looked a little dazed myself, licking his taste from my lips, wanting more.

Then I watched him pull himself together, until his expression was neutral, until the grip on the back of my neck loosened and then drifted away. I could still feel the warmth pooling in my belly from his kiss, even though it was an inconvenient time to feel the urgency and merciless press of desire.

"Let's begin," he said gruffly, stepping back before rounding toward Samryn's head.

It was a whiplash of sensation. Hot and then cold.

Once I regained control of my breath, however, I knew it was for the best. "I'm ready."

When I felt Alaryk's familiar touch of magic rising in the staticky air between us, my own responded. How easily I could summon it now, as if I was feeding off Alaryk's power. Unlike last night, it felt like a tight ball in my chest—firm, with no soft edges—which threatened to leak out.

I reached out my hand, pressing it against Samryn's flesh, and envisioned the rivulets of magic tracing the edges of his tipped scales, seeking, searching. Looking for a way inside.

And when it found one, that ball inside me loosened, becoming thousands of little threads that went searching inside the cursed creature, though they were all connected to me.

It was easier this time. I could delve further into him, but I knew that was because I'd already cleared a pathway. I picked up where I'd started, dragging in a deep breath, readying myself, preparing for a long night.

And then I began.

"Lean on me when you need to," came Alaryk's voice. "Use me. I'm here."

I trusted that he would be as I slowly sank into the tangle of decay, bracing myself for what I might find.

CHAPTER 26
AMAIA

When I woke next, there was the taste of blood in my mouth. My eyes felt tight in my skull. And a pounding headache made me wince, made me feel like a vise was squeezing around my temples.

"I'm here," came a husky voice next to me.

"How long?" I whispered, my voice scratchy.

"Not long," Alaryk assured me quietly, and I saw the bright blue of his eyes reflected toward me in the darkness. "I brought you back a couple hours ago."

Relief whistled through me. Maybe I was getting more accustomed to clearing the remnants of the curse from my own body. Or maybe it was Alaryk's magic, which I remembered now. Bright and warm, I'd wielded his strength to help me hack away at the curse inside Samryn. I thought we'd made progress…but I couldn't remember much else.

We were lying in his bed. His warm flesh was pressed against me. I never would've thought Alaryk Arn'dyne to be a *nuzzler* in bed, but he had me wrapped up in his arms, solid and secure. If I hadn't been in pain, it would've felt lovely.

Behind him, on the small table next to the bedside, I saw the familiar blue smoke rising from the little pot. I wondered what it was but didn't have the energy to ask.

"Let me try something," he murmured.

"I don't know if…"

I felt a sparking along my skin. His magic. He was funneling it into me, a mere touch. "Take it," he whispered, pressing a kiss to my temple, which throbbed beneath his lips. "See if it'll help you."

Surprisingly, I latched onto that little morsel he offered me, clasping onto it like it was a gift. My own magic rose with it, stoked to life, though it felt like a mere smolder compared to the roaring fire it usually was at its peak.

Gradually, the pain in my temples faded. The muscles in my body loosened, no longer so tight that it felt like a large cramp within me, knots where bones were.

"Better?" he murmured after long moments. He probably felt the way I'd begun to relax in his arms.

"That's…pretty amazing," I settled on, whispering out the words, bright relief mingling with my awe. I felt *good*. "Does it hurt you though?"

"Weakens me, yes, but it doesn't hurt me," he told me. "I have a deep well of magic I keep, so don't worry about me. I only want to help you."

"Thank you."

I finally lifted my head to regard him, feeling his magic begin to fade. It whispered over my skin until I could no longer find the traces of it. And I worried how easily I was getting used to it. Would I be so familiar with it that soon I no longer felt it? Would Alaryk keep his word and not use it against me?

So far he had kept his promise.

"That's what you do for others," he murmured. "You just did it for yourself, finally."

"I don't know anyone else who has heartstone magic," I confessed. "Only you."

He made a sound in the back of his throat, his arm flexing beneath my head. My cheek was cushioned against the rock of muscle there. Not entirely comfortable, but I didn't want to move away. His body, pressed against mine, his warmth, his smell were entirely too tantalizing.

I liked him too much already—even when he made me angry. I'd found him sinking into my thoughts at all moments of the day, making for distracting work in the hatchery.

But he was still a puzzle to me.

Moving my hand between us, I drifted it up the wall of his bare chest. His skin was smooth and searing. He looked as cold as ice sometimes, but really he was roaring like a forge, making me sweat beneath the furs. He was naked too, I could feel the bare stretch of his leg against mine.

His pupils were dilated in the low light, watching me. My thumb dragged just beneath his pectoral, and the pad of it met the steady beat of his heart. I rested my palm there, and the strong thud felt comforting.

Our faces were so close that we were sharing the same breath, and it felt intimate and strange but...*right*. I didn't pull away and neither did he. We only looked at each other. His gaze was soft, running over my features as if he had all the time in the world, settling on my lips before flicking back to my eyes.

"Tell me what happened to Samryn," I said, the words tumbling from me, quiet and hushed, as if someone else was in the room and I didn't want them to overhear us. "Please."

His heart skipped. A little stutter that he knew I felt.

He blew out a rough exhale. "To understand what happened to Samryn, you would have to understand...*everything*. And that's a long story."

"Then tell me everything," I said simply.

I thought I deserved to know, didn't I? I was the only one who'd felt what was *really* roving inside the poor beast. And it was an awful thing. For someone to do that to an Elthika…they'd wanted to make Alaryk suffer too.

For a moment, I thought he wouldn't tell me. In fact, I expected it. The silence stretched so long that I felt a stab of disappointment.

But then he surprised me. In the warm quietness of his bed, he said, "I was born and raised in Harta, as I'm sure you've heard. My mother was Karag, though, and we crossed over the border back to her homeland when I was a young boy. But it was difficult for us to make a new home. From nothing and with nothing."

I listened, rapt, his voice almost trancelike.

"There was once a village. Close to Grym's borders. A couple decades ago, it was a busy, growing town, where Karag and Hartans both lived. Not particularly savory, I'll admit. But my mother found a job working at a tavern there, and I would forage for edibles to sell at the market in the nearby forest. We lived there for nearly a decade. Until I came of age."

Oddly, I could picture him as a wild boy, spending his days in the woods.

"You…you weren't in rider training during that time?" I asked, only knowing what I knew from talk around the village. Most riders came from a lineage of it. They were called blood borns, and they usually entered training as young as twelve or thirteen. Most blood borns had claimed Elthika by the time they entered adulthood.

A small huff of a laugh fell from him. "No, I didn't enter rider training until I was nineteen. After my mother had died."

"Oh," I breathed, feeling my expression pull. "I'm sorry. I didn't know."

"She'd been sick for a while," he told me. "It finally caught up with her. The village was called Gryloth. It doesn't exist now—most of it burned down during the war. But during the last year of my mother's life, and shortly before I left, there was a Hartan witch who came to live there. Her name was Kamora. My mother befriended her, brought her into our home for a while."

I heard a sharp edge of bitterness in his tone.

"She was my first love, I suppose you could say," he admitted to me, a curl of resentment on his lips. "My first everything. But what I thought was love at the time was really only obsession and lust and heartstone magic, all fueled by pain."

"She had heartstone magic?" I whispered.

"Yes," he told me. "She was my tutor."

Dawning realization spread through me.

"She was older than me, by nearly a decade," he continued. "She had lived all her life in Harta, but as a nomad. Traveling from place to place, making a living giving prophecies and using her magic to…persuade people away from their coins and jewels."

My heartbeat was quickening in my chest, as was Alaryk's in his. He dragged in a deep breath, my hand rising with it.

"She could put suggestions into place in a person's mind, but they never lasted long. Not long enough, so she had to be a quick thief, and she needed to leave as swiftly as she came. At least that's what she told me. But in Gryloth…she found me. And so she stayed much longer."

"You took care of her?" I asked.

"Yes," he replied, the word wistful and yet full of regret. "I thought I was in love, remember?"

I frowned.

"My magic had always been an unpredictable thing," he admitted. "Used more for violence and pain when someone wronged me or my mother. Kamora became my tutor, helping me manage it. Which, in some ways, I am grateful for. But I told you that magic responds to different things and for each person, it's individual."

"You said yours was pain," I remembered, brows scrunching.

"We discovered that accidentally," he told me. "She'd been frustrated. We'd been arguing. She'd hit me so hard my ears rang, and I felt my magic surge, like it was trying to protect me."

"Alaryk," I whispered, my heart squeezing in my chest, tendrils of my own magic wiggling.

"After we discovered that, the pain started carrying over into sex," he admitted. "Lust was also a strong conduit for me. Sex became a battleground for our sessions together."

My stomach cramped. I could imagine rough, needful, *can't get enough of you* sex, where you wanted someone so much that your teeth ached. I'd felt that with Alaryk…

But still…it had never turned *violent*.

"And you…liked it?" I found myself asking.

"Truthfully, I don't know," he replied, surprising me, making me wince. "I've thought about it for many years. At that age, sex was so intertwined with what I thought was love…but also with power, with accomplishment, with control, with pain. It's hard to differentiate and untangle it when it was one complete thing, all at once.

"Regardless, Kamora's power was greater than what she'd led anyone to believe. In Harta, she'd been raised in a group called the Idima, who practiced together to create more powerful magic. Darker magic. It was usually built around a sacrifice, to appease their three gods."

What he was telling me…it was frightening. I'd only ever known Kakkari and Drukkar, the two Dakkari deities. The Karag believed in no god, only in their Elthika. But the Hartans? They used blood sacrifice?

I'd heard of Dakkari sorceresses once practicing the same thing. All for power. So perhaps it wasn't so out of the realm of possibility that this would happen in a different place, on a different continent entirely. Perhaps it was entirely *likely*.

"How long were you with her?" I asked.

"A year," he replied. "And it felt like a lifetime."

I exhaled sharply, spreading my hand wider over his chest before I moved it up the column of his throat. I rested it on the back of his neck, feeling his heat and the silky smoothness of his hair.

I was surprised by how much he was willing to reveal to me, only because I'd asked. It was a vulnerable place to be, for someone as private as Alaryk.

He's private for good reason, I couldn't help but think.

"What ended everything between us was my mother's death," he told me. "I'd only stayed in Gryloth because of her, because of her declining health. My relationship with Kamora was already volatile. Twisted. She began to realize the extent of my magic, of what I could *do*. She wanted me to take things from others or persuade them to enrich her own life. She saw me as a tool—a weapon, even. And I found myself not willing to do what she wanted. She started saying that I owed her for everything she'd taught me. She started to think that I would join the Idima. That I would travel back to Harta with her. And that with my power, the Idima would rise together."

The hairs on the back of my neck prickled.

"Needless to say, after my mother died, I wanted to leave Kamora. And so I went to Grym. I wanted to leave the region because I was worried that she would find me. So, in Grym, when I saw there was a band of acolytes leaving for the Arsadia for that year's training, I used my heartstone magic to convince the instructor to let me come."

I was shocked. "That's how it happened?"

He nodded. "It was pure chance, or perhaps fate, that led me here. That eventually led me to Samryn, whose magic bonded with my own on the Tharken cliffs. A Vyrin, when the position of the *Karath* of Grym had been opened that season. I was not, in any way, qualified. But I learned. I had Samryn at my side when my position was challenged. It was not easy. And then the war was growing, tensions rising with my power over Grym. And one day, when I went to the Hartan region of Bral to visit with a council of Elysom's members for peace negotiations, I saw her again."

I nearly jerked, but my hand only spasmed on the back of his neck.

"Kamora. Dressed in silk, silver adorning her. She'd become a mistress to the Hartan king, having persuaded her way into his bed."

He stopped talking for a brief moment. I got the sense there was something he might be leaving out, like he was navigating the thread of the story that could be cut out.

"Tell me," I urged, my voice serious. "I want to hear it all."

His eyes narrowed on mine. "Even if you think of me differently for it?"

I frowned. "Especially."

"It's no secret, I suppose. What I did. Only the circumstances surrounding it," he said gently. Finally, he admitted, "I used Kamora."

"For what?" I asked, shaking my head.

His smile was wry. He threaded his hand through my hair, smoothing it back. "To end a war."

I didn't understand.

"Elysom had been trying to end the war for nearly five years. Gryloth had burned, as had other territories along the border, in both Harta and Karak. They wanted peace because Harta controlled most of the mountain territories. They didn't want to use *ethrall* or Elthikan power to bring them to heel because of it. But for Harta's surrender, they wanted a supply of Elthika eggs to build up their armies. Elysom negotiated with their king, Trekin, for months as more died, on both sides of the border. And so when I saw that Kamora had found herself tucked into Trekin's bed, I used her. I used the very heartstone magic that she helped me discover and hone…and I used it as a weapon against her."

"What did you do?"

I'd heard gossip, cut off before the heart of the matter was discussed, throughout Grymia. Half-hidden truths that seemed to be common knowledge. And yet I didn't know.

"I forced her to murder Trekin."

I stiffened, thinking I'd heard him wrong.

"In his bed, while he slept," he told me.

He was *that* powerful?

"Trekin's commander was next in line to take over Harta's armies and control of the stronghold after him. She was more willing to negotiate because she herself was a soldier. And she had seen the battlegrounds, she had seen too much, knew that Harta could never withstand a war with the Elthika. I knew Trekin's death would usher in a swift peace, no matter the cost. Elysom hadn't been willing to take part in an assassination, but they sure reaped the benefits of one."

So *this* was what people wouldn't give voice to. Alaryk had ended a war with a cutthroat, merciless decision. And he'd used his former lover to do it.

I didn't know what I felt, hearing him speak about it now. I didn't know how I felt being in his arms as he admitted these things to me…but I'd asked. And the truth was ugly, as it always was.

"Kamora hated me for it, naturally," Alaryk told me, but his lips quirked, as if remembering her ire brought him contentment. "I wiped the memory of the actual act from her mind, but the knowledge that I'd used her as *my* weapon, for once, really stung."

I was surprised that his responding smirk—over such a dark thing he'd done—made a sense of *rightness* rise in me. He'd taken his vengeance and ended a war at the same time. But the morality of it all was…gray and hazy.

"She'd rejoined the Idima already. What I think she was really angry about was that she still hadn't secured me for them. She saw my betrayal as just that. A slap in her own face. She knew about Samryn. Like before, she thought I owed her some of my success. She told me she would forgive me—if I took her back with me to Grym. If I installed her in my citadel, in my bed. If I kept her happy in gold and pretty things. And when I denied her all of it, she vowed that I would regret it. That she would take everything from me and leave me poor and broken and alone, just as I'd been in Gryloth."

I could guess what happened next. He'd told me once that Samryn had been cursed by a witch, but what he hadn't told me was that the dark magic had been fueled by many. Everything suddenly slotted into place. The mystery of the ugliness inside Samryn.

Softly, I asked, "The Idima cursed Samryn, with her at the helm?"

Alaryk traced my brow and the curve of my cheek with his finger. "Yes. They killed one of their own to do it too."

That was why the magic was so powerful. It hadn't just been one sorceress, one witch. It had been many. Funneling their magic to bind the curse, a tangle of threads from not one but a group of powerful individuals, fueled by blood sacrifice.

"You should've told me," I whispered, meeting his eyes. "From the beginning. How will I ever undo this, Alaryk?"

His eyes sharpened. "You already are, Amaia."

My lips parted, hearing the strength, the certainty, in his voice.

"You are more powerful than any of them. Even more powerful than I am," he told me. "I've felt it. I feel *you*. Never doubt that. And you're only getting stronger."

I wanted to believe him. Everything in me wanted to believe him.

"What do you think of me now, *mariss*?" he asked me, his palm resting against my cheek. "What do you think about sharing your bed with a Hartan bastard whose hands are stained in blood? I've done many terrible things…and I would still do a lot more if it meant saving Samryn."

"I know," I replied. I thought of my own family, of why I was here. "I would do a lot to save the people I love too. And I can't pretend to know what it's like to be a *Karath*. The sacrifices needed. The decisions you have to make. I don't know what war is like. I've never seen one. And so I have no idea what needed to be done."

Alaryk's gaze flickered.

"But it does scare me," I whispered. "Because I know the lengths to which you'll go to get what you want. And I can't help but wonder…how far you'll go with me."

Alaryk's expression didn't change. His gaze only flicked down to my lips. "You think I'll hurt you?"

"I don't think you'll hurt me like Kamora hurt you," I said. "But…maybe you'll use me. Like you did her."

"You're nothing like her," came the sternness of his voice. "I used her for a purpose, yes, but also because I *wanted* to hurt her. I wanted my own revenge because I can be a callous bastard. And I got it. She betrayed me long before I ever betrayed her. That's what cut the deepest."

But how would he feel if he knew about why I was here? I couldn't help but fear. Would he consider *that* a betrayal too?

A surge of panic rose in my breast. I thought he might've seen it flash across my face because I caught his brief frown.

But I didn't want him asking me questions I couldn't answer. And so I tilted my face up, pulling down on his neck, to capture his lips in a swift kiss, stealing them before they could form words.

His surprised huff drifted across my tongue, but then his was stroking mine, taking advantage, the other arm beneath my head pulling me closer.

"Sex will always be complicated with me, Amaia," came the sudden words against my lips. Soft and hushed, like a prayer.

Pulling back to look into his eyes, I said, "It doesn't have to be with me. I want only pleasure. I only want to make you feel good too."

His eyes closed at that, his brows pulling toward one another.

Hesitantly, I leaned forward and brushed my lips across the cut, sharp lines of his cheekbones. The scar on his jaw that wound its way down his neck looked silver in this light, and I kissed it too.

"Where did you get this?" I whispered against his skin, my hands moving between us.

"Her," he grunted.

My nostrils flared, anger rising in my breast that she would mark him like this. I kissed the line of it gently, making his breath hitch.

"I worry I'll lose myself with you," came his gruff tone. "That I'll hurt you. Get too rough. I don't want that. You only need softness, gentleness. I can't be that for you all the time."

"I can handle myself," I told him, thinking I'd liked it when he had been rougher with me last night. "Don't worry."

I wanted to lose myself in him again. I wanted to banish the rising panic in me. The warm little ball that was building inside me, that told me I was coming to care about a *Karath* too much, that I was worried how he'd look at me if he ever discovered my betrayal.

I shifted over him, suddenly hungry.

"We shouldn't," he grated, his eyes flying open to stare up at me, though his hands settled around my hips, gripping me there like an unyielding lock. "You're recovering—"

"I'm recovered, thanks to you," I said, cutting him off, my hands slipping beneath the fur covering his bed. "And I want you entirely too much," I confessed.

"Don't sound so perturbed when you say that," he

murmured, his hands sliding to my backside, *squeezing*. His hands were so big they covered my ass entirely, and I wanted them all over me.

"Be quiet," I ordered, trying to stifle my laugh behind the rebuke, and then I cut off whatever he was about to say next with a hard kiss.

CHAPTER 27
ALARYK

"You like to be touched," came the words, guttural from my throat, sucking in a breath as one of Amaia's hands trailed down my abdomen, tracing the rivers and valleys of the muscles there. Like a road, she followed the path they made until her small finger brushed the head of my cock.

My breath hitched.

"You like to be admired," I continued, trying not to choke on my groan.

She is a beautiful female, I thought. Not just because *I* was attracted to her, but because of the warm light in her eyes, the way her smile made others feel relaxed. I'd watched her interactions with others, could glean enough to know that she had a beautiful soul. Others knew that too.

"And people do admire you," I found myself saying.

"Do *you*?" she asked, raising her brow. Seeing her like this, her cheeks flushed, eyes wanting…it made my cock bob and pulse.

"Oh, yes, *mariss*," I rasped. My little ember, burning bright for me. "I admire you more than any of them."

She smiled, so beautiful and shy that it made my insides twist with an emotion I didn't want to give a name to. Not yet.

Amaia had a temper, yes, but she could also be as docile as a baby shearling. She didn't *need* to be cared for, but she *wanted* to be loved.

And on Muron, I wanted to be reckless enough to give in to her.

When she shifted down to kiss the tip of my cock, a low growl rose from my throat.

"Take that off," I ordered, not even trying to hide the urgent demand in my tone. "Let me see those perfect tits."

Her green eyes flashed up to mine, her lips hovering over the sensitive tip of my cock, her hot breath drifting over the pre-come that was already beading. I didn't think either of us should be expending our energy on anything but sleep…but now that we were on the precipice of *this*, nothing would claw me away from it. I wanted to be inside her. I wanted to hear her moans drowning out all sound, feel the bite of her nails raking across my skin, her legs wrapped low around my waist, not letting me escape.

Amaia sat up, releasing my cock, which dragged out a shuddered breath from me, and peeled off her tunic. I'd taken off her tightly laced pants and boots when I'd brought her back from the landing field, so after she threw her tunic onto the floor, she was suddenly naked in my bed.

I admired her for a brief moment. The remnants of the fire in the hearth made her light brown skin glow, softening her features. Her green eyes were half-lidded, her full lips darkened from my kiss. Her soft belly, her long legs, which were tucked beneath her, her perfect breasts, tipped up toward me, her back arched subtly as if she knew how much I liked to look at her.

Her beauty had snuck up on me, slow and gentle. But now?

I thought she might be the most lovely creature I'd ever seen.

I shot up from my prone position, dipping my head as lust

swarmed my mind. Her gasp made a sizzle of desire shoot through my belly, funneling straight to my cock, as I wrapped my lips around one nipple. My other came up to cup and squeeze her other breast, plucking at her hardened peak, making her squirm.

"Stroke my cock," I purred.

"Bossy," she choked out, even as her warm hand closed around my thickened shaft. When her palm dragged down, the piercings pulled, and sparks lit up my vision. My spine bowed, a near gasp tumbling from me. "Even during sex."

"That's the best time for it," I argued. "*Harder.*"

"I don't want to hurt you."

I nearly chuckled against her breast as I laved my tongue around the brown-tipped peak. "You won't—believe me."

As if hearing the assurance in my tone, her hands tightened and she gave a few experimental pumps, which had me whispering out curses against her skin. Her fingers found my *syn'ra*—which I knew the Dakkari called a *dakke.* Sparks skittered up my spine when she pressed the sensitive bump.

"*Yes,*" I hissed, my hand falling from her other breast to dive between her legs, parting her slick folds.

She jolted when I found her clit, and then ground down against my hand when I toyed my thumb against it, a gentle brush, a light tease. Her hand glided away from my *syn'ra*, her pace falling out of rhythm as she worked my cock, slickening her own hand with my pre-come.

Keeping my thumb on her clit, I pushed two fingers inside her, hearing her shuddered gasp, feeling the rocking of her hips against me, wiggling. The sound of her arousal as I pumped my fingers into her filled the space between us, but she didn't get shy. If anything, she moved against me more and more brazenly, pleasing me.

"The things I want to do to you, *mariss,*" I breathed against her nipple, lapping before closing my teeth around it gently. I squeezed, not hard enough to hurt much but enough to make her gasp.

But she surprised me when she pushed me back onto the bed and pulled my hand from between her legs. It shimmered with her wetness in the low light, and I popped a finger into my mouth, swirling my tongue around it as she watched with parted lips.

"Come up here," I said, narrowing my eyes on her, my cock jutting like a pillar between us, my mouth watering for her, sweet and divine. "I want to taste more of you."

I saw the flash of intrigue cross over her expression, and I laughed low.

"Did you like when I was eating your pretty little cunt last night?"

"Yes," she breathed. "But I want to taste *you* now. And you're much too demanding. Maybe you need to learn you don't get everything you want."

I stretched out, my leg sliding up as she settled between them, lying on her stomach as she gazed up at me.

"If this is your idea of punishment," I began, gritting my teeth when her hand fisted around my cock, "then by all means, continue."

"I've never seen piercings like this," she whispered, her hot breath drifting off the sensitive head of my pulsing cock. It was so hard, so hot, I could feel my heartbeat throbbing there. "Did they hurt?"

"You want to talk about my piercings right now?" I asked low, my hand coming to her hair, gathering it back. I saw her pink tongue flash out, watched it drag up the unpierced side of my shaft. I held my breath, my gaze glued to that tongue, feeling it spark up my spine like she was tracing it there too. "*Fuck,* Amaia. Do that again."

She did, even more slowly, as I held my breath. Then said, "I'm just curious. About you. About why you got them."

"Wrap your lips around it, and I'll tell you," I rasped. Her eyes sparked, nearly making me smirk, but then all thought left my mind when she did as I requested. My back bowed when she sucked on the head. The little delighted, surprised moan in the back of her throat was the sexiest thing I'd ever heard.

"You like the way I taste, *mariss?*"

"Mmm," she hummed, not even lifting off my cock to give a proper answer. I felt my sac squeeze, a rush of more pre-come spilling. She tightened her hand at the base of my shaft, her thumb rubbing one end of a piercing at the very bottom. A pulling, aching tease that rivaled her seeking, enthusiastic tongue.

On Muron, it felt *too* good.

"It's a Har—*fuck*—Hartan rite of passage," I rushed out, my voice dark and husky and wobbly, my gaze rapt on her sucking my cock. "Look up at me."

Her green eyes met mine, the erotic sight she presented scrambling every thought in my brain.

"It's an ancient custom," I continued when she squeezed harder at the base of my shaft, pumping her fist. "I'd always… been pressured to choose between two worlds. Getting them was my way of saying I could be both."

Her eyes were warm as she regarded me, a spark of under- standing in them. Those eyes made my heavy sac tighten, the first hint of an orgasm growing, coiling in my belly.

"And yes, it did *fucking* hurt," I growled. "But I *liked* it."

There was a challenge in her eyes. She finally lifted off my cock to ask, "You always need pain to come?"

"Yes," I replied immediately, answering on instinct, because I couldn't remember the last time I hadn't needed some sort of stimulus to reach an orgasm. When I'd come with Amaia last night, the bite of her teeth had gotten me there. Relatively tame, but just the hint of pain had been there, shoving me over that invisible threshold to completion.

"Interesting," she whispered, a small tug of a devious smile on her lips.

"What are you up to?"

"Nothing at all," she replied before her lips wrapped around me again.

I closed my eyes for a brief moment, letting the sensation of simple pleasure swarm me. The heat of her mouth, the silky tease of her tongue dragging up the line of metal piercings, the delicate sound of them hitting her teeth.

She grew more comfortable, taking me deeper, her jaw widening as she sank down. She found a rhythm that had me squirming underneath her, that had me cursing all her previous lovers—a ridiculous sense of possessive jealousy filling me at the thought of *anyone* but me experiencing her like this.

It didn't make any sense, but she had my mind scrambled.

"I'm going to come," I breathed a handful of moments later, my hand tightening in her hair, being a little selfish as I guided her down. She tugged on a piercing, a sharp jolt. "Amaia—"

Just as the burn started to sizzle its way up my shaft, she pulled back, making me growl out a curse. My abdomen clenched, frustration rising.

As I fought not to come, she rubbed the tip of my cock across her lips, watching me.

"So it's like that," I breathed.

"Will you let me do what I want?" she asked, letting me come down from that near explosion. "Or will you get demanding again?"

"Is this punishment for ordering you around?" I asked.

"Maybe a little," she said, a flutter of a smile crossing her lips. "But I also just want to see if you really do need pain to find your pleasure. Or if I can just make you mindless enough that it won't matter."

Fuck.

Make me mindless, mariss, I thought, a new bead of silvery pre-come dripping down the side of my shaft. Amaia watched it with fascination before she leaned forward, lapping it up.

I leaned back, an arrogant smirk crossing my features, one I didn't feel. Settling in as I challenged her. "You're certainly welcome to try."

"Gladly," she whispered, her head lowering, her own sensual smirk on her slick lips.

"Amaia," I grated, fisting the furs beneath me, unable to stop moving. Torn between shoving her mouth over my fucking cock and exploding down her throat—*finally*—or letting her complete her twisted little experiment, one that both frustrated me enough I wanted to bellow and tantalized me enough I wanted to torture myself longer.

I loved it. I was mindless with it. I couldn't form a single thought, a deconstructed form of myself whimpering beneath her, torn between prolonging this madness or letting her claim her victory. Even the furs beneath me felt too rough, my skin overly sensitized.

And truthfully, I didn't know how much more patience I had left. The frayed strings of it had been thrummed so often that they'd all snapped like twine.

I'd lost count of the times she'd brought me close to the edge before she'd backed off. She was an erotic mess, her lips flushed red, her eyes wild with need. She'd been squirming herself between my legs, rocking her hips against the bed, as if she needed the merest stimulation to help relieve the burn between her lush thighs.

I could make her come in a single thrust, I knew. I could see the aching desire on display, her body so sensitive and stimulated as she dragged her nipples against the soft fur beneath her, desperate. She hadn't expected to *like* this as much as she did, I knew.

No lover had ever edged me like this. Had ever dragged me up the climb of my orgasm so many times, only to leave me gasping for breath as I fought against ruining it.

There was a part of me that was nothing but a beast, one that wanted to take what my body so desperately needed. *Release.* Sweet *fucking* release.

I envisioned flipping Amaia over, shoving my aching, sensitive cock deep inside her, using her pussy for my own pleasure. It would take nothing at all. One, maybe two pumps. I'd only need to feel the merest squeeze of her, and I'd be *gone.*

Even now, as moment after moment ticked by, as the moonlight drifted across the floor, the merest whisper of her lips could have me poised at the edge.

I was a growling mess, bellowing out Hartan curses—which I could've sworn I'd forgotten after all these years—when she denied me again, but the only thing I hadn't done was beg. We were locked in an erotic game, one neither of us wanted to lose. But as each promise of an explosive orgasm died, I didn't know who was *really* losing anymore. And I was perilously close to snapping.

My cock was throbbing. So hard it was almost painful. So engorged with blood that the head was nearly purple.

Amaia's eyes were half-lidded when she looked up at me. I swallowed hard, my mouth dry, my chest heaving, sweat glistening.

"Beautiful little monster," I rasped. For a moment, we stared at each other.

Then Amaia's grin spread. Tired—her jaw must've been aching—but delighted.

"*My* little monster," I growled.

That grin alone finally made me snap. I didn't care if I lost this drawn-out battle between us. I would gladly surrender if it meant finally getting *her*. I needed to come. She did too.

And then when I've recovered, I will spank her so fucking *hard for this…until she promises to do it again,* I thought, a dark need rising. *She won't be able to sit for a week.*

Amaia gasped when I moved. I pushed her back, crawling over her until her head was hanging off the foot of the bed, and I had her thighs locked around my waist before she could blink.

"A-Alaryk," she breathed.

With a bellow of relief, I pushed inside her slick cunt, hard and fast.

"Oh, fuck," I rasped. Sensation assaulted me. The searing heat of her, the tight, seeking squeeze, my overly sensitive flesh rubbing inside her. "*Oh* fuck, Amaia."

There wasn't a thought in my mind—she'd banished them all. A sweet reprieve. I was nothing more than a rutting, mindless beast, and her slick, tight cunt was making me see stars.

Her sudden orgasm ripped through her. I felt every facet of it, every miniscule change. The shudder of her body. The tight twitch deep inside, the flutter of her cunt, the way her breath was ripped from her lungs.

My pelvis ground into her, stimulating her clit, my chest rubbing against the taut peaks of her nipples. Her face was scrunched up, a silent scream making her mouth drop open.

And when the spark of my own pleasure began, I was almost afraid what it would bring.

My roar echoed. My body felt ripped apart. Sublime ecstasy was between her thighs.

I'd never felt anything like it before as I chased it down. And all I could do was surrender to it, all I could do was let it drag me down before it brought me back to life.

I shuddered when it finally began to fade.

Amaia was spread out on the bed before me, her breath heaving, her eyes wide. A sheen of perspiration made her skin glisten. Her hair was a wild tumble beneath her head.

I felt a swell of deep affection settle into my chest, too exhausted to feel wary about it.

"Kiss me," she whispered.

I lowered down on my shaking arms, feeling her clench around my cock. So out of my mind for her that I'd spilled myself deep inside and hadn't even realized it until now.

And I knew that she'd worked me over so thoroughly because I didn't even have it in me to *care*.

I poured a lot into that kiss. It was both soft and hard, punishing and sweet. I breathed her in, our magic tangible, like it covered our skin and we were spreading it between us.

Whatever had just happened…I feared that I was already addicted.

To her too.

Guess I don't need pain to find pleasure, I thought.

And I fell into a dreamless sleep.

CHAPTER 28
AMAIA

Another week, another trip to the cropland, I thought, gritting my teeth against the strain of the basket of hatchling feed. This particular batch stank even more than the last.

Even though I'd woken this morning feeling untouchable, the high from last night had slowly descended into a brooding mood. When Syris, Moak, and I had reached the farmstead, expecting to see Brune, we'd been informed by one of the tillers that he'd been sent away from his duties. Nysa and his son, who Brune had been assigned to live with, didn't want him under their roof any longer after what Ryak had done.

As such, I'd learned that Brune was living with Ethrisha but was evidently keeping a low profile around the village until it was a certain decision about his return to Dakkar.

The snickering stares as I lugged the feed back up the pathway, past the rider acolytes—Nevin *not* among them, making me think that he, too, had been driven from his post—and through the roads of Grymia, only added to my mood.

"Ignore them," Syris panted, glaring at a small group of younger Karag who made snide remarks as I passed, laughing when I turned my back.

It didn't stop there, however. As we rounded the corner near the washing house, a steam-filled dwelling solely for laundry, one of the workers outside spat as I passed. Actually *spat*. I was so shocked, his spit narrowly missing my boot, that the feed bucket nearly tumbled from my hand when I tried to swing back.

"What's wrong with you?" Syris hissed out at the stranger, surprising me because she was not someone who liked to be confrontational. But she was mad, her yellow eyes spitting fire. Her bucket dropped as she put her hands on her hips and glared.

"Whoa, whoa," Moak said. He pushed between the Karag male and Syris when she stepped up to him. "Hold on there," he murmured down to Syris, his brow raising in what I thought was intrigue. "As much as I would love to see you take him on, I don't think you'll be happy about it when the dust settles, all right?"

"And it's not your fight," I added quietly. "Just leave it alone, Syris."

She pushed Moak's hands away. "Fine. I'm just tired of…of… small-minded, judgmental bastards like him who think it's okay to spit at anyone."

"They fucking deserve it," the male said, glaring. "They don't belong here."

"What's going on?" came a familiar voice, calling out from down the pathway. An angry voice, cutting and sharp.

When I turned, I saw Alaryk, Myzalla, and another male that I knew was one of his riders, heading toward the landing field. Dresnar was his name, if I remembered correctly.

The washhouse male tilted his chin up. "Nothing, *Karath*. Nothing at all."

"I highly doubt that," he said, breaking away from the others to approach, his strides quick.

Alaryk's gaze cut to mine, and I felt it whittle me down to bone, like he could see everything I was feeling. How could he do that?

But I was looking straight back at him. When he stood an

arm's length away, I was reminded of the tingling between my thighs. Remnants from the night before, like my body had been held suspended on the precipice too long. I hadn't seen him since last night, which likely also accounted for my brooding mood. I'd swung my head to try to spy him in Grymia, my cheeks flushing at Syris's teasing. I'd *wanted* to catch the merest glimpse of him. It was alarming how quickly he'd settled into my mind, a permanent fixture.

There had been a guard to greet me this morning, but Moak had assured him there wouldn't be any trouble on his watch as we ventured to the farmlands, so he'd stayed behind at the hatchery, finally taking his meal for the afternoon.

Alaryk would likely have his head, now that I thought about it, which spiked my worry.

"What happened?" Alaryk's clipped voice came, standing close enough that I could feel his heat. I wanted to reach out to touch him, the impulse so instinctive, but I was aware of the dozens of eyes on us.

Belatedly, I realized his voice was raspier, smokier than usual. Because of last night? Because he'd been groaning and bellowing out his pleasure as the moonlight had crept up the wall of his dwelling?

Part of me was proud I'd made him come undone, unraveling all his threads for me to see. Alaryk Arn'dyne, in the daylight, seemed untouchable. Physically large and impossibly intimidating, like the golden statues in Dothik, where you could look but *never* touch.

But in the hushed darkness of night? He was someone different. Someone who'd lain his past out before me, to prod and judge. Someone whose hand had tightened in my hair as I lapped at the metal piercings lining his shaft, trying to make him squirm beneath me, trying to elicit that half moan, half gasp that I feared I'd become addicted to hearing. Someone who'd held me tight through the night, wrapping his furnace of a body around me like a fur, not moving once.

When the sun had risen and I'd woken to an empty bed, I'd had the alarming thought that I could fall in love with him and not even know it. How *easy* it would be.

"He spat at her feet," Syris helpfully supplied when I didn't say anything. I sighed, cutting her a sharp look of warning, which she shrugged at. She'd been in a foul mood all day, likely due to another hatchling birth in the middle of the night. They'd all gotten only a few hours of sleep, and I'd felt immensely guilty when I'd discovered that upon my arrival. I should've been there to help.

"He did *what?*" came the quiet words from Alaryk, staring directly into the male's eyes, making him freeze.

"N-Not at her," the male stuttered. "She just happened to step there as I was spitting."

Syris scoffed. "What a bucket of lies."

"Leave it," I said softly to Alaryk, looking up at him with pleading eyes. I didn't want to make anything worse in the village, especially since this incident was already attracting a large crowd of onlookers. One of them was the female from the feast, one of Alaryk's lovers, and seeing her made my gut twist as jealousy tangled with the mess of emotions inside me. I forced myself to look away from her, to meet Alaryk's eyes.

I felt like we were all holding our breath still. The tension was rising, and I just wanted peace.

"Please," I said quietly, the word meant just for him.

"Potra," came Alaryk's icy voice, though his eyes never left mine. His arm brushed my side.

"Yes, *Karath?*" the male asked, trepidation in his voice.

Finally, Alaryk's gaze cut to him, a cold glare in his eyes that had *me* even shuddering. "Some livestock gave birth this morning on the farmlands. Some of the dressings need to be picked up, washed, and delivered to Gralkin before nightfall. Take care of that."

Potra's shoulders fell. "That's usually Hethro's responsibility, and—"

Alaryk's glare cut off whatever he was about to say. "It's yours now," he said, his withering tone allowing no further questions.

"Yes, *Karath*. Right away," Potra squeaked and headed off down the road that led to where we'd just come from. I imagined him carrying up armfuls of stinking, bloodied bedding from the births and only felt marginally better.

"Serves him right," I heard Syris mutter.

"What has gotten into you today?" Moak asked quietly. His voice lowered, deeper. "And why do I like it?"

My friend's face flamed red, but I was already looking back at Alaryk.

"Where is your guard?" he asked, peering around the small group as if making a point.

I nearly gulped. "I, uh, wanted him to stay back at the hatchery while we went to get the feed. No use in all of us suffering. And he hadn't eaten all day."

Alaryk's nostrils flared. "He doesn't leave your side when you're not with me," he rasped. "And I'll make sure he remembers that."

"I insisted," I said, seeing Moak's color drain a bit from the corner of my eye, since he was the one who'd convinced the guard to stay behind. "I'm *fine*. A little spit doesn't worry me when I've had my arm up inside a *pyroki* giving birth."

"You did what?" Moak asked, his tone sounding like maybe that knowledge made him respect me a little more.

Alaryk looked over his shoulder to Myzalla and Dresnar. "Go on without me—I'll meet you down there."

Myzalla inclined her head, her gaze flitting to mine briefly, brows pulling down, before they left. "Break it up," she grumbled to the crowd, who slowly dispersed as she waved her hands at them.

"I'm fine," I insisted. The stink of the feed was starting to permeate the air around us, stagnant. Alaryk took the bucket from me, hoisting it effortlessly, like it weighed nothing. And he took Syris's too.

"I'll see you there myself," he rasped, jerking his head in a movement that made it clear I should start walking. "Get moving."

His lips *nearly* twitched at the sharp look I cut at him. We didn't need to bond our magic for him to hear the thought, loud and clear, that went sizzling through my mind.

Bossy.

His eyes dropped to my lips, his pupils flaring. I nearly sucked in a squeaked breath, but then I turned on my heel and trudged up the path, falling in line with Syris, who looked back and forth between Alaryk and me.

"I don't want to hear it," I said quietly.

"I wasn't going to say anything," she whispered back. She flexed her hand, a line of red cutting across her palm from the bucket's rope handle. "I'm just glad I don't have to lug that thing around."

"You're the one who offered to help Moak," I pointed out.

She was wisely silent.

I cast a look over my shoulder. Moak was ahead of us on the pathway, but Alaryk was directly behind us. His blue eyes were piercing when they connected with mine. Then they flicked to my backside before running down the line of my long legs. Then back up again.

My belly fluttered. I could feel my pulse between my legs. If I swayed my hips a little more, knowing he was watching…well, I would never admit to it.

With Alaryk walking with us, no one looked in my direction

once as we passed. And the time to the hatchery was short considering I wasn't carrying the hatchling feed up the incline.

My guard—Tybor—straightened, a look of dread passing over his face when he saw Alaryk with us. He'd been waiting at the entrance of the hatchery. Moak clapped him on the shoulder, as if in apology, and Syris followed behind him as they entered the door.

"I'll speak with you later," Alaryk told him.

"Yes, *Karath*," Tybor said, keeping a brave face.

I gave Tybor an apologetic smile as I passed him and sensed that Alaryk was right behind me as I entered the atrium.

"You can just leave that here," I told him, oddly feeling a little shy when I found we were alone. Ahead of us, I could hear Syris and Moak passing through the incubation room, their voices echoing before a door shut, and then there was quiet.

"Come with me," he said instead, leading us through the hatchery as I followed behind him. Past the incubation room— six eggs left, I counted, most of them Rythbacks—we entered the hallway that led to the kitchens and the courtyard, the sleeping-quarter doors shut.

Alaryk left the buckets of hatchling feed in the hallway and then pulled me into my old room.

"What are you—"

The moment he shut the door, his mouth was on mine. And I'd never thought of myself as *easy*, but I submitted to his kiss almost immediately, folding like the fur blanket I'd straightened on the bed that morning.

He pushed me back into the door, the gold handle pressing hard into my spine, but I didn't mind. My hand dove into his hair as he crouched, as I went on my tiptoes for more.

His tongue was hot as it tangled with mine, kissing me harder, a low growl starting in his chest, one that I knew might bleed through the wood door, out into the hallway.

When he tore his mouth away, it seemed like it was nearly in frustration. With my pulse jumping in my throat and my lips reddened, I watched him run a hand through his hair, looking around my old room with unseeing eyes, the front of his trews tented, his cock straining the laces.

I didn't know what was happening, but this was Daylight Alaryk…and I hadn't expected Daylight Alaryk to push me into a room and kiss me senselessly, *hungrily*, against a door. As if he couldn't go a second longer without it.

I nearly grinned in victory.

Darkness Alaryk would do that. Darkness Alaryk would slip his fingers between my legs and squeeze my ass with his other hand. Darkness Alaryk would smirk as he watched me tug on his metal piercings with my teeth.

I'd been twitchy and aching between my thighs all throughout today already. He'd only made it worse.

"It's flattering how much you want me," I found my glib tongue commenting, trying to keep a straight face and failing. My words were meant to lighten the tension strumming between us.

Alaryk glared after he ran a palm down his face. "Just you wait until tonight," he growled. He returned to me, pressing me back into the door. "Does that please you, *mariss*? That I've thought about you all *fucking* day?"

"Yes," I breathed, meeting his eyes, tilting my head back against the wood of the door, hoping I appeared calm and collected and not like I wanted to come out of my skin and crawl into his.

"You've had my mind in knots all morning," he confessed to me, his breath a caress against the side of my cheek as he leaned down. The tip of his nose trailed along my jaw. I felt the bite of his teeth on my neck as his words made warmth bloom.

I'd done that to him? It relieved me to know that he felt the same, then.

"Have you been replaying it in your mind?" I teased gently.

My hands came to his chest, and I curled my fingers so that my nails dragged against the material of his vest as I trailed them down. And down. And down…

Alaryk's breath hitched, a Hartan curse whispered against my skin, before his teeth squeezed harder. I teased my nail across the leather laces of his trews, hearing a ragged sound drop from his lips. I could feel the heat of his cock just below the material, perfectly hard, and my hand nearly curled on instinct, wanting him in my grasp.

He tore my hand away, wrapping his palms around my wrists, giving them a warning squeeze.

I nearly grinned in satisfaction, seeing his frustration on display. The only thing that had it dying on my face was that I was denying *myself* too.

It was fascinating to watch Daylight Alaryk regain his brief slip of control. And I was only mildly disappointed when he moved away. It was for the best. Another moment more and he might've been deep inside me, his thrusts banging me against the door, alerting the entire hatchery to what we were up to.

The burn of embarrassment made my cheeks heat, thinking about how I would never be able to look Tarkosh in the eye again.

"Did you bring me in here just to kiss me a little?" I asked.

"No," he rasped, once he was back in control. "Your guard stays with you at all times."

"Ahh, so you came to reprimand me," I said, my heart still throbbing in my throat as I rubbed my finger against my slightly swollen lips. "Your favorite thing. Well…one of them."

"That's our deal," Alaryk said sternly, eyes rapt on my lips.

I didn't know what made me do it. Maybe it was the indifferent stiffness with which he held himself, when he'd been passion and trembling *need* just moments before.

I was getting better at calling my magic forward, especially when Alaryk was near. I felt it drift up, all around me like a veil, simmering in the air between us, making Alaryk cut me a sharp look when he could feel it too.

"Amaia," he warned.

I envisioned it trailing against his skin, like my own touch, stroking him in all the places I wanted to, to see if I could scrub away some of his coldness.

Alaryk closed his eyes, his jaw twitching, and I nearly smiled in accomplishment.

"If you're trying to distract me—"

"It's working?" I finished for him, a tendril of smugness entering my tone.

His eyes opened. I thought I spied a little amusement in them.

"Amaia," he murmured. And I finally let it drop.

"I'm getting better at it, don't you think?" I asked.

"You are," Alaryk agreed softly. He sighed, a little of his sternness shaking away, when he tipped my chin up to his. "Promise me you won't try to convince your guards to leave you be. They're there for a reason."

"It's sweet how much you worry about me."

Alaryk blew out a sharp sigh.

"Fine." Then I remembered something. "Did you know that Brune was sent away from the croplands?"

His lips pressed. "Myzalla informed me this morning."

"And Nevin?"

He drew himself up to his full height. "Myzalla thought it might be best for him to stay away from the other acolytes while we settle things in Grymia. Temporarily."

I frowned. "You'll send them away, won't you?"

"They might want to leave, Amaia," Alaryk replied, his eyes sharpening. "Have you thought about that? Brune is hiding away in Ethrisha's dwelling. Why be there when he can go home? I cannot control the opinions of my people, nor would I want to. I can only make the decisions that will keep people safe—Brune included."

"Hence the guard for me," I added, his answer bringing about a slice of sadness. Brune had become a close friend. Maybe not as close as Syris and I had become, but a good friend nonetheless. And he might be sent away, for something he didn't even do.

Maybe it's best, came the unwanted thought. *Considering what our true purpose was here.*

My stomach roiled. Guilt swarmed me as I met Alaryk's gaze.

"You're right," I said.

His eyes narrowed.

I changed the subject before he pressed. "Are you leaving somewhere? With Myzalla and Dresnar?"

"I said I wouldn't, didn't I?" he murmured. "I told you I was staying in the Arsadia, and I meant it. Gevanth, from Elysom, is leaving. Myzalla is accompanying him." Right, she'd told me that last night. "I was going to see them both off."

"Oh," I said, the knowledge that he was keeping such a small promise to me warming my chest while also deepening my guilt. "All right."

He released my chin.

"Stay out of trouble," he told me.

Then he was gone, and I was left skimming my fingers over his bite, trying to fight my smile and failing.

CHAPTER 29
AMAIA

Alaryk didn't return to his dwelling until after I'd already washed off the day and was tucked into the lounge area, the fire in the hearth already lit. I had already gobbled up my dinner at the hatchery—Syris having made her stew again—but was picking at a tray of food I'd found rummaging through Alaryk's own stores. A soft, pillowy loaf of seeded bread, dried meats, and cured cheeses.

That was how he found me when he came trudging through the door. I tried to ignore the way my heart leaped at the sight of him.

His eyes were assessing when they met mine. I drew my knees up to my chest, popping another morsel of dried meat into my mouth as I regarded him, wondering who would break the silence first.

And how.

I'd be lying if I said I didn't want him to come straight over so we could finish what we'd started in the hatchery earlier. No one was here to interrupt us. No one would hear my moans and gasps.

Alaryk undressed, shrugging off his vest. His tunic dropped

to the ground as he approached me, displaying his broad, bare chest, the glint of metal through his nipples. I swallowed hard as his hands began untying his laces. Anticipation rose, making my nails curl into my palms.

When he reached me, his laces were undone, the tip of his cock head peeking out from the waistline of his leather trews, but he didn't move to push them down. Instead, he stayed standing above me in the lounge, and his thumb came to my lips, rubbing against the soft flesh.

My tongue darted out, and I heard his sharp intake of breath when I nipped gently at the calloused flesh, my eyes never leaving his. A silent invitation.

But strangely, he didn't initiate anything beyond that.

Ever so quietly, he told me, "My council and I have decided it's best for Brune and Nevin to be sent back to Dakkar. Before Ryak's execution in two days."

I pulled away.

I processed that new information, though a large part of me wasn't surprised by it. Not in the slightest.

"And what about me?"

"Your place here was never in question," Alaryk replied. "They'll leave tomorrow morning."

My brow furrowed. My shoulders slumped. "So soon."

Part of me was relieved. Because without Nevin, with Ryak's execution…the *Dothikkar*'s mission had failed. My brother would be safe, wouldn't he?

But the Heartstone Accords would likely fail between our two nations. Perhaps no more Dakkari would be sent to Karak. What then? Would a peace even be possible? Or would it only further motivate the *Dothikkar* to believe the Karag were our enemies?

Alaryk sank down beside me, stretching his longs legs out, heat radiating off his chest.

"It's for the best, Amaia," he finally said.

A tiny bubble of unease spread through me.

I glanced over at him, my gaze gliding over his bare chest, his half-unlaced pants. The perfect distraction. Maybe he'd meant it to be one as he'd broken the news of his decision.

When my fingers trailed to his thigh, he cut me a look in assessment. I shifted, swinging my leg over him until I was settled in his lap. Was it selfish that I wanted his arms around me? Was it selfish to want that when they made me feel safe and protected?

He was always everything to everyone else. A leader, cold and unyielding, the one who had to make the tough, unpopular choices, despite the consequences. He carried the weight of Samryn's curse on his shoulders, the weight of a *war*, I knew, on his shoulders, using someone he'd once loved as a weapon. His people respected him, though it had been difficult as a Hartan boy growing up in Karak.

"I've never known anyone like you," I told him softly. "I doubt I ever will again."

His eyes flickered silver, a mere flash. Had I surprised him? But I couldn't understand why that would be. He had to know that he was singular.

And I will miss him terribly when I have to return to Dakkar, came the certain thought.

My heart had already sunk into him. How deeply, I didn't know.

But maybe I should leave with Brune and Nevin.

I might be able to move on with my life if I was able to salvage my heart *now*. Leaving him would break it, but it wasn't too late, was it?

Then I chastised myself because there was still Samryn to consider. I wouldn't leave him to suffer his curse. Not for anything.

Even if it frightened me how much I'd come to care for Alaryk Arn'dyne.

He must've seen the peculiar expression cross my face. "What is it?"

"We were never meant to meet," I said simply, trying to keep my morose thoughts away from my tone. "If I'd had my way. It's strange to think that now."

"What do you mean?"

I had to tread carefully, I realized belatedly. But I could give Alaryk a half-truth, even though my belly roiled with it. I hated lying. And being here, being with him…it was the biggest lie of all.

Could I tell him? I wondered, debating for a brief moment. I *wanted* to. Desperately. But there was too much I didn't know happening in the background, in the shadows of the *Dothikkar's* palace. There was something happening I couldn't see, something I didn't understand yet. I'd sensed it since we first arrived. So far away from Dothik, I wouldn't be able to protect my family if their lives were at risk—so I had to protect them from afar.

It was safer to lie.

"My brother was meant to be here," I confessed softly.

His head tilted as my hand skimmed his chest, the pad of my finger brushing the metal through his nipple. "You have a brother?"

"Yes, I suppose I've never said," I murmured, darting a look up at him. "His name is Kiron. He's a guardsman."

Alaryk stiffened slightly under me. "Oh?"

"That was all he ever wanted to be," I continued. "We were inseparable growing up. He was my best friend. And I saw his eyes as he watched the patrols through the city. Their glittering armor. And to a boy from the Market District, living in the *Dothikkar's* palace must've seemed like a grand adventure. So when he came of age, he worked hard, harder than anyone else, to achieve what he wanted. Even if it broke our hearts."

"What do you mean?"

I sighed, sitting back on his thighs, my hands dropping away from him. One came up to my pendant, rubbing at the fire gem out of habit until Alaryk's face glowed with it.

"Training is intense. You're required to choose, essentially. Your life…or the king. All of them swear their allegiance. And when Kiron did the same, it was like one moment he was there, the next he was gone from our lives. It was like a death in a way. When you spend time with someone nearly every waking moment, when you can read them as easily as you read yourself, every twitch of their face, every movement, when you can identify them from five blocks down just by the way they walk. And then to…not. When Kiron went to training, we didn't see him for four months straight, even though he wasn't far. It…it broke my heart a little. It really splintered my mother's, though she would never say that."

"You felt abandoned," Alaryk said. "You felt he chose a stranger over you, your family. That's understandable."

"But it's what he always wanted," I said. "And as the years passed, it got easier. My mother still had a place for him at our evening meals. But I stopped looking for him walking on the streets, coming home. I started to get angry. Bitter. Then I realized it didn't matter. He'd made a choice. And I could also choose to not let it eat me up either. So I forgave him instead. When we saw him again, he acted like everything was normal. Working for the *Dothikkar* was all he could talk about. With no mention of his absence. I don't even think he knows how much he'd hurt us, but what can you do?"

Alaryk's brows drew down. His hand had slowly stroked up and down my back, pushing my tunic up so he could touch my bare skin. It felt wonderful, the rasp of his rough hands, calloused from dragonback.

"Anyway, it's because of Kiron that I'm here," I said, remembering my original point, a wry smile quirking my lips when I circled back around. "He was meant to be in rider training with Ryak and Nevin. And…" I trailed off. "My mother threw a fit when she found out. No Dakkari has ever survived, except for the princess. We thought it would mean his death."

I dragged in a deep breath. Not entirely untrue.

"Kiron found out about the position in the hatchery. He said that he would stay in Dothik if I took his place here."

Understanding dawned in Alaryk's eyes.

"And I was angry at first, because I felt I didn't have a choice. I'd worked so hard in Dothik. My *mrikro*…the *pyroki* master…I was to be his replacement when he resigned his post. A highly respected position, one I'd worked so hard for, and it was to be mine. I would like to think that that remains when I return, but there was another strong contender for the position. And well, a season is a long time to be away."

"Do you resent him for it?" Alaryk asked. "Kiron?"

Hearing him say my brother's name was jarring. A bridge connecting my two lives—Dakkar and Karak.

"Yes," I whispered, pressing my face against his warm neck, the confession falling like a stone from my lips. "And I feel terrible saying that out loud."

Alaryk's hand slid into my hair.

"But if it hadn't happened…I would have never met you," I pointed out, an obvious truth. I leaned back to look in his eyes. "Or Samryn. Or experienced working in an Elthikan hatchery. Or found a dear friend in Syris. Brune. Ethrisha. Tarkosh. The truth is that…I resented my brother until I saw the Elthika land outside the East Gate in Dothik."

Alaryk exhaled a sharp breath, one of understanding, mingled with amusement. "Were you frightened?"

"Of you," I admitted.

His smirk told me he liked that, and my gaze drifted to his lips. I pressed my finger against them, feeling their surprising softness. His smile slowly died, and I felt a familiar energy rise between us. One of awareness.

"I was terrified of you," I said quietly. "But not of the Elthika. I looked at them, at Samryn, and I thought…this was what was meant to happen. The path I was meant to take. Kiron was meant to be a guardsman, if only so I would be *here*. That single decision led me across the sea. Right here. With you."

Something shifted between us. An acknowledgment, perhaps, of what we were to one another. Of what it was we actually felt for one another.

I hadn't expected someone like Alaryk to ever appear in my life.

Yet here I was, in his lap, my hands running down the wide berth of his chest, my fingernail clicking over his nipple piercing, making his abdomen tighten against me.

His eyes came to my pendant. He reached for it, running his thumb across the gem. "Who gave this to you? A lover?"

I heard a roughness in his voice I hadn't anticipated. I chuckled low. "Would you be jealous if that were the case?"

"Yes," he replied simply.

I tried to bite back my soft smile. "You're one to talk about lovers. Speaking of, I saw one of yours today, watching the confrontation with Potra."

Alaryk's brows furrowed. "*One* of my lovers?"

"One of your harem," I teased with a pointed, dry look.

He bit out a frustrated sigh. "You know I've been with no one since…"

"The feast night?" I asked.

He rubbed his thumb over the fire gem. "Watching me? Even then?"

I wouldn't let him distract me. "That was the last time you were with her?"

That was the night I'd seen Samryn crash into the forest. It had only been half a moon cycle ago, but it felt like so much longer.

"Yes," he replied. "The arrangement I had with Rivenna was sex and nothing more. I'd only been with her a handful of times over the course of two seasons. Besides…"

"Yes?"

He rubbed the back of his neck. "I ended our arrangement after the night in Ny'am with you. I saw her in the village the next day and told her."

I jerked back, surprised. "You did? Why?"

"Because I knew it was inevitable between you and me," he said. And I…liked that way more than I should. "I felt it then. I know you did too."

For a long while, I regarded him with my insides fluttering. He was still holding my pendant between his thumb and forefinger, and I looked down at it.

"My parents gave me the pendant," I finally told him. His eyes were molten as he absorbed the words. "My parents saved every piece of gold they could to buy me the fire gem. My father is a talented metalworker. He works in the forges in Dothik. He set it into the backing, and my mother crafted the chain, piece by piece. They gave it to me when I got accepted to my apprenticeship."

For the first time, I saw a soft smile cross Alaryk's face, one only of gentleness.

"It's my most cherished possession," I said, looking down at it. "I like having a piece of them here."

"Have you ever given thought to if they'd like it in Karak?"

The question made me still as I searched his eyes. I swallowed as he dropped the pendant, and it hit the space between my breasts, his words permeating the air.

"I haven't," I replied honestly. "They have community in Dothik. Lifelong friends, especially my mother. I don't ever see them giving that up."

He knew what went unspoken…that I didn't know if *I* would give them up to stay here. I didn't think I would. I would feel too much like I was leaving them behind. I didn't want my mother to feel like she had in the aftermath of Kiron's leaving. It would break my heart.

I tried to change the subject, away from something I didn't even know how to answer.

"We're close to the center," I said, past the lump in my throat. "Did you feel it?"

He knew exactly what I was talking about. And thankfully, he let the prior subject drop. "Yes."

Samryn's curse. We were nearly there, untangling the Idima's curse within him. And once we found the center, we could eradicate it completely. I didn't have a doubt in my mind now. Not with Alaryk's support, not with his strength.

"We will save him, you know," I said. "I feel certain of it now. And I promise that I won't leave until we do."

Alaryk's hand tightened in my hair, and he drew me forward. Our lips met in a crash, and a low groan tore from his throat, but it sounded like one of relief, not pleasure.

"You like me too, don't you?" I couldn't help but whisper against his lips.

"Too much," he growled, sounding perturbed by that fact, and my laugh made his kiss turn even fiercer, like he was trying to punish me for it.

For a brief moment, as I sank into him, I let myself imagine it. Staying.

Days in the hatchery, nights in Alaryk's arms.

But eventually, we would have to return to Grym. The Arsadia was only a temporary home for him after all. This wasn't his stronghold.

But I imagined it nevertheless…loving him.

I sighed into his mouth, liking the feel of him between my legs, the heat, the bulk, the strength. I felt exposed like this, but protected. It was freedom, but it was safety. Like running off a cliff, knowing he'd be there to catch me.

Alaryk pulled back. Suddenly and strangely. When I moved to try to catch his kiss again, he held me back.

When I opened my eyes, confused, I saw his head was cocked, his gaze directed at the wall of his dwelling, his body stiff.

Alarm went through me. "What is it?" I whispered.

"Samryn," Alaryk said. "He's…warning me."

Just then, in the distance, I heard bells ringing, hard clangs that echoed throughout Grymia.

"Fuck," Alaryk growled, rising with me in his arms until he righted me. Already lacing up his trews and snatching his tunic off the floor quickly, his movements jerky and hurried.

"What's going on?" I asked in a rush, going to my boots by the door.

"You stay here," he growled. "We're under attack."

"What?" I breathed.

Shouts and commands funneled inside the dwelling when Alaryk tugged open the door. A breeze whistled inside. It was dark, only a half-moon illuminating the quiet road beyond.

"Stay here," he growled. "Promise me."

But I did no such thing, and he was already out the door, racing into the darkness beyond.

The hatchery, I thought, a twinge of fear filling my insides.

I couldn't break a promise I'd never made, after all.

And so I ran out the door, my eyes on the glowing dome in the distance.

CHAPTER 30
AMAIA

"Amaia," Syris gasped out when she saw me, relief in her eyes. "Help me with the eggs—we have to bring them down."

"Down where?" I asked, already going to a Rythback egg, its glittering shell hard beneath my touch.

Syris was in her nightdress. The incubation door was open to the main hallway, and I saw Ulin race down it, could hear Tarkosh giving orders.

"There's a cellar in the kitchens," she told me. "Hidden."

I nodded. I didn't ask any more questions, not until the eggs were to safety. I felt a strange sense of calm overtake me. I had a purpose. And while I worried about Alaryk, about what could possibly be attacking Grymia, I knew that he would be safe. My priority was the hatchlings, getting them secure. Then I would figure out what came next.

Even still, I felt my magic rise around me like a simmering veil, at the ready. Such a strange, new thing, but I felt more comfortable with it around me.

Syris gasped when she looked over. "Amaia, your eyes…"

"Ignore it," I told her. "Here."

I passed her the Rythback egg, and she tucked it into a

satchel, one likely insulated since I saw glowing starstone frag-ments nestled at the base.

The light of my heartstone magic—glowing in my eyes—illu-minated the incubation room in the darkness. But after Syris's initial surprise, she paid it no mind, and we quickly gathered the remaining eggs, placing each one, carefully insulated in one of the enclosed satchels, in the hallway, where Ulin was transporting them down to the cellar.

Working together, we got the incubation room cleared out.

"Where's Moak?" I asked.

"Getting the hatchlings down with Tarkosh."

I nodded. I followed her to the kitchens, seeing Moak with a leash and chain around Kyr, trying to get him down the stairs of the hidden hatch that had been covered up by a rug.

"Kyr," I rasped. When he saw me, he stopped fighting against Moak, prowling toward me instead. He was too big to carry, even for Moak, who seemed relieved to see me, handing me the leash and chain.

"Get him down—he's the last one," he told me.

"Where are you going?" Syris demanded when she regarded Moak.

"Down to the village," he said, squeezing her arm as he passed. "Ulin will stay behind."

"You're not a rider, Moak," Syris argued. "Leave it to them. Come down with us."

"I'll be fine," he assured her.

She stared at the door after Moak went through it, leaving just the two of us—well, three, including Kyr—in the kitchen.

"He'll be fine," I assured her, guiding her down the stairs. "Come on."

Kyr followed me down without a fight, his bulk making him clumsy as he navigated the stairs. Down below, Tarkosh was lighting oil lamps, illuminating the small barren space. There was a rack of shelves pressed against one wall. Old provisions, I saw, along with barrels of water and dried hatchling feed. Ulin had lined up the remaining eggs, warm in their insulated satchels, along the wall. And there was chaos with the hatchlings themselves, all running around, climbing the stone.

"What's going on?" I asked when I got Kyr down. He was settled, however, staying by my side, thankfully, and not exploding with energy. "What's happening?"

"Two wild Elthika formations converging over the village," Tarkosh told me. "A lot of them. They've already burned most of the cropland."

My belly squeezed. How was that possible? "Burned?"

"There's a Redback among them. At least one. They breathe fire."

"Not *ethrall?*" I asked, confused, my mind swimming. I didn't know such a thing was even possible.

"Only Vyrins have *ethrall*," Ulin corrected me, wrestling one of the hatchlings away from the shelving. "Redbacks are rare, but they're only here in the Arsadia. They can't fly very long distances, so luckily they can't cross into our other territories. That's why we have this cellar. This stone," he said, knocking his knuckles against the walls, "won't burn. When Grymia was built, there were Redbacks all over this territory. Most of the dwellings are made of this stone."

I still know nothing at all, I realized.

"I have to go back out there," I said.

Tarkosh looked at my sharply. "No, Alaryk would want you down here."

"People could be hurt," I said, determination rising. "I won't make the same mistake again."

Her lips pressed together.

"If I'm needed, I can help," I said, handing Kyr's chain to Syris, "but I won't know that if I'm down here."

Syris looked worried. "Wild Elthika are unpredictable, Amaia. What if you get hurt?"

"Luckily I'm more resilient than anyone I know," I answered, giving her a quick quirk of my lips. "Don't worry about me."

"I'll go too," Tarkosh said, squeezing Syris's shoulder as she passed. "There could be injured Elthika."

"Be careful," my friend said, inclining her head. "Both of you."

When Tarkosh and I got to the top of the stairs, she said, "Close that. I'll see you down there—I have to get my supplies."

"Right," I breathed, not watching as she sprinted down the hallway, firmly tugging on the hatch door until the hinges squealed. The door was heavy, made of the same stone. Fireproof. Knowing they were safe—the eggs, the hatchlings, my friends—I ran out of the hatchery and immediately smelled the smoke.

I skittered to a stop, dread settling deep in the pit of my stomach when I saw the battle in the sky.

Elthika, flashes of talons and scales, locked together, a twisted tangle in the sky. Some I recognized, even in the darkness. Some had riders on their backs.

"Gods," I whispered, scanning the sky desperately for Alaryk and Samryn as I began to run toward the landing field. The croplands were on fire in the distance, illuminating the night in a dangerously orange glow, shadows deepening, ash swirling like mist. "Kakkari, save us all."

The smoke was acrid and bitter, and my lungs were pumping full of it as I sprinted. There was an Elthika down in the landing field, lying on their side, a stream of Karag all around them. *Hurt?* I wondered. *Or dead?*

My legs pumped harder until I was gasping. Overhead, I heard a whistling scream, the flash of an orange Elthika, the likes of which I'd never seen, and I watched in horror as a stream of fire billowed from its jaw, aimed directly at another Elthika flying toward it.

The heat was *searing*. Luckily the other Elthika dove, swirling in the air, escaping the fire. *Myzalla*, I saw, recognizing her

Elthika and her dark figure on its back. But she had it under control, and I heard the impact her Elthika made as it careened into what I could only assume was a Redback.

Where is Alaryk? I thought, looking for the merest glimpse of Samryn in the sky, my head swinging. As I neared the landing field, more Karag were milling around, the sound louder as they rushed buckets of water forward, trying to put out the floating embers from the farmlands.

I saw a familiar figure.

"Brune," I gasped out, racing toward him.

His face was smeared in ash, but there was determination lined in his expression as he passed a bucket to the next person, more Karag villagers making a line that funneled its way down toward the croplands.

"Trying to save the grain field and livestock pasture," he gasped out, hacking up a cough through the smoke. "There's a chance. The Elthika, Amaia." He jerked his chin toward the landing field. "They're hurt. *Go.*"

I sprinted away, nearly running into a familiar Karag, who took the bucket from Brune. The male who'd spat at my feet today.

The landing field was close, and by the time I reached it, I was panting hard. Even more chaos exploded here. Elthika were battling above us. I could hear the snapping jaws, the terrible sound of scales meeting scales, the scratch of talons, and the screams of fire. The Grymian healer—Raran—was kneeling over a prone rider, wrapping his arm in a bandage to stop the bleeding from a large gash.

When Raran saw me, she pointed to a large Elthika on the far end of the field. "The bleeding won't stop. Can you help him?"

I nodded, racing to him, drawing my magic up. It was fed by my sheer determination, my need to help these creatures.

Villagers were surrounding him, climbing up to keep cloths —anything, really—pressed to a deep gash along his side, to keep him from bleeding out onto the earth. But they all backed away when the glow of my eyes illuminated them all.

They gave me space, and when my magic spread over the panting Elthika the healer had directed me to—one with black scales tipped in silver, a Rythback—I felt it *flood*. It poured out from me, as if before I'd only controlled a mere trickle and now it was a rushing river.

As I did with Samryn, I looked for a way inside, my magic crawling up the rivulets in his scales, little rivers and pathways, all following the blood that was dripping.

When I dove into the wound, the ache and weakness hit me like a wall…and yet it was nothing compared to Samryn's curse.

I can do this, I thought, determined. Even without Alaryk's aid.

I didn't know how long I worked on the Elthika, envisioning a weave of thread, looping my magic back and forth to close it, just as my mother would do as a seamstress. I did this though, all around me, I felt the heat of a Redback's fire, narrowly missing another Elthika's body in the sky, knowing that at any moment, it could aim its weapon at us on the ground instead, incinerating us where we stood. While I heard the terrible screeches and animalistic groans as the Elthika of Grymia defended themselves against the wild packs.

And then, there in the sky, I saw the familiar red of Samryn's scales, flashing in the fire's light. He appeared to glow, like a beacon in the night. And Alaryk was on his back, a dark shadow, locked into a riding position as Samryn swooped and veered, hunting down a large wild Elthika whose scales shimmered blue.

My magic slipped as worry rammed into my chest, but I shook myself, focusing back on the Elthika before me, whose wound had finally stopped bleeding. The flesh beneath the scales —which had been ripped away—closed like a scar.

I blew out a breath when it was finished, stumbling back when my vision swayed. A Karag male caught me, holding tight onto my arms as I blinked away the ache, though it lodged itself deep into my insides.

"You all right?" the male asked, his voice hushed and hurried, his red eyes bright in the night, like Samryn's.

"Fine."

"*Amaia,*" called a familiar voice. Tarkosh. She was huddled over another female rider, who'd been dragged in from the outer fields.

Though my legs were still wobbly, I raced over, skidding to the ground, my magic already rising, a warm ball that I spun outward when I saw shredded flesh on the rider's leg, white bone peeking from the wound. Nausea rose. I'd never seen anything so terrible, but I swallowed down the flood of saliva, closing my eyes, Tarkosh's presence beside me as she comforted the moaning rider helping to center me.

I heard the gasps from a few other huddled Karag. Time had stretched and slowed in my mind, but I knew what I would find when I opened my eyes. I was weaker than before, a sharp sting throbbing down my own leg, mirroring the rider's injury.

Smooth skin greeted me, the rider's gaze one of disbelief. Her eyes flashed up to mine.

"Th-Thank you."

I'd only healed two…and already my stamina was waning. These were deep wounds, though, and one had been Elthikan.

And I was still needed. I would use my heartstone magic until I collapsed.

Alaryk could help take away the rising pain, I knew, but he needed to defend his people, his outpost. And when I saw another Elthika—and its rider—fall to the earth halfway between the cropland and the landing field, I knew I *had* to push through.

There was no choice.

I took off running.

CHAPTER 31
ALARYK

The last of the wild Elthika fled just before dawn.

And on Samryn, high in the sky, watching the shadows retreat into the lightening sky speared with blues and pinks, I felt a deep seed of worry take root.

My heartstone magic hadn't worked on the Elthika. For the first time, I'd snapped out my power with the intent of making them retreat before there was more bloodshed, more destruction.

But what I'd felt had been concerning.

The heartstone magic that was born within each Elthika was so depleted, a mere wisp, that I'd had nothing to latch onto, nothing to guide.

It confirmed what we'd already known for years: The heartstones were very nearly spent in the Arsadia. The *thalara* trees from the seeds we'd cultivated in Dakkar wouldn't grow new heartstones for another decade, unless we could somehow discover a way to speed their growth.

The Elthika were *starving*. They were starving to death. They needed the heartstone magic to fill that void…and there was very little left. And none would come for years. No reprieve.

What would happen then?

They'd sensed the lost heartstone in Ny'am. They'd likely wanted it for themselves, but we'd been able to defend our home. For now.

When I was certain that the wild packs had crested beyond view, I turned Samryn back around to look at Grymia. A smoldering, smoking Grymia. Much of the farmlands had been wiped out, though the grain field closest to the village had been saved. A surviving herd of livestock was being corralled to the landing field, the fencing having burned. Luckily much of the village hadn't been touched by the Redback's flames. And other structures that had, the villagers had been able to extinguish quickly.

The watch tower was burned, however, crumbled to the earth in a smoking pit. We had been fortunate. Though if more wild packs came, I didn't think we'd be so lucky.

But there was something more pressing—the dread that had been present in my innards for hours, ever since I'd seen the glow of her magic.

I maneuvered Samryn down to the landing field, where most of the villagers were still milling around. Everyone was exhausted, but there was still a sense of urgency. The fires had been put out, but there were still a lot of people who were injured and plenty of work to be done.

I wondered how many were dead.

I could sense the tiredness in Samryn, his strength waning, still too quickly for a Vyrin. Though without Amaia's influence over the curse, he wouldn't have been able to hold the line against the wild packs for as long as he had.

I leaped from the riding seat, landing on the hard ground in a crouch before rising.

Myzalla was the first I saw, her face streaked in ash, sitting on the earth as she tried to recover for a brief moment, leaning back against her Elthika, who was sleeping—passed out—on the field.

"Where is she?" I asked.

She cast her arm out, too tired to speak it seemed, toward a group of Karag who were huddled around something. *Someone.*

My chest squeezed, and I ran. When I reached them, I pushed through the gathering crowd, which only parted for me when they saw who was barreling through.

A strange panic was tangling and twisting my heart.

Amaia lay on the ground, her head resting in Syris's lap. Tarkosh and Brune were standing nearby, in the inner circle around her, but the rest backed away when I neared.

Her skin was ashen, leached of color, and streaks of dried blood were coming from the inner corners of her eyes, a familiar sight to me. She was barely breathing, a slight rise and fall of her chest—the only thing that didn't make me fall to my knees on the earth. Because at first glimpse, she looked dead.

Her hands were covered in dried blood, likely having needed the physical contact with the villagers and the Elthika as her magic had begun to wane more and more.

"Let me have her," I rasped, my voice so deep it felt like a string of growls. Syris gently eased Amaia's head off her lap as I sat down on the earth, gently maneuvering her limp body to me.

When we'd done this the first time, she'd been awake. But nevertheless, I called up my magic for the hundredth time that night and tried to press it into her. It was met with a wall, but I kept the warmth there, like a touch, hoping it might rouse her.

"*Mariss,*" I whispered. "Wake for me. Let me help you."

She didn't stir. I touched her chest, just to be certain her heart was beating. I felt the dull thud and closed my eyes, uncaring that there were dozens and dozens around us. I shifted her in my arms until her back was against my chest, the earth hard beneath me as the sun crested over the taller peaks in the valley.

I kept my magic as a presence, something to guide her back to me. I wasn't a patient person, but I had to be now. And when the sunlight finally touched my skin, I felt her shift in my arms.

"Amaia," I murmured quickly, my heart jolting. I could hear

Syris's sharp intake of breath. When Amaia's bloodshot green eyes blearily opened, just a fraction, I took advantage, casting my magic over her like a blanket. "Take it, *mariss*."

Like she was starving, I could feel the way she grasped onto me, like I'd given her a tether to this world and she held on for dear life.

She drank in my magic, letting it fill all the aches, all the corners of pain that she'd had to absorb into her body.

I didn't know how many she'd healed tonight. But I remembered seeing the glow of her magic, reflecting down on the darkened battlefield—because that was what it'd become—more times than I could count. And every time I'd wanted to go to her, to help her recharge her magic or to berate her for leaving the safety of my dwelling, another Elthika had veered for the village and we had needed to chase them down.

"That's it," I breathed. "Take it all."

She gasped, like it was the first deep breath she'd been able to take all night. And while her face still looked pale and sallow, some of the life returned to her eyes and she was able to stay conscious.

"Better," she said, her voice quiet, shaking. "*Kakkira vor.*" Thank you.

But I could see the pain she was still trying to shield from me, even if she was able to sit up.

"Are they all right?" she asked.

A sound left my throat. I looked up at the gathered crowd.

"Amaia," Tarkosh said, crouching down to meet her eyes, "you saved five Elthika, four riders, and nine villagers. No one has died tonight *because* of you."

No one? There had been no casualties from the attack?

I closed my eyes, a prick of relief, of gratitude swelling in me. And when my gaze flashed open, I saw the Grymian villagers had their heads bowed, a sign of respect.

When I looked at Amaia, there were tears ushering into her

eyes. Clear ones. When they dripped down her cheeks, they helped wash away some of the crusted, red blood. The tears, I thought, were in relief. A weight lifted off her shoulders, perhaps, when I knew Gethrin's death sat heavy on her.

I rose from the ground, cradling Amaia in my arms.

"She needs rest," I said. "All of us do."

"What if they come back?" came Dresnar's question, his jaw tight. "I'll take the first watch."

I nodded. "I'll join you, once I get her situated. But I don't think they'll be back today. Hopefully for a while."

There were two dead Elthika lying on the outer fields. Two of the wild Elthika, one of them Samryn had killed, his jaws clamping deep.

I didn't like to see *any* dead Elthika. It was a tragedy. They'd been desperate. I'd felt it myself. But it still didn't change the fact that Grymia had been in danger. They could've killed many more of my people.

I left the landing field, knowing Myzalla would organize tasks, though I knew the priority was rest for most of the villagers. My riders had fought valiantly and endlessly tonight.

We were silent as I navigated us back to my dwelling, cutting through the village off the main road, the quickest path. When I brought Amaia inside, into the cool quiet, I released a breath I hadn't known I'd been holding.

I took her into the washing room, undressing her carefully as the bathing pool filled with steaming water. Every wince she tried to hide from me made my gut twinge.

I carried her into the pool after I undressed. Though I knew I needed to get back to the village, to help with the repairs, I would allow myself this moment with her. I needed the brief reprieve, if only to assure myself that she was...*well*. Alive. Breathing. Warm. The vision of her sprawled on the landing field was still quick in my mind.

"You're all right?" came Amaia's quiet voice when I settled us back, when I began to scrub at the dried blood covering her hands.

"I'm fine," I answered, water trickling.

"And Samryn?"

I met her eyes. The green against her blood-streaked face was vibrant. "He's unharmed."

"Good," she breathed.

"Amaia."

"Hmm?"

Pausing in my scrubbing, I pressed my forehead to hers, feeling her heartbeat against me when I dragged my palm to it.

"Thank you," I said quietly. Her breath hitched, and I saw my eyes reflected in her own. "You saved many of my people. I won't ever forget that."

For once, she seemed at a loss for words.

"But don't *ever* do that again."

She frowned.

I grabbed a clean cloth from a basket next to the pool, dipping it into the warm water. Gently, I dragged it against her face, trying to erase all evidence of her bloody tears and ash and grit and soot.

She took my wrist to still my actions. "I won't ever hide again when people need me. You have to know that."

"I asked you to stay here," I merely said, my tone coming out harsher than I'd intended. My hand was shaking, and I couldn't make it stop.

Amaia seemed to notice too, and she took my palm in hers, squeezing tight. "Alaryk."

"Fuck," I murmured softly, releasing the cloth, letting it float on the surface of the water as I scrubbed my free hand down my own face. I thought maybe the shock was catching up with me. I didn't want her to see it.

"I'm here," she said, taking my jaw into her hand. She pressed her lips against mine, and I immediately clutched her to me, trying to be conscious of my own strength so I didn't hurt her accidentally. "I'm here," she murmured against my lips. "I'm okay."

"I saw you," I murmured. "On the field. And I thought how easy it would be to lose you. How quickly it could happen. And it fucking *terrified* me, Amaia. Don't ever do that again."

Her eyes widened.

"I wanted to help," she argued. "I *had* to. You said yourself— my magic is rare. So why not use it to help your people?"

"Because I don't want to lose *you*, Amaia," I snapped, my voice harsh and guttural, but I knew the intent of my words landed. "I can't lose *you*. And it's not just because of your damn magic."

Time seemed to pause, like we were both holding our breath.

"It's not?" she whispered, strangely still and rapt on my words.

"No," I bit out.

She'd become more to me than I'd ever imagined…and I couldn't quite pinpoint when it had even happened.

Only when I'd thought she was dead, lying listless and unmoving, her head in Syris's lap…I'd had the dizzying sensation that I had splintered into two.

One moment into the next. One realization, and now I would never be the same.

Both of us were quiet after that, ruminating in our own thoughts, at the unspoken confession I'd just made.

Quickly, I finished up in the bathing pool, scrubbing at us both until we were clean of the grime. And only when I had her dried off and clothed in one of my tunics did I feel marginally better.

"Do you have to go back?" she asked softly, pressing her forehead into my chest, her arms coming around my waist. I was dressed in my riding vest, having just finished clasping the catches. "You need to rest too."

"I'll try to be back as soon as I can," I told her. I nudged her until her face was tipped up to me. I kissed her gently, feeling her sigh. "I promise. Sleep. And don't you dare sneak off to the hatchery. Tarkosh will handle it."

When I pulled open the door, she said, "Alaryk."

Looking over my shoulder at her, I raised my brow as ash danced inside.

"I was terrified for you too," she finally said.

Our eyes held. My chest felt tight. Walking a few paces back, I grabbed her, pressing another hard kiss to her lips, one she returned eagerly.

Then with a small curse, I left because I knew if I didn't, I might never again.

Closing the door behind me, with her taste still on my tongue, I turned my sights toward Grymia, knowing there was much to be done. And though my heart was still with Amaia, I needed to be calm and focused for my people, bracing myself for the work ahead.

Halfway down the main road, I heard a rush of voices ahead. A few guardsmen were arguing in front of...

Fuck.

"What's happened?" I growled, stalking toward them, fearing I already knew.

Jirin was the brave one to meet me, to break the news, his expression braced, his jaw tight.

"I'm sorry, *Karath*," Jirin said, meeting my eyes. The dwelling behind him was dark, the door busted in by brute force, hanging off its hinge. "He's gone."

I could see it play out in my mind. When the Elthika had attacked, the priority had been Grymia. Not guarding a prisoner. They'd made a choice. They'd left their post to join in on the fight.

And I couldn't even say I blamed them.

"Ryak is gone," Jirin told me. "And we can't find Nevin either."

CHAPTER 32
AMAIA

The summons to Grymia's council—made up of Alaryk's riders and a couple trusted advisors—felt daunting, a gnawing of worry deep in my gut as I followed the road down the rebuilding village.

The fresh morning still smelled like smoke and burning wood. The scent of death—from the two wild Elthika that had been brought down by Grymia's riders—permeated the air, though their bodies had been disposed of, laid to rest in the forest beyond the village's borders.

Dresnar followed behind me, his booted feet making me tense. After the Elthika attack, I'd slept the day and night solidly, only waking to discover that Ryak and Nevin had disappeared.

I hadn't seen Alaryk since he'd brought me back to his dwelling. Though, judging by the imprint of his body and the rumpled furs on his side of the bed, I assumed he'd returned to me at some point in the night.

This morning, instead of waking to Alaryk, Dresnar had been outside, informing me that the "Dakkari prisoner" had escaped, Nevin with him, and that my presence was requested among the council.

Worry and dread had made me nearly sick.

But as I walked through the village, what surprised me most was the reception I received from near strangers. People who even recently had whispered as I passed or simply ignored me.

Now I got the inclining of heads, greetings of the morning, well wishes that I'd recovered. There was an older Karag female who I'd once seen Ethrisha speaking with, who pressed a fresh-baked loaf of bread into my palm as I passed, saying that it was mixed with *naro* seeds, which would help me find my strength again.

It was a strange contrast—the warm reception of Grymia, while also feeling like I was about to be sick.

Did they know? Had they found Ryak and Nevin? Did they uncover what the *Dothikkar* had sent us here to do? To spy on the people I called my friends? My…lover?

"Through here," Dresnar's voice came from behind, leading me to a tall dwelling, an oil lantern installed in the roughened stone near the steel door. I'd seen it in passing, considering its close proximity with the landing field.

Before I entered the dwelling, I noticed there was a blue-scaled dragon, the color like midnight, nearly inky black, on the landing field. One I'd never seen before. And another black dragon, with eyes as gold as the sun. Had more representatives from Elysom come? There was a group of Grymian villagers gathered, breaking in their duties, to stare at the two Elthika.

Dresnar led me inside. Down one of the hallways, I could hear the low murmuring of deep voices.

The room that I entered was rounded in shape, a high circular table in the center, a map of what I assumed was the Arsadia spread out, the edges of the parchment frayed and curling inward. There were no chairs in the room and so the inhabitants were all standing.

My eyes found Alaryk's immediately. His expression was unreadable, so unlike the rawness in the bathing pool yesterday, the tremble of his hand against me, the sheer relief that I was alive palpable and pouring from him. He cared for me. *Deeply.*

The only thing more frightening than that was that my own feelings mirrored his. I thought it surprised the both of us what yesterday had revealed.

Looking at him now, however, didn't assuage the worry gnawing in my belly. If anything, it made it coil tighter.

Myzalla was in attendance, standing next to…*Brune.* His lips curved up in a quiet smile, but mine pressed when I saw him. He gave a soft shake of his head, as if that would answer anything for me.

What had he told them?

As for the other two males within the room…

Both were similar in height, build, and coloring. Black hair, sun-kissed skin, sharp, cutting features that speared me in place as they regarded me.

For a moment, I thought they might be brothers. But as I stared, I began to notice the differences that told me the two couldn't be more different.

"This is Sarkin Dirak'zar," Alaryk told me, gesturing to the male closest to me. He had short black hair that curled at the nape of his neck and piercing, beautiful eyes. Golden in the center, molten brown, and dark forest green. I watched the pupils narrow on me, his riding vest creaking with his smooth shift. "You know of him, I'm sure."

"I do," I said quietly. I recognized the name. He was the *Karath* of the southern territory of Sarroth. The Karag king who'd come nearly a year ago to take the princess of Dothik, one of the *Dothikkar's* own daughters, Klara, to wed. Of course everyone knew the story. An act of punishment that had led to love.

I remembered the night when he'd come to Dothik, demanding the princess. It had been all anyone could talk about for *weeks.*

And here he was, the villain made flesh.

"And this is Vaedrin Malik," Alaryk continued, gesturing to the other male in the room.

The name didn't register with me, not in the way Sarkin's had…but there was no mistaking what he was. A king in his own right. A *Karath*? I wondered.

"He is the *Karath* of the northern territory of Kyloth," Alaryk answered for me, as if hearing my wonder. "Rider of Aeras."

Now I realized why the group of Grymian villagers had gathered to gawk at the Elthika. Because how often was it that you saw two Vyrin next to one another, up close and in the flesh?

That was how I felt faced with not two but three *Karaths*.

Vaedrin Malik had black hair, wavy and wind-swept, that brushed the tops of his broad shoulders. There was a cloth hood that was draped around them and thick hide leather that molded to his chest like armor. A silver buckle was strapped around the middle of his chest, the hilt of a dagger flashing when the cloak's fabric shifted.

And his eyes…they were *purple*. A soft violet that was almost too pretty for such a brooding, stark face. I'd never seen their likeness before, not here or in Dothik. His face was perfectly symmetrical, too handsome to be real, not a single flaw. It almost hurt looking at him, and I had to look away.

I averted my gaze back to Alaryk's, just as he said, "This is Amaia of Rath Savenal."

"Savenal?" Vaedrin's voice came, deep like thunder but strangely smooth like glass. "You're from the West Lands?"

I cut him a sharp look, surprise making me forget his beauty. "My family, *lysi*," I replied. "How…how did you know that?"

Vaedrin spread his hands over the table as he leaned forward. "I am fond of the West Lands."

Sarkin cut him a sharp look. "Elysom gave you orders."

"And I haven't been back, have I?" Vaedrin replied, but he kept his eyes on me. His piercing observation made me squirm in place.

I cleared my throat. "My family lived in a horde there once, decades ago. But I was born in Dothik. I've never stepped foot in the West Lands."

As much as I wanted to.

"A shame," Vaedrin replied. "There is much beauty there. In the land and the people."

Then he fell silent, staring down at the map.

I licked my lips, looking back to Alaryk. "You needed me for something?"

My voice sounded strained, even to my ears. Nervous too.

"Something about Ryak?" I asked, very aware of Brune's presence. "Have they been found?"

"No," Alaryk replied. His thumb traced the edges of the forest on the map outlining Grymia. "We have searched the outer borders, but there is no sign of them. We can't spare many riders to look for them, with all the work that needs to be done."

I looked to Brune, a quick flash, but one that Alaryk caught.

"Did you know anything?" came the question, rasping from my lover's throat. "About what they planned?"

My brows drew together. Something I wouldn't have to lie about, thankfully. "Of course not."

"Did you ever speak to Nevin?"

"I—" I cut myself off, thinking fast. The truth wasn't enough to expose Brune or me. But I did hate the deception. "He did speak to me. He asked what would happen to Ryak. He knew I was…close to you."

Alaryk's eyes pinned me. "And what did you say?"

"Alaryk," I said quietly, spreading my hands out, even as my gut churned. "I certainly didn't suggest that he break Ryak out at the first opportunity he had."

"I didn't say that," he murmured, not looking away from me.

I began to feel like I was under interrogation. My heart was pounding harder in my chest, a sensation that I was going to be sick the longer Alaryk looked at me like that. With…caution. I hated it.

"I told him that I thought it was very likely Ryak would be executed," I said, the truth tumbling from my lips. "But I didn't think it was a secret. That was what Grymia wanted."

I still couldn't read Alaryk's face.

"I think it's more likely," Sarkin said, cutting through the tension that had suddenly seeped into the circular room, "that this Nevin saw an opportunity to save his friend…and he took it. I don't think it was planned. And I certainly don't think these Dakkari were involved."

I jerked, my eyes flashing to Alaryk's, frowning. "You thought we had planned this with Nevin?"

Whatever Alaryk saw in my face, it made his shoulders loosen, but only slightly. "I wanted to be sure."

Did I even have a right to be angry and hurt? When I was the one stepping gingerly onto a battlefield, afraid I'd misstep at any moment?

Ryak and Nevin were gone. Which meant Brune and I were no longer bound to fulfilling the *Dothikkar's* orders. Ryak had made a mess of this. It was he who would answer to his king…if he ever made it home.

My brow furrowed.

How *would* they make it back home?

"I had no idea that Nevin would do what he did. Or Ryak for that matter," I answered, because, with the eyes of the Karag on me, I felt like I was on trial. I wondered if they had questioned Brune already. "Like I said, I hardly knew them."

So why was my gut churning? I looked down at the table to avoid meeting Alaryk's eyes, dragging in a deep breath. Because he would be able to see right through me. Panic was rising.

"Are you all right?" Brune asked, touching my shoulder when it slumped.

"Fine, just tired," I replied, not meeting his eyes either.

Because I didn't know what he had told them. But judging by the way he had shaken his head subtly when I'd stepped foot inside the room…I thought nothing. I thought that maybe Ryak had also threatened him, perhaps concerning his own father. Like me, maybe he'd do anything to protect his family.

Even though the true threats were no longer here, we *still* had to go back home. There might still be consequences.

And who knew what blame would fall on us when we returned…

I wondered if Brune had thought the same. I *had* to keep it together.

When I looked back to Alaryk, I felt more centered and in control. "You've found no sign of them?"

"They can only get so far in the Arsadia," Vaedrin murmured, his gaze on the map. "There are steep valleys, mountain ranges, lots of perilous land that's hard to navigate if you aren't on Elthika-back. They're hiding somewhere. A cave system, perhaps? Ny'am was searched?"

"Dresnar searched it this morning," Alaryk said, nodding toward the rider who stood guard at the door.

"No sign of them," Dresnar answered.

"I don't understand," Myzalla chimed in. "Nevin and Ryak are guardsmen for their king. They have survival skills, surely. How far did they think they would get? They have no food or water or shelter. Not to mention they're on an island in the center of our nation. To get back home, they need…"

"Help," Sarkin finished for her. "They need help from the Karag. They need Elthika. So was Nevin's decision based on the fact that they had already secured help? Or was it desperation?"

"Desperation," Vaedrin answered, scoffing. "No Karag would help them. Especially here, in the Arsadia."

I bit my tongue. I thought they *might* have help. Because Ryak had been getting messages back to Dothik, hadn't he? He'd seemed to have some way of communicating. I just hadn't been privy to that information. Besides, a big part of me had thought he might've been lying in an attempt to control me. A bluff.

"What if it's the Dakkari?" Vaedrin asked. "They don't have Elthika, but their vessels have landed on our southern shores before. If either of them has a beacon of some sort, it's possible they could find their way here by sea."

"Our patrols would've spotted a ship by now," Sarkin murmured, shaking his head.

"Not if they came up from the east," Vaedrin replied. "We don't have regular patrols there."

Alaryk was looking at me. I only hoped he didn't catch the flicker of guilt.

"What do you think, Amaia?" he asked. But his voice was cold. *He knows,* I thought. I only hoped it was my paranoia.

"Me?" I asked, swallowing. I blew out a breath, shaking my head. "I have no idea where they could've gone."

Brune chimed in. "Is it possible that they learned enough in training to claim an Elthika of their own? To leave the Arsadia?"

"Doubtful," Myzalla said, sniffing. "But not impossible. Even still, it's suicide. You'd have to be desperate."

"They are," Sarkin merely replied. "If they don't have outside help, they are most certainly desperate."

A wave of dizziness made the room spin, and I clutched harder at the table so I didn't fall. It was getting harder to breathe, but I thought I was able to hide it well.

"Amaia," Alaryk murmured.

I lifted my gaze.

"You know nothing about this? The *Dothikkar* never spoke to you? Ryak and Nevin never spoke about their plans here or hinted that they had allies here?"

Brune's hand brushed mine beneath the high table.

With the eyes of the Karag on me, I looked at Alaryk and said, "No."

And the lie tasted like bitter ash on my tongue.

CHAPTER 33
AMAIA

Alaryk was in a strange mood that night, but I thought it was because of the meeting earlier with his council.

Sarkin and Vaedrin had already departed. It was a lucky happenstance that they'd both been meeting with Elysom's council when news of the Elthika attack had spread. They'd come straight from Elysom, and they would be lending support from their own territories to help with our food supply, the crops of which had been decimated during a single night. There were stores deep underground, of course, that would last months, but next year's supply was precarious without aid.

So whether Alaryk was in a brooding mood because he was tired or because of the emotional aftermath of the Elthika attack on his people or because of the questions and concerns that Ryak and Nevin's escape brought forward, I couldn't be certain. Likely all three. I didn't know how he carried it all on his shoulders. How strong he was.

I gave him time alone in the washing room, the trickle of water every now and again my only indication that he was still in there. But I grew more and more impatient and eventually ducked inside, slipping past the gossamer curtain to find him reclining on the ledge, arms spread out on the stone edges behind him, his head tipped back. I thought he might be sleeping, his eyes closed, but when he heard the merest whisper of my approaching footsteps, he tipped his head forward to regard me, the burn of his blue eyes spearing me in place.

"I was worried," I said. "You've been quiet. Are you all right?"

I wanted to know what was going on in his head. His expression was…distant.

Maybe…he'd seen through me today. And that made my insides twist.

I opened my mouth. To tell him what, exactly? I didn't know. I *still* had to go home. If I spilled the *Dothikkar's* secret plan to someone he viewed as an enemy, what would happen? To me? To my family? Even though Ryak and Nevin were gone, I had to be careful. Alaryk wasn't Dakkari. He was a king of a nation that could decimate my homeland if they so chose. And for the first time, I understood the *Dothikkar's* own fear and paranoia. I'd seen the might of the Elthika, the strength of the Karag firsthand.

The Dakkari?

We'd never stand a chance against them. All we had as protection was a signed accord between us, rooted in heartstone production.

Which was already flimsy and precarious…as Ryak's actions had proved.

"Why are you so opposed to me using my magic on you?" Alaryk asked suddenly. Warning pricked my mind. Something was wrong.

My nostrils flared. "I told you. Because I didn't like how it felt. It felt violating. You inside my mind, your voice filling me up like a water jug. And…"

"And what?"

"And I have good reason to be afraid of you," I finished. I didn't know if he'd take offense to the words. He'd confided in me about his actions concerning Kamora. Would he think I was trying to throw them in his face as a weapon?

I might've had rare magic…but his was more dangerous and powerful. His could topple kingdoms. What could that same magic do to me? I'd be like moldable clay in his hands.

I couldn't read *how* the words landed. He wouldn't give me that insight. He felt closed to me. Like a book. So different than yesterday, in this same place. A contrast so sharp and stark that I wondered if it had been real.

His eyes raked up my body. "Undress."

My stomach was curling. I hesitated. "You're acting strange."

He stood, wading toward me slowly in the bathing pool, steam curling all around him, making my hair frizz and my clothes dampen. When he reached where I was standing at the edge, his hand touched my ankle, skimming up the side of my leg as I held my breath.

"I want to be inside you if I cannot be inside your mind," he murmured. My breath hitched, surprising heat unfurling like a bloom within me. "Undress, *mariss*."

"What's wrong, Alaryk?"

"Undress for me," he purred, reaching up to untie the laces of my trews already, droplets of water running down the material. "I'll tell you when I'm deep between these pretty thighs. When all I can feel is you. That's what I want."

I shivered, biting my lip. When he pulled my trews down, his lips brushed my calf muscle, sensitive beneath the cool press of his kiss. He trailed his mouth up as I sighed, and I felt his tongue lap behind my knee, making me jolt. Hesitantly, my hands went to the hem of my tunic and I had it off, stepping out of my trews until I was naked, my bare feet on the stone of the pool's edge.

Maybe we both needed this, the feeling of connection during intimacy and sex. Maybe I could unravel what was really bothering him when both our walls were down, when it was only sensation and pleasure and heartstone magic between us.

As I stepped into the pool, he returned to his place on the ledge opposite me, sitting back in anticipation.

I could feel the way his crystalline-blue eyes roved over my body, unable to hide the appreciation and desire in his gaze as I waded toward him.

Alaryk's cock was already hard, poking above the edge of the water. When he saw me watching, he gripped it hard, stroking himself until a bead of pre-come shimmered at his tip.

I pressed my hands to his chest, still feeling uncertain, though the familiar lust and need, running like a current between us, was comforting. My thumb scraped over his nipple, and he hissed with pleasure when it tugged his piercing.

Then he groaned, his hand leaving his cock to pull me against him, squeezing my ass. I felt a thrill go through me. I loved when he got like this, when he acted like he needed me close, when he got possessive with his touch.

He was unashamed of his desires, which allowed my own to feel freed. It made my belly swoop, made me throb between my legs…even though I was wary of his distant mood.

His magic spread over my skin like a body oil, shimmering and thick. It felt good, warm like a fur wrapped around my shoulders on a wintry day. My own responded, greeting Alaryk's in anticipation, in *relief.* I was a little greedy, taking some of it for myself because I still felt spent from the Elthika attack, letting it fill the tired places until I was arching against him, until he made me feel strong and desired and whole.

My head dipped. My tongue found his nipple, and I rolled the metal with my tongue. A deep, ragged huff left him.

But then his hand was tangling in my hair and he jerked my head back. Not hard, but firm enough that I gasped, that my neck was exposed, and I looked at him half-lidded, my lips parted.

Alaryk leaned down, keeping my hair taut in his grip, licking and sucking at the column of my throat. His teeth bit my skin, like he wanted to mark me. I didn't expect to like it, that little flint of pain.

But it made the heat in my belly mutate into an inferno, and my nails dug into his shoulders, leaving half-moons in his flesh, making him groan.

Maybe a little pain wasn't so bad.

Maybe we would mark each other with it.

Why did I *want* that?

Why did I feel this rising desperation to claim him in some small way?

But I knew the answer.

I wanted to remember these moments with him. I wanted to remember them when I was back home and missing him… longing for him enough that I would still taste him on my tongue, the jagged pieces of my broken heart aching for him.

Tears pricked the back of my eyes, and I squeezed them tight.

"Tell me," he whispered. Because of course, I could hide nothing from him. Except maybe my own betrayal.

"This wasn't meant to happen," I breathed, my throat bobbing against his mouth as I swallowed. "I wasn't supposed to find you."

His magic surged, and I gasped. I could feel it like a little ball inside my chest. Like a seed that would grow. Like a heartstone that would radiate its warmth and light and power until I was glowing.

I gasped when he lifted me—

Then all thought left my mind when he swiftly entered me, his thick cock eliciting a sharp moan.

I became a wild creature, owned and controlled by Alaryk. I used his shoulders as leverage to ride him, my knees not quite meeting the stone of the ledge because his thighs were as thick and strong as tree trunks. I was spread wide over him. He only gave me the illusion of control, but really, *he* was fucking *me*.

It was fast and desperate. It made my spine tingle, my toes

curl. He felt so good inside me, all that metal hitting and sliding deep, making me clench, making me *come* unexpectedly, like I was a tight string he only needed to pluck. I was his plaything. The control he had over me was shocking.

My cry echoed until it returned back to me off the stone, flooding my ears. His magic was hot, searing. It grew and grew, and I continued to squirm through the pleasure that billowed out from my core.

"I told you I would tell you when I was between these thighs," he growled. His lips came to my ear, and he bit down on the lobe, making me jolt. He continued to fuck me, bouncing my body, using me as the orgasm never ended. But he didn't come. *Wouldn't.*

"What?" I breathed, words a confusing jumble in my addled brain.

"You're lying to me, Amaia," he said. His declaration was punctuated by a sharp snap of his hips. "About everything."

The words broke through the haze of pleasure. I stiffened, my body falling out of rhythm over his.

"I know you are. Am I so far gone for you that I don't even care?" he continued, followed by a dark chuckle that made my throat tighten. "I'll find out what you're hiding."

His magic surged.

That was when I felt what I'd felt once before.

His presence, strong and certain and roving, in my mind.

I gasped, bucking off him. He let me slide off him. Shock, disbelief, and betrayal cut through me, mingled with my own guilt as tears welled in my eyes.

I flung myself away, turning my back as I hunched, trying to focus, trying to get him out of my mind.

"Stop!" I pleaded.

I know you're lying to me, mariss, came his voice, whispered through the thick wall of disbelief.

He'd broken his promise.

He'd broken his promise!

He knew what this meant. He was willing to sacrifice Samryn for *this*? It didn't make any sense. Unless…

Unless he thought that my feelings for him were strong enough that this could be forgiven.

Unless he thought that I cared for Samryn enough that I wouldn't let him fall to the curse.

He knew that I didn't want to see his Elthika suffer. So he was taking what he wanted…all while knowing I'd kneel to him anyway.

My chest twisted. Hurt speared me.

Had…had it all been a lie? I wondered. Had this been his intention all along? Had he suspected all along?

Suspected what, mariss? he questioned.

I closed my eyes, envisioning the blade in my mind as I'd done on the wildlands. He wanted my mind laid bare, but I surprised him.

I severed the connection, just as he likely knew I would.

"Get away from me," I rasped, but it was me who rushed to the edge of the bathing pool, pulling myself out on trembling arms, still feeling the way his cock had filled me, a deep twinge at the sudden emptiness.

I didn't bother to dry myself off. I dressed quickly, even though my hands shook, as hurt made me shiver.

"Think you can hide now?" came his guttural voice. I heard the malice in his tone. When I turned, I saw him stepping from the pool. Dripping wet, still naked—and hard, as he rounded on me. I swallowed, hearing my rough breaths as he backed me up. Until I was pressed against the wall of the washroom, the stone hard and unyielding against my back.

"What are you hiding?" he growled, lowering his head until our eyes were level. "Tell me, Amaia. This isn't a *fucking* game."

I turned my face, but he captured my chin. "Let me go," I hissed.

"Tell me right now. Did you come here with a purpose? Did the *Dothikkar* give you orders? Are you under his command as well? Was everything you told me a lie?"

My eyes widened, but the anger rose in place of my hurt. "Of course not."

"But you've been lying about so much," he said in disgust, his voice twisting. "I thought you were different. I thought I could *believe* you. But now I'm forced to go over every single word you've ever said to me, to try to differentiate what was real and what wasn't."

I pushed at his chest. I was shaking. "Let me go!"

"What was the strategy, exactly?" he continued, as if I hadn't even spoken. "Was it planned? Your place in my bed? Did you plan it with your *Dothikkar*? With Ryak? Nevin? Did you promise to spread your legs for a *Karath*, to get his secrets?"

I felt like he'd slapped me across the face. "How *dare* you."

He laughed, bitter and dark. "How dare I?" He shook his head. He glared, cold as steel in winter. "The *fucking* audacity for *you* to say that to *me*."

"You used your magic against me," I hissed. "The *one* thing I asked of you. You…"

His expression was edged in icy mockery. "I…what? Betrayed you, Amaia?"

Tears swam in my vision.

"Now you know how it feels. You're just like her, thinking you can have whatever you want, thinking you can use me for your gain," he growled. He meant Kamora. Despair cut deep, mingling with my anger. "Tell me what you were sent here to do!"

"Or you'll what?" I hissed, mad enough to poke at him. Hurt enough to want to burn it *all* down between us. Fuck it. Nothing he could threaten me with scared me more than the *Dothikkar's* threats against my own family. "I didn't ask to be here. I didn't seduce my way into your bed. *You* brought me here. *You* asked for my help. *You* broke the promise you made."

His expression was thunderous.

"So fuck you, Alaryk," I said softly, enunciating each word as tears dripped down my cheeks. "I trusted you."

"And I trusted you not to fuck me for your king," he said, the words clipped, as bitter as ice. A shuddered, shocked breath escaped me, a pitiful little sound dying in my throat.

"You…you think I'm a whore," I rasped. "Is that what you're saying?"

His head tilted back slightly, peering at me with narrowed eyes. The cool glare told me exactly what he thought of me. That *gutted* me, that he would think me capable of something like that. As if I was this scheming, manipulative person.

In a low tone, he said, "You're no better than Kamora. At least she was always honest about what she wanted from me."

Something in me broke. And I thought he might've seen it splinter in my eyes because his grip on me loosened, his pupils dilating as his eyes flicked between my own.

I pushed past him, dripping wet and shivering in my clothes —my tunic I might have put on backward, my laces undone on my trews.

"You're not going anywhere," he growled.

I didn't reply. I didn't even put on my boots. I pulled open the front door, a breeze whistling inside, before closing it behind me. I ran down the steps, shock mingling with my own sense of guilt.

I heard him throw back the door, coming after me.

"Amaia, get back here," he called.

Over my shoulder, I saw he was still naked, standing at the bottom of his dwelling as his cold gaze tracked me.

"We're not done," he said.

"No," I said. "I don't want you near me again."

Frustration laced itself into his sharp exhale. "Amaia—"

"Leave me *alone!*"

Then I was running toward the hatchery, the glow of the dome of the incubation room a welcome reprieve in the cold darkness of the night.

I could feel his eyes on me until I reached the hatchery door. When I slipped inside, I crumbled onto the floor. It was there that Syris found me, likely having heard a noise and coming to investigate.

"Amaia?" she breathed. "What's happened?"

"N-Nothing," I said, though it was obvious that it was a lie. Another lie…among many. Alaryk wasn't the only villain here.

And I couldn't quite meet Syris's gaze when I said, "I'd like to sleep here again."

"Of course," she said quietly, her voice tranquil and hushed. I liked that about her. She was calm in the face of uncertainty.

Moak was a fool for seeing past her all this time.

"Come on," Syris said, helping me up. "Your quarters are just as you left them."

CHAPTER 34
ALARYK

I was sitting in the lounge in nearly pitch-black darkness, staring at the empty bed across the way.

My hand was wrapped around an almost-empty goblet of wine. The biggest goblet I had, trying to do anything to dull the sharp ache inside, to mute the rage, to forget the *wrongness* I'd spied in Amaia's eyes, to erase the words that ran on repeat in my mind.

I was exhausted.

I was *fucking* hurt—the familiar feeling of betrayal and loss cutting more than it ever had before. Like shards of glass against my chest, trying to dig straight to my heart.

And all I wanted to do was go after her. Drag her back to my bed, pin her beneath me, and demand that she tell me everything so I could understand *why*. So I could assess if I could get past it. If *we* could get past this.

Because right now I didn't know if I should exile her or demand her as my wife.

I still didn't understand it. I'd caught a merest glimpse, a confession taking shape in her mind when I'd delved my magic deep, in the brief slip before she'd severed the connection. There had been a plan, one that she'd known before coming here. She'd been trying to hide it all this time.

Only Amaia was a terrible liar. I'd already known that, but during the meeting with Sarkin and Vaedrin, I could practically feel it seeping from her flesh.

A sound rose from my chest. One of restless ache and frustration.

Why couldn't she just come to me?

Why couldn't she have just trusted me?

Letting my goblet tumble to the rug, I closed my eyes, squeezing them shut tight, rocking forward to press my hands around my temples.

I'd been inside her mind and felt her raw shock, her wild hurt at what I'd done. For a moment, she hadn't been able to believe it. Struck dumb by my betrayal, that I could be the villain, the threat, one she'd let between her thighs.

I'd *felt* how deeply I'd hurt her. It had mirrored my own pain, my own hurt.

And I'd been the bitter, callous bastard to lash out at her. Her face had paled, her eyes softly vulnerable when I'd implied she was a whore, when I'd said she was no better than Kamora. I flinched even now, standing from the lounge as if I could physically get away from what I'd done, from what I'd said.

But the truth remained…if she'd been capable of lying to me this entire time about a plan she'd had with the *Dothikkar* and the guardsmen…what else had she been lying about?

I'd like to think that her feelings for me had been real and not faked.

But I was so fucked in the head right now, between the confusion, the wine, and the sheer responsibility of what would come next, that it all blurred together.

And maybe I was weak because all I wanted was her back in my bed.

What kind of *Karath* did that make me?

What kind of protector of my own people did that make me? Choosing a potential enemy over them?

I couldn't be in here, staring at the place where she *should* be. I wouldn't be able to stand the smell of her lingering scent because it would only make me ache for her more.

So I stalked from my dwelling, turning down the dark road toward the landing field. The cool air felt good, stinging enough to cool the heat of my flesh. Grymia was quiet, save for the regular patrols I'd assigned. I wound down to the familiar dwelling at the edge of the landing field, one that thankfully *hadn't* burned.

Inside, I found the training bag lined in Elthika scales, and I dragged in a deep breath. My tongue was bitter with wine. But the promise of pain centered me.

And as I struck out at the sand-filled bag, I remembered that damn Hartan witch's prophecy. One I'd thought about more than I cared to admit.

That I would cut out the heart of my first love, before I offered her mine in return.

Years ago, I'd thought that maybe she'd been talking about Kamora. After what I'd forced her to do. But Kamora barely had a shriveled heart to cut out and I'd *certainly* never given her mine as payment.

Now, however...I wondered if she'd been speaking about Amaia all along.

Amaia of Rath Savenal. Who could fit in with any crowd but whose eyes betrayed a deeper loneliness when you got close enough. Who was brave and giving and kind...all things I didn't think she could've faked for a moment.

I loved her temper, her sharp tongue. I loved the way her eyes widened in awe when our magic intertwined, as if I was revealing a hidden world to her, just for us. I loved her determination to learn, to experience everything she could in Grymia, as if at any moment it might be taken away.

It couldn't have *all* been a lie, right? She couldn't have faked what she'd felt for me. I would've known…unless I was the biggest fool in history.

Was I to be cursed in love too?

I slammed my fist into my bag, a guttural sound wrenched from my throat.

I wanted her back.

But I shouldn't.

And none of it mattered anyway. Because I'd broken whatever had been inside her eyes, whatever she *might* have felt for me. I'd watched it shatter into millions of fragmented pieces. Her heart had felt like it was bleeding in my hand as I'd squeezed my fist around it.

My fist connected with the scale-lined bag again and again, the hard reverberation sliding against bone. I nearly sighed in relief.

And I have no one to blame for that but myself, I thought grimly.

CHAPTER 35
AMAIA

In the early hours of morning, I still couldn't sleep, tossing and turning on my firm mattress, which I'd dragged to the floor of my sleeping quarters again.

Belatedly, I'd realized I hadn't minded sleeping on a raised bed with Alaryk. Those nights, as long as his heat had been seeping into my skin and his presence had been strong and certain behind me, I'd felt perfectly content and at peace, lulled to sleep by his even breaths.

A sharp pain in my chest made it hard to breathe, and so I tried to forget, rolling again on my mattress, feeling the hard press of stone just beneath it.

I wondered how much longer it was until dawn. I could get the morning chores done now because I knew that sleep wouldn't come. Maybe it would exhaust me enough so I wouldn't constantly think of Alaryk's magic, like a striking serpent, seeking in my mind. It wasn't the magic that made tears drip down my temple, onto the pillow. It was the betrayal. The shock that he would willingly and knowingly do something that he knew would hurt me.

I'd hidden something from him, yes.

But he'd gone too far.

He'd thought he could control me. Thought he could control me like he'd controlled Kamora.

The realization was heinous. Cutting. It would fester and ache for a long time, especially when my heart had been involved. Especially when he had splintered it apart with a single decision.

Tap, tap, tap.

A series of soft thuds at the window. My breath hitched, and I tilted my neck back sharply to peer through the darkened glass.

Was it him?

I cursed myself for thinking it might be Alaryk. Come to apologize. Come to…take me back to his bed, when all I wanted was to forget that this night had ever happened. I wanted him to wrap me in his arms and tell me that it'd just been a nightmare, that it hadn't been real, that he would've never done that to me or that he didn't think of me as a whore, slipping into his furs for his secrets. That he didn't think I was as wretched as Kamora…a vicious person who'd hurt him, who'd preyed on him, who'd *used* him.

A weak part of me hoped for that. That none of it had happened.

But the face I spied through the glass, cut sharply in moonlight, wasn't Alaryk's.

My heart gave a lurch when I shot straight up, my mind reeling.

Ryak.

He tilted his head, his meaning clear. He was out on the courtyard behind the hatchery. Had likely scaled the half wall.

Dread crept in my belly. For a moment, I debated even going out there. For a moment, I debated waking Tarkosh, who would undoubtedly find Alaryk. Ryak could be captured again tonight.

I could prove my loyalty to the people who I called my friends.

Not to a murderer, who'd threatened my family.

But it was the memory of *that* that had me quietly tugging on my boots by the door…and sneaking out into the hallway, heading toward the bolted door that led to the courtyard. I only prayed to Kakkari that no one was awake at this quiet hour, in the dead of night.

I winced when the door hinges creaked, but I left it open a smidge after I wiggled through the crack.

Ryak was waiting for me beneath one of the trees, away from any of the other hallway windows, just in case someone woke and decided to peer out at the moonlight.

And he wasn't alone.

Nevin was with him.

There was a tightness to Ryak's face, a mottled bruise over his cheekbone that had me thinking his guards might've taken their frustration out on him during his imprisonment.

I felt like I was walking into my own.

"Listen to me carefully," Ryak said, his voice hushed like a whisper but somehow even more frightening. "After I'm done speaking, you will go back inside the hatchery and you will take three eggs."

I stiffened, all the blood rushing from my face as I felt rooted to the stone beneath my feet, unable to move. Behind him, Ny'am seemed to spin.

"One I will carry. The other Nevin will carry. And the third you will carry," Ryak said softly.

I swallowed, my nostrils flaring, panic rising though I tried to keep it from showing. I tried to *think*, willing my sluggish mind to churn.

How could I stop this?

"Ah, ah," Ryak murmured, taking my chin between his fingers, pinching hard enough that I winced. "None of that."

His hand smelled metallic, like blood. When the moonlight flitted over his knuckles, I saw they were raw.

"And don't you dare think of waking your friends," Ryak said.

He looked at Nevin, who grabbed me by my arm and pulled me —roughly—over to the half wall. "Because if you do, we'll finish the job and kill him."

Nevin had me look over the wall. Behind the hatchery, there was nothing to see. No road that led anywhere, only the mountain. And there, half-slumped against the wall I peered over was a dark mass. A familiar figure.

"Brune," I breathed, though it sounded like a whimper in my throat.

His face was bloodied and beaten, some of his clothing torn, like he'd tried to fight back. Maybe the bruise on Ryak's face hadn't been from the guards.

Anger and horror and desperation rose.

"What did you do?" I demanded. Nevin jerked me back around so that I glared at Ryak. "What did you do? Is he okay?"

Ryak's eyes narrowed. "For now. We'll let him return to his little Karag whore if you do what we say without a fight."

I peered back over the wall at Brune and could only feel a spiral of relief fill me when I saw the rise and fall of his chest.

Ryak's tight grip tugged my back, and I gasped.

"Don't waste our time," he growled in my face. "Go get the eggs."

Desperation was rising. "You…you know I can't… It's…"

Ryak let out a sharp exhale.

"They'll die away from the hatchery," I insisted, though it was a half lie. They needed the heat from the starstone, yes, but I knew that they could be transported in the satchels Syris had used during the Elthika attack. "They won't survive the journey."

I assumed that was what this was *all* about.

From the moment that the seed had been planted about the hatchery? When Kiron had mentioned me to the *Dothikkar*?

Had it all been planned, from the very beginning? Had Kiron *known*?

This had always been about the *eggs*. The *Dothikkar* wanted to steal Elthika eggs. And that was what he'd sent his guardsmen here to do.

Ryak's grip on my arm tightened, pulling me more firmly against him. "Go get the *fucking* eggs."

"Just listen to me—"

A sharp crack of pain exploded against my temple, and the breath whistled from my lungs. I registered the cool blood that was already covering Ryak's fists, now smeared against my face.

I whimpered, cradling my face with one hand, hot and throbbing, as I stared at Ryak in shock.

As if he hadn't just punched me—hard enough that my vision blurred—he said, "Go get the eggs, Amaia. If you say another word, I'll tell the *Dothikkar* myself that you're a traitor to your own people. Kiron will be thrown into the dungeons. Your father, your mother…well, they'll be turned from their home, everything stripped from them. They'll be banished to the Dead Lands like the Market District filth they are."

My breath rattled from my throat.

"Don't dishonor your family," Ryak murmured, brushing his thumb against my throbbing face. "Because if you do what the *Dothikkar* wants, he will instead reward them greatly, for raising such an outstanding citizen as yourself."

Hatred burned deep in my gut. Ryak nearly grinned, splitting his deceptively handsome face wide, when he saw it.

I had a choice to make.

To betray the Karag. To commit a crime they saw as comparable to murder itself, to steal Elthika eggs. To betray Syris, Tarkosh, Moak, Ulin. To betray Brune.

To turn my back on Samryn.

To betray Alaryk.

A bitter pain twisted my insides.

Or…I would save my family and Brune's life.

I thought of the shimmering eggs in the incubation room. If I stole them, what future would await them?

A sound came from across the wall. Brune. A gentle groan, a wheezing breath.

"Shut him up," Ryak ordered Nevin.

"Wait," I pleaded.

But Nevin was already jumping over the wall, swinging his legs effortlessly before dropping down to the other side.

I heard the squelch of blood as Nevin hit him, the sound of Brune's head meeting stone, a wet cough tumbling from his lips.

"*Stop*," I breathed, glaring at Ryak through a veil of tears. "Enough. I'll do it. Stop now!"

He help up his hand, and Nevin ceased.

"I'll be right back. But don't touch him again," I hissed.

Ryak tilted his head back in an affirmative. "Be quick. And nothing funny, *pyroki* girl."

I turned on my heel, my gut churning, making saliva pool in my mouth like I would be sick.

I had a choice...but I wasn't strong enough to make the righteous one.

And so, I squeezed back through the courtyard door and slipped into the incubation room, the heat of it feeling suffocating.

I was crying as I gathered the satchels from a cabinet near the door. The same ones we'd used to transport the eggs into the cellar. I figured it was their best chance of survival. I slipped my hands into heat-proof gloves, lined in hatchling scales, and scooped up starstone fragments from one of the empty alcoves, filling the bottoms of each insulated bag as quietly as I could.

If Syris woke...or Tarkosh or Moak or Ulin...Brune was dead. My family would be in danger back in Dakkar. I couldn't afford that, so I worked as quickly as I could with shaking hands, determination feeling like a stone lodged in my breast.

When the satchels were filled, my gaze went to the Ryth-backs. The other egg in the room was a Redback, I'd only discovered recently. I sure as hell wouldn't give that kind of power to the Dakkari. The Rythbacks were the most logical choice.

But even as I stole the eggs from their pedestals in the quiet alcoves, I was still crying. I was thinking of Kyr. All the hatchlings I'd seen break from their shells. I didn't *want* to do this. I wanted to remain here, to finish what I'd begun.

I wanted to see Syris one last time. All my friends.

I wanted to see Alaryk again.

And now I never would.

My vision was blurred when I tied up the bags, making sure the eggs were nestled deep in the starstone. When I straightened, I touched my pendant, hanging around my neck. My most cherished possession, from my family.

As though it was an apology, I tugged the chain from my neck and laid it in one of the alcoves. I hoped that, at the very least, they would know what I was trying to say. How sorry I was. How truly sorry I was.

The firestone in the pendant glowed from the heat. I felt disgusting, my flesh crawling. I felt empty, scraped from the inside out.

It felt fitting. It felt like I'd cut a piece of myself out, that I was leaving it behind here in the Arsadia.

It would be a beacon to whoever woke in the morning first, to find three of the Elthika eggs gone.

CHAPTER 36
ALARYK

I woke to pounding on my door.

When my eyes flashed open, for a brief moment, I didn't know where I was. I stared up at the familiar ceiling of my dwelling, my hand reaching out next to me to find the furs empty.

Fuck.

Reality came flooding back. I felt hungover, like I'd partaken in too much wine on a feast night, my body battered, my fists raw, the flesh shredded.

I must've come back and passed out from the sheer exhaustion. My clothes felt grimy from the sweat, blood dried along my knuckles.

My head pounded, mirroring whoever was at the door.

When I swung my legs over, my strides ate up the distance quickly. I tugged it open with enough force that the hinges nearly broke off, only to find Myzalla's wild expression, the grim set of her mouth.

Immediately, I tensed.

"What's happened?"

"Three eggs from the hatchery have been taken," she reported quickly.

I was already out the door, not even bothering to close it in my haste.

It was still early morning; most of the village hadn't even woken yet.

"Where is she?" I growled, my legs eating up the distance to the hatchery. The morning was brisk. My mouth tasted sour, which mirrored the churn in my gut.

"Gone," Myzalla said quietly, keeping pace.

I didn't know what to think or feel. But I would save my disbelief, my anger, my bitterness for later. I'd been betrayed by a lover before.

How foolish was I to have it happen a second time?

And why did this time feel so much worse?

Because I actually believed she had a kind soul, I knew. *Because I'd actually thought I was falling in love with her.*

Now I had a duty to my people. How many more things would go wrong? First Ryak, then the Elthika attack, and now *this?*

Elysom was already looking for any excuse to null the Heart-stone Accords, to take the *thalara* trees from the Dakkari.

This might be the tipping point into war.

And Amaia…had she really betrayed us all?

It didn't make sense. How could I have been so *wrong?*

Tarkosh's expression mirrored Myzalla's when I saw she was waiting for us at the entrance of the hatchery. She must have woken to the discovery.

"Show me," I said to her.

She inclined her head and led me through the quiet hatchery.

"Does anyone else know?" I asked.

"Syris. She's inside," Tarkosh explained.

Inside the incubation room, the heat was like a wall. Syris was standing, stock-still, a drawn expression on her features as she stared at the remaining eggs.

"Here," Tarkosh murmured, gesturing to three of the alcoves carved into the stone walls. Starstone was still at the base of each small nest, where eggs would've been nestled. "Three Rythbacks are gone. Three satchels were taken," she said, gesturing to a black, open cabinet. "And this…"

She went over to one of the alcoves and plucked something from the starstone. She quickly moved it between her hands, likely hot from the stones.

I held out my hand, a sharp spear of rage going right through me.

When Tarkosh dropped the object into my palm, it was still glowing red. A fire gem, she'd called it. A precious gift from her parents.

She'd left it here.

To…gloat? To stamp her mark on her crime?

Or…was it something else?

"I didn't even know she was here," Tarkosh said quietly, her voice bubbled up with something I recognized as…grief. Because she'd trusted Amaia too. And this betrayal would cut all of them deeply.

"She came here late in the night. To sleep," I answered, my voice sounding hollow, trying to make sense of it all.

Syris was crying, and through her sniffles, she said, "I don't believe she would do this, *Karath*. I just don't believe it."

"People can surprise you with what they're capable of," I answered woodenly. "With what they hide."

I'd experienced it plenty of times. Too many.

It all made sense. It was why she'd made me promise not to use my magic on her. Because she knew she couldn't hide her true intentions for long. I just wanted to know *why*. I just wanted to know if *this* had been the plan all along. To steal the eggs.

Because there was a part of me that echoed and felt Syris's words.

The Amaia I'd thought I'd known…she wouldn't have been capable of this.

"But why would she take the Rythbacks?" Syris asked, turning to Tarkosh, her expression almost pleading. "It doesn't make sense. The Redback is ten times more valuable. She would've known that."

I stared down at the pendant.

No.

Something was wrong. I knew how much this pendant meant to her. She'd never taken it off. Not once. I knew that it was her most cherished possession. So why would she leave it here?

"How was she capable of carrying out three satchels, packed with starstone *and* eggs?" Myzalla asked. "She's strong, but she's not that strong."

"She had help," I answered. "Ryak. Nevin." My head snapped up. "Where's Brune?"

Myzalla said, "I'll go see if he's with Ethrisha."

"Go," I murmured. I turned my gaze to Tarkosh. "Was anything else out of the ordinary this morning?"

"The door to the courtyard," Syris murmured for her hatchery master. "It was unlocked this morning when I woke up. I bolted it myself last night. I know I did."

"Let me see."

So Amaia had left through the courtyard, over the wall. Still, each satchel, loaded down…it wouldn't be easy.

Which meant they couldn't have gotten far.

Outside in the courtyard, the cool morning felt icy with the storm coming. Sarkin had warned me that the system was moving east from Elysom. They'd gotten caught in it as they'd departed the capital.

Ny'am Mountain greeted us through the canopy of the trees planted back here. I walked down the length of stone pavers, looking for anything that might give me more insight into what happened last night.

And I might've missed it entirely—if it hadn't been splattered onto a white stone.

Three droplets of black blood, dried down, next to a tall tree. It was at the back of the courtyard, away from the windows of the living quarters. Beyond the wall led directly into the eastern forest.

I crouched down, looking for anything else.

Blood…it wasn't Amaia's. These drops were black. Hers was red, given her human ancestry.

Relief strummed through me. She wasn't hurt.

What is going on? I thought, frowning when I touched the dried blood. Whose blood was this, if not hers?

I heard something right then.

My head snapped up, holding my breath, the tip of one ear twitching. My brows furrowed, trying to place it.

It sounded like movement, clothes shifting.

Then…a rasping breath.

I rose swiftly, pressing my front to the half wall of the courtyard, peering over it.

"Brune," I growled. I looked over at Tarkosh. "Go get Raran. Hurry!"

I jumped and hurtled myself over the edge of the wall, crouching in front of Brune. His face was bloodied and swollen. His lip split, his eyes closed. His breathing sounded wet, gurgled.

Fuck.

"Brune," I murmured, taking him by the arm, shaking him.

He was alive, but barely.

His one eye that wasn't swollen shut opened, and I saw the red of his iris peer at me.

He made a sound in his throat when he saw me, his single eye flitting wildly.

"It's okay. The healer is on their way," I told him, keeping my voice calm. I heard a gasp from above the wall, saw Syris looking down at Brune, her hand coming up to her mouth, her face paling.

"Go get some water," I ordered her, if only so she wouldn't be sick.

She retreated swiftly with an affirmative squeak, and I turned my attention back to Brune.

His voice was so husky and raw that it sounded like another person's. "He came back…Ryak. Nevin. They…they…"

A rattled wheeze gurgled up from his throat.

"Where's Amaia?" I asked urgently.

Another rasping deep breath. "They were coming here…to use her. To take the eggs."

My nostrils flared, my fist clenching around Amaia's pendant. Brune's grip on my arm was surprising, considering his state.

Hope rose in my chest…but then it was flooded out by cold panic.

"Find her," Brune pleaded. "They'll kill her."

Ice froze my veins, and I rose as I saw Syris skidding back into the courtyard, sloshing a water goblet over her sleeve.

"Where did they go?" I asked.

His eye flitted to the dark brush of the eastern forest. "There," he rushed out. "They're…they're meeting riders."

"Riders?" I growled. Unfathomable. "Mine?"

"Don't…know," came his answer, his breathing labored.

Which meant I didn't have much time to find them…if they were still in the Arsadia. Urgency pressed down on my shoulders.

I needed to find her before it was too late.

"Syris, stay with him," I ordered. "Raran is on her way."

"I will," she said, her tone determined though she looked like she might faint from all the blood as she climbed over the wall, trying to keep the goblet steady.

I didn't wait for another moment, already calling for Samryn in my mind, feeling him awaken as the bond pulled tight between us. There was nowhere for him to land back here, so I raced toward the landing field.

I caught Myzalla on the way.

"Brune's gone too," she breathed, panting as she sprinted back up the hill.

"He's hurt. Beaten," I told her, gesturing back at the hatchery. "Tarkosh is getting Raran, but we have a bigger issue. Brune said riders are helping them. I don't know who."

"On Muron," Myzalla breathed, shaking her head. "Ours? How will we find them before they leave?"

I had an idea, but I didn't know if it would work. Heartstone magic was unpredictable, after all, but it could also feel like a familiar touch. A summoning, just as a bond would.

"Get only our most trusted riders and get them in the sky," I growled. "They cut east through the forest."

Samryn's roar overhead, as he careened through the sky, nearly shook Grymia. If anyone wasn't yet awake, they would be now. The dark clouds in the sky warned of the storm that Sarkin had mentioned to me. The day might be as dark as night soon. I worried about the visibility.

"I'll find her," I told Myzalla.

I only hoped I wouldn't be too late.

CHAPTER 37
AMAIA

When the rain started, it came pouring down over us in sheets. Icy and prickling, it was nothing like the gentle storms in Dothik during the warmer months, when the drizzle felt more like a enveloping fog.

This was a punishing rain, and in no time, it soaked me through to the bone, even beneath the protection of the trees in the thick forest.

I was sandwiched between Ryak and Nevin, in a single-file line as Ryak led the path through the dark woods. The only thing that didn't make my teeth chatter was the hot satchel against my back, keeping the core of my body warm.

My eyes were on Ryak's back, glued to the satchel. They were frustrated that I moved so slowly, but the starstone and the eggs were nearly as heavy as a newborn *pyroki*. Carrying one on your back for hours, with very little sleep and trembling limbs? I was surprised I hadn't collapsed before dawn had broken over the Arsadia.

My head was pounding still from when Ryak had hit me. Every drag of my legs made me want to curl into a ball. I wanted to huddle all the eggs to me, to try to shield them, to protect them. I wanted to return to Grymia. I wanted to wake up beside Alaryk and pretend that he hadn't betrayed me, that I hadn't betrayed him, that we hadn't fought.

I wanted to pretend that I'd never done such an awful, awful thing.

But this was my own punishment, wasn't it?

It was an act—a decision and a treachery against people I had come to love—that would haunt me for the rest of my life. Every day, I would remember this.

I went to grip my pendant, a habit when I was feeling lost, only to feel the bare flesh of my neck. A reminder. Another loss.

"Hurry up," Ryak growled when I fell behind, again.

"I can't go any faster," I panted, nearly doubled over on the trail that wasn't really a trail. Only a temporary one made with Ryak's heavy footsteps, the brush already springing back into shape. Something slimy was crawling along my leg, and I was too tired to shake it off. The rain was making the forest floor as thick as mud. Every step felt like wading into sludge.

My only small victory was that the journey also seemed to tire the guardsmen. I didn't think either had the strength to even take the satchel from me. They needed me to transport it…to wherever we were going.

Ryak looked up at the sky as I caught my breath. "We have to keep moving. They'll know they're gone by now."

I wondered who'd discovered my theft this morning. Was it Tarkosh? Or Syris?

"How much farther did they say?" Nevin asked.

They?

"The edge of the forest cuts away down to a valley," Ryak answered. "I checked it. That's where they'll be."

"Move," Nevin ordered me, finally ending my brief reprieve. The tip of his mud-covered boot prodded the back of my thigh. "Hurry up."

I didn't know how I found the strength to pull my leg from

the muck where I'd begun to sink, but I continued. I wondered about Brune, hoping that he wasn't dead. Hoping that someone would find him quickly. Before we'd left, I'd tried to funnel as much of my magic into him as I could, to try to keep him alive until he was discovered. At least until Ryak had noticed the glow of my eyes.

What would Alaryk think when they found the eggs gone? When they knew it was me who'd done it?

Would he believe that I was truly the treacherous, lying bitch he'd made me out to be last night?

He would be proven right. I wished I could've explained.

Now…I would never see him again. Maybe it was best for both of us that he hated me.

Overhead, I heard the familiar swooping of wings. My heart jolted, my head snapping back. There was an Elthika.

My heart only sank when I realized it wasn't Samryn or an Elthika I recognized. From this vantage I couldn't even tell if it had a rider or if it was wild.

Though I was tempted, and though I thought about it, I knew that if I screamed up for help, it would certainly mean my own death. And I knew that Ryak was a hateful bastard, that he would make good on his promises of ruining my family when he returned to Dothik.

So I bit my tongue, watching the Elthika fly out of view, something shriveling in me at its retreat.

"That's him," Ryak murmured.

Good thing I didn't call out, I thought, my heart swimming in dread.

"We must be close."

They *did* have help from the Karag. The stunning realization made my gut feel like it was coiled tight. There was more happening here than I'd even known.

And that was the first moment when an inkling of doubt began to spread. Was *I* in danger?

Questions raced in my mind on a loop. Until long moments later, I heard the familiar sounds of an Elthika or two and the low murmuring of voices just through the tree line.

The forest finally gave way to a wide, flat, rocky ledge that dropped straight off into a deep valley, just as Ryak had said. I wondered if this was what they'd done since Nevin had broken him out of his prison back in Grymia. Biding their time, looking for an opportunity to get to me. Had they been watching the village? Watching me? How had they not been caught?

There, standing along the sheet of the ledge, big enough for two Elthika to land, were two Karag riders. One I didn't recognize, with long brown hair, partially braided away from his face and steel-gray eyes, but one I did.

Dresnar.

One of Alaryk's own trusted riders. Just yesterday morning, he'd led me to the meeting with Sarkin and Vaedrin. I would've only been more shocked if I'd seen Myzalla herself standing there.

"*You?*" I breathed.

His lips were pressed tight, the flint of his eyes unreadable.

I wasn't thinking when I asked, "But why? He trusts you."

And maybe it wasn't my right, but I felt sinking dread for Alaryk. That one of his own riders, his own friend, would do this to Grymia.

Dresnar stepped forward toward me. He'd been the one riding on Elthika-back, coming from the direction of the village. He took the satchel from me, though his movements were careful, as if he didn't want to disturb the egg.

"Let's not pass judgments on trustworthiness, Dakkari," he replied. I flinched, the words like a dagger.

"We can still stop this. We can leave and return the eggs," I said softly, looking at Dresnar. "I don't know why you're doing this. But surely you know that this will start a *war.*" I cut a look over to Ryak and then to Nevin. "Is that what the *Dothikkar* really wants? He won't win a war with the Karag. It'll be a *slaughter*. Of our own people. We can still stop this!"

"That's not your concern," Ryak answered, his voice a dismissal. "We have our orders."

Dresnar's voice was impatient as he cut a look to Ryak, the satchel securely in his grip. "We need to leave now. They have patrols all over this forest. They found Brune, and he told Alaryk which direction you'd gone."

"*Vok*," Ryak cursed, glaring over at Nevin. "I knew we should've killed him."

The words twisted my belly. Brune's father was a guardsman. They would really kill their own brethren's son? His flesh and blood?

And if they were willing to do that, what were they willing to do to me?

Already Ryak hadn't seemed to have much respect for Kiron. Maybe…maybe I was never meant to come back from the Arsadia.

The thought hit me like I'd run into a pillar of stone.

Maybe I was a liability. A loose end.

I shook myself, thinking I was being silly.

Still, my feet stayed rooted along the forest's edge, watching as Ryak and Nevin kept their satchels on their backs, as Dresnar took my egg and looped the straps over his own shoulders. Nevin cut me the smallest glance. I noticed the brown-haired Karag was watching me carefully.

This was wrong. Everything told me that there was something wrong about this.

"What now?" I forced myself to ask, even as the hair on my arms stood on end, even in the steady rain, which skimmed off my skin in thick droplets.

"Now we go home," Nevin said.

But no one moved.

And that was when I knew I'd made the biggest mistake of my life.

My magic was wiggling in my chest, spurred on by the sudden threat, the icy fear. When my eyes began to glow, Dresnar took a step toward me.

"We can still use her," Nevin said, looking to Ryak. "Her power is rare. The *Dothikkar*—"

"No," the other Karag said. "She's seen our faces."

My heart was pounding, and I took a step back. "You need me," I told Ryak, but I hated that it sounded like a plea. Trying to bide time. "I'm the only one who's worked in a hatchery here. What are you going to do with Elthikan eggs when you get them back home? You don't know what they need, but I do."

"So do they," Ryak said, tilting his head to the Karag.

My gaze flitted to Dresnar. There were four of them. I was already so tired. I wouldn't be able to outrun any of them for very long.

They would kill me, I knew.

But why?

"What did they promise you?"

Dresnar's jaw ticked. He was the only one who looked like he was hesitating, like it disgusted him that he was even here. He didn't *want* to betray Alaryk. So why was he? What was in it for him?

"Your people have mature heartstones. We've only been given the seeds," he replied. "Do you how long it will take for those seeds to grow? Do you know how long it will take until our Elthika are sated again? *Decades.* And as you witnessed yourself from the attack, the wild Elthika will only get more violent. I won't see my people plunged into conflict with them again."

Again?

Understanding went through me.

Ryak had made a deal with these Karag. Maybe it was a deal that the *Dothikkar* had given him license to make. In helping to steal the eggs and transporting them back to Dakkar…they'd be rewarded with mature heartstones.

"And what are you going to tell Alaryk when you suddenly possess a heartstone?" I asked, watching Nevin edge toward me.

"There's one in Ny'am," Dresnar murmured. "That's where I've been, after all. Looking for it after the Elthika attack."

"It belongs in the mountain," I argued. "For Grymia's own Elthika."

"Don't talk to me about what's best for *my* home, Dakkari," he said coolly. "I love my people. I love our Elthika. I won't see Grymia in danger again. And if this is what it takes, to do what others are afraid of doing so that we are safe again, then I'll do it."

"You're stealing Elthika eggs," I breathed, needing to break through to him. "Giving them to a nation who wants to start a war. If he finds out, it'll mean your death."

"Which is why he won't find out," Dresnar said, expression grim.

And suddenly it hit me, as rain pelted against my skin, dripping into my eyes.

That's why I can't live, I realized.

He knew I was close with Alaryk. He knew I'd been forced to do this, that it wasn't my own choice. Dresnar wanted to procure a mature heartstone for his people, the other unknown Karag perhaps wanting the same, and the *Dothikkar* would offer them one as payment for their service, for their crime.

But Dresnar also wanted to return home. Back to his village, back to his people.

He wouldn't be able to do that unless I was silenced. Because if Alaryk ever came to Dothik to find me—for Samryn or for himself—I would give him the name of his rider who'd betrayed him in a heartbeat.

And it would mean Dresnar's death.

"They've seen you too," I told him in a rush, gesturing to Ryak and Nevin. "They aren't exactly trustworthy either."

"We have our own assurances in place," Dresnar said, making my shoulders tighten.

Raw panic flooded my veins, adrenaline pumping through my system. Ryak took a step toward me, edging the Elthika egg satchel off his back slowly.

"Stay back," I told him, though I heard the brittleness in my tone.

"Amaia, we're all going home," he told me. "Stop wasting time."

I wasn't a fool, even though I'd played one up until this very moment.

Ryak took another step toward me—

And I turned and *ran*. As fast as my feet would carry me.

"*Vok*," I heard Ryak curse from behind me. "I'll get her. Just be ready to leave."

And then I heard his body crash through the forest brush behind me.

My heart was pumping madly, thudding in time with my swinging arms as I used them to propel me faster. Sprinting with all my might, with the last of my strength. Because if Ryak caught me, it would mean my death.

Exposed branches and sharp foliage whipped across my face, slicing into my cheek and whacking hard enough against my legs that I knew bruises would bloom there.

The remnants of the makeshift trail we'd made were still evident, but eventually I couldn't see through the rain and I deviated, traveling into the deeper part of the woods, caked mud clinging to my boots, starting to weigh down my legs.

I had no weapon. Nothing I could use to defend myself. Except my magic, but that would only help Ryak, not hurt him.

If only Alaryk were here, came the sudden thought, aching and desperate.

My magic was rising, trailing over my tired body. I was panicked, and I couldn't sever it. My eyes were glowing, lighting me up like a beacon for Ryak in the dark woods. And I could do nothing about it.

He was closing in. I could hear him. Quickly, I looked over my shoulder, seeing the dart of his body through the trees, his eyes pinned on me. He was hunting me down. I shuddered, whipping back around, determined to go faster—

My shoulder slammed directly into the wide trunk of a tree, toppling my balance, sending me careening into another. My face hit the rough bark. I heard a crunch—the bone of my nose —as pain exploded, the warm trickle of blood running over my lips.

I made a sound, dazed, staring up at the tree that had felled me.

Get up, I thought.

Desperately, I scrambled on the ground, my hands sinking into mud and muck as I tried to rise. I ignored the pain and the blood. I needed to get *away*. Could I make it all the way back to Grymia?

I didn't think so, but I had to *try*.

I had just gotten off the ground, had just started to run again, when I felt him lunge for me.

I cried out when his body crashed into mine, heavy and unyielding like a boulder.

He sent me flying back to the ground, the force of the impact and his weight sucking the air from my lungs. I hacked and choked, trying to breathe again.

Ryak flipped me around, using his weight to keep me pinned as I desperately struck out, trying to dislodge him. It was strangely quiet in the woods. Just the sound of rustling clothes and flesh on flesh as I tried to get him off.

I felt the squeeze of his hand around my throat.

No.

I gripped at his hands with mine, raking my nails across the flesh, thrashing my legs to try to get him off. I was tall and strong…but for someone like Ryak, a trained warrior, cutthroat and ruthless, he barely budged.

Pinpricks sparked in my vision. I couldn't breathe. The pressure on my throat was crushing. I thrashed my fist out since I didn't have the strength to pry his hands away from my neck. My punch connected, but there was no force behind it. I tasted blood, dripping from my broken nose. My eyes felt tight in my skull, the air depleting, the panic rising.

But his face was lit up from my eyes, bright enough that I could see every pore, every drawn line, every scratch, and the color of his bruises. I hoped they were from Brune.

I thought of my mother, my father. Kiron. I wondered what they would tell them, what lies they would spin. I wondered if Kiron could keep them protected. Because I hadn't been able to.

My hand grappled along the ground as my vision darkened. My lungs felt so squeezed, like shriveled, deadened things. I hated that the last thing I'd see was Ryak.

Then I felt a familiar touch against me. Warm and seeking.

I thrashed.

Alaryk.

His magic. He was close!

My hand found the curved edge of a stone, jagged on one end and perfect. Another chance. In the sky above me, I saw a flash of red. Red scales.

Samryn.

And if I was going to die, then I would rather Samryn be the last being I saw in this life.

I tried to cry out. He was right there. Alaryk had come. He was looking for me. Or looking for the eggs. But no sound came.

I gripped the rock tight, and with the last of my strength and will, I hefted my deadened and tingling arm up…and I struck Ryak on the side of his temple. As hard as I could.

His hands loosened, a rough curse sounding. I took advantage, dragging in precious, cold air through my bruised, aching throat, choking on rain drops. It felt like I'd swallowed blades. I was dizzy, the forest swirling, and I tried to crawl away, to put distance between us.

"You *vokking* bitch," he roared.

My magic was flooding now. I couldn't cry out for Alaryk, but he would feel my magic. I was certain of it.

Ryak's hand gripped my ankle, and he tugged hard. My front thumped to the earth, my jaw snapping, and I bit my tongue, a sharp pinch, more blood.

He must've risen because the swift kick that he landed into my abdomen made me wheeze and hack. Before I could drag in another breath, he landed another. And another.

I caught a glimpse of him. His eyes so dark they were black. The extent of his rage was terrifying, the monster beneath capable of anything. I understood now what it was that Gethrin Osa had seen that day on the landing field. What Brune had seen.

He will kill me, I knew. *And he will like it.*

Alaryk's magic was sinking in my chest. I grasped at it, a lifeline, tucking it inside me like it was something I was trying to protect. I curled into a ball as Ryak continued to kick me with all his strength. I heard bones cracking, sharp pain that made me want to stop breathing.

He turned me over with his boot. I tried to lift my arms but couldn't. I tried to fight back, but I was so tired, my body battered.

There was blood running into his eye from his temple.

At least I drew his blood before he killed me. That brought a sense of satisfaction.

And maybe he saw that realization in my eyes when he stared down at me. Because I saw that rage deepen.

When his fist connected with my face, it was sharp and oddly dull-sounding. A *thump* of flesh and bone. My heart was racing in my ears, and Alaryk's magic was bundled inside me.

And when Ryak became even more violent, I retreated

inward. I pressed into Alaryk, letting the warm current soothe me as I gritted my teeth and felt some of them loosen from the brute force of Ryak's punches.

"*Vokking* bitch," Ryak hissed. "Don't you dare look at me like that. Red-blood Market District filth!"

Hold on for me, came Alaryk's voice, sharp and clear in my mind. And instead of being frightened, I reached for him like I was wrapping my arms around his energy, trying to guide him to me. *I'm here,* mariss.

I closed my eyes because it was too difficult to keep them open.

Stay with me, Amaia, came Alaryk's command, urgent.

Another hit came. It sounded like a wet squelch. I couldn't feel anything anymore. I wondered if that was because of Alaryk's magic or because my body was shielding it. All I knew was that I was tired. So very tired. I wanted to sleep.

That was when I felt something I'd never felt before with Alaryk. A rushing of power, hurtling and forming into the sharpened end of a blade, like it was about to strike. The length of his strength, the sheer magnitude of it, was surprising.

Order him to stop, Alaryk told me. *Use me, Amaia.*

I couldn't speak. Could only think the command, envisioning the spear of magic cutting straight through Ryak.

The sounds stopped. When I managed to open one of my swollen eyes, I saw Ryak had stopped, as though he were bound, his eyes bulging with confusion, frustration.

I could feel the brief flash of Alaryk's relief. Through my dim vision, I saw Samryn circle back around, having pinpointed where I was. Nowhere to land here…and I swore I saw a figure leap off his back, the white flash of his hair illuminated by a lightning strike in the sky, the rolling roar of thunder like an Elthika's warning.

I focused on my breath as Ryak hovered over me, trying to break past the bonds of Alaryk's magic.

I could feel his presence, sprinting through the forest, wherever he'd landed. He'd jumped off Samryn to reach me.

I'm sorry, I thought, tears mixing with my blood. *I'm so sorry, Alaryk.*

Stay with me, mariss, was his only response.

He entered the clearing. I saw the glowing blue of his eyes first, his nostrils flaring when he saw me, a brief flit of shock, which steadily turned into his own form of rage, carefully coiled and ready to strike.

I wondered what he saw. I wondered what I looked like.

Alaryk, the eggs, I thought, thinking maybe I'd spoken out loud, but my tongue wasn't working. *They have them. Dresnar—*

Alaryk unsheathed a long dagger from his riding vest.

A weight was lifted from my body, Alaryk plucking Ryak off like he was nothing.

All I heard was the whistle of a blade, followed by the shocked gurgle dripping from Ryak's throat. I saw his body slump forward, Alaryk's eyes on mine over his shoulder, his dagger deep in the Dakkari guardsman's belly. His arm moved. Twisting. Making it hurt.

Then he shoved Ryak away. He dropped close by, limbs sprawled, eyes staring unseeing, frozen in his last expression of shock.

Dead.

Alaryk dropped onto his knees beside me in the mud as Samryn roared overhead. His hands shook when he took mine. I could feel his anger, carefully honed by his shock. A maelstrom of emotions that washed through me.

His magic rose, like a sparking of flint, and all I felt was peace. There was no pain.

I'm glad it's you, I thought, my fingers finding his wet hand. *You're all I wanted to see.*

Then I remembered nothing at all.

CHAPTER 38
ALARYK

A hand came to my shoulder, breaking my gaze away from Amaia.

I frowned, and when I turned my neck to regard the intruder, it felt stiff.

Myzalla was looking at me, concern etched deep into her expression. Not for Amaia, but for me.

"Tarkosh said the eggs look healthy," she reported. "They're back in the incubation room. Safe."

I cleared my throat, my eyes returning to Amaia. To her chest, specifically. The way it rose and fell, the only thing that loosened the fist around my heart.

"Good" was all I said.

"Dresnar—"

"Don't," I murmured. "Not now."

Myzalla sat on the edge of the bed where Amaia lay.

"We don't have the luxury to wait," Myzalla said. "We have both being guarded. But Sarkin should know that one of his own riders has betrayed us all. Let me send a missive to Elysom. He's still there. Let him come and take away his rider, so we can deal with ours."

"Fine," I rasped. The tangle of politics, of hard decisions, weaved in my mind…and right then, I didn't have the stomach for it as I usually did.

Not when Amaia had been so badly beaten that she was hardly recognizable. Not when I could still see her, *feel* her, in my mind, battered and bloodied and full of sorrow. Her death had been a certain thing in her mind…and because *she* had been so certain, it had stamped itself into mine, and I couldn't shake it. The rain had been so cold, and though it had been hours since I'd discovered her lying in her own blood in the forest…I couldn't get warm.

I'd done something I never thought I'd willingly do again. With Samryn, it had been inevitable.

But Amaia had been close to death. In that singular moment, clarity had struck. I knew I'd rather be part of her for the rest of my life than lose her forever. Otherwise she would've gone where I could not have followed.

"Why don't you go bathe?" Myzalla's voice came. My brow furrowed, and I wondered how long the silence between us had been. "I'll watch over her."

I looked down at myself. I was still in my riding vest. Caked in mud and forest sludge and blood, dried down so that it felt like plaster, splintering off me whenever I moved.

Syris had been here shortly after we'd returned to Grymia. It had been Syris who'd cleaned Amaia's face. Her friend had sniffled, tears rolling down her cheeks, as she'd swiped the cloths across her skin, dirtying the basin with enough blood to need it refilled three times. Raran had come, but she'd said there was nothing she could do except try to reset the bones that had been broken.

Amaia could heal herself if I fed her my magic…but she wouldn't wake. Nothing would wake her.

"Alaryk," Myzalla murmured, catching my attention. "Go clean yourself up. I'll be here."

I rose from the chair I didn't remember dragging up to the bed. My eyes flickered to the *sersa* pot, the dark smoke rising from the small ember burning the powder. My mother had once believed it kept away death. And while I didn't believe that, *sersa* smoke had been proven to keep the lungs clear and to strengthen the body, to help fight off sickness and disease. It had been used all throughout Harta for centuries. I always kept a store of it, even now, so many years after my mother had died. I always purchased more when I was back in my birthland.

In my bathing pool, I scrubbed off the mud, remembering the events that had come after I'd found Amaia, in brief flashes. I remembered the cooled rage as I'd raced to the open clearing where Samryn could land, with a bloodied Amaia in my arms. Myzalla and two of my riders had already been there, having caught Nevin, Dresnar, and Sarkin's rider from Sarroth. When I'd appeared on the ledge, Dresnar had emptied the contents of his stomach, narrowly missing Myzalla's boot, and Nevin's face had paled, though he'd never taken his eyes off Amaia.

And that had made me even angrier.

My magic had been swift and sharp. I'd ordered Nevin to jump off the cliff, a steep drop into the valley below. He couldn't even scream on the way down, and Sarkin's rider had started to piss himself when I'd turned my glowing gaze to him.

Myzalla, however, had stopped me before I'd dealt with the Karag myself. She'd told me to get Amaia back to Grymia, to get her to Raran.

Even now, after my mind had cooled, I still wished she *hadn't* stopped me. It would have taken me *seconds* to kill both of them. Hesitation had gotten me here. I should've executed Ryak the night I'd returned from Elysom. Maybe then this wouldn't have happened.

We'd retrieved his body from the forest. And since Nevin's body was at the base of the eastern valley…I would send Ryak's back to the *Dothikkar* with a letter of my own.

Across my magic, I tested Amaia's again, only to feel a cold wall.

After I bathed and dressed in clean clothes, I returned to Myzalla. She was still in the same spot, and she met my eyes when I appeared.

"You care for her," she said. "Truly."

I didn't think I needed to respond to that.

She sighed. "This will mark her, Alaryk. Always."

"I know," I replied.

Myzalla meant in Grym. Among my people. Amaia's actions would always be whispered about, no matter what good she did here. The theft would follow her, no matter what the circumstances had been. With time, it would lessen. I knew that first-hand. Shortly after I'd become *Karath*, shortly after what I'd done in Harta had spread throughout my own people, no one would meet my eyes anymore. It had taken years, but eventually they had.

It would pass.

My people would learn to accept her again. Because I didn't intend to let her go.

Myzalla knew that. She could see that clearly. Her words were meant as a small warning, nothing more. But she knew my mind was made up.

All of this was dependent on if Amaia woke again, I knew.

It didn't matter if she hated me when she did. I'd said horrible things to her when I'd seen her last, betrayed her trust, done the *one* thing I'd promised not to do. It had made me a villain in her mind. It had broken something in her. I'd seen it fracture. I felt that realization go through me, even now, like a cold wind.

Had I broken her completely, though?

All I knew was that we had two injured Dakkari and two dead Dakkari. We had a nation across the seas that might've just sparked a war, a swift punishment necessary on the heels of a foolish king's greed and lust for power.

"Whatever comes, I'll stand by you," Myzalla told me.

The words made my throat tighten.

"I don't ask you to," I told her.

She scoffed, standing from the bed when I took my place back in the chair. "I don't need you to," she replied.

With that, she left. And I reached forward to take Amaia's cold hand. I pressed my warmth into her, spreading my magic like a blanket, in hopes it might root itself.

Maybe it was a fruitless effort, but I'd keep trying nevertheless.

We were bonded now.

I had bonded my magic to hers in the forest.

To save her life, I'd made that unthinkable choice for both of us as lightning had flashed and rain had battered down on our bodies.

She might hate me for that, too, when she woke.

And if she died…I would feel the loss of her forever.

CHAPTER 39
AMAIA

For a brief moment, when I thought my eyes had opened only to find darkness, I feared that I'd gone blind. I blinked, pain and panic surging forward.

My whole body felt like one big *ache*. Throbbing and pulsing. At least I wasn't dead. Because if death felt like this…I'd feel cheated.

I must've made a sound because a warm bulk next to me moved. I reached out, skimming my hand along solid flesh.

That was when I saw it. A little blue glow next to a bed, a familiar smoke rising from a small ember in the pot. And as my eyes adjusted, though they still seemed dim, I saw Alaryk's eyes begin to glow in the darkness.

"Amaia," he breathed, a relief so strong in his voice that it almost trembled. My throat felt tight with that singular word, and my eyes started to tear up.

His magic flowed into me, and I grasped it. I felt him flinch, a deep ragged breath torn from him, which I thought was strange. But I used his magic, as we'd always done, to heal my body. Like a parasite, I fed off him…but he only gave willingly.

The forest returned to me in flashes. Ryak. The flash of his fists, the sickening sounds. Samryn, with glittering scales. Alaryk, the whisper of a dagger. Brune—

I sucked in a breath. "*Brune.* The eggs."

They are safe, Alaryk told me, his voice clear. *All of them.*

I was too relieved to realize that he hadn't spoken at all.

I felt bones crack, the sound startling. Despite the sharp pain at first, the pinch slowly faded into nothingness. My body was resetting itself, the bones snapping back into place. So many had been broken—my ribs, an arm, my cheekbone, collarbone, nose. I wanted to scream, but no sound came.

I kept my gaze on Alaryk, and with every snap, I felt the flare of anger within him though his expression never changed. He wanted to kill Ryak all over again. He wanted to kill him again for every time a bone had been broken. Every time he'd marked me, every time he'd made me bleed.

The length of Alaryk's anger and need for vengeance was staggering. What shocked me even more was that I could *feel* it. It intertwined with my own sense of relief, my own sense of sorrow. So vastly different, and yet they all melded together until it felt like one big wound between us, gaping and raw.

I almost lost you, he told me. His eyes glowed brighter, nearly blinding. *Never again.*

Tentatively, his hand reached forward to skim over my healing face. There was a rawness in him, like the scraping of bone, when he looked at me. I felt the surge of affection, the need to protect me, the sheer unfathomable relief he felt.

"What's happening?" I asked, confused, my voice rasping and husky, like I'd been wailing for days on end.

I felt his emotions retreat until they were dulled enough to be mistaken for my own.

"Heal, *mariss,*" he murmured, his voice richer, his breath floating over my skin. His lips pressed to my temple, where I remembered Ryak splitting the skin.

In his arms, I was cocooned by warmth and memory and

magic. I closed my eyes, feeling Alaryk radiate like starstone. My hand came up to my neck out of habit. The cool touch of my pendant made me want to sob. Someone had returned it to me. And I longed for my home, for my family. Would I forever be torn between two places now?

I will bring them to you, Alaryk said, *so you don't have to miss them, Amaia.*

I slept again.

When I woke next, it was to warm oranges and pinks. Sunset. The bed was empty, and my body felt…better. So much better. Enough that I had the strength to push up in bed. I went dizzy, sucking in a breath as the dwelling swayed. There was a metallic taste in my mouth, and my head pounded something fierce. But I was dressed in one of Alaryk's soft, clean tunics, and there was a large jug of water next to the bed.

A small gasp came. I looked over, only to see Syris rising from the dining table, where she'd been sitting. My hand froze, half stretched out for the goblet, as a tumult of emotions flooded my mind.

"Syris," I breathed.

"Oh," she said, racing for me. There were tears shimmering in her eyes, and she was gentle with her embrace, though it was tight.

I didn't know what to feel, but I didn't feel like I deserved her kindness.

"I'm sorry," I whispered into her hair. "I'm so sorry."

Syris didn't say anything, only pulled back when I gave a small wince. My back muscle pulled tight from the strange position.

"You're here," she said, giving me a wobbly smile. "That's all that matters, all right?"

"How is Brune?" I asked quickly.

"Recovering," Syris answered. "Ethrisha has been by his side night and day. You look better than he does."

I struggled to get out of the bed. "I'll go to him now and help—"

"No, you need to rest," she said firmly, pushing me back. "He's fine."

I saw the determined set in her shoulders. Alaryk had probably told her to keep watch and to keep me here.

"And the eggs," I said quietly. "They're safe?"

"Yes," she replied, her smile dying. "The eggs were recovered. Ryak and Nevin are dead." I flinched, remembering the shock on Ryak's face, though his eyes had been lifeless. *What happened to Nevin?* I wondered. "The other two…Sarkin collected his rider for trial. As for Dresnar…he was executed yesterday."

I blew out a breath of disbelief.

I'm sorry, I thought again, though I knew she wouldn't want to hear it.

"I—I…"

But I didn't know what to say. How to explain it. That I had been sent to betray their trust, that I'd told Ryak how many eggs the hatchery had, that I'd promised I would tell him anything he'd wanted to know.

But Syris placed her hand on my arm and said, "Brune told us everything."

"Everything?"

She nodded.

"About what the *Dothikkar* wanted us to do?"

She took a deep breath. "Brune said Ryak and Nevin threatened him. That your king would throw his father into the dungeons and persecute his mother if he didn't do what they wanted."

So…he had been threatened too.

"I'm assuming they did the same to you?" Syris asked softly. Gently. Carefully.

"Yes," I whispered. "Alaryk knows?"

She nodded.

"How long have I been asleep?"

"Nearly a week," she answered. "You woke for the first time a couple nights ago and managed to start healing yourself with Alaryk's help. But you've been asleep since then."

I nodded.

"I must say," Syris murmured, her yellow eyes tracking over me, "your magic truly is remarkable, Amaia. You'd never be able to tell…"

"What?"

Her brow furrowed. A flash of despair, so brief that I thought I imagined it, crossed her features. "I couldn't even recognize you. When he brought you back that night."

My belly tightened.

"I'd never seen anything like it before. How someone could do that to another person."

My eyes filled with unushered tears, my throat tightening.

"Looking at you now…it's like it never happened," Syris finished, wiping at her cheek, sniffing. "I couldn't believe my eyes when I walked in here this morning."

"You should be at the hatchery, not tending to my bedside," I told her.

"Alaryk wanted a familiar face here if you woke while he was gone," she informed me. "Tarkosh understands. They're all busy, but they'll make do."

"Does she hate me for it?" I couldn't help but ask.

"Of course not. But…she'll come around," Syris answered, making me bite my lip.

"I have to go home anyway," I told Syris. She frowned. "I don't know what will happen now that Ryak and Nevin are dead.

I'm worried about my family, about Kiron. I need to leave. And soon."

You're not going anywhere, came Alaryk's voice, deep and certain in my mind. I gasped, memory pushing to the forefront.

"What is it?" Syris asked.

Just then, I heard the thud of boots on the stone stairs outside before the heavy door was pushed open.

Alaryk stood on the threshold, looking like he'd been sprinting here, his breath a little heavy. When he stepped into the dwelling, Syris rose.

"Thank you, Syris," he murmured, holding the door open for her, his intention clear.

My friend looked back at me, inclining her head. "I'll see you soon," she assured me. "Rest."

I nodded, watching her slip past Alaryk's wide berth until she disappeared out the door. The light of the setting sun flooded in, but curiously, Alaryk kept the door open.

"I want to take you to Ny'am," he told me. He pressed his pointer finger into the pot beside his bed, which had once been filled with blue powder but now lay nearly depleted. "I've used up all the *sersa* powder, and I think the heartstone will help you."

I shook my head. "Alaryk—"

"Can you stand?"

"There's so much we have to talk about," I breathed.

"Then we'll talk there," he replied, voice determined. When I didn't move to stand, he plucked me from the bed himself, and I gripped onto his shoulders in surprise, though I knew he wouldn't let me fall.

"Seems I don't have a choice," I murmured.

His face was unreadable.

"No, you don't."

Then we swept out of the dwelling, and Alaryk closed the door with his foot. Luckily this area of Grymia was away from the hustle and bustle of the village's center. The only other things back here were the hatchery and a few scattered dwellings, so no one was around to see Alaryk carry me toward the mountain.

The shade of it felt cool, sliding over my skin. Though I was only in a tunic, my skin felt hot. The shade felt like a relief, which was only deepened when Alaryk guided us to the familiar cavern entrance, hidden in the rock face, and down the narrow stone stairs we'd once traveled together. Alaryk said nothing, and even though the darkness enveloped us, I didn't mind it, only pressing my hands into his shoulders harder.

The cavern looked more brightly lit in the light of the setting sun, casting rays of gold and pink to illuminate the dark stone and blue, trickling water.

Like before, I felt the heartstone magic skim across my flesh —a whisper, a summoning. I felt it so much easier now, as if my entire body was tuned to it, anticipating it.

In a way, it felt like sinking into a hot bath after a long day. A comfort. A relief.

Alaryk had been right to bring me here.

Along one of the stone walkways, toward the center of the cavern, there was a series of crumbled pillars that appeared to have once made a ring around the landing. Perhaps a pavilion. Alaryk brought me to one, toppled onto its side, the small slab a perfect bench. The pillar was cool beneath me, and I gazed up at Alaryk, a thousand unspoken things between us that seemed dammed up in my throat.

Instead of untangling them, I remained silent.

It was strange being so close to him again. Strange and achingly familiar. So many hurts and so many apologies and so many wants jumbled in my brain.

He went to his knees before me so that he wasn't looming, until our eyes were level with one another's.

His hand came to my unmarred cheek as Syris's words returned to me. I could almost hear his thoughts. He'd seen me like that too. Beaten so badly that my features weren't familiar.

I said the only thing I could think to say.

"I'm sorry."

"Don't," he replied. His hand skimmed over my cheek.

"Alaryk—"

"I bonded our magic together."

At first I thought I hadn't heard him correctly.

"What?" I whispered, my brow furrowing.

"You were dying," he said. I felt the sharp cut of grief pierce my mind. *His,* I realized. "And I couldn't lose you. So the choice became a simple thing."

"You told me you never wanted to bond with anyone," I said. "That it would…it would mark you forever."

Because it was like a piece of your soul was willingly given to another. You would never be whole again. Always…fractured.

He…he'd saved my life? But he'd made that choice for the both of us. I didn't know how to feel about that.

"We can still break it, can't we?" I asked, remembering what he'd said once.

He shook his head. "Even if I wanted to, it's latched itself and it'll hold. Can't you feel it?"

Even if he wanted to?

"What…what does this mean?"

His forehead came to my own. And he didn't have to say anything. I felt it.

He wanted me to remain at his side.

Always.

I gasped.

"I know there's much I have to make amends for," he murmured to me, his brows drawn. "I've made so many mistakes with you. But I want to start new. With no secrets between us."

My vision went blurry.

"Because there can't be now," I whispered, so incredibly torn and confused. My temple throbbed. "You're in my head now. You'll see everything, feel everything. I—I didn't ask for this."

"I know," he growled, his grip tightening. "And I'm sorry for forcing this on you. But Amaia, I *saw* you. I *felt* you in that forest. I felt your resignation, your realization of your death. Your grief for your family. I felt the pain. I felt your magic, reaching for me. And I reached back because I *couldn't* lose you. Ever."

My lips parted, hearing the rawness in his voice. The turmoil.

"I made a choice," he continued, voice guttural. "Perhaps a selfish one. But I made it only with the purest of intentions toward you. To save you. There wasn't anything malicious about it. The answer was clear, and I chose it."

I looked down at my palms spread open in my lap. Alaryk took them in his, his hands so big they completely enveloped mine. His lips brushed my cheek.

"You know what I did," I found myself murmuring. "You know what I did, and you still choose this?"

"Yes," he said without hesitation.

"Why?"

"Because I love you, Amaia."

I sucked in a sharp breath, reeling back so I could look him in the eye. He said the words so casually, so matter-of-factly.

But I didn't need to see his face to feel the truth of his words ringing through the bond. Molten and warm, they flowed through me like a river current, washing away my own doubts.

"You do," I whispered. Not a question. An acknowledgment.

His smile was wry. "And I never thought I'd say those words."

Except to his mother, who'd long passed, I knew. I could hear what went unspoken. And even then, she'd been a difficult female, one who'd rarely expressed her own emotions.

My lips parted, knowledge that I shouldn't have had being recognized as truth. *This* was the power of the bond.

"There was a Hartan witch that my mother consulted, shortly before we left my birthland," Alaryk told me. "The witch said that I'd become a king in my own right...but that I would forever be torn between three worlds—Harta, Karak, but the third... I know what she meant now."

My heart squeezed. I heard his answer reverberate between us. "Us," I whispered.

"Our bond," he said. "A world of our own making. One that will anger many, but one that will make us all stronger."

"I don't want to be your burden," I told him. "I know what I've done, Alaryk. One of the highest crimes someone can commit in Karak. I'm not hiding from that. I know what your people will demand."

"And you think I have it in me to kill you?" he asked, a spark of his temper igniting the bond. "How could you ever think that?"

"I didn't say you would do it," I amended. "I *know* you wouldn't. But you are also a king to your people. You answer to them too. You would look weak if you let me stay. That's why I have to go back. One reason of *many*."

The refusal was in his mind.

"There's no going back, Amaia," he said. "For either of us."

That was what I feared.

"My family—"

"Don't worry about them," he told me. "I've handled it."

My brow furrowed. I didn't even realize I did it, but I dove into his mind, trying to find the answers I sought. And most surprising of all, he let me.

His mind was a beautiful tangle, one like the chaos of Samryn's curse, but one that was inherently *him*. Sharp but gentle, cutting enough that it bordered on ruthlessness, but driven to do right by his people. To make Grymia *better*, to keep the peace, even if it meant he had to be merciless.

He held himself to the highest standard. Unrelentingly. And I wanted to embrace him, because no one could sustain that for long. Though Alaryk had...for nearly all his life.

And in his thoughts, he projected what I wanted to know.

That he'd sent Myzalla herself and proven, loyal riders of Grymia to fly to Dothik. To deliver Ryak's body, a warning to the *Dothikkar* himself…but to also…

I gasped.

"You're bringing them here?" I asked.

"And Brune's family as well," he said. "He told me everything. Their lives were at risk. Your *Dothikkar* has proven to be unpredictable. So until we can decide what needs to happen next, I thought it best that they come here. They'll be safe here."

I couldn't believe it. Couldn't believe that I might see my family soon. *Here* in Karak.

But what about our home? My mother's friends? Their *lives*?

And Kiron…what would he have to say about all of this?

And what if something went wrong trying to get all of them out of the city?

"I have it all handled," Alaryk assured me. "Don't worry."

My mind was spinning, but I felt his influence. Calming me down. I dragged in a deep breath…and let myself sink into him. Gently, hesitantly at first, until I just let go.

Alaryk's arms came around me as he soothed me from the inside out. As Ny'am's lost heartstone pulsed with life. Somewhere near. Somewhere hidden.

Which made me remember…

"You executed Dresnar," I whispered. "I'm sorry you had to do that."

He tensed. In my mind's eye, the flash came. Of Dresnar's bowed head, Grymia in attendance, his Elthika circling overhead. The flash of his own blade, black with blood.

My chest squeezed.

"He made his choice," Alaryk murmured.

So did I, I couldn't help but think.

His arms tightened. "No, it's different."

"Is it?" I wondered. I breathed him in. "I was trying to protect my family. Dresnar was trying to do the same."

For a heartstone. To protect Grymia. To help the Elthika.

"And he was willing to murder you himself if it meant he could get away with it," Alaryk finished. I flinched. Because that *had* been the difference. A pretty stark difference at that.

"You're right," I said.

"He'd wanted the mountain searched time and time again. But the heartstone doesn't want to be found. And our Elthika need it here. He never understood that," Alaryk said. "Even still…I never expected him to betray us like this."

It had cut him—and his riders—deep. All of them had been in attendance at Dresnar's execution, stone-faced. They'd been his friends, his allies.

"But you never really know someone," he said.

That's not true, I thought, deep in his mind. Because here, there was nowhere to hide, nowhere to run.

He huffed out a small breath. "You're right, *mariss.*"

Would I ever get used to this?

I wasn't certain.

"This is a lot, Alaryk," I whispered. "Too much."

I pulled away, catching the way his lips pulled down. I pressed my hand to my forehead to keep the quiet cavern from spinning.

"You don't want this," he murmured. Because he could *feel* it.

"It's not that," I said. And because I didn't know *how* to express all the thoughts fighting and pushing and pulling at each other in my mind, I imagined inviting him inside it so he could decipher it for himself. Letting go so everything could be revealed to him all at once.

It was because he'd told me he loved me. It was because I'd just woken after a guardsman had nearly beaten me to death— Alaryk huffed out a deep breath at that one.

It was because my family was in danger and that they were having to leave their entire lives behind because of me. It was that Dresnar had been executed. It was that I'd been sent here to spy on the Karag, that I'd stolen eggs that I'd only ever wanted to protect, that I'd seen Brune bloodied and slumped against a wall, and that the cavern was whispering to me. It was my raw guilt, the friends I'd hurt, the trust I'd broken.

It was *that night.*

The night Alaryk had used his magic as a *weapon* against me, a choice that he'd known would hurt me when I had been most vulnerable. And he hadn't cared. He'd compared me to Kamora, one of the most vile people he'd ever known, who'd taken so much from him, who'd cursed Samryn.

"Amaia," he growled. I felt the rise of his own grief when he discovered that.

It was just too much.

I just wanted it to *stop.*

Alaryk's breath evened out. His head slumped down onto my shoulder, his forehead pressed to the exposed skin there.

"All right, *mariss,*" he murmured.

And just like that, I felt the connection sever, making me shiver.

I was…my own again. My mind was my own. Alaryk was *gone.*

"I can keep it controlled, for both of us," he murmured. In assurance, I realized when I gazed at him wide-eyed. *Relieved.* "Until you decide what you want."

"You'd do that?" I asked.

"Anything you ask," he told me. "Because I know what I want. For the first time in my life, it's a decision *I* want to make, not one that was chosen for me. But I realize that I've never given you the opportunity to decide the same for yourself."

It was almost on instinct, me reaching out my magic toward him. But it was met by a cold wall, and I wondered if he could even feel it.

Oddly, it felt like a loss.

"Take the time you need," he murmured. "I'll be here when you decide. I promise."

CHAPTER 40
AMAIA

My room at the hatchery was quiet, the single candle that was flickering on the table less bright than my pendant, which I'd worked up to a solid red glow.

I was lying in bed—which I'd kept on its frame instead of dragging the bedding to the ground—staring up at the ceiling.

I sighed, letting the silence sink deep. But it was better. I realized that it wasn't a terrible thing to be alone here, alone in one's own mind, alone in one's own thoughts. The silence wasn't quite so pressing, so threatening as it had once been.

I realized now that maybe I'd been afraid of the silence because I'd been afraid of my own thoughts. I'd been afraid to confront the fact that I'd come to Karak on false pretenses. My being here had been a lie from the very beginning. To my friends and to myself.

But now…I'd done the unspeakable. Syris had forgiven me. Moak and Ulin were coming around. Tarkosh had agreed to let me return to the hatchery at Alaryk's request, though beyond asking me if I was recovered, we'd barely spoken. Ever since I'd come back a couple nights ago, she'd taken to locking the incubation and the nesting rooms. She was the only one with the master key. Not that I could blame her. Every time I heard her lock it, I felt my gut twist, mirroring the turn of her key.

I'd made a mess of everything. Nothing had gone right.

And yet…it wasn't the end of the world. I was still *here*.

I was wading through the muck and aftermath of my decision, taking on the consequences in my own way.

Perhaps a part of me was punishing myself by staying away from Alaryk. The situation between us was too complicated to untangle. I didn't trust him. He didn't trust me. And yet he'd decided to choose me. To work through it. Together.

I hated that I was afraid to make that leap with him. Part of me was still hurt by what he'd done. The other part thought I didn't deserve him. It was one big mess in my mind.

So what had I done?

I'd taken time. I'd returned to the hatchery, resuming my duties. Most of the time, I just ended up watching over the hatchlings in the courtyard, very aware that Tarkosh would come more frequently to check up on me.

I'd thought keeping myself busy would help me feel more normal after what had happened. But all it'd done was highlight how *other* I truly was. How quickly I'd healed, how quickly I tried to smile at people who didn't trust me anymore, how often I looked toward the sky, hoping my family would come that day.

The other unshakeable thing I couldn't escape was how much I missed Alaryk.

Our relationship looked *other* to anyone looking in. How strange it must've appeared, how mismatched we were.

Then again, both Alaryk and I were *other* too. We'd never quite fit in anywhere. Alaryk had used his ability to earn people's respect, people's fear, but he would always be the Hartan that people gossiped about. And me? I'd hidden my true self for so long that I didn't know who I was anymore. I'd faked smiles in Dothik so people would like me, a shapeshifter who could make friends with anyone. I enjoyed being in people's company, but I'd always felt like I couldn't be myself—not truly—because of what I was hiding.

Here in the Arsadia, I'd felt free. But now? It was like I was trying to keep myself small so I wouldn't anger anyone, tiptoeing on glass, afraid to get cut.

With Alaryk, I'd never felt that way. We'd *worked*. Our otherness finding another half in each other. I thought we were both surprised how easy it had been…even when he'd made me so mad I could spit.

I remembered the first night we'd had sex. The rage that he'd morphed into desire. How out of control my magic had been, overwhelmed and spiraling. And he'd been my pillar, as he'd always been. He'd pushed me enough but then given me what I'd needed.

We had worked perfectly.

I remembered his kiss, firm and unyielding. Wanting. Gods, how he'd *wanted*. How strong he was, how his big calloused hands rasped across my skin, gripping me tight like he was afraid I'd leave.

My breath hitched. My hand trailed beneath the coverlet, finding the space between my legs, already beginning to heat and throb. A tiny little coil inside my lower belly, getting tighter and tighter as I thought of Alaryk, alone in my bed.

I stroked and pressed, wanting him to be beside me so I could reach over and feel him. I wanted his mouth on mine, telling me it was going to be okay.

I should've told him I love him too, I thought.

A sharp stab in my chest made my hands drift away. My body was wanting but my heart was heavy. Frustrated, I got out of bed and went to the window, sitting on the stone ledge as I peered out into the dark courtyard.

I didn't know how long I stared out the window, but my heart jolted when I saw movement beyond the half wall—a torso that I spied moving beyond the trees, and it wasn't until they walked beyond one of the trunks that their head came into view.

I saw the silver hair first. Even in the dim moonlight, it glowed like a beacon. My heart gave a pang, not out of fear this time but out of nerves.

I hadn't seen him since Ny'am a few days before. I'd stayed within the walls of the hatchery, like it was my own prison, only leaving once to go and see Brune.

What is he doing here? I thought.

And just when I thought that, his eyes flicked to me over the wall—blue, but not glowing-heartstone blue.

I hesitated for only a moment, feeling slightly guilty sneaking out of my room to slip into the courtyard after dark. Tarkosh had her ears perked, and surely she'd hear the creak of the door.

But I only debated for a moment before I slipped away from the window and did just that: sneak out of my room, pad down the quiet hallway with held breath, and slip through the courtyard door after I unbolted it, the sound loud enough to make me grit my teeth.

The last time I'd done this…it had been to meet Ryak and Nevin. Had that been nearly two weeks ago now?

Outside, there was a chill in the air. The changing of seasons. The riders would be heading to the Tharken cliffs soon for the *illa'rosh*, the choosing, or so Syris had mentioned to me. In another few short weeks, my time would've been up here in the Arsadia.

Never to return. Never to see Alaryk again.

"I thought you'd called to me," Alaryk murmured when I met him at the wall, pressing my front to the stone. The wall came up to my shoulders, but Alaryk could easily perch his arms across it, peering down at me, a barrier between us when I only wanted to feel those arms around *me*.

My hand was close to his wrist. I rested my little finger against the skin there. His lips quirked, and instead of playing a coy little game, he reached out and grabbed my hand. He rubbed it between his own, callouses rough but he was so warm, and I nearly closed my eyes at how good it felt.

He brought the back of my hand to his lips, which felt equally as good. Then he paused, his eyes flickering and sharpening. It took me a moment to realize why. He could *smell* me. I remembered…I'd been touching myself.

My cheeks flamed and I gasped, snatching back my hand, a low, embarrassed laugh sounding next.

"I see," he said, his voice a little huskier than it'd been. "That's why it felt like you were calling for me."

In a way, I supposed I had been.

"You…you could feel that?"

He inclined his head. "I've kept the bond dampened for both of our sakes," he told me. "But heightened emotions can always peek through."

That didn't do anything to calm the heat running up my neck.

"I was worried. I was just going to check to make sure the hatchery was secure," he said.

That made my heart flutter. I'd been so miserable the last few days, trying to come to terms with everything that had happened. *How* I thought I should feel after the violent assault versus how I actually felt. Syris seemed to tiptoe around me, like any moment, she expected me to crumble to the floor. Tarkosh too. Though she didn't trust me, the hatchery master had pushed another bowl of stew over to me at dinner, saying I needed to keep up my strength. Had she noticed I hadn't been eating?

Maybe she thought it was because of what Ryak had done.

But it was strange. It *had* happened. I'd almost *died*. At night, I still had nightmares of that forest, the mud, the rain. And yet life was pressing me forward, as it always did. I didn't want *Ryak*, of all people in this world, to make me feel afraid for any longer than he already had. *That* was my choice. My power over him.

He was dead. And I was still here.

Truthfully, my appetite had been diminished because my heart was still a little broken. Alaryk was offering me the pieces, but…it was my choice to puzzle them back together.

"I'm fine," I said to Alaryk. And I meant it.

I miss you, I thought next.

And maybe he felt the strength of the sentiment of that feeling because his expression flickered, a warmth rising in his eyes.

I perched my chin on the stone wall, as close as I could get to him, and he stooped down so he was doing the same, our eyes level. His hand reached out to trace my unmarred cheek, as if he still needed to make sure I was whole, flesh unbroken.

"I wish that I could go back to that night," he told me quietly, gently. "I think about it all the time."

The night he'd broken his promise to me.

"I've never regretted anything I've done when it comes to protecting my own," he said. "People think that I had doubts when I used Kamora to kill the Hartan king. I didn't. I never did, not once. And I don't have remorse that I did it either. If people knew that, they'd think I was heartless. How could I do that to someone I'd once cared for? How could I be that callous, that ruthless? Sometimes I think Myzalla even questions that. I occasionally see it in her eyes when she speaks to me."

My lips parted. So…maybe he'd really felt alone.

He took in a deep breath, which lifted his shoulders, his hand leaving my face. I reached over and took it in my own this time, not letting him escape.

"But that night," he murmured, closing his eyes briefly. "I can see the moment so clearly. The moment when you realized what I'd done. The sharp hurt. The fractured betrayal. It hit me like I'd run into a mountain wall, and I remember thinking… *What have I done?*"

"Alaryk," I whispered, my chest squeezing.

"I broke something in you that night," he told me, his voice firm, his eyes finding mine again. "And for that, I'm sorry, *mariss*. I am deeply sorry. I can't ever make it whole again. I will see that expression on your face forever imprinted in my mind. I will feel the shock and disbelief and hurt when I betrayed your trust, as if it were my own. And I never even explained why I did it."

"I know why," I said, squeezing his hand. "I understand. You didn't *have* to explain."

"But I want to. I was angry that night. I *know* you're not anything like her," he said softly. *Kamora.* "But that night, I remembered the way I *used* to feel with her. Uncertain, diminished, desperate, angry, where all I wanted to do was lash out. So I did. I wanted to hurt you. I'm not proud of that. I knew exactly how to do it…but it doesn't make what I said true. I *know* you're not *anything* like her, Amaia. And every day, I will regret those words because I know I can't ever take them back."

I took in a deep breath, feeling a hard knot release inside me.

"I realized, in that meeting with Sarkin and Vaedrin, that you were lying to me. You're not good at it, *mariss*. And I started to wonder what you were lying to me about. And the thought of *you* not being someone I could trust, when I feel the way I do about you," he said, his lips in a bitter twist, "it hurt more than I thought it would."

I swallowed hard, needing to own my part in this. "I made you promise not to get inside my head because I knew you would figure me out in mere moments," I confessed. "You know that already."

"I heard it from Brune, but I'd like to hear it from you too. Not in thought and feeling, like what you revealed to me in Ny'am. But in words. Your own words."

I blew out a breath.

Where to even begin?

"Try," Alaryk murmured quietly.

"It was mostly true what I told you the night of the Elthika attack. I took Kiron's place here because we feared that he wouldn't survive rider training. But the circumstances of him needing to be here at all, I hadn't told you. The *Dothikkar* was assembling a close circle of spies to send over to Karak during the exchange periods. But too many guardsmen might've been seen as suspicious, so they opted for family members in different fields, with different specialties, but still family with close ties to the throne."

"Go on," he urged, his eyes pinned on me.

"I...I would've done anything for Kiron. Even after everything I told you about...he's still my brother," I said. "So, given the choice...I would've still chosen to protect him. I knew that we were meant to come here and gather information that would be relayed back to the *Dothikkar* and his advisors." I took in a deep breath. "But believe me, I had *no idea* that this was what they wanted to begin with. To steal the eggs, to kill, to hurt anyone who stood in their way? *Never.* Please tell me you believe that at the very least."

I didn't know why it was so important, but I knew I'd cut into Alaryk's trust deeply, gouging it with my perceived loyalty to my homeland. But it had never been about the *Dothikkar*. It had only ever been about my family's safety.

"I do believe that, Amaia," he told me. "I promise you I do."

Relief coursed through me. I cleared my throat. "It became clear that something else was going on shortly after we arrived to Grymia. Ryak approached me one day. He made threats—against Kiron, against my own family, promising that their lives would be destroyed, my brother's career over—if I didn't do what they wanted. He asked me that day how many eggs there were in the hatchery." Alaryk's gaze narrowed. "Obviously I understand why he asked that *now*. But at the time, I just thought it was to test me, to test if I would do what they wanted. Because...the thought of stealing Elthika eggs? From the Karag? How foolish do you have to be?"

"Some of the biggest fools in history have been leaders of their people," Alaryk told me. "You'd be surprised by what weak kings are willing to do for power—and the lengths to which they'll go to attain it."

I still didn't understand the madness of it.

"You didn't know that Nevin was planning to break out Ryak? Or that they had gotten to Dresnar?"

I gasped softly. "*No.* I saw Dresnar on the cliff that day, and I knew how hurt you'd be once you found out his betrayal. After Ryak killed Gethrin, I only saw Nevin once more. He came here to the courtyard"—I swept my hand behind me, to the far corner —"and he asked what you were planning to do with Ryak. I...I told him that it was very likely you'd execute him. Nevin asked me when. And I said I didn't know. That was the last I saw of him before that night. I swear it to you, Alaryk. And that's all that I told him."

He nodded, squeezing my hand.

I took in a deep breath. "And that night...they'd already gotten to Brune when they told me to go get the eggs. They were going to kill him. He was still alive, but barely. They threatened my family again. And I felt hopeless. I felt scared."

"I wish you had come to me. Before all this," he murmured, leaning over the wall to press his lips to my face, to take the sting from his words. "I wish you could've trusted me, Amaia. You know I would've protected you."

I shook my head. "I wanted to. But I had my family to think about. You don't understand. Dakkar's different. The *Dothikkar's* power in the city—it's frightening. Even up until recently, if you showed heartstone magic, you disappeared overnight. He had that kind of power. The only ones with the strength to stand up to him are the *Vorakkar*, the horde kings. But they live out on the wildlands with their people. Most just keep their heads down. And I feared for my family—if I disobeyed the *Dothikkar*. I feared what his retaliation might be."

"I understand," Alaryk murmured. "You were right to be afraid."

"I'm sorry," I whispered. "I never wanted to deceive you, to lie to you."

My eyes met his in the darkness. I bit my lip, debating my next words.

"You *did* hurt me that night, Alaryk," I said quietly. "Deeply. But I want you to know that what I feel for you…it had nothing to do with them. What I was sent here for."

"I know," he growled, his gaze flashing. He pressed even closer to the wall, his hand cupping my chin. "I'm sorry, Amaia. Let me make amends. Let me prove that you can trust me again."

"How?"

He bit out a sharp exhale. He went quiet for a moment, his thumb sweeping over my cheekbone. "Only with time, I suppose. I know that's not the answer you want. But it's the only one I can give."

It *would* take time. We'd both made mistakes, grave ones that would be difficult to come back from.

But…

I wanted to try with him. We both did. That was the most important thing, if we were both willing to move past this, to build a future together, to see where this path, and all the others that would come, would lead us.

And so I turned my head to press my lips to his palms. His breath caught in his throat.

"I never thought that I would find you here," I murmured, similar to the words I'd said to him that night, when everything had changed. "That I would care for you as I do. That I would…"

My heart was thudding rapidly in my chest, and I took in a deep breath.

"Can I show you?" I asked, feeling my magic rise.

Alaryk's eyes narrowed when he felt me. I felt the barrier that he was sustaining to keep the bond dampened, a constant effort on his part. Just as I could feel a bit of his relief at not needing to hold it when he let it fade.

And I let it unleash inside me, everything I'd kept so tightly locked away and hidden and tamped down. My respect for him, my desire for him…

My love for him.

He closed his eyes when it hit him. When he felt it swell in his chest, as tears pricked my own eyes. I'd never been a crier. I'd cried more times in the Arsadia than I thought I ever had in Dakkar. But they came so easily for him because I didn't feel like I had to pretend. He wanted to see all of me, every little place I'd kept in the dark. He demanded it.

I whispered, "I'd never given much thought to love. I was so focused on *hiding*. But with you, I feel like I don't have to hide anymore. You see all of me."

His eyes were glowing when they fastened on me. His face was unreadable, but the bond was lit up like a star storm, bright and beautiful.

My smile was wobbly. I was officially turning into one of those weepy, sappy females, but I didn't care. Not a single bit when it came to Alaryk.

"I love you," I told him, though I didn't need to. He could *feel* it across the bond. "And I made such a mess of it."

We both did, he told me across the bond. *But it's* our *mess.*

His lips were on mine before I knew it, warm and firm. It wasn't even quite a kiss, it was a meeting of our mouths, a sharing of our breath, a mingling of our bond. We held each other there, his neck uncomfortably craned down over the wall while I went up as high as I could on my tiptoes.

I smiled at the ridiculousness, as tears dripped down my face from the rightness of it.

Come back home with me, he said in my mind.

I pulled back, a shy smile flitting across my face. This was all so new. I still didn't even know what this meant for us.

"I can't," I said. "If Syris woke up and found me gone in the morning, she'd worry herself sick. Tarkosh already keeps two eyes on me at all times. I don't need to go disappearing in the night again."

"I meant back to Grym," he murmured.

My breath hitched, surprise widening my eyes as they flickered over his serious expression.

"After the season is over," he continued, his eyes drifting to my lips, pressing a small kiss there. "But we can discuss it later."

Right.

The Arsadia was only his temporary home. I hadn't given much thought to what would come beyond the next moment these days. So the fact that he was thinking of the future, of *our* future, made my insides feel a little melted.

"Even when everything is so uncertain between us?" I asked.

"I don't feel uncertain about us, *mariss*," he replied. "Not at all. I made my decision when I bonded our magic. It was simple for me."

Was it as easy as that? A simple decision?

Maybe it was me who was overcomplicating it, overthinking too many things when maybe it was so incredibly simple.

"It is simple," he agreed. "Move back from the wall."

I frowned, confused, but did as he asked, pacing back a few feet, watching as he jumped and swung himself over it effortlessly.

"What are you doing?" I whispered.

"I don't intend to sleep without you tonight, and you will not leave the hatchery. So it's simple," he said again, taking my hand, guiding me back to the hatchery door, which was still ajar.

A small bubble of a laugh rose in my throat, though I tried to stifle it. "No outsiders are allowed in at night."

Not that Moak ever abided by those rules, judging from the sounds I sometimes heard coming from his room. Though none recently, strangely enough.

Alaryk gave me a dry look. "I think Tarkosh will make an exception for me."

"The bed is so small," I added, following behind him. "You'll barely fit."

"Then you'll sleep on top of me," he answered. He raised his brow over his shoulder. "Simple. Anything else?"

No, I thought, making my decision as I slipped into the hallway behind him. I didn't have it in me to stay away from him.

Good, he replied silently.

Inside my room, I watched as Alaryk quietly bolted the door. The candle had burned further, the light of the flame dim. He undressed, hanging his tunic and trews over the back of the chair.

I watched from the foot of my bed, my eyes skimming over hardened planes and deep ridges of muscle. My fingers curled into my palm, and when he approached me, knowing in his gaze, I tipped my head back, baring my throat.

His thumb rested on the indent just below my lip as he stared down at my face, his eyes flickering across it like he was memorizing every line, every dip, every swell.

"*Beautiful,*" he whispered. I realized it was *awe* in his gaze, and it made me feel like an explosion had gone off in my belly. No male had ever looked at me like he was looking at me, like he couldn't believe that I was real. "*Mariss.* My little ember that sparks flames."

My lips parted. *That* was what he'd been calling me? This entire time?

Heat licked at my belly. I wanted to show him just how brightly I could burn for him.

I pulled him down for a kiss. Deep and languid and slow. We were in no rush. And tonight wasn't so much about sex as it was about connection. Reconnecting.

I wanted to feel the weight of his body pushing me down. I wanted to be bathed in his scent until it was all I could smell. I wanted to memorize the way his wicked, hot tongue would trace over the curve of my hip or between the crease of my thighs. I gripped him tighter, *needing* that.

And when we were both naked in my bed, when he was swallowing my moans and gasps to keep us quiet, when he pushed two fingers between my lips to keep me from screaming to my goddess while he lapped away between my thighs, taking his sweet time, as if dawn was eons away...I *still* needed more.

After he made me come on his tongue, I dragged him up with strength that surprised me, given how boneless my arms felt. He sat, his bare back against the stone wall of my sleeping quarters, which the small bed was pushed up against, and I straddled his lap. My breasts were pushed against his chest as I plastered my body against his, winding my arms around his neck.

Our kiss was a battle, an apology, a beautiful twisting of our hearts, tangling as the bond pulsed to life, threading us together as one. I'd never felt anything like it before. So sweet and pure and tangible that it made my eyes sting and the back of my throat tingle. I didn't have to doubt what he felt for me. I felt it like it was my own truth, ringing bright and clear through every vein.

I sank down onto his cock as a tear dripped from the corner of my eye. He kissed it away, murmuring his own truths across my cheekbone, hissed little confessions of his love as I rocked my hips over him. Harder and faster, chasing him down.

His lips returned to mine. Our eyes, half-lidded, met and never strayed.

And when we both came, there was no pain, only pleasure. I felt his orgasm spark inside him, a wonderment as much as a release, and we saw it through together.

Hours later, as dawn was breaking over the Arsadia, pink light creeping across the floor and over our naked, damp skin, I finally fell asleep on his wide chest, exhausted and sated and wanting even more, with him still deep inside me.

His simple solution to my small bed made reality.

CHAPTER 41
ALARYK

I stayed back, leaning against the rebuilt fencing around the landing field, as I watched the Elthika circle overhead.

Amaia was trying to keep herself back, but her jittery nerves were seeping into the space around her.

They won't land if you're in the way, I told her through the bond.

Then I'll get squashed, she snipped back. Even still, I stifled a grin when she scooted back a few paces, her neck craned up at the sky like a child watching a star storm. Anticipation was coursing through her, so much that she trembled with it.

Other Grymians had gathered to watch too, though they had the good sense to stay far back from the landing field since there were so many Elthika. Myzalla and my selected riders for the journey landed first, rattling the earth. My second-in-command looked tired from the trip, but when she met my eyes, she inclined her head, telling me all was well.

Amaia's gaze was rapt on a single Elthika, carrying not one but six, all tucked safely behind the rails of the transport harnesses.

Brune was standing close to me, and I cut him a look.

Ethrisha was standing beside him, her arm tucked around his waist. Amaia had helped heal the worst of his injuries shortly after she'd woken. Though I could only use my ability on those with heartstone magic, I didn't need to root around in his mind to know that he was relieved to see his parents. He, too, must've thought the threats against them, the *Dothikkar's* retaliation, would be severe.

And so did his family, if they thought leaving their home behind was the safest option. I wondered what Myzalla had told them, but I could only guess the truth.

The Elthika landed.

I felt a surge of emotion well up in my chest when I watched Amaia sprint toward them. Both hers and mine. I rubbed at my heart, feeling the ache of it as I straightened along the fence line. Brune broke away from Ethrisha to approach.

"Amaia!" called a female voice, watery and loud. "Amaia!"

"*Lomma!*" she cried back.

A Dakkari female, who looked very much like my Amaia, came skidding down the Elthika's wing, having scrambled over the seats. Though her mother's skin was darker, her body smaller and thicker, there was no mistaking their resemblance in their features.

The swell of love, of relief, of joy was so bright as it filled Amaia as she raced toward her mother and embraced her so readily, so fully.

And I stamped down the bond, because it was a moment best shared between them. I waited, holding it back, observing the scene in front of me as Brune's parents descended next. His father was nearly as wide as him, his mother tiny in comparison to both males. Brune wrapped his arms around them both, his mother's hand resting on his back, running up and down. His head sank toward them.

Amaia's father descended next. An older male with graying hair, who Amaia went to more slowly than her mother but with just as much emotion, wrapping her arms tight around his neck. She got her height from him, I noticed. They were nearly eye level with one another.

The last to leave the transport Elthika, save for the rider, was Kiron.

Amaia looked up at him as he navigated down the wing, his eyes darting to the village beyond before they refocused on his sister.

There was a slump in his shoulders, many words that went unspoken as the two siblings regarded one another. I remembered the hurt that Amaia had revealed to me when it came to her relationship with him. How abandoned she'd felt, how he could've taken better care with his family.

But blood was blood, I knew.

And despite everything, I knew in that single moment as Kiron's expression crumbled that he'd had no idea what had awaited Amaia here. If he had…he never would've asked this of her. He would've rather died.

It was what *I* had needed to see.

Amaia went to him. Her head nestled into his neck as his arms came around her shoulders.

I let go of a breath I hadn't known I'd been holding. Behind me, the nosiest of the Grymians were watching as well. I wondered what it was that they'd report to their friends and neighbors.

I knew that they talked about Amaia around the village. About Brune, too, but mostly Amaia. Stories and opinions about her were varied. Unsurprisingly, most still had a favorable view of her, seeing the theft of the eggs as coercion by her Dakkari kinsmen, an impossible choice, especially with Brune's life held in the balance.

Most had *seen* her when I'd brought her back to Grymia that stormy day. I'd had to race from the landing field with her enveloped in my arms, unconscious and bleeding. Most had gasped, faces paling, horrorstruck at what she'd endured. The news of the eggs hadn't broken until the next day, but by then, everyone had known what state she'd been in. Brune too.

And so, it wasn't as it had been, as it could've been. Amaia's choice that day might always follow her, as Myzalla had warned —not just here in Grymia, but throughout all of Karak. But… the Grymians had seemed to make up their minds. And they'd stood behind the Dakkari they had once mistrusted.

Some, of course, like Gethrin's mother, still spread vicious lies whenever they could. But most merely listened, knowing she was only a grieving mother while shaking their heads the moment she turned her back. I'd watched it too many times to count.

My people's acceptance of Amaia had lifted a weight from my shoulders because it only meant her life here would be easier. I didn't want her fearful every time she left the hatchery. I didn't want to worry that she'd be spit on or called a disgusting name or forced to keep her head down after everything that she'd already had to experience.

It was *enough*.

Grymia had seemed to decide the same, especially given her actions the night of the Elthika attack. How many lives she'd saved, how tirelessly she'd worked, even at her own expense.

I felt the prickle of her familiar gaze, and when I turned back toward the landing field, I saw she was looking straight at me, her arm around her mother's waist, her hand in her father's.

And I'd almost asked her to give them up, I thought, thinking of how foolish that would've been. *To remain here, she would've had to leave them behind.*

I approached her and her family, and we met halfway across the landing field.

As I neared, I saw her mother's reaction to me. A widening of her eyes, the shadow of doubt and fear flickering across her expression. I wondered if she'd been outside the East Gates that day when I'd come to collect the Dakkari. I wondered what she thought of me now.

I inclined my head to all of them, meeting the eyes of Kiron when I lifted my gaze, knowing he *definitely* remembered me. Brune led his family forward as well until they hovered behind Amaia's.

"I am Alaryk Arn'dyne," I greeted, my eyes going to Amaia, whose eyes were filled with warmth and unushered tears. "I know your journey has been long, and you must have a lot of questions, all of which we will address after you're rested. But for now…"

Amaia smiled, and I released the bond, letting her flood back in. I ushered out a sharp breath of relief when I felt her.

"Welcome to Grymia," I finished.

A new home and a new beginning for them all.

Later that night, I stood outside the quiet dwelling where Amaia's family were situated. A large one, with three separate rooms, to comfortably accommodate all of them. They'd been resting for most of the day, having bathed and slept. Amaia had just prepared dinner, and while she'd asked me to join them, I'd thought it was best if she had the time with her family.

So they could talk freely about everything that had happened without a stranger looming. I got the sense that Amaia's mother was furious with Kiron, but she was determined to smooth it over.

Amaia took my hands. "You're sure you don't want to stay?" she asked.

I knew how much her family meant to her. This was what she'd looked forward to. I knew how worried she'd been, thinking that something might've gone wrong when Myzalla was retrieving them out of Dothik. Every day that had passed without sight of them had only made her fears more pronounced.

So today had been a relief. A joyous one. Her family was here, reunited. I didn't want to stand in the way of that.

"Be with your family," I told her. "You should sleep here tonight. I know how much you've missed them."

She frowned, biting her lip in indecision. "You're sure?" she asked.

I smiled and tilted her chin up to mine. The sun had long set, and Grymia was quiet, smoke rising from chimneys and muffled talk and laughter floating out to the road from various dwellings.

I pressed a long, lingering kiss to her lips.

"I'll have you for the rest of our lives, *mariss*," I told her. Her breath hitched, and I felt how much she liked that sentiment, spreading like ink through the bond, permanent and certain. "I can be patient."

"*Kakkira vor,*" she whispered, pressing another kiss to my lips, and I held her against me.

"Go," I murmured, nudging my chin toward the door.

I waited until she scurried up the steps, throwing me an appreciative smile over her shoulder before she disappeared inside.

I tilted my head back toward the sky, feeling the contentment swell through Amaia and feeling Samryn resting within Ny'am. They were well…and so I turned down the road, heading back to my dwelling to sleep.

But…well past midnight, when the last embers in the hearth glowed dully, the front door creaked open and a chilly breeze pushed inside with it.

I was awake in a flash but then relaxed when I realized who it was.

"What are you doing here, *mariss*?" I murmured, my voice husky from sleep, still half held in dreams.

Amaia slipped into our bed after she closed the door and toed off her boots. Her flesh was cold, her feet like ice, but she was only wearing a nightdress, so I wasn't surprised.

Her hands spread over my chest, and I grunted, capturing her palms to warm them in mine. She crawled against me, cuddling close, nuzzling her face into the crook of my neck and breathing me in.

"What's wrong?" I murmured, turning so I could hold her, my arms coiling around her.

"Nothing at all," she whispered against my skin. "This is where I want to be at night. I belong with you."

The sudden swell of affection and love I felt bloom was either hers or mine. Or a combination of both.

I tightened my arms around her, tucking her closer as she sighed in contentment.

"Sleep, *mariss*," I murmured into her ear.

"Bossy," she whispered back. I smiled into the darkness.

But I felt her drift off mere moments later while I held her. I knew that this was exactly how I wanted every night of my future to end too.

I would demand nothing less.

CHAPTER 42
AMAIA

The night that we broke Samryn's curse, it was clear and quiet, the moonlight and stars reflecting off the glass-smooth lake, a place we'd been before.

We'd been chipping away at the curse more and more, nearly every night, after my parents had arrived in the Arsadia. The *illa'rosh* would begin soon, the choosing for the acolytes, and I was convinced that we could end this tonight, before all of Grymia would make the journey to the Tharken cliffs in a few days' time. I felt it, had thought of nothing else nearly all day, practically bounding with energy when Alaryk returned from his patrol.

The only thing that had broken me from my determination was witnessing Kyr take flight this morning. I'd known that today would come all too soon. I'd known that I would feel the chipping of sadness, deep within my breast, to watch Kyr's uncertainty, his fear at being presented to the elder Elthika.

Another Rythback, one belonging to one of Alaryk's own riders, had chosen to take Kyr under his wing. It had been a beautiful thing to witness, to watch them take their first flight together, Kyr clumsy but growing stronger with every passing second. I'd anticipated the sadness. But I didn't anticipate the pride.

Tarkosh had reached over to squeeze my hand afterward. I'd been surprised, but she'd only inclined her head, looking at the tears dripping from my cheeks. *You did well with him, Amaia,* she'd said.

The first words of praise she'd said to me since I'd taken the eggs from the hatchery.

And I'd known then that everything would be okay. I'd watched Kyr until he'd disappeared into Ny'am with the elder. I missed him…I was proud of him…but I also knew there was much more work to be done. He would be one of many that I would watch take flight over Grymia.

At least I hoped.

Feeling that love for Kyr helped my own determination when it came to Samryn, the Elthika that Alaryk loved and respected. And now that I knew the depth of a bonded pairing and how much it would hurt Alaryk to lose him, I knew that I would do anything to break the Vyrin from the curse.

And so, on that night, I was determined to do just that.

Alaryk felt it within me. We'd been strangely quiet as we rode on Elthika-back to the lakeside. We didn't know what we'd find at the center of the curse, so we got as far away from Grymia as possible.

Alaryk pulled me to him, pressing his forehead against mine, before we started. I felt everything roiling within him: his fear for me, his uncertainty over the curse, but also his love, his support. He'd be the pillar that I needed, and he would pick me up when I, inevitably, fell.

And as the night drew on, I needed to lean on him more and more.

The curse grew in power the closer I got to its core, a tangled ball of rot and muck and dark magic. Being near it, strangely, made me feel like I was in the forest again with Ryak. My feet getting weighed down by mud, my body aching, cold from the icy sheets of rain and fear.

Stop this, Alaryk told me across the bond. I could feel his own rising panic. The more I hacked away at the curse, the more it took from me.

Once the *Karath* of Grym would've used up every fragment of my heartstone magic if it meant saving Samryn's life.

Now I could feel the choice looming in his mind. My safety…or Samryn's life.

I *refused* to make him choose…though I knew which he'd pick. He'd told me so himself a few nights prior. That if worse came to worst…it would be me. It had been a terrible thing, hearing that confession fall from his lips, whispered in the reprieve and quiet of our bed after lovemaking, because I knew how much he loved Samryn. Yet he would choose me.

But I couldn't allow that to happen. It would tear him in two. I could do this. *I would* do this. Not just for Samryn, but for the *Karath* I'd come to love.

Trust in me, I told Alaryk, feeling the wiggle of Samryn's own heartstone magic, inherent and wild in all Elthika. It had been so diminished, so weakened by the curse that when I brushed my own against it, I was *amazed* at the raw power I felt. It was breaking through, becoming stronger as I held the curse down.

I do, mariss, Alaryk told me, frustration lining the bond. Then determination. *Let's finish this. So you'll never be in danger again.*

With the tendrils of Samryn's magic, with Alaryk, strong and stable and certain at my back, I imagined a blade, sharp as slivered glass, feeling the last of the curse wiggle in my grasp. I was stronger than it now. Once it had seemed insurmountable. Overwhelming. A forest of violence and betrayal and cold vengeance meant to kill.

But with Alaryk, with Samryn, its death and demise was a

certain thing. We had worked hard for this moment. Weeks of pain, of struggle, of grief…and it would all end tonight.

And so, with the peaceful lake glittering with starlight nearby, not even the hint of a breeze threatening to disrupt its calm, I plunged the last of the magic I'd built, spearing the curse straight through. Like a beating heart, I felt it spasm. I felt it wiggle like an animal, a wild beast against me, trying to escape, trying to *survive*.

I twisted. Just as Alaryk had twisted the blade in Ryak.

A deafening sound exploded in my ears, but I thought to an onlooker it might've been silent. My eardrums popped and crackled, pressure rising in my temples.

An unseen force rippled out from the heart of the curse, physically knocking me back, sending me straight into Alaryk as my magic overflowed from me like a flooding river, glowing and seeping.

"I have you," he growled into my ear as the sounds grew louder and louder, all around us. A violent wind was rushing, twining my hair up around my head like it was caught in a tornado, whipping against my cheeks, harsh enough to sting. Alaryk huddled me closer, protecting me, his hand cupping the back of my head, pushing me into his chest.

A roar, booming and ground-shaking, cracked open my very soul, filling it with hope.

No, not a roar. An assured *victory*.

And with Samryn's final attack on the curse, banishing it with his own unearthed and undiminished heartstone magic…the world went silent. The wind died. The quiet of the night returned as if it had never been interrupted.

I sucked in a breath, my ears sounding stuffed with cloth, but I hesitantly looked up at Alaryk. Immediately, I felt him drifting over my skin, feeding me his own strength, letting it fill all the places that the curse had eaten away.

I closed my eyes as he healed me, my hand winding down to

wrap around his wrist, holding him tight. When it was done, I nearly sagged in appreciative relief.

"Did we…?" I whispered.

Alaryk's gaze was bright and warm. I felt the answer reverberate across the bond.

That was when I heard something different. A whispering sound. *Familiar.* At first I thought it was a heartstone, the energy near like it'd been in Ny'am.

But when I turned, I saw Samryn's red eyes in the darkness. He was still lying down on the earth, but his head was raised as he regarded the both of us. His scales were thrumming, creating a song of his own. A beautiful one, haunting and hushed. One I thought I could listen to forever.

"What is that?" I whispered, not wanting to break the spell.

Alaryk's hand wrapped around my hip as he moved into place beside me.

"His *sy'asha*," he said, the quiet reverence in his voice unmistakable. "An Elthika's song."

A deep breath fell from him, one of relief. Pure and beautiful.

"It's gone," he told me. "This is his thanks. His blessing. Meant for you and you alone, Amaia."

"His blessing?"

Alaryk turned me toward me. "He knows I've chosen you as my mate. He knows I intend to take you as my wife. To be mine. For the rest of our days."

My heart gave a little throb, a swooping in my belly accompanying it. I tried to fight against the grin that threatened to crack my face open. I felt like I was floating, light as air after what we'd accomplished. "Oh? You do? And do I have a say in this decision?"

Alaryk grinned. "You do. And you'll undoubtedly give me your strong opinion about the matter."

"And you'll just be bossy about it regardless," I breathed, wrapping my arms around his neck.

"You do like that," he whispered, the words drifting across my lips when he leaned down.

The kiss was soft, bordering on sweet.

"Thank you, Amaia," he breathed against me, as Samryn's *sy'asha* wrapped around us like a veil. "Thank you."

"Alaryk."

He dragged his lips across my cheekbone, across the bridge of my nose.

"I want you to be mine too," I told him. An answer to his unspoken question, one I felt thrumming within him.

I felt his grin more than saw it.

Across the bond, he replied, *I already am,* mariss.

EPILOGUE
AMAIA

I wanted payback, and Alaryk knew it.

So it delighted me to watch him squirm.

His irises were so dark they were inky pools of blue. Briefly, they shuttered from my view when he closed his eyes, his neck tilting back, a deep exhale tearing from him, followed by an anguished moan.

The bonds around his wrists were tight. I'd worried that I'd hurt him, but he liked the scraping of the rope digging into his flesh. One thing about sex with him, which I was still coming to learn, was that his needs were still *him*. There were times, like tonight, when he craved the roughness, the torment, the biting surprise of sweet pain followed by teeth-gritting pleasure. Other times he liked it slow, liked to savor the feel of my body around him while he was deep inside my mind, consuming me in totality as only he could.

All I knew was that both versions of him made me shiver uncontrollably, made me hunger, made me wet, made me see dizzying stars.

I nibbled on his bottom lip, drawing it into my mouth, sucking. He breathed into me, a constant rumble reverberating through his chest, vibrating my hands.

Slowly, I sank my hips down. And when he tried to thrust up, tried to get *deeper*, I laughed and pulled up.

"Amaia," came the growled, dark word. A warning.

I gave him a soft kiss. He was seated in the chair I'd tied him to, and I felt him struggle against the bonds. We both knew, no matter how tight I'd tied them, he could still snap them with his strength if he wanted to. He could break the whole damn chair if he wanted to.

And he was getting perilously close to that breaking point.

"It's only fair," I whispered.

Before this, he'd held me on the edge for seemingly hours. I'd gotten back from the hatchery, my second to last day working there, and he'd pressed me back into the bed, his face sinking between my thighs. Every gentle lap of his tongue, every spine-bending suckle had made the pressure rise. And just when it had been about to explode, he'd stopped.

Another game we liked to play. Another game that left us panting for each other, frustrated and delighted and trembling.

"It was retaliation," he informed me, glaring up at me, the tendons in his neck strained.

I grinned, rubbing my nipples across his chest, the cold metal through his own teasing mine. I knew what he was referring to. This morning we'd had one of the rare moments where he was still in bed when I woke. I'd taken advantage, still half-asleep, relaxed, my body languid and well-rested. I'd woken him by strumming my fingers across his cock, which had been half-hard against his thigh. My fingernails had clicked against his piercings, one by one, and he'd pulled me to him greedily.

But it had been the morning that we'd be presenting another hatchling to the Elthika, who'd been ready to take flight, and so I'd been needed on the landing field. I'd slipped from his grip, dressing as his cock bobbed against his abdomen, his eyes promising revenge as I'd giggled my way out the door.

"I did deserve it," I admitted, kissing him in apology. His tongue stroked against mine, and my pussy tightened around the head of his cock. He groaned, and I knew I'd teased him long enough. His cock was so hard, the flesh dark, a constant bead of pre-come pushing from the slit. "Will you forgive me?"

"Untie me and I will," he rasped.

His hands were tied together behind him, and I had to rise to loosen the thick strands, weaved through the rungs in the chair back. The moment he was released, he was standing and I was up in his arms. The bed was too far away—I could see that calculation in those primal eyes. Instead, he went to the closest stone wall, using it to keep me pinned in place, my legs spread wide for him to wrap around his hips.

He thrust forward with a victorious groan, and my head fell back, a bloom of pain coming when I hit it against the wall. I barely noticed it.

"Don't stop," I breathed, my voice a plea.

"*Never.*"

He used his body against my own as our pleasure rose together with the bond. Every tingle, every deep pulsing wave, every thread of lust and excitement—I could feel it all.

He pounded into me mercilessly, those piercings rubbing me *perfectly*, making me cry out as my hands scrambled around his neck, trying to hold on for dear life.

The orgasm came swift and fierce, robbing me of breath, my lips parted in a silent scream. I felt a deep throbbing, felt *and* experienced Alaryk's own pleasure as mine sparked his. The flint to the blazing fire…and we both burned together.

I didn't know how long it went on, but eventually I came back to reality, my heart thundering, my skin damp. Alaryk's face was pressed into my neck, his rough exhales drifting across my throat.

You forgive me now? I asked through the bond, exhausted and alive.

He grunted.

I'll take that as a lysi, I thought, smiling.

Well past midnight, I was lying against Alaryk's chest. We'd dozed a bit before having a late-evening meal, which I'd been ravenous for. But now, sated and full, I got to relish the feel of him against me, the quiet moments where it was just us two.

Especially when everything else was so uncertain. Alaryk was my one constant, my never-ending support.

"I think you'll like the citadel," came his rumbled voice, running his thumb down my spine, back and forth. "It's not quite so imposing as the name suggests. It's a beautiful estate, tucked against the mountains. The view of Grym is unparalleled."

"I will miss the Arsadia," I told him, sighing as I pressed up onto my elbow to look down at him. I could feel the spark of indecision in his chest. He knew I was sad that we were leaving in two days, but I wanted him to understand something. "But I don't want you to worry. I *am* excited to see your territory."

"*Our* territory," he corrected gently. "You will be my *Sorrina*, after all."

I tried to hide my smile and failed. "Yes," I whispered, almost shyly, which I knew drove Alaryk mad. We were leaving early from the Arsadia, and the rest of the traveling party, including Alaryk's own riders, would depart the day after. Now that the *illa'rosh* had finished, the choosing ceremony for this year's riders, there was no more need to remain in Grymia for much longer.

We were going to bind our marriage in the temple of Lishara before we traveled to Grym. The temple for the first female

Elthika was located in the Arsadia, toward the center of the island, where heartstone magic still flowed freely.

It was, of course, only a formality. A *sy'asha,* an Elthika's song, was almost as binding as the actual ceremony at the temple. It was a blessing, after all. Samryn had given me his blessing, and for a bonded Elthika, a bonded Vyrin, I knew that wasn't an easy choice to make. He'd honored me with it.

But for me to take my place at Alaryk's side, to become his queen, his *Sorrina,* the formal ceremony was necessary. The last valley that lay between us.

In two days, I would be his wife. And he would be my husband.

Only formalities…because he was already mine. And I was already his.

He felt that knowledge flow through my mind, that assurance, and he rumbled his approval, his agreement.

"I know you'll miss Syris. And Brune. Tarkosh," he told me.

"Yes," I replied. *But I'll have you,* I thought. "But you visit the Arsadia nearly monthly, and I'll come with you when you do. Simple."

He chuckled. *Simple.* A word he'd said to me, a realization, really, that could answer nearly anything. How simple everything was, truly, when you just…let go.

"Besides…Syris is traveling to Grym with Moak to help her mother with her shop until the nesting season," I answered, strumming my fingers against his chest. "I'll see them often."

The day before the horde had traveled to the Tharken cliffs for the *illa'rosh,* I'd caught Syris and Moak in the kitchen. When I'd entered, Syris had sprung back from Moak as if he'd been on fire, while he'd greeted me with a wide grin, his eyes twinkling. My friend's lips had been kiss-stung, a bright flush blooming across her cheeks. My own lips had twitched in knowing amusement. All I'd said was, "Don't let me interrupt," casting Syris a look that told her I'd need *all* the details later, and I'd left the kitchen, as quickly as I'd come.

Ever since, they'd been inseparable, though Moak knew exactly how to push all of Syris's buttons. I was happy for my friend. I might not understand it, but I knew she'd cared for Moak for a long time, saw something in him that I didn't. Everyone knew it. I only hoped he didn't break her heart and that he would love her as she truly deserved.

I continued, softly saying, "Brune is still so wrapped up in Ethrisha I doubt he'd notice I was gone for *at least* a week." Alaryk chuckled. Sighing, I added, "As for Tarkosh…maybe some distance will be good."

The hatchery master still didn't fully forgive me for what I'd done, the only bleakness in my life at the current moment. She had warmed to me. She'd at least stopped locking the incubation room at night when I worked late with the hatchlings…but I feared there would always be a wall between us. A betrayal that she might not ever forgive.

I couldn't blame her. That was why I didn't push. I only did what I could, hoping that maybe one day she might trust me again.

Alaryk told me, "She'll come around."

I smiled down at him, flickering my gaze over his face. His warm eyes did the same to me. I brushed my thumb against his lips, trailed it down to the little divot in his chin and then across the silver scar that trailed past his jawline.

There were times when I thought Alaryk might still be haunted from the events of that defining night. Sometimes when he looked at me, I knew he was lost in memory. In the pained memory of finding me in the rain-drenched forest, mud caked over my body, Ryak looming over me, his fists bloodied and splattered. Sometimes he had nightmares of it. Sometimes I did too.

I knew the guilt that still plagued him…because it mirrored

my own. We might always feel it. But it had smoothed with a little time, and now it was only a mere ripple whenever the memory surfaced.

It would mark both of us forever. What Alaryk had done, what I had done. It was like two scars that branded us, that perfectly aligned themselves when we pressed against each other. Matching scars, matching regrets.

But our love was like the press of lips against those scars. An apology, a promise, a recognition, a forgiveness.

I dipped my head now, giving him a sweet kiss, my lips lingering.

"I am relieved to go back to Grym," Alaryk admitted to me. "And I'm excited myself to show you the territory. To show you Harta, even."

Though only on Samryn's back, he added silently. Tensions with Harta were still simmering in the background with the knowledge of the heartstones' discovery in Dakkar. They wanted a piece of the power. Much like the *Dothikkar*, the Hartans believed the Karag held *too* much power. I understood the paranoia, the fear.

But the *Karaths* were good leaders. As long as they were in power, they wouldn't exploit or overstep. Regardless, the Elthika themselves were the gods of the land. *They* chose their representatives for the nation. They chose the *Karaths*.

It was not the Karag who held the power at all. It was the Elthika.

But with the heartstones' magic dwindling from the land, there was unrest among their wild hordes, becoming more difficult to contain. It would be another decade before the heartstones would mature into usable energy.

I knew that Alaryk was worried what would happen until then. Elysom had called a meeting once the moon was full to discuss it. We'd barely be settled in Grym and Alaryk would have to leave again.

But that was his responsibility. His duty to his people, to his nation. I understood that.

Tensions with Dakkar and Harta were high and might always be. The Heartstone Accords would continue, given the other terms in the agreement, but with even more vetting. The *Dothikkar* was apparently furious over what had happened with his guardsmen here but knew that an outright war with the Karag was a death sentence. His back was pressed into a corner, his control slipping over his kingdom...and it was never more apparent than now.

I might never see my homeland again.

And that was a strange realization.

I was only thankful that my family had decided to come. To leave their lives, to venture into the unknown.

My mother still grieved her friends, her neighbors, her community. Her *life*. All her life, she'd known one place, and now...she might never see it again. But she'd told me that she would choose it all over again. To come to Karak on the back of an Elthika, armed with nothing more than words from a stranger.

For me.

"You are my life," she'd told me a few nights ago when we'd come over for the evening meal. "All of you. That's all that matters. As long as we're together."

It had been Kiron's idea for all of them to make their permanent residence in Grym as opposed to the Arsadia. I would be in the capital city most of the year, after all. At Alaryk's side, where I longed to be. And instead of working at a hatchery, I would instead be working with the mature Elthika directly, which apparently kept the healers quite busy, my ability a welcome reprieve.

We would all be together. Though they wouldn't live in the citadel with us, Alaryk had homes set up for my parents and Kiron separately, close to the bustling Market District. My mother liked the excitement. She liked people, activity, and she was thrilled at the prospect of living close to all the noise. The Arsadia was too quiet for her, though I thought my father preferred it.

She had already packed her meager belongings two days ago, eager to see Grym. Alaryk had promised that she'd be able to raid the Market District at his expense to furnish her home, to replenish their left-behind clothes, her jewelry, her spices and cookware…and I thought her eyes had glittered at the prospect. She wasn't used to getting whatever she desired. My parents had lived modestly and worked hard all their lives.

But now…everything was different.

We were all different.

In our warm bed, I settled back into Alaryk's arms, my cheek pressed to his bicep as I skimmed my hand across his abdomen.

Across the bond, I knew he felt my excitement, just as I could feel his relief. It would be a change, certainly, starting a new life in Grym…but it would be a welcome one. A fresh start for all of us.

For now, I relaxed against Alaryk, in the quiet of our home, listening to the steady beat of his heart, turning off my mind from anything but him.

"No matter what comes," I whispered, feeling his fingers tracing across my skin, "this is exactly where I want to be."

With him. My pillar to lean on, my strength.

In this beautiful world of our own making, where our love was…

Simple, he answered across the bond.

NEWSLETTER

Want to hear about new releases, exclusive giveaways, and get access to bonus content, like extended epilogues and character art?

Sign up for my newsletter:

If you're already subscribed to my newsletter, access all bonus content here:

www.ZoeyDraven.com/bonus-content

CONNECT WITH ZOEY
Scan the QR code with your phone to access her links:

I'm mostly hanging out on
Instagram. Come say hi!

ABOUT THE AUTHOR

Zoey Draven has been writing stories for as long as she can remember. Her love affair with the romance genre started with her grandmother's old Harlequin paperbacks and has continued ever since. As an Amazon Top 50 bestselling author, now she gets to write the happily-ever-afters—with an otherworldly twist, of course! She is the author of Sci-Fi and Fantasy Romance books, such as the *Horde Kings of Dakkar* and the *Brides of the Kylorr* series.

When she's not writing, she's probably drinking one too many cups of coffee, hiking in the redwoods, or spending time with her family.

Website: www.ZoeyDraven.com
Facebook group: Zoey's Reader Zone

www.ingramcontent.com/pod-product-compliance
Lightning Source LLC
Chambersburg PA
CBHW030103310726
48970CB00004B/1127